Worlds Apart

Luke Loaghan

ISBN: 1-4611-6965-8
ISBN-13: 9781461169659

Dedicated to:

My wife for her love and patience,

My five children for the inspiration and happiness they provide on a daily basis,

And to my best friend who cannot stop talking about high school… ever.

Preface

The more you reach, the more it pulls away. The universe contracts and strips away everything you have left. Happiness can come as close as a finger tip away, as near as a glance, or as far as a single breath can travel. I had nothing left to lose, and yet, I still lost everything. The night of the prom remains the single worst night of my entire life.

Where did I go wrong? How did I end up here? It is twenty years later, and I am the antithesis of who I intended to be. I had a plan. I had a future. I had so many things going my way. Now I'm just another person obsessed with high school, wishing that I could go back and do things differently, make better decisions, better choices. I am still haunted by my senior year of high school.

My senior year started out ordinary. I was a regular kid with normal ambitions, with aspirations of college and a career and so much more. Everyone experiences stress and pressure in their lives, and sometimes more so during their last year of high school. I had the normal pressure, the normal work load, and the usual decisions that had to be made. But it all became very complicated, very quickly. We all make mistakes; we all have regrets. Time has given me new perspective, but nothing has changed, and nothing ever will.

It was such a crazy time to be in high school. Everything changed that year; music, technology, the way we talked, the way we dressed, the way we saw the world. The world always changes for kids graduating high school. I think about my teachers; I think about my friends, and the choices I made, the people I knew, and of course, I think about her...all the time.

I could not attend my reunion this year; it's hard to believe that twenty years has passed. It's hard to believe that all of this happened so long ago and yet the memory is fresh; the wounds are unhealed; and for me, the bleeding never stopped.

It all seems like a myth, like a dream, like a story that is a reflection in a mirror.

Some say that they can leave high school without regrets, just like I tried to do. Go ahead and avoid your destiny.

It was the beginning of senior year, and there were only ten months to go until I could really begin living my life. Only ten months until I was out of high school, out of my house, and moving on to bigger and better things. I had hoped to leave New York City behind and never look back. I was seventeen, and practically an adult, though only in my eyes, and definitely not in my father's eyes.

That past summer, I had a job at a bar in the city, but for one month. There just weren't many summer jobs available. It was the end of the 1980's, the local economy was awful; the country was in a recession, and most businesses did not hire for the summer. The housing market had crashed two years ago, and foreclosures were abundant. Instead of making money and saving for upcoming senior year expenses, I spent a month at home with Harry, my younger brother by one year. I studied for the SATs with books I borrowed from the library. And as usual, I practiced my musical skills.

I felt privileged and fortunate to attend Stanton High School. Our principal, Mr. Mash, instilled in us that we were the chosen few, the diamonds in the rough. Nearly a million students in New York City attend their local neighborhood high schools, but the best of the best attend Stanton in downtown Brooklyn.

Admission to Stanton required passing a rigorous entrance exam and obtaining letters of recommendation from the principals and teachers of our middle schools. The admission process filters out the academically weak and creates a highly competitive environment. Stanton had a one hundred percent graduation rate, and a ninety-nine percent college acceptance rate. One percent of the graduates go to the military. By military, I am referring to West Point or Annapolis. Stanton was unique for a public high school. One thousand students gain admittance into the freshman program annually. By senior year, the attrition process whittles the graduating class to about seven hundred students.

There was an exceptionally high statistic at Stanton—the number of student deaths. The suicide rate in particular was the highest of all high schools. There have consistently been nine deaths in every senior class. Stanton students are like eggs boiling in a pot. Sometimes the heat can cause an egg to crack.

Mr. Mash, a Stanton alumnus, was very proud of the school. Mash was of stocky build, and waddled when he walked. He wore old tweed jackets with elbow pads, wrinkled oxford shirts, pilled sweater vests, argyle cardigans, and worn out penny loafer shoes. He had white hair, longer than traditional length, that he wore brushed straight back down to the nape of his neck. He was most easily recognizable for two features: his glasses, which always rested midway down his nose, and his long gray eyebrows that protruded in opposite directions. Mash's official title was Principal, but he looked more like a private boarding school head master from the last century. Students often referred to him as the Head Masher.

Mash was the most gregarious principal that anyone could ever meet. He was well known for standing in the lobby of Stanton's beige, twelve-story brick building, and talking to students as they entered in the morning; although, it could have been better described as barking rather than talking to students. Mash would point out the school's hall of fame wall, in the main corridor on the first floor. The most famous and notable of Stanton's alumni were photographed, framed, and mounted on this wall, along with their graduation year and notable career achievements.

"Look at these photos!" Mash would shout with much exuberance as students entered the building. "Look at this great and stupendous hall of fame. Scientists, Nobel Prize winners, chief executives, the world's greatest engineers, captains of industry, and published authors..." Mash would often lean into a student, usually some unsuspecting freshman, look him or her in the eyes, and ask, "Will you be on this hall of fame one day? Will you be in our Canyon of Heroes?"

Mash knew most of the students by name, that is, if they were ranked in the top of their classes. Mash would seek out these elite students and get to know them, sometimes giving them public accolades, which were highly sought after by all students. He managed Stanton like he was captain of a large sea vessel. It was his way or the plank.

Some kids and teachers couldn't take the workload or the mental stress. But the board of education never responded to complaints about Mr. Mash from students, parents, or teachers. In other schools principals get tenured, but at Stanton, Mr. Mash was fixtured into the school; brick by brick, limb by limb. Although a senior citizen, he had no intentions of retiring and demonstrated no signs of slowing down. Mash tried to make arrangements to be buried on school grounds, but was denied by the mayor of New York (who, incidentally, flunked out of Stanton many years previously.) The rumor circulating back then was that upon his demise, he was going to be cremated in the school's furnace, thereby granting him unprecedented permanent access to the infrastructure of the landmark Stanton building.

Mash sometimes slept in the school, and showered and dressed there as well. There was nowhere else he would rather be. As for a wife or children, Mash was married to his job, and the thousands of students at Stanton were his children. When it came down to dedication, to duty, Mash was second to none. Mr. Chronus Mash was a titan amongst educators.

The students of Stanton spoke various languages, representing the melting pot of the five boroughs of New York City. Stanton sold academic prep books and materials needed for science and engineering classes. These books, tools, and materials were not cheap. Many students were enrolled in private study classes offered by the school, and needed money to pay for these classes.

The official school day at Stanton began at eight in the morning and ended at four in the afternoon. However, seventy percent of the student body was already in the building at seven a.m. when the prodigious steel doors opened. We were there for early morning cramming, and many of us stayed for activities well past six p.m. An eleven hour unofficial school day was the norm. If you didn't spend at least eleven hours in school, a school official might ask if you were taking it easy or enjoying a half day.

I had learned to study on the subways and while eating dinner. Sometimes I even studied while taking a shower. I studied while walking from the subway to the school and in the hallways and stairs from class to class. I learned to live with just a few hours of sleep. I was a very good student, and could've been valedictorian at any other high school, but for all my Herculean efforts, I ranked nearly three hundredth in the senior class. Why was I unable to break into the top three hundred? The answer laid in the minutest of numbers. All that separated me from being in the top three hundred was a two point increase in my overall grade point average. The way I saw it, if someone missed an exam, I would move up. If someone committed suicide or suffered an unfortunate nervous breakdown, which happened more often than one might expect, then I would also move up in the rankings.

Every day that I went to school I studied hard, prayed for luck, and tried to spot the next kid heading to Belleview Mental Hospital. Sometimes I would glance out of a window during class and see a padded wagon, and know that my stock was rising. I wasn't cold or callous, just indifferent. If it was me heading to Belleview by chauffeur, at least ten of my rivals would sleep better that night. Stanton was a very competitive school.

Test papers at Stanton were returned in descending order. The test scores and respective student names were announced by teachers. This was the case for every teacher, in every class; it was required by Mr. Mash. Public humiliation was a way of motivating students not only to do better, but also to go to another high school. When I was a sophomore, I received my test results at the top of the heap. But during junior year, I started receiving scores in the middle of the distribution. This was considered average at Stanton. I didn't score below a 90 on any test that year.

Names, grade point averages, and rankings were on full display, from top to bottom outside the principal's office. Mr. Mash made it a point to update the list every Monday morning. Exaggerating your rank was futile.

Stanton is the greatest public high school in the State of New York, and perhaps in the entire country. But if one wanted a Stanton education, one had to risk going to school in the most dangerous neighborhood in all of New York. In the 1980's New York City was the murder capital of the world. Street gangs, drug dealers, robbers, muggers, and other nefarious creatures, were in control of the streets. Overcrowded housing projects surrounded the school, as well as a halfway house for the recently incarcerated. It was like going to school in a war torn city, like Beirut or Saigon. A Stanton education did not cost money, but it wasn't free. Students came from Staten Island and the Bronx, and the outer parts of Queens. They came from Manhattan and Brooklyn, and a few even tried to sneak in from New Jersey. Most students commuted an hour and others as much as two hours. We risked our money and our lives for a Stanton education. There were students that came from far away nations like China, Russia, and India. Stanton produced more future doctors, engineers, and scientists than any other high school. It was a factory, a high pressure laboratory, and a competitive school for only the brightest students with the greatest mental faculties.

One learns the hard way about Stanton's competitive environment. My fellow students were ruthless. In past years, castor oil was dumped in the food at lunch, causing hundreds of students to get diarrhea on important exam days. (It was official Stanton policy that make up exams were not allowed.) Book reports and final papers had been stolen from lockers, resulting in lower grades for missed assignments.

I'd seen unattended backpacks become the object of arson. Pages from important text books and library books were often ripped out, resulting in incomplete studying. Tests had been stolen from teachers' bags and from their homes late at night. These occupational hazards, compounded by the normal stress that came with being a teenager, caused students to crack, to break down mentally, to lose their minds. There was a direct correlation between a student's ranking and their likelihood to have emotional problems.

chapter 1

"A MAN WITHOUT regret never looks back."

In my hand was the small strip of paper from my fortune cookie. My eyes held its message; my mind held its meaning. I do not pay attention to fortune cookies. Who does, anyway? Why read too much into randomly generated wisdom? I am not and never have been superstitious, nor am I one to read into trivial, ancient Chinese secrets. My father is a different story. He glanced at the paper for some time, reading my fortune cookie as was his custom. My father searched deeper for its meaning, as if it was a message from the gods, fate, or the universe, and maybe all three at once. My father pointed out that there was an extra fortune cookie on the table. My brother laughed. I opened the superfluous fortune, ate the cookie, and read the message. It said, as the first one had, "A man without regret never looks back."

One of our few traditions was to eat Chinese food the night before the first day of school. We ate at a low-priced Chinese restaurant called Ho Lee Kitchen in Astoria. My father considered eating out an unnecessary expense, as money was tight. Much was considered unnecessary by my father, who was frugal and firm.

The fortune cookie was not a big mystery, just a random message from thousands that made its way into my hands, albeit twice.

School began on a cold autumn week in September. I went with a new jacket—not too expensive, but a good, warm jacket. I looked really good in it, more sophisticated, and maybe even suave.

In front of the mirror in the boy's bathroom, I remembered the classic Greek myth about a boy that fell in love with his own reflection. I knew students who thought too highly of their intelligence, too highly of their athletic abilities, and too highly of themselves. They were Narcissus by different means.

I placed my new jacket in my locker, secured the lock, and then went to each class on the schedule, obtained my books, and met all my teachers. This was the last time I saw my jacket; it mysteriously vanished before the end of the day. When I returned to my locker, a live snake had taken the place of my jacket. The snake hissed, I gasped, and jumped back. The snake fell to the floor and slithered out of my sight quickly. It was a calling card from the thief, a member of a street gang called the Deceptors. This was part of high school in Brooklyn. I should have known better and not left my jacket in my locker. Over the years I had lost so many things. It was frustrating and I was sick of it, but I was accustomed to vanishing possessions.

My English teacher, Mr. Zoose was drinking a Coke. He waved hello and smiled as he walked into his classroom, and as always, he placed an apple on his desk. He was one of the best teachers at Stanton.

I should mention that I played guitar. My musical ability was what I was most famous for in high school. Everyone gets a reputation for something in high school. Some kids are well known for being the class clown, or for their excellent grades. Some are well known for their heroic accomplishments on the football field or for who they date. Some kids are well known for how they dress, how they wear their hair, or who they befriend. No one at Stanton reads the school newspaper, so hardly anyone cared that I was the sports editor. Ask anyone who I was, and they'll tell you that I was a great guitar player and a pretty good singer as well.

The guitar is not even considered a serious orchestral instrument; but the way I played, it brought tears of joy and sorrow to those who listened, and always brought down the house at school shows. Sometimes my music even tamed the wild beasts on the football team. It surprised me how many people really listened. In past years, I have played in the cafeteria, on the subways, on the street corners, in the park across the street, and whenever and wherever I could. I didn't need to find an audience; whenever I played guitar or sang, an audience found me.

I was not one of those eccentric, self-indulgent, artsy-fartsy types. I didn't dress *avant garde* or like a homeless hippie to play music. I dressed like a normal teenager from a poor family. I played from my heart, with hunger and passion, and that was good enough to be a great guitar player without dressing the part. Besides, it was expensive to dress like a starving artist.

Don't get me wrong; I did take pride in my role as the sports editor. I exercised poetic license when writing about the exploits of our school's athletes. The athletes always liked my articles; after all, it was about them. I made them seem like heroes, but that's the job of a sports writer. I was rarely complimented on my writing. Most of my fellow students congratulated me on my great guitar playing, even though I had not played for them since the previous year.

I had a solo in each of the past three school holiday performances and also at graduation each year. My singing was improving. This was my only talent, but it carried little significance on a college application. What was the likelihood that I could make a living in the future playing guitar? Slim. There were enough starving musicians in the world. It's hard to risk my future on the guitar or even a career in music. Besides, classical guitar was dying, destined to be an antiquity like its predecessor, the lyre. It was already replaced by its electric versions in school events. I could play electric and acoustic guitar better than anyone I knew, but I decided to put the guitar aside to focus on graduating high school.

I did not look like I was about to graduate high school. I had not grown into a man like other boys had. To tell the truth, I was still waiting for puberty to fully kick in. I was medium height, thin, and insecure about my build. Actually, I was insecure about lots of things. I wished I was built faster and stronger, that my body had produced more testosterone. I wished that I had developed hand-eye coordination like a short stop or a point guard. If that had happened, I could've been a great athlete. But I can't waste anymore time looking back at what could've been. No more looking back, only looking forward.

There was a school newspaper meeting after school. Not only was I the sports editor, but frankly, I was the only normal person on the school newspaper editor's staff. Everyone else was uptight, never smiled, never joked around, and only talked about how important they were to the fate of the newspaper and the minds of the students. The other senior editors on the paper talked about how they were prepared to work on the school newspaper all night. It was not the New York Times; it was just a crappy high school newspaper that no one read.

The editors were engulfed in a media power struggle existing in their own minds. Each tried to prove that they were smarter and knew better than anyone else. They would debate headlines for hours. I was part of a staff of pretentious type-A personalities. As far as the notion of working all night on the paper, it was for not me. I was leaving by six p.m. no matter what. I had to get home to study. I also had to prepare dinner two nights a week.

Besides, the other editors on the school paper were Ivy League types. They were smart, annoyingly so, tightly wound, pedantic, and mentally disturbed; a winning combination for acceptance at an Ivy League school or for living in Manhattan.

I couldn't even apply to the Ivy League schools. I didn't have the grades or the money for the applications. The little money I had made during the summer helped pay the bills at home. I couldn't ask my father for the money; he was too busy reminding me that we didn't have any. My father worked hard, but we were barely getting by. Our family went from middle class to poor when my father lost both of his jobs, and we took on boarders to survive. This happened a couple of years prior, and we'd been playing catch up ever since.

I felt too guilty to ask for money for another reason. How could I convince my father that I was an adult, capable of living on my own, and then ask for money for college applications? I needed to make my own money. I had to make smart choices in life. If I was accepted to an expensive college, how would I even pay for it? I suppose that I could have taken loans and spent the rest of my life in heavy debt. This was something that he would not understand. My father didn't even use credit cards.

Besides, I didn't want to be another poor kid doing dishes at a college for rich kids. It was not a question of placing my ego within harm's way; rather, I wanted my college experience to be different from the poor life I was living. Already humbled by my family's lack of money, I didn't need to get humbled at college as well. Private schools were out for me.

What was the difference anyway between a private college education and a state college education, other than price? Exclude the brand name recognition, and just consider the actual education. Were their books different from the ones at state college? If so, I'd just read their books. Were their professors smarter than the state college professors? I read somewhere that many state college professors actually went to expensive, elite schools. What's the point of going to an elite private school, if all you aim to do in life to teach at a state school?

I was determined to be a self-made success story no matter where I attended college. College was my ticket to the middle class and beyond. I had to also avoid membership in the growing class of people that were educated and poor that drive beat up cars with multiple bumper stickers from various private universities. We lived on the same block as a guy with a PhD from New York University in mechanical engineering, a Master's degree from Columbia in Applied Sciences, and a Bachelor's degree from Dartmouth in Early Languages. He drove an old clunker with a bumper held up by duct tape. So much for his degree in mechanical engineering. That will never be me. He needs a bumper sticker in sanskrit telling him to get a new car.

I still didn't know what I wanted to do with my life. But I knew that I needed to be smarter, make money, and not end up like my father, my grandparents, or my aunts and uncles. I came from a long line of hard working poor people. What good was that? They all dropped dead of exhaustion at an early age, never getting to enjoy retirement.

Some of my teachers had graduate degrees from expensive universities. They wore clothing from twenty years before and took the subway. It was like they had a degree in being poor. Why can't there be a PhD in being rich? There wasn't a college offering this degree. There is no crime in being poor, but there are serious repercussions. *Poordom* prevents people from pursuing their God-given talents and dreams, such as playing the guitar for a living. The most serious consequence of *poordom* was the inferiority complex that I had developed which prevented me from asking out the girl of my dreams.

Delancey was a girl I had known throughout high school. I'm not one for clichés, but she was different from all the other girls. She wasn't necessarily the prettiest girl at Stanton, though she was in my eyes, and she wasn't the highest ranked either. Delancey had never been a cheerleader, but she brought a cheer wherever she went. There was a certain quality about her that everyone noticed and some boys chased after. Perhaps it was the way she smiled. Often friendly, she was a regular Miss Congeniality, like a ray of morning sunshine after a long, dark night. I liked so many things about Delancey, but especially the fact that I could talk to her about anything.

The previous year we had talked about her dreams of success, her addiction to Coca Cola, and her infatuation with everything British. Her favorite band was Journey, and her favorite song from that band was "Separate Ways." Delancey and I had been in so many classes together that I actually knew a lot about her. Junior year, she dressed as the Statue of Liberty for Halloween, and it really didn't seem out of place or even out of character. If it wasn't for the green makeup, no one would think she was wearing a costume. She had thick, brown locks of hair atop her tall, demure figure, and she walked with a certain regal gait. Delancey almost always wore blue jeans and sometimes a tee shirt emblazoned with a rock band. She dressed bohemian, and that was by design. She had the long, elegant fingers of the aristocracy. Delancey went out of her way to look like an average girl, but there was a soul behind her eyes, something far above average, that made me yearn for her to be closer to me.

Delancey was an average tennis player, and I wrote a few articles about her tennis accomplishments last year, which annoyed the good tennis players. I really didn't care; I wanted to write about Delancey, and made a five minute interview stretch for an hour and a half. She could trace her genealogy to the Mayflower. She belonged to a country club in Long Island, where her mother lived. She once mentioned this in passing. No other student at Stanton, or all of Brooklyn for that matter, belonged to a country club on Long Island. She was a true American beauty, having grown up on Long Island, and moved to the city to live with her father when her parents divorced. Sometimes I thought that she liked me too, but I could never believe that. What would a girl like Delancey see in a poor boy like me? Although I really liked her, my malevolent friend, Sam, was obsessed with her.

Sam, like most kids at Stanton, was hell bent on getting into an Ivy League school. Sam's parents would have to struggle to pay for it, but he was more than okay with that. Sam boasted that his father was a doctor, but his father was not the kind of doctor that made a lot of money. Sam's father, an immunologist, did mostly research at a hospital in the city. His family had recently spent their life savings to pay for his sister's hospital bills. She had died of cancer the previous year. It was ironic that an immunologist's daughter died from a cancer of the blood. The death of his sister left his family mentally off kilter, and financially and emotionally broke. Sam once said to me, in a rare moment of sincerity, he felt his parents would never recover from his sister's passing. A family can recover from financial hardships, but tragedy lingers in silence for generations.

Sam definitely had the grades and the motivation to get into a top school. He planned on writing his college essay on his sister's health crisis, and how it motivated him to become a doctor. Sometimes

I believed him, sometimes I didn't. Sam would say or write anything to get into Harvard. He was the quintessential Stanton student. He wanted to be a doctor to satisfy his parents, and to make lots of money.

Sam, Carlos, and John were already at lunch sitting at our usual table when I arrived at the cafeteria. There are only two times in life that people have a 'usual table.' The first is in the high school cafeteria. The second is when you're rich enough that people who own restaurants remember who you are, where you sit, and what you like to drink. Most people only experience the first. The boys and I were discussing our classes and teachers when Delancey walked in, unseen by me.

"Wow," said Sam, "Delancey really grew over the summer...in all the right places." Carlos, amused, agreed with Sam and then went back to eating. This was typical of Carlos, always in agreement with Sam, and never really saying too much. Some people are leaders; Carlos was definitely a follower.

John, my closest friend, asked if any of us had classes with Delancey this year.

"I have English class with her," I said with a sheepish grin. We kept eating, none of us saying another word on the subject. The wheels were turning in Sam's head. I was friendly with Delancey, and found her very attractive, but never had asked her out, chased after her, or expressed my feelings. She was out of my league. I was a realist, pragmatic to the core. She was too much of a long shot, and too much of a dream. She was someone I could reach out towards, but never hold.

September was shaping up to be a busy month. I had to work on the paper after school and could not go with the guys to the park. I told them I'd see them tomorrow, and explained that I had to "work all night on the school newspaper." They laughed, detecting my sarcasm and what I was alluding to. John had to work at his strict Korean parents' fruit and vegetable store, which was usually the case.

After gym class, I was in the boys' locker room changing out of the required Stanton gym t-shirt. The room smelled like jock straps and sweat, and that was with the windows open. The boys were talking about a street gang attack after school and the best ways to leave the school and head for the subways. This street gang, the Deceptors, was infamous.

The Deceptors always planned a secret attack on the first day of school. Everyone always knew about it, except the police and school officials. I was more than familiar with the gang's well deserved reputation for terror. I wasn't concerned. By the time I finished my sports articles, the gang would be long gone.

At six o' clock, I exited the newspaper office. Bellicose voices roared in the background. They continued to argue about the lead story, sounding like a parliament meeting of a third world country. The only thing missing was fisticuffs. The editors smirked and made snide comments that I didn't work as hard as they did and that sports was easier than the news or the entertainment section. This of course, wasn't true, but probably was not false either. I never had the patience for office politics.

I walked my normal route to the subway on Dekalb Avenue. There was a clairvoyant's store front I was accustomed to passing. I don't call them fortune tellers because that would give them credibility. The psychic was a slightly chubby woman, probably in her late thirties. She wore black clothing, and often sat outside her storefront. She smiled a sexy smile and asked if there was anything she could help me with. I said no, thank you. She smiled back, and continued with her sales pitch.

"I could tell you your future. It's very interesting." Or, "Maybe I can help make your dreams come true." Or, "I know what you'll do after high school. I know the right path for you to study. I have the answers to your questions."

I never paid her any attention. Her customers always looked desperate. Sometimes her clients were high school students. When this was the case, the girls always came out crying, and the boys always came out nervous. I may not have had all the answers to my future, but she didn't have any. Her profession implied that the future is already written, and ready to be foretold. I made my own future and not a single person could convince me otherwise.

I rode the subway home that first day of school. One day down, three hundred to go. No sign of the Deceptors, just as I had predicted. The first day of school and the last day of school were always wonderful; the days in between were a problem. It's not that I disliked school. I saw it as a means to an end, a necessary odyssey. School is penance for being young.

I had made a promise to myself that if I was going to have a successful career one day; I needed to get in the habit of never missing a day of work or school. After all, I would never have this opportunity again. Once high school was over, it would really be over. No one can go back in time and relive high school. No one can ever bring something back once it is gone. Too many people come to this realization when it's too late. Like at their twenty year high school reunion.

After much reflection over the summer, I had made it a point to stop hanging out with the negative people in my life. This included those who did not share my ambitions or desire for a better future. This meant not hanging around some of the losers I knew the previous year. This also meant that I was running out of friends fast. John Donne wrote "No man is an island." In other words, I still needed to sit with someone in the cafeteria during lunch, or risk appearing to be a total loser.

Sam could be construed or misconstrued as a really negative personality type. He was kind of apathetic and expected everyone else to be apathetic as well. At the same time, there were few students in all of Stanton who were better academically, or more driven to succeed. No one was more determined to go to Harvard. Sam was hard to explain. Rather, my friendship with Sam is hard to explain.

During sophomore year, whenever I tried to sign up for a club, or try out for a team, Sam showed up to talk me out of it. Sam knew exactly what to say and when to say it. During football tryouts, Sam walked by. I was already nervous about the tryouts because I was not as big and strong as some of the other guys. Sam shouted out, "Don't waste your time...you are too small, too weak, and too slow. You're just going to embarrass yourself." Everyone laughed. I walked off the line and went home. It wasn't always what he said; sometimes it was the way he said it.

Sam had the uncanny ability to be very convincing and spoke with conviction. He would bad mouth every student trying their best or striving for greater achievement.

Sam had a problem with anyone who achieved any form of success. When I had announced to Sam and John that I'd been named Sports Editor of the school paper, Sam threw a fit. He tossed my backpack across the hall, yelled obscenities, and stormed off. John, on the other hand, congratulated me and said I deserved it after all my hard work. John was a much better friend, and I liked him better than Sam. But for some reason, Sam was always around, and it was hard to cut the cord. My father always said, "Show me your friends and I'll tell you who you are." Well, that may be true, but looking back, I can take it a step further. Your friends in high school are a reflection of your insecurities, self doubts, and vulnerabilities. John believed that the prettiest girls always hung out with the not so pretty girls, in order to make themselves look prettier. I think the pretty girls sees themselves as the not so pretty girls, and birds of a feather flock together.

My father warned me about my friendships, and I heard his voice in my head often. I hope I'm not making him out to be Polonius, because he was, in fact, the opposite. My father was quiet, blue collared, and rarely offered advice. My father's best friend had betrayed him in high school over a sports competition. His friend had tricked him to believe the competition was moved to the next day because of rain. Guess who won the competition? "Never trust your best friend," my father would say.

Sam hated the fact that I participated in school activities. He spent all his spare time chasing girls and smoking. Sam was not a good looking kid, and was physically awkward and socially inept, more so than the rest of us. Sam tried his best to get any girl to like him and to be their friend. The truth was that people, often found him a little creepy. He was famous for emotional meltdowns in school, which often left him red-faced and in tears. At the end of last year, I had promised myself that I would never surround myself with people like Sam again. Already it had cost me a lot of wasted time...time that was now running out. But Sam just wouldn't go away. He was like a leech.

I had to interview Michael Noah Torres this week. I had known him since freshman year, and like everyone else, I called him Mino. Mino was the star running back for our football team. Two things were consistent about him: he was always fast, and was always in the weight room. Mino took football very seriously. His mother was often at school for practices, games, and to talk to the guidance counselors and coaches. She was determined that her son would go to college and play football on scholarship.

When we were freshmen, Mino and I were almost the same height. He had a real running back's build, like a bull about to break out of a stable. His legs were thick like trees, and he had a neck to match. I hadn't seen him in a while—Stanton is a big school, and it was not uncommon to not see someone for an entire year.

My eyes almost popped out of their sockets when I walked into the weight room. Mino was lifting more weights than anyone I had ever seen. He was enormous; his wide back was shaped in a perfect V. I waited in awe for a half hour for him to finish his workout. Mino squatted more weight than two average football players could lift. He was clearly the strongest kid in the school, maybe even in all of Brooklyn. But he had not really grown and was six inches shorter than I was. I marveled at his bench presses, military presses, and bicep curls. His biceps were bigger than my thighs. I never felt so weak in my life.

My interview was not going well. Mino was pensive. Clearly distracted, he found my routine questions about school and college annoying. This was not like him. I asked how much he was lifting. The numbers were staggering. He had just completed a set of 400 lb bench presses. He was squatting more than 600 lbs. Mino's arms were pulsating and trembling. I asked him about his speed. Mino could run the 100 yard dash in 11 seconds. I was amazed at the results of his hard work and training.

We talked about college. The tone in his voice seemed like he was about to blow a fuse. With intensity, he described how he had to get bigger and stronger; many scouts had told him so. If he did, it may guarantee him a full scholarship. Mino was working out 3 to 4 hours a day.

"If I were just a few inches taller, I'd get a scholarship anywhere," he said.

As I exited the weight room, I looked back and saw him remove his tee shirt. On his back was a large constellation of acne. I wondered if Mino was completely natural.

I wrote an article stating that Mino was looking forward to a great season and that he was training harder than ever for a scholarship. I wrote about his enormous strength. In the weeks that would follow, Mino broke every school record for the Stanton Serpents.

The first week of school was over, and I was heading home on the F-Train. The ride home started over the Manhattan Bridge. There were spectaculars view of the East River, lower Manhattan, the South Street Seaport, and the World Trade Center. It was breath taking. The graffiti-filled F-Train then crept slowly into a tunnel, and made stops in Manhattan.

More people and more police rode the F-Train. The shorter way home was the G-train through Brooklyn. This was more dangerous, as it traveled through tough neighborhoods with thugs, muggers, and drug dealers. They all took the G-train, and high school kids were easy targets for them, especially at the Brownsville stop. The G train was nicknamed the Gangster train, for good reason.

I was alone on the F-Train, with fifty other people, when I saw my neighbor's son. He had just started Stanton.

"So I see you took my advice and took the F-Train," I said to Theodore Carl Smith.

"Yeah, I definitely don't want to get killed trying to get home from school," said Carl. Looking at him reminded me of how much I had grown since I was a freshman. He had baby-faced good looks and an athletic build.

"Any more advice?" Carl asked.

"Well for starters, don't carry that T-square everywhere. You don't want everyone in New York City knowing that you're a freshman. And try to get involved in as many clubs as you can. Join a team and play sports," I said with a touch of regret.

"I am going to play baseball and football," smiled Carl. "What about girls?"

"Carl, forget the girls at Stanton. They are only interested in guys with the highest grade point averages. The guys that do well on the SATs get all the girls here." I looked at him, and he put his head down. The poor kid didn't stand a chance.

"I'm so glad that I'm not going to Rikers," said Carl. Rikers was the nickname for our neighborhood high school, named after the prison. It was a dangerous high school, packed with juvenile delinquents, gang wars, robberies, shootings, and stabbings. Rikers was about survival and Stanton was about education.

"Focus on Stanton. Although we don't have to worry about getting jumped inside school, you still have the pressures of keeping up academically, and keeping your rank at the top." I wondered if Carl would make it or if Mr. Mash would eventually pull him aside and "suggest" a different high school.

Stanton was especially challenging on freshmen, and many first year kids suffered mental breakdowns before Christmas. When I first entered Stanton, I thought all my problems were over, and that I wouldn't have to put up with the bullies and jocks that other high school kids had to put up with. Instead, there was Sam, and others who ranked higher than I and gloated about it.

Stanton teachers were not inhumane, and took it easy on us the first week of school. That week, I finished my homework by eleven p.m.—just under four hours.

I met a kid named Maurice that first week. He was famous for his brightly colored yarmulke, and for being the only religious Jew at the school. The Stanton hours and schedules were not kind to the Sabbath and religious holidays.

I also met Sal, perhaps the brightest student at Stanton. He was from Sheepshead Bay, Brooklyn. Sal was always ranked in the top five, but this year he was in the top three. He was involved in an engineering club that was creating a risk assessment of city bridges, tunnels, and landmarks. Sal hardly spoke, and when he did he mostly mumbled. He always carried surveying and engineering tools on him. Sal was famous for being the weirdest student in all of Stanton. He often sat alone at lunch.

I saw Mr. DeJesus, my former wood shop teacher, who was also the school's carpenter. He built the stage sets for the school plays.

As September rolled on, I attended all my classes while continuing to look for a job. I quickly re-acclimated to the Stanton workload and the lack of sleep. By the third week of school, I was firing on all cylinders.

Mr. Mash announced that seniors were now required to meet with a designated school psychologist. Stanton was getting bad press because of the suicides and the number of mental breakdowns. I laughed it off, because that would never be me. My mind was made of iron, my soul of steel. I could easily pick out five kids that might break down soon, the way engines would if they were running out of motor oil. Nonetheless, I had no choice; it was mandatory for every student to meet with their designated psychologist.

During my lunch period, I met with mine, Ms. Eris. She was a young woman, no more than thirty years old, and seemed pleasant with a plastic smile and neatly brushed hair. I typically don't smile when I meet someone for the first time, and when I meet someone who does, I automatically don't trust that person.

"David, I just wanted to talk to you for a few minutes." She motioned that I should sit down. These people are often out of sorts if you stand up and walk around. She started chewing her nails.

"So what can I do for you?" I asked.

"I know from your file that you had an incident sophomore year…"

"That was not an incident. I just wanted to take a break and play guitar in the cafeteria. It was nothing serious, just a lack of sleep."

"It's just you and your father and brother at home," she said as she looked at my file. "Your mother passed away a few years ago."

"I'm fine; my family is fine, and I'm not going to have a breakdown. Don't worry about me. This school has enough students that will keep you busy." I was in a hurry to leave.

"David, Stanton is a high pressure environment. If you feel stressed, you can always come and talk to me, and I can arrange a few days off for you." She seemed too nice, speaking so slowly.

"I play guitar. There is nothing wrong with playing it in the cafeteria."

"This is Stanton, and kids normally use their lunch hour more wisely."

"I can assure you that I am mentally fine."

"David, most students do not commit suicide or end up at Belleview. They exhibit no obvious signs of mental breakdowns. Instead, they lose control of their emotions, and make illogical, irrational decisions and exhibit strange behavior. They do things that they normally would not; they rebel in strange ways, but continue with their normal lives."

"Thanks, Ms. Eris," I said. This was precisely why I no longer brought a guitar to school. High school was hard enough without having to answer to a quack.

chapter 2

THE LAST WEEKEND of every month we visited my grandparents on my father's side. This had been our tradition for as long as I could remember. This weekend was different; it would be the last time I would see my grandfather.

My grandfather, David "Lake" Arfayus, had immigrated to the United States many years ago. He was born in a South American colony then called British Guiana. Lake had worked six days a week for as long as anyone could remember. My grandfather was a blue-collared guy, and had worked in the furniture refinishing business. Most people from the Guianas were brought over by the British who were searching for gold. The British claimed they never found any gold.

Lake had lived without electricity and plumbing most of his life, and had worked on several sugar cane plantations while in British Guiana. He was the only boy in his village that had learned to read, and actually earned money reading newspapers and letters to people in the village. Lake also earned money as a bare knuckle boxer, as he explained that "Englishmen liked boxing and scotch and paid good money for both." Sometimes he boxed three fights a night, just to make enough money for a week's worth of food.

Grandpa was exposed to many chemicals in his line of work and as a result had become severely ill. But he confessed that he was really sick because he was being forced to retire the next month. "A man's body can't just stop working one day. Been working my whole life, without vacation, or sick day, and now no work. No work makes men sick." He spoke in broken English, similar to that spoken in the Caribbean. I used to chide him about his accent, but he explained that it was hard to make your tongue move like an Englishman if you were born outside of England. He was sitting on the couch watching the Yankees. I was taken back by how much weight he had lost since the last time I had seen him. This once mighty figure in my life now looked frail and weak. He put his glasses on and recognized me instantly. His mind was sharp, but his body was deteriorating fast.

"Eldest grandson…me need talk to you badly," he said sharply.

"It's great to see you, Grandpa," I replied.

"Me not have much time, but listen me before ya speak or say anything. Just lemme finish." He took a sip of hot tea and continued, attempting his best to speak American, as he referred to my language.

"David, such high hopes for you, and me just wanted to tell you few things. First, in my life, have seen so many people succeed and fail. Most of the time, the same people doing both. But me wanted to tell you that you are getting older and you are now grew up and me don't want you to make the same mistakes me make in me life. First, think your actions through. It will always be your actions that count, not your intentions, or your thoughts, even though they may be all well and good. So much time is wasted wondering and thinking about the right decision or the wrong decision. Me know that you want to go to college, and that you want to go away, some place far. You going to be the first member of our family—ever—going back generations, ever go to college. That's what I'm talking about. Go and get an education. Become smart in life, and learn to speak and write clearly. There are people I've met that have been to college, and they really don't impress me at all. They can't speak or communicate properly. Don't be one of those people. In life, many people become rich then lose it all. Me lived through some tough times. Through race riots between the blacks and the Indians in my native country. Lived through famine and drought. People are quick when they judge you. But when you walk into a room full of people and start speaking, everyone knows if you are a fool or an educated person. They know right away based on how you speak. Your mother was so smart. She spoke so well. She taught piano and music to so many. She read poetry for pleasure. Get educated. Make good decisions in life and then pursue the decisions you make. Don't be one of these indecisive persons, like you uncles or you father. They have spent nearly ten years thinking over things and trying to make decisions that successful people make in one hour. Even if you don't know something for sure, trust you instincts and just go for it." Other people then entered the room.

"Also, and this is the most important thing. I see your father full of regret. His mind is stuck in the past, and he can't live in the present because of it. What's over is over. Don't spend your life like your father, always looking back. David, just promise me that you'll take my advice."

"I promise," I said. "I swear it."

Grandpa took a sip of his tea, handed me some money, and started talking to everyone else. I could tell that he wanted to finish our conversation, but now my aunts, uncles, and cousins were in the room, and he was not free to speak.

That night, I kept thinking about his advice. He wanted me to be educated, to speak like an educated person, and to carry myself as such. And he emphasized that I should be a decisive person. I can seem a little wishy-washy. I usually answered important questions with "I don't know," like I sometimes did when people asked me, "What are you going to do after high school?"

I really didn't know if I wanted to go to college or if I needed a year out of high school to work. When people asked me, "What college are you going to?" I replied, "I don't know." I wondered if my grandfather was disappointed in me, and that's why he was giving me this advice. I hoped he did not foresee that I would become just like my uncles or my father. My father was stuck in the past, always lost in thought about my mother and their short life together. My relatives were very careful decision makers and often spent more time unable to make decisions than they did making the decisions. I didn't want to be indecisive any longer; especially if it meant that it would disappoint my grandfather.

The next morning, the phone rang at six a.m. with the news that my grandfather had passed away in his sleep. I was devastated by the news, although I tended to exhibit a lack of emotion when it came to death. I would miss my grandfather. He meant the world to me. All I could do was make good on my promise to him.

At the funeral, I told the story of how my grandfather had once bought me a fancy jacket when I was in the fifth grade. Lake was in the city working at a fancy law firm, refinishing their conference table. The head lawyer had just bought his own son a fancy bomber jacket, but realized it was the wrong size. It was Christmas Eve and too late to return the jacket, so he sold it to my grandfather at a tremendous discount. When I received the jacket on Christmas Day, I was stunned. It was the most gorgeous leather jacket I had ever seen, the kind worn by Air Force fighter pilots. It was heavy, thick, and had wool around the collar, and patches with names of flying squadrons on the sleeves. It was a jacket I had only seen in the movies and in clothing catalogs, not something my family could otherwise afford. When I wore the jacket to school, some kids liked it, and some loathed it. The fifth grade bullies decided to tease me about it. I felt angry, but also dejected, because I knew how incredible it was that my grandfather was able to get me this jacket.

I complained that I didn't want to wear the jacket, that it brought me unwanted attention. Lake put his hands on my shoulders and lowered himself to where he could look me in the eyes. He said that if I couldn't wear that jacket in the fifth grade, then later in life I wouldn't be able to wear success either.

"It's not about the jacket, it's about having confidence. There will always be people that will have something nasty to say when you have something good in your life. You have to be able to block out these people and walk in confidence. That's how you'll get to the Canyon of Heroes in Manhattan one day. And they'll throw you a ticker tape parade." I kept wearing that jacket, even after one of the bullies slashed it and ripped a hole in it.

His casket was lowered into the ground at St. Michael's cemetery in Astoria. He had a small, engraved piece of brick instead of a fancy headstone. After everyone left, I approached the burial spot. I was ashamed that we were so poor that we could not afford a nicer headstone. He deserved better and one day I hoped to make enough money to buy him the best headstone in the entire cemetery.

Death is a reminder that life is short. When I returned to school, I was determined to ask Delancey out on a date.

Consumed with nervous energy and anxiety, I paced non-stop outside her last class of the day. Breathing no longer was automatic for me. Perspiration trickled down my temples. The bell rang and her class dispersed. Stampeding students savagely exited the classroom, and within seconds their bodies evaporated from the hallways. She was still inside, speaking to her teacher. Peering conspicuously, my eyes fixated on her long hair and her long legs. Forcing breath to fill my lungs, I repeated the lines I had rehearsed all night. Inadvertently, some of the rehearsed lines could be heard outside of my head, as I mumbled the phrases that I no longer felt would adequately suffice.

Delancey walked out of the classroom. I called out her name. The world slowed down for me, and as her head turned in my direction, I abandoned my seasoned script.

"David? What are you doing here?" she asked, smiling, but looking mostly confused.

"Delancey,...uh...how's it going?" I asked.

"Fine. I had to talk to Mrs. Moynihan about a project due for her class next week. How's it going with you?"

"Great. So busy. Looking for a job on the weekends. You know... need extra money for senior year."

"Well...it was good seeing you." Her intonation indicated the conversation was over. I was losing an opportunity that I desperately needed to seize. I had a chance right here, right now, and needed to make the most of it. There was no turning back; the time was right.

But only seconds remained, as she was headed into the abyss of the school stairwell.

Her back was to me. Several paces of empty space separated us in the otherwise empty high school hallway.

"Delancey." She turned around slowly when I called out her name. "Would you like to…" I started asking, voice cracking, throat dry, out of air and moisture at the same time.

"David, I really don't know. I think you might be better off asking some other girl." The words fell from her full lips, like grenades from a B-52 bomber. I stood in silence, dejected, rejected, and crestfallen. I could see that she understood my pain, and as the seconds of awkward silence lingered like poisonous gas, there was a change in her countenance.

"How did you even…"

"Know what you were going to ask me? You're so obvious. I've been on to you for some time now," she said. I couldn't even finish a sentence. "David, I'm heading home; if you want we can ride the train together."

I heard the words, and saw them leave her lips, one syllable at a time. A sheepish grin escaped, and I nodded yes, for my throat was still too parched to speak.

Delancey and I walked four blocks to the subway, making small talk about school, teachers, the upcoming SATs, and college. I flashed my student train pass and entered the turnstiles; Delancey used a token. The platform was overcrowded.

We boarded the train without speaking, standing just inches apart. I could smell her sweet breath, as well as her subtle citrus perfume. We remained silent, until I shut my brain off, and just let my emotions take over.

"You smell so good," I said. She blushed, glancing downwards.

"Are you upset that I turned you down?" she asked.

"Technically, I didn't ask you out, and you never said no." We both giggled.

"There are so many other girls in school, why don't you ask one of them out?"

"I appreciate your interest in my love life, but I can take it from here, thanks," I said curtly. The F-Train was now over the Manhattan Bridge, and we were awestruck as usual by views of the Brooklyn Bridge, the East River, and all of lower Manhattan, including the World Trade Center.

"I never get used to this view, even though I see it every day." Delancey's eyes lit up with the awe that filled my vision.

"I know what you mean." I asked her about her family.

She talked about her father, who owned big, expensive restaurants in the city. She was being pulled in different directions by her divorced parents. Her mother was remarried and living on Long Island. Delancey lived with her father in the city during the school week.

"Why did they divorce?" I asked, realizing that it was none of my business the moment the question was asked. Delancey paused.

"I'm sorry I asked the question; it's none of my business."

"It's okay...I just...well, I really don't know what would be the best answer. There were so many reasons, like years of constant fighting. I could go on and on. But I guess the best way for me to answer is to say that they never should've gotten together in the first place. They were doomed from the beginning. My mother is so different from my father. She is...well....I wouldn't say that she's a hippie, but she's definitely a free spirit...free willed, and just not really the kind of woman that I could ever see my father with. He is regimented, a workaholic, with very specific routines, and structure...a pragmatist. My father had plans for my entire life laid out on paper before I was born. He wanted me to go to the private school in the city that he picked out when I was two years old. He plans well, even for a divorce."

Delancey's expression seemed to change when she discussed her father. I could sense they were close, much closer than she was to her mother.

"It was a really big argument when I told him I wanted to leave private school and go to Stanton. It was like my entire future was over for him. But I threatened to live with Mother full time on Long Island, and that's all he needed to hear before he relinquished. But that's my dad. Very possessive and controlling. And my mother, the free spirit. How does anyone control a free spirit?"

The F-Train was in Manhattan, and I asked her where she lived.

"Upper West Side, I have to change to the number two at Times Square. What about you?"

"I'm in Astoria, over the 59th Street Bridge," I replied.

"That's not what I meant. How about your parents?" she inquired.

"It's just my father, brother, and I. My mother died when I was eleven."

"Oh, David, I'm so sorry."

"It's okay. We're surviving without her."

"What happened, if you don't mind me asking?" She seemed concerned.

I really didn't want to get into it. "Let's just say that your mother is a free spirit, and my mother's spirit is free." Delancey exited the train and waved good-bye. I stayed on, and headed home. The double doors closed, and through vandalized windows I watched her walk up the platform as my train pulled away.

"Delancey!" I called out, but there was no answer.

chapter 3

A HARD, COLD October rain fell on the first day of the month. October is such a great month. Gone were the summer strolls, now replaced with brisk walks. The brightly tinted treetops dripped with the changing of colors, signaling autumn in New York. The girls on the subways looked better in the fall. They wore sweaters and fashionable full length clothing, but they weren't covered up with coats. It was a great time to be a boy in high school, and although I liked baseball and basketball, girl watching was my favorite sport.

There was only one month to go before the SATs, and it became easier to study when the weather was dreary. Studying was all on my own, nightly, with books borrowed from the local library in Queens. The absence of part time employment meant I did not have the money for SAT prep classes. Studying for the SATs was difficult and slow going. I consistently put in three hours a night, in addition to my normal workload of five hours of studying and homework daily. Math was my strength. The reading and vocabulary parts were more difficult.

My body had acclimated to the lack of sleep and coffee was my elixir. Stanton students learn early that sleep is a luxury. Sleep can be taken with short naps on the subway, to and from school, whether sitting or standing. Many of my deepest sleeps occurred when I was standing on a crowded subway train in morning rush hour.

The truth, deep down inside, was that I dreamed of becoming a professional musician. I loved playing guitar and singing. If I had attended a normal high school, one less academically intense, I may have been more inclined to pursue my musical aspirations. In reality, Stanton and its students frown upon idyllic notions like musical careers. College was not optional at Stanton; it was required, and instilled within each student's psyche from the beginning. We were all expected to be future engineers, doctors, scientists, etc., not musicians. A lot depended on my scores on the upcoming SATs. I felt the pressure to do well weighing on my shoulders and aching in my joints. Bile from anxiety filled my digestive system.

My work on the school newspaper was about the football team. Our football team was having a winning season, suffering only one loss thus far. My articles were a little grander than reality, as I painted a picture of heroes winning battles with my stylistic writing. The football team's record was deceiving. If you are unfamiliar with high school football in Brooklyn, you would think that our team was fantastic. In reality, our rivals frequently were missing their best players, due to incarceration. However, a win is a win. Stanton did not have its own football field, as was the case with most other New York City High Schools. The Stanton Serpents played football on a field they leased from a nearby college. Like in the Middle East, land was at a premium in Brooklyn.

Sam was weighing heavily on my mind. He was becoming a pain in the neck. I'm not sure if he knew or even cared about my feelings for Delancey. He had tunnel vision, which was required for him to succeed in his elected future field of medicine. Tunnel vision was also necessary for success in the field of high school romance.

Sam discovered that Delancey's birthday was that week. He was unusually enthusiastic about making yet another move on her. Sam's parents never gave him any money, and he never held a job a day in his life. He was a bit lazy, and really did not believe in the concept of working for a living. Sam would often say, "Most people work because they believe it will lead to money, and yet they are still broke. Logically it is flawed, and therefore the opposite should be true." The logic tables we had learned in school could not be applied to real life.

Sam's attitude had to do with being born into a wealthy family in Iran. With the overthrow of the Shah, they had fled, taking some of the wealth with them to England. But like most moderate Iranians fleeing in the dark of night, the majority of the family fortune was left behind. Sam's family only recently immigrated to New York. He joked that his family left the magic carpet behind, and as a result wasted their money on airplanes. He once had servants and chauffeurs. The lavish lifestyle he was born into was gone forever, but he did not accept that in America, he needed to work. He accused me of having a poor man's mentality. Sam could not grasp the idea of America as a place where people start over.

Instead of getting a job, Sam mooched off the rest of us. He always said he was good for it, and that he would repay us when he was a doctor. Carlos usually lent him the most money, banking on their friendship lasting into the future. But that day, Sam needed a lot of money. He planned to buy Delancey something special, something expensive. He asked me ten times for money, knowing which buttons to push when he said, "Don't be cheap."

I gave him a five dollar bill; it was all I had on me. I asked for change; he said he didn't have any. Then Sam asked other kids for money. This went on for two days.

The day of Delancey's birthday, Sam and Carlos were not at lunch. John explained that they had gone to Bloomingdales to buy a very expensive bottle of perfume.

"How much money did the Persian Prince get begging?" I asked.

"About $150 dollars," John said. That was a lot of money for a kid without a job or an allowance. When Sam put his mind to something, he usually pulled it off.

I went to my next class, health education. This was a brutally embarrassing and visually vivid class. It was mostly about sex, pregnancy, AIDS, and birth, though not necessarily in that order.

The health education teacher was a young, beautiful woman named Mrs. Bulzer. Her good looks didn't help the situation for most of the boys. We were all dreading that day's class: the birthing video. I had made sure to eat a light lunch.

Howard Moh was a small, nerdy kid and very uncomfortable discussing the topic of sex. Howard asked questions that led the class to realize he had literally not hit puberty yet. He had no clue about sex. When he saw the infant delivery during the video, he vomited and fainted. The class laughed; it was bad enough his nickname was HoMo, but now this incident would follow him wherever he went. Mrs. Bulzer had succeeded in associating sex with something disgusting, and in this case Howard had helped. She had spent the past few weeks stirring up fear of AIDS, and now pregnancy and birth could be feared as well.

We had to write a one page anonymous essay on our views of sex. I contemplated writing the word "none" in the middle of the page and then handing it in. I would not have been exaggerating. I started writing that I had not had sex yet, and wasn't planning on having sex until I was older, perhaps 19 or 20. Don't get me wrong, I was as big a day dreamer and fantasizer as anyone else. I sometimes daydreamed that Delancey and I were on a deserted island, the result of a fortunate accident. Anyway, the fear of AIDS and pregnancy overwhelmed me.

I was not sexually attracted to the girls I knew in school, except for Delancey, and she was out my league. I also did not want to get involved with someone in high school and carry on a long distance relationship at college. I felt that I wanted to really be in love with the first girl I had sex with. It was a silly romantic notion that I had carried with me for a while. I included all of these points in my essay.

My grandmother, Calli, had done a great job of convincing me that sex was a bad thing. She always mentioned that only bad people had sex. She never mentioned married people having sex, just "bad people." This was not a conversation I could ever be comfortable having with my grandmother. At that point, I was willing to wait a few years.

I wrote that I was afraid of getting AIDS or any other sexually transmitted diseases and be sick for the rest of my life. This was actually true. A guy on my block had died of AIDS the year before. I folded the paper and handed it in.

I really didn't care that I was still a virgin or that I was willing to wait until I met the right person. I had bigger fish to fry. College applications were due soon, as well as the SATs, midterms, the prom, finals, etc.

In a school like Stanton, I would guess that most of the kids were still not sexually active. Sure, there were some who were, but this was not your typical high school in America. Sex was not the priority; success was the priority. The two might be mutually exclusive. Who really had the time or the opportunity? When I came home from school every day, my younger brother was home and I had chores. Besides, it's not like I would have ever wanted a girl to see the poor neighborhood and sloppy, small house we lived in. Try that for an anti-sex campaign suggestion. The class dragged on forever, until the bell finally rang. I had sports articles to write and headed to the pool.

The best boys swimmer was Jacob. He swam for two hours straight on most days. I was in awe, because I loved swimming. However, Jacob made it look like art, and I made it look like an act of survival. If I could swim like him, maybe high school would've been different.

Jacob took a break, and I sat down to interview him. Jacob was good looking and full of jokes. He had rock star hair; that's how the girls described him. I could never picture him without a smile on his face, exposing his large teeth. Sandra joined us—she was the captain of the girl's swim team, and Jacob's girlfriend.

Sandra made me nervous. Trying to interview a beautiful girl who happens to be soaking wet in a swimsuit was not easy. She was also intimidating when she was dry and fully clothed. Sandra had curly, dark hair and naturally dark skin. She was tall and muscular, with a swimmer's wide back and shoulders. Sandra had a physical presence about her that let you know she was in charge. It was in the way she walked, and the way she sat, always with perfect posture. Her commanding presence led some of the guys to nickname her The Amazon. When I was around Sandra, I always felt that I might be slouching, or that I could use about twenty five pounds of muscle on my body. But the truth was that there were hardly any girls in school quite like Sandra. She seemed deliberate in her speech and actions. Sandra also radiated self confidence and pure raw feminine energy, and that's what probably intimidated most of the boys. In a few years, Sandra would become the ideal woman for any heterosexual male, but at that time she was surrounded by insecure boys.

Jacob was sure he would get a full swim scholarship to Cornell. Sandra had a half scholarship to a small liberal arts school in Ohio, but was still waiting for decisions from other schools. They asked about my college choices and I mentioned that there were no scholarships for sports reporters or guitar players. They laughed, but I wasn't joking.

I asked Jacob why the Stanton Serpents swim team was the best in NYC and he answered, "It's because of Coach Don Poseye. Coach uses techniques including summer training at Coney Island Beach on Neptune Avenue. The riptides are very strong, and during the summers we train there for about three hours a day. It is brutal. All the other swim teams in NYC train only in a pool. We're at an advantage."

Jacob flashed a smile and shouted, "You can quote me on it!"

These two were nice kids, and clearly athletically gifted. Graduation would probably mean the end of their relationship. Stanton was not the type of school where high school sweethearts ever got married or even stayed in touch. Jacob left the interview and dove back into the pool, immediately splashing us with a series of thunderous dolphin kicks. I was alone with Sandra.

I said, "You must be so happy. You have such a bright future ahead of you. I'm sure lots of good looking guys are waiting for you in college." She smiled. Sandra and I barely knew each other, but the topic of going off to college was a sore spot. Her demeanor became less Amazon princess, and more vulnerable young woman.

"I really want to go to Cornell with Jacob, but can't afford it without a full scholarship. I'm just three seconds short of qualifying for a full scholarship," she said. "I'm realistic. We're going to meet other people in college. It's just a shame. We really have a great thing here."

"I know all about it," I said. But the reality is I didn't have a high school relationship, or a half scholarship, so I really didn't know anything about it. Sandra finished her interview and dove into the pool with a huge splash. I wondered if the few minutes I had spent interviewing student athletes would be remembered. In the future, when student athletes look back on their high school sports life, I hoped they understand that sports reporters recorded their own personal history.

I was leaving the pool area when Delancey entered looking gorgeous. She was dressed very feminine, not a hair out of place, completely well put together. She had on make up, which was rare, and looked like she just walked out of a fashion magazine.

"Hey, David, what are you doing here?" she said with a pleasant smile.

"I had to interview Jacob and Sandra. I hear it's your birthday. Happy Birthday!"

"Thanks. Sandra, Jacob, and a few of us are going out for pizza; do you want to join us?" she asked.

"I can't, I have to write an article for the next issue, but thanks anyway." I didn't have any money; I had given Sam my last five dollars.

"So what did you get me for my birthday?" she asked coyly.

"I'm so sorry, I didn't get you anything," I stuttered, completely embarrassed.

"I'm joking. I didn't expect you to get me anything," she laughed.

"Oh sure...I knew you were joking the whole time," I said. I tried to play it off, but I looked embarrassed.

"Maybe you can play your guitar for me sometime as my birthday gift," she said. She definitely knew me well.

"I'd like that. Anytime you want. You know, I was considering giving up guitar to focus on more worthy things in life," I said.

"Don't ever do that. You have a God-given talent, and you should really see it through." Her reflection in the pool was that of a beautiful nymph, airy, and erudite.

The next day at lunch, I asked Sam about Delancey's present. He was angry.

"I'm so pissed. She's such a typical you know what. I got $150, cut school with Carlos, and bought her a bottle of expensive French perfume. I gave it to her in front of all her friends. She said no thanks, that she's allergic to the perfume. In Iran, no one is allergic to anything. I'm done with that girl, man." Sam was brooding.

Served him right. Sam did nothing in school for the previous three days other than borrow money in an attempt to impress Delancey. He got nowhere fast. I didn't think he had real feelings for her. He only knew that I found her attractive and that was enough to set him off. It was a game for him.

"Don't even think of asking out Delancey; she would reject you instantly," Sam said out of the blue, and his words resonated deep within my head.

The school workload was starting to pile on. I had eight classes, papers due, and tests coming up. Senior year at Stanton was meant to prepare students for college, and the normal heavy workload increased. In addition to state tests, I also needed to take Stanton's final exams, which were famous for being more difficult than any state exam.

In gym class, some students discussed an assault on a student who was on his way home the day before. It could happen to anyone, and they discussed self defense options. The Deceptors had hospitalized the student. The sophomores in the locker room were in shock.

I felt indifferent, having had heard similar gang stories for years. I rarely saw a policeman on a school street. It was equally rare to see police on the subway, with the exception of Manhattan. I guess their job was to protect the working wealthy of the big city, and everyone else had to fend for themselves.

The boys in the locker room were planning to carry weapons for protection. A few months remained until graduation, and I didn't want to ruin my chances of getting into a good college by getting caught with a weapon at school. I was too close to the end of high school to make such a stupid mistake. The best way to deal with gangs was avoiding them.

It was common to see a student showing off a knife in the cafeteria. Weapons have become a mundane showpiece; someone always had one. Anyone could buy a gun for fifty dollars in the park across the street. A masked student sold guns in the park every Friday. No one knew who he was, but everyone knew where to find him. He was Stanton's very own arms dealer.

The kids of Stanton were smart enough to have their brawls outside of the school building. I had never seen a weapon pulled during an after school fight. Brooklyn had turned into the Wild West and if someone were to pull a gun, ten guns would immediately point back in their direction. Most of the fights involved fisticuffs only. The longest fight I had personally witnessed lasted sixty seconds. I could defend myself for sixty seconds without a gun.

In gym class, I lifted weights to exhaustion, but still looked like puberty had lost my address. I'd been lifting weights since I was fifteen, with minimal results. Guys like Mino and Jacob increased my insecurities, and skewed my body image. "A sound mind in a sound body" was engraved on a plaque outside the weight room. I could no longer feel my arms, but still did not resemble a classic Greek hero. Perhaps I never would.

The school employment office finally had good news. That weekend I would start working part time at a café in the city. The owner of the café hired me without an interview. It was good enough for him that I was a Stanton student. I needed to be at the café at seven o' clock Saturday morning. It was great to finally be earning some money, but the new job also reduced the time I had to study for the SATs.

chapter 4

SATURDAY MORNING, I eagerly rode the subway at six a.m. to the World Trade Center. An hour later, I was running through the ground floor of the Twin Towers, crossing a sky bridge over West Street, and jogging down the marble steps of a monumental glass and steel building called the Winter Garden. The Hudson River shimmered in the early morning sunlight.

An information kiosk explained that the magnificent building I was standing in was built on a landfill, using dirt excavated during the building of the Twin Towers. It was designed by Cesar Pelli. The newly constructed World Financial Center was like an entirely different world, a different dimension.

The owner of the café promptly started training, teaching me how to bake cookies, muffins, croissants, and operate the register. I was to start baking at seven a.m. every weekend. At eight a.m. a second shift would start. The owner of the café created a four page list of instructions. The first sentence read, "If you can't stand the heat, get out of the kitchen."

At eight o'clock, three high school girls and one guy started their shift. They were all Chinese Americans, all young, all pretty. They did not need training and were from his other café at the Seaport. The girls had known each other for years—from Chinatown, elementary school, middle school, and, currently, the same local high school.

They spoke a mix of Cantonese and English. I was listening from the back of the café, shocked by their conversations. They were discussing night clubs, parties, sex from the night before, and how exhausted they were from the whole thing. At times, the girls told dirty jokes to each other and laughed intermittently.

I was feeling awkward around them. I continued to listen, surmising that "Dai Lo" was the head of their gang. They were just teenagers, but had already lived ten years more than anyone I knew. They were hardworking, smart, well spoken, some with ambition to attend an affordable college in the city. Family and gang obligations required that they stay close to home. I spent the first day on the job just listening, hardly speaking.

I was feeling like an outsider on many levels. Toward the late afternoon, about a half hour before my shift was over, Christine asked about my high school. When I told her I went to Stanton, they all laughed. Christine was the most loquacious, and the prettiest of the girls. She said they knew a lot of boys from Stanton. Kenny, the boy in their group, was displeased.

It made sense that they would know students from Stanton. Many kids from Stanton were from Chinatown, and a few were Chinese gangsters. These kids were smart enough to pass the entrance exam to get into Stanton, and smart enough to keep their grades up, but rumors always swirled about their involvement in nefarious activities.

Not all the Asian kids at Stanton were in gangs. The gangsters were easy to spot because they dressed the same. They dressed like the kids I worked with at the café. The gangster dress code included tight black pants tapered around the ankles, plain canvas sneakers, either a plain white or plain black tee shirt, and oversized denim or nylon jackets. Their hairstyle was blown dry very high, spiked, with lots of hair spray and gel. Some gangsters' hair stood six inches high or more. Most of the boys had earrings in their left ears.

My first day at work ended at 5pm. Exhausted, I fell asleep on the subway ride home. My first weekend at the café ended at 5pm on Sunday. I still had six hours of homework, and three hours of studying to do. Upon arriving home, I did not spend much time with my brother or my father. In the past, the three of us had always spent Sundays together.

The ensuing week at school was typical. I studied for the SATs well past midnight. Sleep was the least of my priorities. The unofficial Stanton policy on sleep was, "you can sleep in the afterlife." I wrote a few articles for the newspaper, and went home to study and make dinner on my designated nights. I deftly avoided the robberies and gang attacks on the school's perimeter, and on the subways. More stories circulated about the Deceptors.

The Deceptors were a unique New York City street gang, because no one knew who they were. They operated out of many city high schools, and were always in disguise. It was rumored they had over a thousand members. Stories swirled that kids in school were the same Deceptors robbing and attacking other students. When they attacked, they wore face paint, ski masks, or bandanas. They wore hats and big coats. Some of the Deceptors were students gone evil, some had been co-erced, and others were just students who wanted to be in the gang.

Fear grew with each more incredible story about the terror of the Deceptors. Exaggerated stories became oral traditions, and freshmen often quivered in their shoes at the mention of them.

On Saturday, I went back to work at the café. I quickly started my job, baking an assortment of foods, and making several urns of coffee. I made bagels as well, some with butter, some with cream cheese. At eight a.m. the rest of the crew arrived.

They were talking loudly about the Dai Lo. I listened, but did not participate in the conversation. Their Dai Lo had stolen some clothing from a department store and was tackled by a security guard before getting away. The work day was slow and dull. I kept listening;

it was fascinating stuff. Christine said that the Dai Lo was going to miss a couple of days of school.

"Where does he go to school?" I asked. Everyone dispersed. Christine smiled.

"Where DO YOU go to school?" she asked, and I inferred that the Dai Lo went to Stanton. They did not speak too freely for the rest of the morning. I may have overstepped my boundaries.

Kenny felt that one of us would be fired unless business picked up. I hoped it wasn't me. It wasn't cheap to be a high school senior. Expenses like college application fees, trips, the prom, and more, added up. And I just needed money to buy things. I couldn't ask my father for money. I could hear him now saying, "money doesn't grow on trees."

The next day, Sunday, there was a new manager for the café named Mike. He was tall and lanky, bald, with glasses. I would guess he was close to thirty years old. Christine said that Mike always arrived late, and slept at work. She had worked with him at the café's other location.

She was right. Mike was a disaster. He never actually did any work. Mike was the only adult at the cafe, and was friends with the owner. In the real world, it paid to be friends with the boss.

Christine and Kenny were talking in Cantonese and laughing. I asked, "What's so funny?" She said that I dressed funny. They giggled again.

"You guys dress funny, like typical Chinese gangsters," I said. They were offended and threw wet sponges at me. It's not okay to tell Chinese gangsters that they actually looked like Chinese gangsters.

"If you wanted to be incognito, then why dress this way?" I asked. Christine explained that everyone in Chinatown dressed this way.

"It's incognito in Chinatown."

Later that day, Christine remarked that I wasn't bad looking but needed to do something with my clothes and my hair.

"I know a backhanded compliment when I hear one," I said. She asked if I wanted to go shopping after work. I was a little surprised by how forward she was, but agreed. I had just been paid, and liked the idea of hanging out with her. She was a very pretty girl, with a slender build, and a smile that made her look like a child at times. Her skin was remarkably smooth, despite the make up.

Christine and I went to Chinatown. We walked to Hester Street, an old street with small stores and traditional Chinese restaurants. The entire population was mostly non-English speaking Chinese immigrants. We shopped at a store she suggested. Christine spoke to the store clerk in Cantonese. I tried to speak to the clerk but she ignored my questions about the prices. I figured she did not speak English. I asked Christine to ask her how long she'd been in New York. Christine asked in Cantonese. The clerk crossed her arms, and responded, "I was born in Brooklyn, you idiot!" I bought a cool outfit from her, like nothing I had ever worn before. I had always been a Levis and Tee shirt guy, until now. These threads I bought were the style of Christine's choosing, and reminiscent of Chinese gangsters.

Next we went to a barber shop. They only spoke Chinese, as a far as I could tell, but I didn't want to assume anything. I told the barber, "Give me a trim, nothing drastic." He looked at me puzzled, unable to understand. Christine told him in Cantonese how to cut my hair. Ten minutes later, I was shocked by my haircut. My hair stood tall on top, spiked to the max, and cut to the scalp on the sides.

I thanked Christine for her help and told her I'd see her next weekend. I gave her a hug goodbye, and almost didn't want to let go. I had never embraced anyone so soft and tender before.

On the subway ride home, people kept trying not to look at my hair. New Yorkers rarely stare, but the people on the subway were obviously not told about this rule.

When I arrived home, my father was concerned. He was not accustomed to his oldest son not showing up for dinner. I explained that I bought some clothes and went for a haircut. He asked if I had looked in the mirror before I left the barber shop. I said I liked the cut and this would be my new look. My father looked at me, shook his head in disbelief, and walked away.

On Monday at school, I had a new found sense of confidence. I wore my new clothes, and sported my new hair cut. I was wearing black khaki pants, tapered to the ankle. I wore an oversized t-shirt, and an oversized denim jacket. The other kids stared and some even giggled.

Delancey approached me at lunch and said she liked the new look. Her opinion was the only one that mattered. Several people asked if I had joined a Chinese gang. The Chinese gangsters giggled every time they saw me.

Sam was quiet after overhearing Delancey's comment. He looked irritated. We kept eating lunch. Carlos asked where I got the new clothes and haircut. I told him about Christine, the café, and the shopping trip. Carlos said it looked "bad in a good way." Sam said I looked like an idiot.

It seemed the wheels in Sam's head were turning.

"You can't pull off this look. It's not you and it works better for other people. Besides, why are you wasting money? You should be helping your family with their expenses and saving for college." That was classic Sam. He always knew my real concerns, and which buttons to push to activate my self doubts.

"To each their own," I said.

I've never been the type of person that sought after attention or relished it. I'd been perfectly happy being incognito my entire life, but at this point things were changing. The way I felt about drawing attention and the comments that came with it, also changed. I liked the fact that Delancey liked my new look, and that Sam didn't. Anything that irritated Sam meant that I was doing something right.

Sure, I was thinking that I should've used the money for something better, something more long term. But, I experienced something new that day. I had lifted some of my inferiority complex, even if it was temporary. I had more confidence, and even walked with a little swagger. Not bad for a poor boy from Queens.

"So, what's with the new look?" asked Delancey. I told her about Christine, and working at the café.

"I wanted something different," I added.

"You look so much more grown up." She giggled as she said this, and Sam glowered.

"I wasn't going for more grown up, just cool," I said.

"Oh, excuse me. Definitely cool!" she said.

We all laughed, except for Sam.

Later that day, I had to write an article on the basketball team. Stanton's basketball team was one of the best in Brooklyn. For the first time, I interviewed shooting guard Eddie Lo.

I didn't know Eddie Lo well at all. I knew who he was, but who didn't? Eddie was famous at Stanton. I don't want to sound like I had a crush on the guy, but he was everything I wished I could be. Eddie was the coolest guy in school.

I would describe him as good looking, with an overabundance of testosterone. He was stylish, wore the latest fashions, including a very expensive leather jacket. No one messed with Eddie, either in school or out of school. Eddie Lo was the only Chinese-American member of the basketball team and was hard to miss at six feet four inches tall and a bulky two hundred and twenty pounds. He had fully developed muscles in parts of his body where I didn't even have tissue. He also had a long scar across his neck, and a necklace consisting of a jade pendant tied around a red thread. Eddie Lo was also a dangerous Chinese gangster with a tattoo of a large snake on his arm.

During the interview, he said a few colleges had contacted him about playing basketball. However, he wanted to stay close to home to help his family with their business. He needed to go to college in the city, close to his family's clothing store in Chinatown. He had seen me at his family's store over the weekend, and joked that I looked like a Chinatown gangster.

"You should talk," I said. He accused me of wanting to look like him. We both laughed.

Eddie wanted to play basketball for St. John's University in Queens, but he felt his reputation and tattoos eliminated him from most college basketball programs.

A few days later, when the paper came out, Eddie thought the article was about him, and thanked me. I had intended for the article to be about the basketball team, but since Eddie Lo was the only player interviewed, I could understand his interpretation. Eddie said his father was really proud to see an article about him, even if it was just the school newspaper.

I loved basketball, but I had not played for years. I did not have a basketball hoop in the driveway of my home. As a matter of fact, I did not have a driveway either. I'm not sure we even had a basketball. For me to play basketball meant going to a nearby playground or park. These basketball playgrounds were always a hub for criminal activities and drug dealers. My father was very strict about my brother and I avoiding these places. Fights usually broke out during the games.

The next day, Sam was in the hallway wearing tapered black pants. He even had my hair cut. He said he got the clothes from the same place I did. I was confused. Sam said I looked stupid, but he went out and bought almost identical clothing, and got the same haircut. He stole my look!

Maybe Sam was jealous. Maybe he was gay. Maybe he was just trying to get Delancey's attention. How many other guys would deliberately go out and steal my look?

Three days later, Carlos also had the same haircut. It was becoming normal for Carlos to do whatever Sam did.

Carlos said the Deceptors were going to attack Stanton on Halloween. Fifty kids were sent to a hospital the year before during a similar Halloween attack on a different school.

"I'll worry about it later, as we get closer to Halloween," I said indifferently.

Sam thought about getting jumped and said he would probably cut school on Halloween. Carlos could not cut school that day; he had a big math test. I asked John what he thought.

John and I were always practical, no matter the circumstances. John was planning on coming to school and going home. He wasn't about to worry about an attack that may or may not happen, and even if it did, he would just avoid it. My mother's words from long ago came into my head. She had said, "you always find what you are looking for when you go looking for trouble." The kids most worried about the Deceptors were the ones likely to get assaulted.

Delancey asked if we would attend a march after school to raise awareness for a charity for disabled kids. Sam jumped up and shouted that he wouldn't miss it for the world. Delancey laughed, aware of Sam's insincerity. She could see right through him. She mentioned that she would be taking pictures of the march for the yearbook. I told her that we were all headed to play billiards after school. She said the march wouldn't take long. I agreed to attend; after all, it was Delancey asking.

Mr. Zoose's English class was my favorite part of school. Students sat anywhere they wanted; desks were not organized in any sequence. I could even sit on the floor, or near the window. Mr. Zoose usually walked in a few minutes late, placed an apple on his desk, and then began teaching. He preferred we only took notes if we had to, otherwise, it would distract from his class. We were reading *The Stranger* by Camus. I couldn't relate to the character's motives or philosophy. I was indifferent to existentialism.

Delancey also liked the book, but could not really relate to the main character. I wondered if an existentialist could even fall in love. Delancey said that not even an existentialist could avoid certain basic human experiences such as falling in love.

"It's an event, it's an emotion, it's iconic, and uncontrollable. Love is in a category by itself," she smiled at me. "Are you an existentialist?" she asked.

"Probably the opposite," I said.

At the end of class, Mr. Zoose reminded us that he was directing the school play. Mr. Zoose was the head of the drama club, and consistently put on a great show every year. He had asked me to perform "Ave Maria" in the play.

"No. Not this year. I have to focus on more serious things in my life," I said. Mr. Zoose seemed disappointed.

After school, I marched with hundreds of students for 45 minutes around the block. The blustery weather made for complaints that the march was taking too long. I was missing my jacket that had been stolen the first day of school. Delancey took hundreds of pictures.

Sam sat smoking on a nearby brownstone's front stoop. He finally had an audience watching him try to be cool. He was a brilliant student, could possibly have been valedictorian, and yet his constant need for attention led to stupid behavior. I think the only motivation behind his desire to be valedictorian was the opportunity to make a speech at graduation and all the attention that goes with it. He had all the brains in the world, and all the potential that comes with high intelligence. Sam was on cruise control and still getting high grades. I was pushing full throttle with my studying and still couldn't break into the top three hundred on the rankings list.

Delancey asked about our billiards game, and I told her about our favorite pool hall in Manhattan's West Village.

We arrived at the pool hall on Christopher Street, and took our usual table in the back. Sam, Carlos, and I had played pool at Tekk Billiards for the past three years. Carlos and I were playing eight ball, when Delancey entered with ten of her friends. She snapped a picture of me taking a shot. She said that it was for posterity.

"Posterity?" I asked.

"Yeah...the yearbook, silly."

I banked shot after shot. Carlos was standing right next to me, with a smirk on his face. Sam spent the entire time trying to talk to Delancey. She did not take a photo of him, and he did not get anywhere with her.

That weekend at the Café, Mike the manager arrived late, and was soon asleep in the back. Christine and the crew arrived late. The work day was slow, and we talked a lot. The topic of the Deceptors caused Christine to giggle. "The Chinatown gangs would destroy them," Christine said.

Later that day, Christine asked if I had ever dated a Chinese girl.

I had not. I explained it would not be a problem if it was the right girl. I asked her if her friends would give her a hard time about dating a non-Chinese boy. Christine explained it wasn't a big deal because she wasn't one hundred percent Chinese. Her mother was Chinese, but her father, who she had never known, was Japanese. Her mother worked in Japan before coming to New York. Christine revealed her real name was Izanami.

After work, we went to a Japanese restaurant in the World Trade Center. Christine ordered sushi for both of us. I had never had sushi before. She couldn't stop smiling as I tried to get used to the chopsticks. Christine said that in California everyone was eating sushi. I reminded her that we were in New York, where everyone eats bagels and pizza.

We walked onto the plaza of the Twin Towers, and sat under the two-story monumental bronze sculpture of a sphere. Below the sculpture was a fountain.

"Do you have a girlfriend?" she asked.

"No."

"Are you a virgin?" I did not know how to answer the question, but before I could, she said, "Never mind, I already know the answer."

"How could you possibly know the answer?" I asked.

"Boys who are not virgins don't hesitate to answer that question."

"Do you know what the word tact means?" I asked, feeling embarrassed. "I'll be honest with you. I really don't know if I'm ready for a girlfriend or sex. I'm probably going to go away to college and I really don't know if I want to start something that leads to a long term relationship," I said.

"Don't assume I want to be your girlfriend, and don't assume I want to have sex with you either." She punched my arm, laughing out loud.

"Don't assume I was talking about you," I said. She punched me on the arm much harder this time.

"I'm always direct. I hope you don't mind, but I don't understand the need for small talk or for talking around a subject. If I want to know something I'll just ask," she said.

"Do you ever think that being too direct could be a problem?" I asked with sarcasm.

"Yes, I do. But I don't understand why Americans consider it polite not to ask what they want to know, but rather tiptoe around the topic."

"Small talk is an art form," I said.

"Small talk is a waste of time. What about your family?" she asked.

"It's just me, my father, and my brother," I said.

"What about your mother?" she asked.

"My mother died when I was eleven. She was very sick from cancer," I said.

Christine grew quiet. "I am sorry," she said.

"Don't be, it wasn't your fault."

I had a good time with Christine. It was nice to have a female friend.

The long, empty subway ride home allowed opportunity for me to think about Christine. She was so different from Delancey, so much easier to be around. Delancey was one of a kind, but was in a different realm.

chapter 5

ON MONDAY IT was nearly six o'clock when I finished writing articles for the school paper. As I exited the lobby of Stanton, Delancey was leaving school.

"What are you doing here?" I asked.

"I could ask you the same thing," she said.

"You first."

"Why should I answer first?"

"Because I asked you first," I said.

"So what, I asked you second."

"I plead the fifth," I said.

"Well then so do I. If you won't answer, neither will I," she grinned.

"In that case, we should change the subject. Are you heading home?" I asked.

"I'm going to the city to meet my father for dinner at a steakhouse near Wall Street."

"What a strange coincidence, I'm also heading to that very same steakhouse."

"You LIE!" she shouted. We both guffawed.

She punched my arm, and I said, "Is that the best you got?"

She then punched me even harder, and I felt a stinging pain all the way through to my chest.

"Ouch!" I yelled.

"Oh, David, I'm so sorry." She rubbed my shoulder.

"You are much stronger than you look," I said.

"I'm more than I look in many ways," she replied.

"Keep rubbing, it feels good," I said sheepishly.

"I BET IT DOES!" she said as she punched my arm again.

"So are you going to ride the train with me to downtown?" she asked.

"I'll do one better. I will even escort you to the restaurant, Madame."

Delancey held out her bent arm. I wrapped mine around hers, and we started marching in sequence like communist solders. It was great to hold her arm, even if we were just having fun. She was so warm, so full of life and energy. And as usual, she smelled great.

I noticed her jacket's fine brown leather. It was fighter pilot's jacket, very expensive. We were far from a safe neighborhood.

"You look great in that jacket," I said.

"Thanks. My father just bought it for me."

I could feel the icy stares of eyes following us. I glanced back. Three thugs, undoubtedly Deceptors, followed about twenty yards behind us. They were walking much faster than we were, and I didn't want any trouble, not with Delancey at risk of getting hurt. She seemed oblivious to their presence, and I didn't want to alarm her. I knew that her expensive new leather jacket had caught their eyes.

"Delancey, do you think you're faster than me?" I said.

"I know so. I could beat you in a race anytime," she gloated.

"I will race you to the subway on the count of three, and I won't look back," I said. I started counting, "One..." and Delancey took off, running as fast as she could for the subway. When I saw that she was well ahead, I turned around and faced the hoodlums. One wore a belt buckle with a capital D on it. Deceptors.

"Empty your pockets!" one yelled.

I tried to run, but was quickly trampled to the ground. I tried to get up, but caught a few kicks in the chest. I pushed one of the guys down, and ran for the train. They chased after me. I pulled a ten dollar bill from my pocket and dropped it. They stopped chasing and took the money as I entered the subway station seconds later. The Deceptors fought each other over the ten dollar bill, like a pack of wolves fighting over a carcass.

Delancey had already crossed the turnstiles and was entering the platform.

"I won!" she boasted, panting heavily. "Wow, what happened to you?" she asked noticing my disheveled appearance.

"Delancey, I slipped on a banana peel and fell, otherwise, I would've won."

I brushed myself off as we both walked up the platform. I glanced behind me, but we were no longer being followed.

Delancey and I waited for the train, which was delayed. Fifteen minutes passed before a train arrived. I was glad I had thrown the Deceptors the ten dollars. The fifteen minutes that we waited for the train would have been enough time for them to have taken her jacket, and worse.

"David, what are your plans for college?" she asked.

"I would like to go away, although my father objects. I'm going to apply to some state schools. What about you, Delancey?"

"I think you must really like my name," she said.

"Is it that noticeable?"

"Well, you go out of your way to say it, and every time you say it, you smile, like a kid getting candy."

"Well, Delancey, I guess I do like saying your name, Delancey. Such a great name...Delancey how did you get your name?" I tried to change the subject.

"My father picked it. It was his grandmother's maiden name on his mother's side. His family has been in New York, in some way, since colonial times. Even Delancey Street was named after them. But it was not the name my mother wanted for me."

"Oh? What did she want to name you?"

"She wanted to name me Suryanna, after the Hindu God of the Sun. My mother always says that when I was born, it was like the sun came up for the first time. But my father was, and still is, so controlling, that he wouldn't have it. So Suryanna became my middle name."

"They're both beautiful names, and so different from anything I've ever heard. I guess either way, your name was meant to stand out. I was named after my grandfather; he and my mother were really close." We exited the train in lower Manhattan, and we walked four blocks to the restaurant. I wished the restaurant was two miles away. I loved spending time with Delancey.

The icy winds of lower Manhattan picked up, and I shivered.

"You know, we should get something to eat sometime?" I asked, knowing it was a shaky subject.

"David, you should ask out some of the other girls. I'm not what you are looking for." She shot me down again, this time while wearing an aviation jacket.

"I don't understand. You and I get along so well...that—"

"That's just it, David. I really like you. We are starting to become better friends. Why change things? Besides, I'm not girlfriend material anyway. I'm not going to play dumb, and twirl my hair, like other girls. I have no intentions of getting into a serious relationship right out of high school. I have bold ambitions—like college, and law school, and other things. I'm not a follower, like girls who follow their boyfriends to college. Let's be realistic, David, after graduation we may never see each other again. I'm going to some small liberal arts private school in the middle of the Northeast, and that'll be that." She stood in front of the restaurant, hands on hips, eyes emboldened with emotion.

"David, I have a bright future and I'm sure you do too. I'm not looking to settle down and be someone's high school sweetheart. That's the opposite of who I am. I'm not now, nor will I ever be, someone's little girlfriend. I'm a free spirit, like my mother."

Rejected again, albeit with an explanation this time.

"Listen...I'm just saying, let just grab a bite to eat after school sometime." I was trying my best to walk away with a morsel, having lost much of the entrée.

"Fine, but I'm paying, just so you know it's not a date." She then walked into the Sam Hain Steakhouse on lower Broadway. Nearby, the Ferry departed full of passengers.

I went home and studied until late.

Rumors escalated of gangs attacking Stanton on Halloween. It sounded like the Tet offensive was expected. John and I planned to run to the subway together on Halloween, which was the next day. John was at least thirty-five pounds of muscle bigger than I. The subway was four blocks away. As we were walking, the psychic stood outside her storefront. She asked if we would like to know our future. I said no, thank you. She said her answers could help us decide about college, girls, our majors, etc. She had a very flirtatious smile. We kept walking. I looked back and noticed two girls from school take her up on the offer. John said to me, "Those girls are walking in there to find out if they have a chance with a smart, good looking guy like me."

This was a typical John comment. Sometimes he would say things like, "John is too smart for high school" when he'd get a good grade on a test. We got on the F-Train, and discussed college. John had not applied yet, and wasn't sure he would. He was the oldest son, and his family depended on him to run their grocery store. He was not sure if his parents would allow him to go away to college, or even start college the next fall. He was quiet as the train creaked slowly over the Manhattan Bridge. John finally blurted that he'd like to apply to Annapolis.

"The Naval Academy is really hard to get into. Do you have the grades?" I asked.

"I'm the smartest guy in my neighborhood, who happens to be the best looking guy in Queens," said John. That was a good answer, because he definitely wasn't the smartest guy in our high school.

"Are you a US citizen?" I asked.

"Do I need to be?" John answered.

"I think West Point and the Naval Academy only take US citizens."

The color of hope fell from his face and I instantly knew John wasn't a US citizen. John Moon was born in Seoul, South Korea. His shoulders sank with defeat.

"I guess I won't apply there."

I was sorry to burst his bubble. Of all the kids I knew in high school, he was the most genuine and the hardest working. John started to explain the pressures and expectations that came with his status as an oldest son in a Korean family.

"John, it's your future. Your parents will have to survive without you. You should apply to college and start in the fall."

Glancing downwards, he uttered, "Easier said than done."

I arrived home and dove into the books. My homework was a priority, but I also had to study for the SATs. At 6:30, it was time to make dinner and to watch a little TV. I made spaghetti and chicken. We ate everything, there were rarely leftovers.

My father asked about college. I replied that I wanted to go away to school next year.

"David, you are not going away to college. You need to stay home, just do as I say. I won't pay for college if you go away!"

He couldn't pay for college no matter if I stayed home or went away. Angrily, I lashed out "I don't need your help! This is my life and my decision!" This was a typical night at my house. My father insisted that I stay home; I insisted I was going away, and then I would study until midnight. He only insisted that I stay home because he needed me to help out. I desperately wanted to be on my own.

Our upbringing was strict and disciplined. My father worked six days a week, and always had two jobs in case he lost one. When we were younger, our discipline was a firm spanking. I once asked my father, why the corporal punishment instead of grounding us? "There's nothing left to take away from you," he answered sullenly.

I was burnt out from my strict upbringing. The more my father argued against it, the more I felt the need to go away. That's the kind of person I had become, more determined with increased resistance, a contrarian to my father. I credited Stanton for that part of my personality.

I had been studying for three months for the SATS with books borrowed from the library, but my scores on the practice tests were still 100 points below where they needed to be for consideration at a top college. I was concerned, but not too concerned; after all, how would I even be able to afford a top college if I was ever accepted? I thought about the Naval Academy. Annapolis was not out of the question. But if I died in battle, it would crush my father to lose his eldest son and his wife in the same life.

Stanton had a negative impact on my confidence. My life before Stanton was about how smart I was. I was even valedictorian of my elementary school. Attending Stanton was a constant reminder about how smart I was not. I developed a belief that my grades were not good enough, my SATs were not going to be good enough, and discouraged myself from applying to the top colleges. If I had attended a normal high school, I would have believed that I had a chance anywhere. I probably would have been at the top of the class at any other high school. But at Stanton I was average. I recalled a quote from Milton's *Paradise Lost*, "It's better to reign in hell, than serve in heaven." Milton sure was right.

Was college even necessary? I would have rather been a musician. The owner of the café seemed to do well for himself. I was distracted, and found it difficult to concentrate on the studying. I kept thinking about Delancey.

At school, I had to write an article about the girls' volleyball team. I interviewed the captain of the team, Natalie Morales. Natalie was not what I expected—she was now suddenly gorgeous, and it was difficult to do an interview without getting sidetracked and distracted by her looks.

Natalie had blossomed just recently. She was tall, with curly hair, naturally tan skin, and was now on the radar of every guy with a heartbeat. I wrote a great article about her. I had three reporters under me at the paper, and could have assigned any of them to interview Natalie. But why would I want to do that?

chapter 6

EITHER YOU'RE AFRAID of death, or you are kidding yourself.

Today was Halloween, and I carefully arrived at school at seven a.m. Anxiety was everywhere. The imminent attack after school from the Deceptors loomed in the minds of many students. Sam, John, and Carlos were sitting at our usual lunch table.

Sam was there despite intending to avoid school this day. Sam said he had it all taken care of. He mentioned that Carlos was the only one with "any *cajones*." Moments later I figured out that Sam had talked Carlos into bringing a weapon to school.

John and I flashed expressions of surprise to each other. Carlos had grown from Sam's follower to Sam's puppet. I asked Carlos what kind of weapon he was carrying. He just grinned.

"Sam," I said, "what kind of weapon did you have him bring?"

"He's packing heat," said Sam.

"How did you get the money to buy a gun?" John asked Sam.

"Easy. I returned the perfume back to Bloomingdales for a full refund."

"Did you consider paying everyone back? I could use the money," I said, annoyed.

"I will pay everyone back by dispersing the Deceptors on Halloween." Sam sounded full of confidence.

"Where did you buy the gun?" I asked.

"The guy in the park. I think he's a Deceptor."

"So a Deceptor sells you a gun to be used against the Deceptors?".

"How many enemies does America battle that use American guns?"

"Point well taken."

This was major trouble, though a gun in school was not uncommon. It meant instant suspension if anyone got caught, but hardly anyone ever got caught. Only two other guys were caught with guns last year. They were both suspended for a week ending their hopes of getting into a good college. The bigger problem was that Sam called the shots even though Carlos carried the gun.

Carlos needed greater independence of thought, and less interdependence of will. Sam had a powerful effect on people. He had a natural knowledge of the gears and springs of the psyche. It's his true genius. He appeared weak and vulnerable, all the while calculating and devising a system of how to engineer his will upon his foes and allies. Sam had high grades, and could possibly have been valedictorian. He could not risk his reputation or a suspension by bringing a gun to school. Instead, with carefully chosen words, carefully chosen alliances, he manipulated Carlos to carry out his inner desires.

I glanced at the cheerful and the fearful students at lunch. Cafeterias are not for eating, but rather for feeding. Ideas are often spoon fed into the minds of the mentally starving students.

It's fair to assume that many kids brought weapons to school that day. It was Halloween, and I would guess three hundred students were carrying weapons of some sort.

In the past, I'd seen weapons in the locker room. When someone brought a weapon to school, they liked to show it, a necessity when it comes to developing a reputation. The teachers didn't care unless someone used the weapon in school. I would guess that some of the teachers also had some sort of weapons—a club, mace, a knife, or something else.

Halloween was the longest day of the year. As the school day came to a close, fear and anxiety levels increased exponentially. A scared freshmen student was crying in the locker room.

An announcement came from the principal's office that anyone found lingering around the school or participating in any sort of hanky panky would be brought back into school and suspended. There was no mention of additional security or a police presence. By the end of the day, the tension was elevated to high alert. It was as intense as if the Soviet Army was outside the school with tanks and rockets.

At three o'clock I met up with John. We decided not to be anywhere near Sam and Carlos. We were avoiding guilt by association, and we also didn't want to get accidentally caught in the crossfire. Who knew if Carlos could even shoot straight?

I saw Mino, the football player, and felt pretty good walking between him and John. Mino's plan was simple; he said he was going to run to the subway fast. Mino mentioned the football team had banded together and were preparing for a battle with expectations of bloodshed. I instantly had a mental picture of the Alamo. Mino had too much to lose if he fought the Deceptors. I figured he meant his scholarship and college hopes. The three of us stepped outside of Stanton's main exit.

There were about thirty Deceptors across the street throwing eggs, and other objects. They were wearing masks, some Halloween masks, and some ski masks. Plenty of pushing and shoving lead to students falling and getting sprayed with shaving cream. Mino yelled "Run!" and we took off. Mino ran very fast, as I expected a record breaking running back might. John was right next to him, I started to fall back. I looked behind me and not a single gang member was following, just other kids running for the subway.

In the distance, the Deceptors loomed large. Some students were being shoved to the ground and their wallets were ripped out of their pockets. My heart pounded but I kept running. Dozens of students were ambushed. The Deceptors were merciless. I couldn't watch the assaults. They pelted eggs, tomatoes, and used shaving cream to humiliate the students.

I saw Carlos and Sam in the far corner. A large figure stood alone on top of a car. This was the ringleader, a menacing figure draped in dark clothing, and wearing a red Halloween mask. He struck fear in the hearts of every student, as he pointed to his gang members which students to assault. I kept running.

John and Mino were running ahead, with John actually slightly ahead of Mino. He had just beaten the record-breaking running back of our high school football team in a four block race. When I finally arrived at the F-Train station, Mino seemed as shocked as I was at John's speed.

Mino asked John if he ran track. John didn't play sports. Mino was amazed and said John could've been a star on the football team. I compared the two of them carefully, and noticed for the first time that John was about as big as any of the football players on the team, just not as muscular. John had the build of a construction worker, the kind of guy you expected to haul heavy rocks and metal. We boarded the F-Train and John explained to Mino that he did not play sports because he ran his family's grocery store. John described his pace at work, moving fast to unload deliveries, carrying heavy boxes to the basement, and chasing after shoplifters. He unloaded heavy cartons of groceries daily. His everyday life was his weight room.

The three of us breathed a sigh of relief. We were not attacked. Mino left after a few stops, and John and I stayed on the train. I told John that he really missed out not playing sports.

"My father does not see the point of sports when he needs my help at the grocery store." John's father had hindered his son's chances of developing into an athlete and probably getting a scholarship to college.

The day after Halloween it rained, washing away evidence of the egg throwing melee. In the morning, as I walked to school from the subway, the police were questioning students. Gossip spreads quickly, and I soon learned that during the chaos, someone had fired a gunshot, causing a small stampede. Everyone ran, including the Deceptors, but not without firing back. When a gun is fired in Brooklyn, there's a good chance someone will fire back. A Stanton student was shot and killed.

This was the first student death of the year. Carlos immediately came to mind, but I couldn't be sure it was him. The principal made an announcement urging anyone with information to come forward. This served as an unofficial warning for students to keep their mouths shut. Some students laughed out loud, because no one would come forward and risk revenge by the Deceptors.

Delancey was standing in the hallway. She knew the person who'd been shot and killed, a girl named Lucy, but I had hardly known her. I offered my condolences, and told her I hadn't seen anything. Delancey said that Chinese gangs were hanging out at the park across the street watching the entire incident.

"Over a hundred had lined up and were watching the other kids get attacked but they did not get involved," she said.

"It would be easier for the Deceptors to attack regular kids rather than start a confrontation with a Chinese gang member," I said. Delancey was not surprised.

Lucy had been caught in the crossfire. Delancey's explained that her father had sent a car service to pick her up from school and bring her home to their apartment in the city. Tears streamed down her face.

"It's really upsetting. We weren't very close, but it could've been any of one of us. Sometimes I feel like death is all around."

I tried to console her. "I can't help but feel that when your time is up, it's up. I think that's just the way the universe works, and if you try to wonder about any other scenario, you'll just stress yourself out for no reason."

"It was a random gun shot. Any of us could've been killed. I can't help but wonder….," Delancey could not finish her sentence. She apologized and walked away. I was moved by her emotions; I hated to see her so sad.

By lunch, everyone had heard Lucy was dead. Some kids were more upset than others, but everyone was on edge. More students were considering bringing weapons to school as a means of protection.

I disagreed with this notion. The Deceptors might not have fired a shot if someone did not fire first. Fear had engulfed Stanton that day, fear that any one of us could be next. I wasn't worried. Circumstances of one's death can sometimes be controlled, but timing cannot. When my time comes...I'll have to accept it.

chapter 7

IN THE GYM, Eddie Lo practiced his free throws. I needed to write another article on the basketball team and was excited to talk to Eddie again, but he was a little out of it. I asked him what was wrong. Eddie was the first to find Lucy and had called the police. He surprised me by saying that he already had spoken to Mr. Mash about the Deceptors.

"I'm not afraid of the Deceptors. They fired the second shot. After everyone dispersed, Lucy was lying on the ground. She was bleeding badly. I ran into the school and called the police." Eddie kept shooting the basketball.

"You know the Deceptors are going to find out about this," I said.

"I have more to worry about from rival Chinese gangs."

Eddie asked me about my work at the café. He felt Christine needed a nice guy to be her boyfriend. I felt a little funny about his comment. He was either implying that I should date her or I should not date her. Either way I had no response. It's hard to take advice about love from a member of the underworld.

Eddie stopped dribbling and said "You ran pretty fast yesterday."

"How do you know?" I asked.

"I was watching from the park."

I stopped myself short of telling him that only Chinese gangsters were hanging out in the park.

"I'm just happy I didn't get attacked," I said. I shot practice with Eddie Lo. He rarely missed a shot. "You should see me with a gun," he chuckled.

That week at the café, Christine was not her usual loquacious self. She wasn't speaking to me and I didn't know why. The café gradually got busier. Mike the manager woke up around noon looking like hell.

I said, "What the hell happened to you? You look like you slept on a park bench all night."

He answered in a groggy voice, "I slept on a park bench all night." He then washed his face, and walked over to a pot of coffee that I had just brewed for customers. He poured himself three cups and drank them in seconds. He ate a freshly baked muffin, burning the insides of his mouth in the process. He wore the outfit he seemed to wear every weekend, a wrinkled white shirt, and wrinkled black pants.

Mike felt like talking, and asked what my plans were after high school. I told him that I would like to go away to college.

Mike asked, "What are you going to major in? What college are you going to?"

"I am not sure. He asked what field I was leaning toward and I said business.

"Business? What aspect of business? Finance, marketing? Accounting? Entrepreneurship? Real estate?" he said in a weird tone. "How could you go to Stanton and not major in engineering or become a doctor?"

"I don't know," I said.

"You go to Stanton…the finest school in the entire State of New York." I nodded. "Make sure you get rid of your 'I don't know' answers to my questions before you graduate. Don't end up like me; I went to Stanton also."

My heart stopped beating. Did I hear him correctly? How could Mike the sleeping manager, and my homeless supervisor, have gone to Stanton? Stanton is for the brightest minds in New York. Why was he such a loser? There must be some mistake.

A crowd of customers from a tour bus entered the café. It was great to be busy, and we worked fast to serve fifty customers.

After the crowd left, and all the mess was cleaned up, I went back to Mike the Manager.

"Did I hear you correctly...you went to Stanton? When did you graduate?" I asked. Mike said he'd graduated fifteen years before.

"What the hell happened?" I asked.

Mike told me of his average grades at Stanton. He explained that he had lacked direction for his life. He had attended college in Pennsylvania, but quickly discovered that the social aspects were the only part of college that actually interested him. After a year he dropped out and went to another college.

"College is not for everyone. If you really don't know what you want to do with your life...then don't waste time in college. It's better to work for a while until you decide what it is that you really want to do, and then go to college. Or not go to college. This is how it's done in Europe. The kids in Germany and France graduate high school, and then travel throughout Europe and the world, making money as waiters or in hotels, and then come back with a sense of direction."

I was mopping the floors, while listening intensely. Mike continued speaking.

"I left college after a year, and worked at an office here in the city. I drank too much, got fired, and started thinking that maybe I'd like to be a writer. But I didn't know how to write. I went to another college, and I started smoking marijuana and getting high every day. I started off fine, getting high on the weekends at parties, and getting drunk as well. But after a few months, I was drunk or high just about every day. I dropped out of that college and found a job. A few months later, I was fired from that job, and then my father threw me out of the house when he found out I was using drugs. I was then homeless for a summer, sleeping on benches, until I found another job. I worked at bars or restaurants for a few months here and there. Now I work here on the weekends, for a coin dealer during the week, and take night classes at City College about writing. Finally, I have direction."

This was disturbing news. My own lack of direction really scared me. I could end up homeless like Mike the Manager. I spent the next hour in deep thought; actually it was more like deep worry. I eventually shook it off and realized that I had some direction, and was not the type of person to abuse alcohol or drugs. That wasn't going to be me, I'm not going to turn into Mike. I'll have a drink or two with some of my friends, but I know when to call it a night.

"Only here in the great United States of America are we expected by the age of seventeen to make decisions for the rest of our lives. Decisions like where to go to college, or join the military or get a job, or what to major in. I wasn't ready at seventeen to decide my entire future and you sound like you aren't ready either," Mike said, getting louder.

"Well, Mike," I said. "I may not be ready today, but hopefully I'll take some classes in college and decide."

"College is for people that want a paycheck every week for the rest of their lives. I'm talking about doctors, teachers, accountants, office workers, pencil pushers, order takers...they take a weekly paycheck, get married, buy a house, and have kids. And then boom! Life is over."

"What's wrong with that?" I asked.

"If you want to suffer for the rest of your life, there is nothing wrong with that at all. Don't get me wrong; I think society needs people who get dressed in the morning, go to work, eat lunch, go home, and live for the weekends. A part time life, distracted with the demands of a mortgage, and bills, and hungry mouths." Mike drank another cup of coffee.

"What's wrong with it is that no one ever asks if that's really going to make them happy. They do it because it has to be done. They need the security of knowing that they went to college and now they are getting a paycheck, and one day they start asking questions and looking in the mirror. They next thing you know they are having a mid-life crisis, getting divorced, and deciding that all along they just wanted to be photographers or writers or artists. They leave behind a spouse and kids, and they vanish."

Mike was shouting. Everyone could hear him. Christine thought he was yelling at me. But he was yelling at himself, at his life, at his own misfortunes. It was surprising that a guy who had spent the first half of the day catatonic was now doling out advice about life.

"I would love to be one of those people with a job and a paycheck," I said to Mike. "A member of society. A non-homeless member of society."

"A low member of society? Without passion and thirst and pursuing your dreams? It's better to be among the dead than live without doing what you love." Mike walked away.

Christine asked about the shouting.

"So now you're speaking to me?" I asked in complete amazement.

"Why would I want to talk to you? I guess you don't want to date me, and if I needed to know anything about our friendship, I'll just ask Eddie Lo," she said and stormed off.

I kept working, refilling the cups, making more coffee, wiping down all the countertops. I learned not to stand around doing nothing, in case the owner ever walked in. "The secret to keeping a job is looking busy"—good advice from my father.

Late in the afternoon, Mike asked about the SATs. I revealed I have been studying but was scoring average on practice tests.

"People don't care about the SATs in the real world...outside the bubble of high school and college," Mike said calmly. "Its difficult for certain people to do well on the verbal part because it's culturally skewed."

"Culturally skewed in what way and what do you mean by certain people?" I asked.

"Well, let's just say if you grew up in a household with college-educated parents, especially if you live in the suburbs, then the Verbal is easier. Words that you are accustomed to hearing at home are on the test."

Perhaps I was at a disadvantage. No one in my family ever went to college. I started feeling a little depressed about my situation. Was I at a disadvantage in other areas of my life as well? I could not compete with kids that were well off. I never liked rich people, and now I liked them even less. To be truthful, I really did not know any rich people, except for Delancey. I kept thinking about my family's economic circumstances, and how it had impacted my vocabulary, and the way I wrote. Christine seemed to sense that I was taken back by Mike's comments.

"Don't listen to that bum. What does he know? He's doesn't know anything other than how to sleep at work. Don't listen to a loser. The SATs are not much of a test anyway. It doesn't test science knowledge or decision making. So what if you do well on the verbal part? What does that mean...that you can be an English professor somewhere? That you can write poems. Who cares? The world needs scientists and engineers. China, India, Russia, all reward their good math and science students. But not in America...we reward poets and great speakers...with jobs in sales. As if they can create jobs for people. Poets can't feed the mouths of the masses let alone themselves. The kids from my high school ace the math portion every year, and they can't even speak English. If they gave the verbal test in Cantonese, I could get a perfect score. Chinese kids that do well on the SATs can't get into top colleges. There's a quota on Asians, you know. Like there is on immigration." She walked towards a customer.

Several hours passed and I was thinking about the kids at Stanton. Many of them did well on the SATs by just studying hard and building their vocabulary. I went into the rest room dejected, and looked in the mirror. Was I at a disadvantage or was I going to be like the other Stanton Students and study even harder for the SATs? I was through feeling sorry for myself and my social class. I was through taking advice from Mike. I really didn't care if I was at a disadvantage; nothing had changed since the time I arrived at work that morning. I wasn't going to let Mike's advice get me down.

At quitting time, Christine wanted to go for sushi. While I waited for her to get ready, Mike exchanged my paycheck for cash and I couldn't have been happier.

We went back to the same Japanese place. Christine and I talked for a while. She was taking the SATs also, but had hardly studied. Christine had a different approach. While I had spent the past few months studying in the hopes of getting the highest possible score, she was trying to score high enough in order to get into community college. She explained how all the girls in her neighborhood went to the same college to learn accounting or bookkeeping or office skills in order to get a job. Christine planned to study computers in order to get a job in an office.

"Any job, in any office, with benefits. Why are you studying so hard for the SATs?" she asked.

"I want to do really well; I want to do my best," I said.

"If you don't get the score you want, will you be depressed?" she asked.

"Maybe initially, but I'll get over it."

"Why not get over it now? Your score on the SAT's is just a number. It does not determine your life. Your destiny is already decided. All you have to do is show up," said Christine.

"I make my own destiny."

Christine laughed and said that I "drank too much of the American Kool Aid."

I did not find this funny.

"That's a horrible expression. Do you know where it comes from?" I asked.

"What expression?" she said.

"Drinking the Kool Aid."

"It comes from drinking fruit punch?" she said with a smirk on her face.

"It comes from a tragedy in the South American country of Guyana. A cult leader poisoned nearly a thousand people with Kool Aid," I said.

"Where was this cult leader from?" she asked.

"He was a minister from the Midwestern United States," I said.

"American Kool Aid."

I remained silent, and then she apologized.

"All I am saying is that the big things in life are predetermined by destiny. Who you marry, where you live, who you meet, your kids, your grandkids, etc. Maybe even where you go to college. And what is not determined by destiny is determined by luck," she said.

"I don't believe that."

"Believe it or not, it affects you as well. And as for those people who drank the Kool Aid, well, religion is the opiate of the people."

"Thank you, chairman Mao."

"Besides, the whole college admission process is nonsense anyway. My high school had a Chinese girl who scored a near perfect score on the SATs. Her grades were very high, but she was rejected from all the top colleges. They said her essay was no good, and she failed the interviews. But I know the truth; they probably had too many Chinese people already. Instead, a guy that ran track and had average grades was accepted to the Ivy League from my school. What is he going to do after college? Run track to pay the bills, not likely." Christine's stories were taking a lot of the pressure off the SAT's.

"So, is there a girl in your life?" Christine asked.

"Well, not really. There is a girl in school I like, and I have liked her for years, but she's out of my league," I said.

"Out of your league? Is she on the Yankees? Are you on the Mets? Just ask her out or ask someone else," Christine said.

"You need a date?" I asked.

"No, but you do," she smirked.

We ate for a while and then I paid the bill for both of us. She smiled and said, "I thought we weren't dating."

"Don't consider it a date; consider it a loan." We both giggled. Christine loved to flirt.

At home, my father asked where I had been. I told him I ate sushi. He lectured me about getting sick eating raw fish. I told him that Japanese people don't get sick eating sushi. My father reminded me that I wasn't Japanese. "Certain things are built up for generations."

I studied for six hours that night, and felt I made progress on the verbal part of the SATs.

At school, I needed to talk to Mr. Zoose about Mike the Manager's comments. Mr. Zoose confirmed that in Europe they do a lot of things differently. "The SAT's are a big deal, but they are not an indication of how much money you will make or how happy you will be or if you will be a good person. Not everyone fails in life, and not everyone succeeds in life," he said. "Most people settle in the middle. The middle can be pretty good. And you are only at a disadvantage if you see yourself that way."

I really didn't want to be in the middle. "Do you think the SAT's are easier for people from educated families?"

"There are students whose parents are professors, but if they don't study for the SAT's then they won't do well. If their parents were taking the tests for them, they would be at an advantage," he said. "Besides, if you go into a field that you are really good at and passionate about, you will be the cream of the crop, in that field."

"I am not really sure of what to major in, or what career path I want to take, or anything. I just tell people I'm going to study business because I don't want to seem indecisive," I confessed to Mr. Zoose.

"Many kids are in your shoes. Until you try something out, you may never know if it's for you. I once had a job for an airline. I quit after two months, realizing it was not for me. Since you don't know what direction you want to take, do this instead. Write down how you want your life to be in twenty years, and then figure out how to get there. Call it a Life Map." I thought it was a good idea.

"By the way, please do the school play. I wrote it myself." He was pleading with me.

"I won't do *Ave Maria.*"

"You have the right voice for it, and you are the best guitar player I have ever seen at this school."

"I'll do another song," I tried to compromise.

"I only need you for *Ave Maria,*" Mr. Zoose said.

"No deal." Mr. Zoose smiled. As I was walking out, I bumped into his desk, causing the apple to roll off. I picked it up before it could hit the floor and placed it perfectly in its previous position.

Throughout the school, even at lunch, everyone was studying for the SATs. Test prep books were everywhere. In New York City, you know it is SAT season when kids are studying the prep books on the subways.

The anticipation of the test is worse than the test itself. So much rides on one test; so much of the future is influenced by the scores of the SATs. If I did well, I'd get into the college of my choice. College could determine my future career opportunities, not to mention the impact on my personal growth because it would determine the people I would meet in college.

Sam wasn't worried about the SAT. He was taking a private study course in the city and was acing his practice tests. This is one of the benefits of having a father who was a doctor. But he had a different philosophy as to why he would do well.

"Don't forget I went to school in England before I came here. The British education system is way more advanced than the American system. Any junior high school student in England could take the SATs and do well. And before that I went to school in Iran, and their schools were much more difficult than Stanton or any other American high school."

Once Sam started bashing the American education system, he would bash the rest of America as well. He felt crime in America was too high. "People in Europe and other countries are much more civilized than people in America."

He remarked, "I'll never buy an American car when I'm older. The Americans can't make cars the way the Germans or the Japanese can." Sam slammed the subway system. "In London, the metros are so clean, with no graffiti. And the people are much more civilized than the animals that ride the New York subways." I was sick of listening to Sam.

It was hard to argue about the subways. The F-Train was covered in garbage and graffiti. There were panhandlers and the omnipresent smell of urine. He definitely was right about the trains. Sam frequently complained that Americans were deliberately trying to ruin tea. "The rest of the world actually brews tea leaves. You guys stick a tea bag in hot water and call it tea." I told him that he should move to another country.

Sam complained just to complain, like a grumpy old man. He complained about Israel, but complained equally about the Palestinians and Arabic nations. Overall, I did not think of Sam as a bad person. He was adjusting to a new country and his goal was to return to Europe after college.

I fully understood why people who didn't know him strongly disliked him. Sam was hard to take and hard to listen to if you were the type of person that believed what you heard. But half the time he was smiling when he spewed his venom. Sam looked different from American kids. He had short curly hair, tanned skin, and his bushy eyebrows nearly connected in the middle. He had a large nose, and was often mistaken for being an Arab or an Israeli. This would really light his fire. He wore sweater vests and Oxford shirts, not to mention penny loafers. No one in high school—anywhere, with the exception of the suburbs of London, dressed like Sam.

He busted my chops about my proposed career of entering into business. He'd say, "Business, what business? Are you going to sell Coca Cola, Pepsi, or McDonalds? Because that is all this country is going to be left with one day."

Then he'd go on about how America doesn't manufacture anything anymore that anyone wants to buy, except Levis jeans.

Sam's college essay was going to be centered on his sister's death, and how this motivated him to want to treat cancer patients. Sam said colleges loved this sappy stuff, but I knew that he really meant it. His grades were the most important thing in the world to him. Sam often said that a student who doesn't do well in school is like a person who goes to a job and performs poorly. "Like a doctor killing patients," he would say.

Carlos and Sam had a symbiotic relationship. Sam needed Carlos to do the things that Sam couldn't risk doing. Carlos always agreed with Sam's suggestions. Carlos was banking on Sam becoming a rich doctor some day. Sam frequently said to Carlos (whenever Sam needed money) that "one day I'll be a rich doctor and pay you back." John and I often just laughed.

Carlos was an unusual character. He lived in Jamaica, Queens, and in a very tough neighborhood. His mother was Hispanic, and his father looked Indian or Pakistani. As a result, Carlos looked like a gypsy cab driver. He rarely spoke of his father. He dressed poor, and spoke with a strong Queens accent. I once asked him how a Hispanic woman came to marry a South Asian and he replied, "someone needed a green card."

I asked Carlos if he had fired the gunshot on Halloween. He said that his gun didn't have bullets. "What were you going to do with a gun without bullets?" I asked him.

"You were plenty nervous when all you knew was that I had a gun. Besides, the gun cost $50. Sam made $150 from collecting money from the other students. He spent the other hundred on himself. For a guy likely to be valedictorian...he didn't have the brains to save a little money for bullets."

We both laughed. "Academic smarts is not street smarts," said Carlos. I agreed.

"Besides, this is a girl's gun. It's got jewels on the handle. He couldn't even buy a masculine gun." Carlos laughed again.

A college fair had been organized at the school gym. Everyone was attending, except John. He remarked he was too smart for a college fair, that it was for kids who needed a sales pitch. I knew John wanted to go, but had to work at his family's store. I agreed to bring back some brochures for him.

"And posters of the schools," John reminded me. "Something I can daydream about."

At the college fair, Harvard had the center table. Harvard admitted two kids from Stanton every year. That was their limit, and their tradition. Harvard was the goal for Stanton kids; everything else was second place or worse. Harvard would definitely admit the valedictorian. The second admission was up in the air. It was a big deal, not because Harvard was the best, but for bragging rights.

It's an understatement to say that Sam really, really, wanted get into Harvard. It would have guaranteed him admission to a top medical school. If Sam was accepted to Harvard, he'd be keeping pace with his older brother, who was already pre-med at Harvard. Intelligence ran in the family, as did the lack of it.

I asked the Harvard representative about the cost of the application fee. I couldn't afford it, so I didn't bother asking about admission requirements. The rest of the day felt like the wind had been taken out of my sails. It would have been nice just to apply to Harvard, and have delusions of grandeur that I might be miraculously accepted.

Delancey was speaking to reps from small private colleges located in towns hard to find on a map. The reps from these small private colleges all looked like Delancey, all spoke with the same flare, with the same expressions. From a distance, Delancey looked like she belonged to the colleges, not to our high school. When I asked her if she was interested in Harvard, she laughed, covering her mouth to avoid a loud guffaw.

"Harvard is not for me. I just wouldn't be happy there. My father has been pushing me to apply; he has contacts that can get me in Harvard for sure. But there is no way I would feel comfortable in that kind of an environment. I'm looking for a liberal arts school where I can fit in." I guess Harvard was not the goal for everyone.

All Sam could talk about was getting into Harvard. Sam was really juiced up from meeting the Harvard rep.

"If you are, in fact, the valedictorian this year, then you are definitely going to Harvard. Stanton will know who the valedictorian is going to be by the end of June," I said sarcastically.

"And what if I'm not? Then it's up in the air and I can't take that chance," Sam whined. Carlos sat listening, not contributing much to the conversation.

"Well, who else from Stanton has what it takes to get into Harvard?" asked John.

We were all silent.

"There's always Doreen," I blurted out the first name that came into mind. John agreed. If anyone could get into Harvard, it would be Doreen.

"Does anyone know Doreen?" Sam asked.

"She's chief editor of the school paper," I said.

Doreen was a five foot little powder keg, and a super over achievers, even by Stanton standards. She had been junior class president, and on the debate team as well. She was one of the best debaters in the state. But that year, she was also editor in chief of the school paper and had very high grades. She had also spoken with the Harvard rep at the college fair.

Sam became intrigued with the idea of meeting Doreen. I suggested that he stop by the school newspaper office. It was a foolish mistake that I would come to regret.

After school, Sam, with Carlos in tow, came to the office and I introduced him to Doreen. He talked to her about the school paper, and mentioned how he had always seen her around school. What a load of horse manure. Sam seemed friendly and downright cordial toward Doreen. It was an act to anyone familiar with Sam's maleficent personality.

Doreen was not gregarious at first, but toned down her usual abrasive personality. Sam complimented her on her clothes and on her looks. The color on her face changed, as did her gait. She was clearly warming up to him. I was completely in shock when, three minutes later, Sam asked her out on a date. First and foremost, Doreen was not exactly attractive, and second, she was definitely not Sam's type. It was not that Doreen was especially unattractive; she just did not put any effort into her appearance. I suppose if she had put a little effort into make up and hair, and wore nice clothes, she would be quite pretty. Also it would help if she showered before school once in a while. I think the word is unkempt, but I'm probably being kind.

Sam was up to something. Doreen was a smart girl, and I thought she could fend for herself. She and Sam were both ranked next to each other in the top ten of all Stanton students.

It was well after five o'clock, and I headed for the subway, passing the psychic outside her store front. She asked me if I needed a free palm reading. She wore a tight black dress, which placed her chubby hips and breasts on display. She was quite the marketing executive; her outfit was clearly designed to market her services. She didn't lack clients; after all, this was Brooklyn, home of the desperate.

My friendly neighborhood psychic again offered her services. Once again I declined and kept walking. She flashed her sexy smile and asked if I needed anything else, "other than a psychic." I kept walking.

I wasn't completely naïve. But I had mixed emotions about sex, and did not want to have sex with a much older woman, especially my first time. I would never pay for sex. It seemed wrong and I was pretty sure I would get it for free at some point in the future, hopefully the near future. At school we always talked about sex, but most of us really did not have any direct carnal knowledge.

By the time I arrived home, Harry had made his usual spaghetti and meatballs. We ate dinner while watching sitcoms on television. My family could not sit around a dinner table and talk without arguing. Television was a great medium to get my father in a good mood. It was the only opportunity we had to see him smile. After dinner, my father went to the liquor cabinet for his usual glass of bourbon.

That night I studied reading comprehension and vocabulary words until two a.m. My practice tests increased a few points, though nothing really significant. The SATs were just days away; I was running out of time.

I arrived at school at seven in the morning. My eyes were red, my body drained of energy. I had to study for a pre-calculus test. Math was easy for me, and studying last minute was no big deal. John was among the students already in the cafeteria studying or doing their homework.

I told John about Sam and Doreen. He shook his head in either amazement or disbelief; I was too tired to distinguish between the two. We both studied for an hour.

Stanton was a sanctuary for students who wanted to be students. The school opened at six a.m. By seven-thirty a.m. it was usually packed. At eight a.m. I looked out the window, and I could see some of the athletic teams running through the park. I could barely run a mile. My gym teacher often yelled, "Imagine this was a life or death situation and you'll be better motivated!" In my mind, there was nothing more boring than running. I'd rather watch paint dry.

My first class was English with Mr. Zoose. He asked if I had started my Life Map.

"Not yet", I replied.

"High school students with no idea of where to go in life are like drivers in a car without directions. Drivers need a map, some sort of destination, and then they can be on their way. Start at a destination and work your way backwards."

Mr. Zoose explained that he regarded his twenty year high school reunion as the most fascinating experience of his life. His classmates' lives had all taken unexpected turns. "In high school they had it all figured out, and thought they knew how life was going to be. Only those who have not lived life can say with certainty anything about the future."

At lunch, I asked Sam what his angle was with Doreen. Sam said that he needed to know his competition better. Carlos looked up once, like a perky German shepherd, and kept on eating.

The cafeteria was noticeably quiet. Many students were in the library studying. Stanton was offering a free test prep course for the next ten days on how to actually take the test and not waste important time. I decided to attend one of these classes. I needed all the tips I could get.

Global History class was after lunch. It started to feel like the world was changing. New York City had its first black mayor, David Dinkins. The school's black students beamed with pride. Some of the black students followed the mayor's direction and decided to call themselves African Americans.

We had a new president elect of the United States, George Bush, and the students of Greek ancestry were not thrilled about it. He had beaten Michael Dukakis in a landslide. Our new president said that we could read his lips.

Delancey approached me in the hallway. "A woman was elected president of Pakistan. How can a country of people that don't respect women have a woman president, and the United States doesn't even have a woman candidate?" She kept walking before I could think of an answer.

Natalie Morales was in the hallway. She was an incredible sight to behold. She walked in an unusual way; her hips swayed, her feet moved, and her back was straight. She smiled; I said hello, then turned around to watch her walk down the hall. It was just as good to watch her walk from the back as it was from the front. I had known who she was throughout high school, but only noticed her attractiveness for the first time this week. Maybe my eyesight was starting to improve.

I've theorized that one day, girls wake up, and boom—they blossom into women. I don't think it's a gradual thing; it just happens one day, over night. It happens to boys also. Some of the student athletes had tremendous growth in a short period of time. Eddie Lo grew 4 inches and put on 30 lbs in one summer. Sandra from the swim team went from a string bean to a fully grown woman one night last spring. Natalie was an example of this. She used to be a plane Jane type of girl, but no longer.

When would my time come? Better late than never, I thought. Other guys had hit full puberty in high school, but not me. I had not grown facial hair and my voice didn't change until junior year. Sometimes I'd look in the mirror and say "any day now" hoping that my chest, shoulders, and biceps would develop overnight. Weightlifting had no effect on my appearance.

I went to the school newspaper office, and fell asleep in a chair. I think I slept for a half hour. When I awoke, Sam and Doreen were standing next to me. It was odd to see them, sort of like looking at a lion and gazelle together. They had been spending a lot of time together, and Sam seemed more pleasant around her, but he was his usual obnoxious self when she was gone.

Sam claimed that he was only applying to Harvard. "It's Harvard or nothing." I stared at him until he recanted. Sam also had another school in mind, a college that apparently produced a lot of doctors.

"Colleges don't produce doctors; they produce medical students," Doreen smirked. The whole idea of being a doctor was ingrained so deep within his consciousness that he never spoke about another potential profession. This was true with a lot of the kids that wanted to be doctors. They never spoke of a second career option. Tunnel vision was necessary to get through four years of college, four years of medical school, and four years of training.

Sam and Doreen were working on their college essays and finalizing their Harvard applications. It was hard to believe that Sam was dating Doreen.

Natalie was in the SAT class. We were in the same boat; she was not sure where to apply to college, or a even a course of study. We both just wanted to get the SATs over with, and apply to schools based on the results of the test. Natalie was a very bright girl, albeit with soft tanned skin, and long hair. I thought about asking her to hang out after the prep course, but I was very nervous. I summoned all my strength and energy in a single deep breath and said to her, "Let's get a bite to eat afterwards. My treat." It came out very loud, like I was shouting at her. Everyone else turned and looked at me. I put my head down in embarrassment.

She replied, "I can't. I have to be home. But thanks anyway."

Feeling dejected, I tried to play it off cool. Nonchalantly, I said, "You're really missing out. I was going to buy you the best cheesecake in Brooklyn."

She smiled and said, "Maybe next time."

The SAT class was not helpful until the end, when the instructor explained that high scores and high grades weren't enough to make it to the top schools. He said that high school resumes and extracurricular activities were equally important. This sounded preposterous. I wasn't being cynical, but I knew the importance of the SATs. I could not remember if Sam had anything on his resume for extracurricular activities.

The next day, Sam and Doreen were in the newspaper office when I asked Sam about his extracurricular activities.

He glanced at Doreen, and described his four years of working in the lab of the hospital where his father was an immunologist. He said he had a letter from the chief of the hospital. This came as a big surprise, for as long as I could remember, Sam never really did anything after school. If I were to look up "Apathetic" in the dictionary, there would be a picture of Sam next to the definition.

Afterwards, Sam and I walked to the subway together, without Doreen.

"When did you work at the hospital?" I asked and Sam laughed. He said I was too gullible. Sam explained that he wrote the letter of recommendation himself and forged the chief's signature. He had never even visited the lab.

"Welcome to the real world!" he shouted. "It's always who you know and what you dare to create on a resume. There's no way that anyone can deny I worked at the hospital when the chief signed a glowing letter of recommendation. I even got one for Carlos."

We walked by the psychic's store front. She smiled at both of us, her usual sexy smile. The psychic asked, "Don't you want to know what the future holds for you?"

We kept walking and Sam said, "How much?" She replied ten dollars.

Sam liked the way she stared at him, impervious to the fact that she looked at everyone this way. He wanted to try her out, but he did not have ten dollars. As usual, he asked me for ten dollars, and I said no.

"There is something about an older woman that can make a boy stay up at night," he chimed.

I was overly anxious about the SATs, studying until about two a.m. every night. I made up for sleep on the subways, going to and from school. The night before the test, I decided to go to sleep at ten o'clock. I was feeling drained and irritable. The test prep instructor had recommended a good night's sleep. My father asked me how I felt about the SATs.

"I'll do better than average but not as good as I need to do." He asked why, and I explained that I really needed a real test prep course, but it cost too much money. He felt bad about this, but we just couldn't afford it. I dropped the subject. It was my lot in life to do everything the hard way. Maybe Christine was right about destiny.

The next morning I awoke early. My father was already at work driving a cab, his weekend job. I made scrambled eggs, and made enough for Harry. I also made a big pot of coffee, which I could not finish. I left the house in a hurry to take the SATs.

I took the subway to Stanton, and when I arrived an hour later, I was happy to see friendly faces. The test was difficult, more so than the practice exams. Vocabulary words seemed out of left field. Knots tightened in my stomach. It was unfathomable that so many of life's outcomes could rely on one single test.

During a bathroom break, I discovered three dictionaries in the boy's bathroom. Some people were risking everything that day.

Upon completion of the exam, I rode the subway to work. I was mentally fatigued for the last part of the exam, and rushed through it.

As the train rode into Manhattan, with each stop I felt more exhausted and cold. The test was now over; a cathartic sensation of relief came over me. One test can make or break your entire future. The outcome of the test could determine where I went to college, if I went to college, who my future friends, maybe even my future wife and potentially who my children could be. Not to mention my major and future career path. I was growing numb, and was overwhelmed with nausea.

Christine arrived at the same time. She had also taken the SATs that morning and looked exhausted. We took our break together and went outside to the brick-paved esplanade. We stood at the rail, overlooking the Hudson River.

"Don't ask me about the test," she said.

I kept silent.

"I don't know why college costs so much money. It makes no sense," she said.

I kept staring into the Hudson River, and the cold wind felt really good.

"How am I supposed to save enough money to pay for college? And what about books? College books are really expensive," she said. "Where am I supposed to get the money?"

"In God we Trust?" I said.

"Why do we trust God so much in this country? In China the government takes care of the people, not God. In Government we trust." Christine was a little hysterical.

"Why are you so upset?" I asked.

"I'm not sure I can afford to go to college. I need to move out of my mother's apartment, and find my own place, and I really don't know," she said.

"So don't go to college. Save up some money for a year or take out loans," I reassured her. "It's not written in stone that you have to go to college right after high school. Everyone has different circumstances." She wiped the tears off her face, and we went back to work.

On Sunday Mike informed me that Christine called out sick.

"How was the test?" asked Mike.

"Fine," I said. "Just fine."

"You look disappointed in yourself. I bet you blew it, and now your whole future is in the toilet," Mike laughed out loud.

In Christine's absence, the owner sent Vincent, a worker from his other café. Vincent was about my age. He dressed very hip, with fancy black leather shoes, expensive jeans, and sported a very stylish haircut. He said he got his haircuts from Astor Place Hair Studio, in the village.

The work day was very slow; it was almost Thanksgiving, and many people in the complex were already gone for the holiday. I asked Vincent about the SATs.

"I don't need it. I'm planning on taking acting lessons downtown for a year and then heading to L.A." he said, as he kept serving customers.

"What about having something to fall back on?" I asked.

"Something to fall back on is for people who intend to fail."

"I don't think so. I think it's really hard to make it as an actor. What if you don't make it?"

"It is really hard to make it as anything, not just as an actor. I'll just keep trying until I do. I've been acting in small parts in off Broadway productions since I was a kid. I know its going to be hard, but there is no plan B. I plan on making it as an actor, period."

The day brought few customers, and Vincent and I talked a lot to each other. We had to pass the time somehow. He was a very cool guy, different from the academic types that I was used to at Stanton. I told him that I was planning on going away to college. Vincent was not impressed with this.

"College is good for parties and girls and stuff. But anyone that really makes it in life, does it without college," he said smirking.

"I am planning on making it and going to college also," I fired back.

"I bet you have no clue about a future and that's why you're going to college," Vincent smirked.

"So what do you have against college?" I asked him.

"It's four years of wasting money by figuring out who you want to be when you grow up. I want to be an actor, so I'm going to LA to audition. You know...the real world." Vincent had a point. "A college education allows you to walk around Manhattan with a trench coat, a folded *New York Times* under your arm, and you'll look like you read it."

"I'm more of a *Daily News* guy myself," I said.

"I've got talent as an actor. Some people have talent in athletics, or music, or some other field. For people with talent, college is a wasted effort." Vincent kept working with a customer. "Do you have any talent?"

"I play the guitar and sing," I said.

"But are you talented?"

I took a deep breath, puffed my chest out, and said, "I'm talented."

"So why not a career in music?" Vincent asked.

"Because I need college to fall back on, in case I don't make it."

"Sounds like you already plan to fail. Look, even if you don't make it big as a guitar player, I'm sure you can find work."

"I don't want to end up poor and starving."

"You won't if you really are talented."

At school on Monday, everyone was asking about the SATs. I gave the obligatory answer, "I aced it." Sam said he didn't see me taking the exam, but thought he saw me in the boys' bathroom. Sam wondered if I saw anything in the bathroom.

"I didn't see anything." I said stonefaced. He remarked that he did not see anything either.

Sam and Doreen were mailing their Harvard applications together. Carlos perked up; he seemed to be on high alert. Dogs sometimes did the same thing with their ears when something caught their attention.

Delancey wore a tee-shirt with a picture of a large crow on it. Delancey explained that the tee-shirt was for a new rock band. We talked about the SATs. She said she did pretty well on the verbal but she wasn't sure about the math.

"I used to be really good at math. But not anymore. Even my science grades are not what they used to be," she said. She was applying to five colleges. All of them had two things in common; they were all private schools, and they were all very expensive.

It must be nice not to have financial worries, I thought. Natalie walked by, and I waved hello. Delancey noticed that I was checking out Natalie, though I was unaware of my wandering eyes.

"I used to be the girl that all the guys checked out," she said.

I put my hand on her shoulder, and said, "You still are, and always will be." We laughed and went to our classes.

At the end of the day, John and I were walking to the subway together. Smoke was coming out of a nearby mail box. The mail box was on fire and a fire truck quickly arrived to put out the flames. Burning a mail box was a federal crime. When the fire was out, firemen emptied the burnt contents.

"Do you think it was the Deceptors?" I asked.

"Probably not. They're into beating people up, not burning a mailbox," John said. "Besides, there's no money to gain by burning a mailbox."

At the subway station, Carlos stood waiting for a train. The three of us began the long ride home. Carlos hardly spoke. John and I discussed college applications.

The next two days I stayed home with the flu. John called and said that Sam and Doreen were over. Sam had broken up with her during lunch in the cafeteria. I wasn't surprised. I surmised Sam was able to get what he wanted out of the relationship.

Thanksgiving arrived and I felt completely better and healthy enough to go out. My father was driving a cab until three p.m. Harry and I spontaneously decided to go to the Thanksgiving Day parade. We had not been to the parade since our mother had passed. It was still early enough that we may see the end, but late enough that we'd be far away.

We took the subway to the west side of Manhattan and had to push and shove our way out the crowded exit of the station. A million people lined the streets to see the parade. A colossal Superman balloon towered above our heads. One block down, thirty people were barely hanging on to a Garfield balloon. The balloons were twice the size of our house. The wind blew the balloons forward, and the balloon holders struggled to hang on. Harry and I walked north, hoping there were fewer people in that direction. On Columbus Avenue, the frigid winds picked up velocity.

A two-story Snoopy balloon was making its way toward the crowd. It must have been more than forty feet high. In the distance, we could see the last float, Santa Claus in a sleigh. The crowd cheered loudly as Snoopy slammed into a street light, smashing it to pieces. Harry wore a big smile on his face; his eyes lit up brightly, more than I could ever remember. It was overwhelming to see my brother so happy.

After the Santa Claus float went past us, I bought us hot dogs and hot chocolate. It was good to have money from my job at the café.

Someone tapped me on my shoulder. I turned around, elated to find Delancey behind me. Her cheeks were red from the cold, as were her nose and ears.

"Happy Thanksgiving!" she yelled out.

"You too!" I said. "What are you doing here?"

"I live nearby, and came down to see the end of the parade." Delancey asked the vendor for a hot chocolate as well. "What about you?"

"We also came for the parade. This is my brother, Harry." Harry shook Delancey's hand, and commented on how warm her hand was, despite the cold weather.

A large crow flew very close to us, trying to swipe the final small bite of hot dog out of my hands. Delancey was petrified. The bird flew away.

We talked about her holiday plans, and I discovered that she was heading out to Long Island to spend Thanksgiving with her mother and stepfather. After she left, Harry noticed that I couldn't stop smiling.

"She's really pretty, David. How well do you know her?" Harry asked.

"She is, isn't she? I know her from school."

"You should ask her out; I can tell that she likes you. Girls are never that happy to see just anyone," Harry remarked.

"She's always full of exuberance," I said.

Harry looked at me confused. "Is she exuberant around you or everyone else as well?"

"I'm not sure...but she's definitely not that exuberant around Sam." We both laughed; Harry was familiar with Sam. "Besides, Harry, she's out of my league."

Harry chuckled. "What? She's on the Mets? And you're on the Yankees? Don't be ridiculous...there are no leagues..." He sounded a lot like Christine.

"She's rich, Harry, and we're poor. I don't want to embarrass myself."

"You're nuts. Girls are girls, and guys are guys. Who cares who's rich and who's poor? One date isn't going to lead to marriage or a life time of anything. Just ask her out already. She's practically crazy about you." Harry hit me on the chest. He could be right, maybe Delancey liked me too. I didn't bother telling Harry that Delancey had already turned me down once, sort of.

That night, we went to my grandmother's home for Thanksgiving dinner. I saw all my relatives, aunts, uncles, and cousins. It was the first of many holidays without my Grandfather.

One of my uncles offered me a beer, and I drank it fast, hoping my father wouldn't notice. "When parents say no, uncles say yes!" he boasted. I was still smiling from bumping into Delancey earlier.

My grandmother distributed some of my grandfather's personal items. Harry received my grandfather's U.S. Citizenship documents from when he became a naturalized citizen. The name read "David Arfayus." My father received my grandfather's army uniform. My grandfather's college education was on a battlefield in Korea. "He had arrived in New York at a young age, and was drafted for war soon thereafter," my grandmother explained.

At the very end, my grandmother handed me my grandfather's high school diploma from British Guyana. His last name was spelled with an O, and the other letters were different as well.

"That was the original spelling, but when he came to Ellis Island, because of his accent, they changed the spelling of his name to the way he pronounced it." My grandmother was an emotional wreck, everyone tried to console her.

I suggested that we should change our last name to the correct spelling. My father said that he was okay with his last name, but advised me to contact the government to change my name. He joked that even if I changed my name, I still had to obey his rules.

The next day at City Hall, I filled out the application and changed the spelling of my last name, and never looked back. They gave me a copy of the paperwork, which I was to submit to my school. I think my grandfather would have approved.

chapter 8

Sometimes a new month begins, and nothing in the air indicates the change. Some months just feel like other months. This is never the case with December. Whenever November ends and December begins, every kid in school can tell the difference without looking at a calendar. There is a countdown that begins for the holidays.

The café was busy that weekend. Business was booming, largely because New York City, more than any other city in the world, draws lots of tourists for the holidays. I filled the muffin trays with each type of batter. My job entailed baking 200 muffins every morning, which was enough for the tour buses of people that came in for breakfast. Last month, we threw out 150 muffins a day. But lately, tour buses have been arriving on the weekends, and there weren't any muffins to throw out. I also had to bake 400 cookies. The batter was rock hard since it had been refrigerated all night. I learned that by using an ice cream scooper, a little elbow grease, and my hands, the cookies came out perfectly round. I baked chocolate chip cookies, oatmeal raisin cookies, macadamia nut cookies, almond cookies, vanilla cookies, and double chocolate cookies.

The smell of freshly baked muffins and cookies filled the World Financial Center, and even though the building was enormous, and had 35 floors, the smell permeated every nook and cranny of the building.

Music is similar to aroma. Music moves people, whether they are old or young, warm hearted, or with a heart of stone. Music, especially the way I played the guitar, penetrated souls. When I played guitar, it brought joy, and sometimes sorrow to listeners.

The morning crew arrived a half hour late. It's not like Mike would notice, as he was still snoring in the back. The crew looked like hell. Christine explained that they all had a rough night. They drank all the coffee I had brewed. I asked Christine about her night and she said, "You don't want to know," but agreed to tell me later.

Mike the manager eventually woke up, and decided to show me how to make a cappuccino. I took it step by step, loading the espresso, steaming the milk, and learning how to make foam. He drank it and said not bad. I made another one; this time I drank it, and thought it was the best drink I ever had. Mike explained that the cappuccino was a lot like the "people in this godforsaken world." He said that the grinds sink to the bottom, and that the middle part is just for the caffeine and taste, but the part that everyone likes is the foam, and the foam needs to be perfected if it is to rise to the top and stay there. "Foam is like the top 1% of people, there is nothing of substance in foam."

I was prepared for more anecdotes from Mike, but I had grown skeptical of his advice, since he seemed like a big loser. But Mike was particularly loquacious that day.

"So have you given any more thought to your future?" he asked. I told him that I didn't have any answers, but was working on a school project that would hopefully map out what I should do.

"The problem with school is that they always ask the wrong question. The question should not be 'what do you want to be when you grow up,' but rather, 'who do you want to be like when you grow up?' They should ask what source of income you plan on having, rather than what kind of job you are planning on having," Mike said.

I was hoping to avoid Mike having another mental meltdown at my expense. I mostly nodded and agreed, while I continued to work, cleaning counter tops, baking, cleaning the oven, and making more coffee. Still, I gave way to an involuntary grin at the thought of a guy who sleeps on park benches giving me career advice.

Mike continued. "It makes more sense to emulate people that you know, rather than to figure out a career path. Don't make the mistake that the rest of society makes. How you make your living does not define who you are. How much money you make is not who you are. First find out who you are, and then worry about everything else. A job is temporary, but self identity is for a lifetime." Mike seemed pleased with himself.

Mike's voice grew louder and louder, and his face was turning red. A few seconds later he was shouting. "I had a friend who was the smartest guy I knew. He had a full scholarship to Harvard Medical School. You know what happened? He met a girl, fell in love, and decided he wanted to be photographer. He took hundreds of pictures of his girlfriend. Then dropped out of medical school to spend more time with her, and a year later they broke up. His became depressed, turned to pills, and wound up in an institution. You know what the problem was? He never wanted to be a doctor to begin with. The girl he dated was his catalyst to pursue happiness. Today he is an amateur photographer, and he is happy. Imagine that...he could have been a miserable doctor or a happy photographer. It's about choices."

Mike ranted and his sentences became less connected until there was no coherency to the flow of his words. He jumped from thought to thought, starting a new sentence before finishing an existing one. This went on for five minutes. Christine stared at both of us with her arms crossed and left foot thumping the floor.

Mike looked at her and said, "What?"

Christine said, "Mike, are you from Manhattan? Because that would explain a lot."

Mike laughed and said that he was in fact from Manhattan. I didn't get it. This was an inside joke. Mike explained that his mannerisms and tendency to yell, his neurosis and short temper, and ability to get all worked up was part of his Manhattan upbringing. "All the crazies live in Manhattan...we're the norm here...you'll see."

Mike drank another cup of coffee and calmed down.

"I know what you're thinking; that I'm some loser living on a park bench, and here I am, the one giving you advice. But I have learned more from my failures than most people will learn from success. And I still have a lot of life ahead of me, enough time to turn things around. Hemingway was right when he said 'A man can be destroyed but not defeated.'" Mike walked back into the café.

Christine was too tired to have Sushi after work. She described the events of the previous night. Her gang was at a birthday party at a dance club in the city when a fight broke out with a rival gang. Some shots were fired but no one was hurt. She was up the entire night. I thought to myself that my life was so boring compared to hers. I didn't go to night clubs. I couldn't get in even if I wanted to. I was underage, just like Christine, but did not have her connections or a fake ID. My social scene consisted of going to the movies and having pizza with the guys. I felt like a child when I heard about her experiences. I felt deprived of the excitement that Christine had in her life. I really needed to get out more. I really needed to live more. I was seventeen and months away from becoming a legal adult without a social life.

At school, a flyer was circulating about an upcoming ski trip for Stanton high school seniors only. I was determined to go. Listening to Christine's stories about her wild nights at clubs in the city made me want to get out more. The cost was significant, but I could pay for it with my next two paychecks. This would be my chance to get out, even if I had never skied before. All I needed was my father to sign the permission slip.

John couldn't go on the ski trip. His life was pretty cut and dry. John worked every day after school, except for every other Friday afternoon, and was in church every Sunday. There was no way he could get the money. John and I both worked, but I always received a paycheck, and John never did. "Two things in life don't pay," John would say. "Crime, and working for family."

Sam couldn't go either. He had a family trip planned during winter break, and couldn't get out of it. I was relieved to hear that Sam was not going on the ski trip. He was my friend, but he required too much work, and I could have a better time without him.

Carlos wanted to go, but couldn't come up with the money. That's more or less Carlos; he can never come up with the money. My friends were the kids that never went anywhere. They weren't bad kids, just not the kind of kids that went anywhere or did anything. My lack of a social life was related to the company I kept. I had developed socially, accordingly. They were apathetic by default. Delancey and a lot of her friends were also going. I was happy to hear this.

I was nervous about getting the permission slip signed. There was a part of me that knew this was going to be another argument, another battle.

My father initially didn't want me to go. He felt that three nights away from home was a lot, and that since I did not know how to ski, it was dangerous. But he said he would think about it. The next morning, my father shocked me by leaving the signed permission slip on the table with a note. He had written that as long I paid for it myself, I had earned it. "It's your money," he wrote.

At school that day, I told Sam, John, and Carlos that I was going on the ski trip. Sam called it a waste of time. Carlos wished he could go. John said the lodgings were three per room. It would be like college, having a roommate and a shared bathroom. I felt a little awkward about having two roommates. It might give me a sense of what going away to college would be like.

I told Delancey that I was going on the trip. She hoped we could ski together. Delancey had been skiing for ten years, and could not wait to do helicopters. I said, "I'll race you down the mountain."

What was a helicopter? Was I really going to race her down a mountain? I really put my foot in my mouth that time. Nonetheless, I thought it would be great to see some people, especially Delancey, outside school for once. After speaking with other students, I realized that there were a lot of people going, but no one I knew well. I sighed, and wondered if I had made a mistake, and would be alone for three days. Either I would force myself to meet new people and have a good time, or I would stay aloof and alone. I was never good at meeting new people.

A voice in my head started to talk me out of the trip. This voice was powerful, and had talked me out of many opportunities in high school. I stared at the permission slip in my hand, and the money I had in my pocket, and ran to the school secretary's office. Immediately, I handed in my money and permission slip. I needed to do this before the voice talked me out of it. Now it was too late, and there was no turning back. The day wore on, and I felt more comfortable with the idea of going on the trip. I was less nervous about rooming with two other guys, and meeting new people.

Doreen wouldn't talk or even look at me. I ignored her, and continued to write articles. I met with the sports reporters. Finally after an hour, Doreen said that she and Sam were no longer friends.

She said "From the beginning, Sam was fishing for information about my college applications." She said Sam completed his college application similar to hers and even copied sections word for word. This did in fact sound like Sam.

I asked Doreen if she was going on the ski trip, and she said it wasn't her "scene." It was hard to figure out what exactly her scene was. Other than the newspaper office, she couldn't be seen anywhere.

Later that day, Mr. Zoose asked about my senior life map. I said, "It's coming along great. I'm almost done." I hadn't even started it, and didn't know how to begin. As I left school, a sign in the lobby read, "State and City College Applications due by December 21." I didn't even have the applications. I was thinking that a school upstate may have been the right way to go. It had to be a school not too far away either, because I didn't have money for long commutes. I didn't have a car and had to keep in mind the cost of bus trips home. I was a kid from New York City, and the subways were my method of transportation.

A line formed outside the guidance counselor's office for applications for state and city colleges. John was already on line, and said he would pick up an application for me. I said, "Only state not city, I really got to get the hell outta here."

"You and me both," John shouted back. I was serious about going away to college, and John would only do what his father allowed.

I left school and was walking to the subway. The psychic wasn't outside, and the curtains were closed. I guessed she had a customer. Delancey was walking ahead with her friends, and I called out to her. The girls turned around and waited for me to catch up. To my delight, Delancey told her friends to go on without her. I offered to ride the subway with her. Her cheeks and ears were turning red from the cold, but when I accidentally touched her hand, I noticed that her hands were lukewarm.

She said that she had applied to a few colleges already.

"I'm applying to state schools. I have to be pragmatic, and only apply to schools that I can afford," I said.

"I figured you would get a music scholarship somewhere," she said.

"I hadn't even considered it," I replied. "I have to focus on getting a job and making money, and making it in music is a real long shot," I said.

"I think you are too materialistic, and you should forget about the money and pursue your dreams."

"Delancey, we live in a material world and it costs money to rent here. The realm you belong to is a little different." She probably had no idea how difficult it was in a world without family money. But how could she? We rode together, and she switched trains at Times Square.

I watched as she walked on the platform, towards the front end. She was so airy and light, a stark contrast to the grimy and dingy subway. She disappeared into the far end of the station. The second she was no longer visible, I missed her. My heart sank. I was stunned by her effect on me.

At home, my grandmother, Calli, came over to help out. She did this about once a week, and we were all very grateful. My grandmother had to be grandmother and mother. I always looked forward to her cooking. It was the only time we ate well. I asked if she was lonely.

My grandmother replied that she had a lifetime of memories, and still felt my grandfather's presence in their home. She even had dreams about him sometimes. She was all warm with smiles. Sometimes she had to turn around to make sure my grandfather was really not there.

The next day, Sam and Carlos were outside the entrance of the school smoking. This was a first for Carlos and the cigarette looked out of place in his hand. They offered me one, I wasn't into getting cancer. They looked at each other and laughed like I was some kind of fool. Carlos said, "Sam has a great story to tell."

I listened to his braggadocio recount of the previous day's activity in disbelief. Sam stole money from his parents, and went for a reading from the psychic. She said that he would get into Harvard, but he would not be valedictorian. She said that Sam's friends were against him, and that he had a very bright future in medicine. Then Sam told me that they had an intimate experience.

"The horizontal tango."

I asked if this was a joke.

It was no joke. During their session, the psychic explained that she knew a powerful ritual that would make his future brighter and could guarantee one wish. It sounded perverse and nefarious. She offered to make all his troubles go away if he helped her complete a ritual. Sam described magical incantations that the psychic repeated. Involved were cigarettes, rum, beads, feathers, a few candles, and a little drop of blood from his lip. Sam had wished that if he couldn't have Delancey that no one else could either.

"Do you realize that you participated in the occult?" He crudely motioned that he had gotten a lot out of it, and he didn't believe in mumbo jumbo, voodoo, the heebee jeebees, or anything of that ilk. Carlos thought I was freaking out for no reason.

They were losers that would do anything for instant gratification.

I told John about Sam's story. John felt this was evil and was evidently very frightened. His religious background and beliefs were making him concerned. Sam participating in the ritual was a sure sign that he had no morals or ethics. I may have suspected it in the past, but now I knew for sure.

"I thought he was intelligent and religious," said John.

"I don't think he really has any religion," I replied.

John handed me an application for New York State colleges. I took it home and promptly completed it. The great thing about the application was the fact that it was free. I picked a school in upstate New York, three hours away. It seemed like a good choice. There was a picture of a pretty girl in the brochure. I needed to complete the essay. The question read, "Describe a day in your life that defined who you are as a person." I took a deep breath, and stared at the question for ten minutes. Then I wrote my essay.

When I was eleven years old, my mother died. I did everything I could do, but I was not home to make sure she took her medication on time. It was my responsibility to come straight home from school and give her the pills she needed. I was the oldest child, and my father had to work until 6. My younger sibling was too young to be given such a responsibility. She was sick for a long time. I'm not sure if the medication could've prolonged or prevented the cancer from winning the battle. All I know is that I wasn't home from school on time, and when I arrived, I opened the door with my key, and found her on the kitchen floor. I tried to wake her, but I was too late. She had already passed. I called my father at work, but could not reach him. My grandmother arrived shortly. There was no waking her up.

When my father came home, he asked if I had given her the medicine. I told him that I had not, that I came home late, and she had already passed away. "Why were you late?" he asked me. I explained that I was playing basketball with my friends, and was a half hour late. My father was angry with me, but didn't say anything else. He didn't speak to me for two weeks.

At my mother's funeral, I played her favorite song on guitar. It was my way of honoring her memory. My rendition was enough to bring tears to everyone's face. My mother's countenance was peaceful. I have never played that song again, and I never will. It was my way of making a promise that I would never allow myself to be so irresponsible again. I also decided that instead of goofing off, I would spend my life working and helping to support my family. The day my mother died changed the way I live.

I mailed it immediately and went to sleep wondering what I had done. I knew nothing about this school, and had never been to upstate New York, but now I made a decision that put my future in play. I had knots in my stomach all night.

The ball was in motion. I wasn't sure if I was going to be accepted to the college I had just applied to, but it felt good to have at least one college application out there. Acting on a decision changes things.

At work, Mike arrived about a half hour late, and opened the Café. I told Christine about my senior ski trip. She mentioned that Eddie Lo was also going on the trip.

Mike had his routines, and the wakeup routine was one that could be written in stone. First he yawned, and then he stretched. Then he washed his face with cold water. He dried off, poured himself a cup of coffee, which he drank in silence and ate a muffin. He did more stretches, louder, animal sounding yawns, and then decided to check up on us. It was a bizarre routine to which I was accustomed.

Mike asked me what was new. I said that I applied to a college, and that I was going on a ski trip. "What college?" he asked.

"A state college in Albany," I said.

"That's where I went the second time around," Mike said as he walked away.

I had to pick my jaw up from the floor. Not only did Mike go to my high school, but he went to my college? My fear of turning into Mike was first and foremost in my mind. "So what happened?" I asked.

Mike shrugged and said, "Every kid is different. My roommate in college hardly drank, mostly studied, avoided drugs, and had a great time. He graduated and is now a dentist. I would go to the parties with him, and he would stay for three hours and hardly drink. But not me, I couldn't stop drinking and doing drugs."

I asked, "What was the difference was between you and your roommate?" Mike did not have an answer but said that he'd get back to me.

Later that day a customer walked in to the café. He was a well dressed young man, probably in his thirties. I asked him what he did for a living, and he said he was an investment banker. I asked him what an investment banker did, and he said he made money using other people's money. I asked if he was married or had a family and he said that it wasn't in the plan. His words echoed in my head for the rest of the day.

I guess the guy had a plan, and it was time for me to have a plan. On the subway heading home, I pulled out a notebook and pen, and decided it was time to write.

"Life Map, twenty years from now"

1. **I am married with kids**. I am looking forward to a family, and a wife, and this means that I will not hesitate nor put this off. If I find the right person, then I will move forward. I am not going to be the kind of guy that is afraid to get married or have children. I think that I will only date women that have the potential of being my "significant other" and not waste my time with people that are not. I would rather be alone than waste my time with someone with whom I do not want to share the rest of my life.
2. **I have a very good income, though I do not have to go to work every day for a set number of hours.** My father works two jobs, six and seven days a week. This is not what I envision for myself. I am not going to get stuck in the rut of missing out on all the good things in my life and my children's lives, the way my father did when I was growing up. I will need to either have my own business or make a lot of money in a different set-

ting. I will emulate the owner of the café; he has plenty of free time.

3. **I spend a lot time with my kids, playing sports, taking them to activities.** I plan on being an active father, and allowing my kids to play sports, and do all the activities that I never had the opportunity to do.
4. **I have a better relationship with God than I do now.** Many of the kids at Stanton do not have strong foundations, and often have emotional problems because of this. They turn to suicide and drugs. I am not the most religious person. I have to admit I wonder where God was when my mother died, but I also do not wish to stray too far from my belief in God. In tough times, and my entire life has been tough times, it is this faith that has kept my family together.
5. **I am confident in all aspects of my life.** I don't plan to be the same nervous little kid with an inferiority complex when I grow up.
6. **I have good friends that I can rely on.** I don't need a lot of friends, or any fake friends. Just a handful, who I know are good people and that I can count on.
7. **I am educated.** I plan on going to college and actually learning something. I don't want to go to college to just get a degree or to train for a job.
8. **I have good ethics and values.** I don't want to look in the mirror and be ashamed of myself one day.
9. **I am the kind of person that helps others, always shows kindness, and above all else, I have a great sense of humor and I am always laughing and telling jokes.** I don't want to change from the person that I am today. I see too many people unable and unwilling to really enjoy their lives. They are too stressed out to really take a step back and smell the roses.

10. **I have income from various sources such as stocks, bonds, and real estate investments**. This really is tied to not having to work every single day for a fixed amount of hours. Money is important for the quality of life that I desire, but I saw my father work and work and work and never get ahead.
11. **My health is great; I have always taken good care of my health**. I don't plan on getting sick or drinking too much and killing my liver. I don't plan on being a stoner or having no brain cells in twenty years from using drugs.
12. **I drive a car, and no longer take the subways.**
13. **I can hold a conversation with anyone on any topic at anytime**. Maybe this boils down to being educated, and maybe it boils down to being well versed in a variety of topics. I think it also comes down to being better socialized than I am now.
14. **I am not shy, or intimidated by any person or situation**. I am never going to shy away from a confrontation or a fight.
15. **I have never been arrested**. This is important because I've seen too many people get arrested over the years, and I am intent on staying out of jail. The best way to not get arrested is to walk a straight line.
16. **I am successful in business**. I'm not sure of the business, but I don't want to be an investment banker. Maybe I'll own a café. Maybe the music business. But I think that business is the way I want to go.
17. **I have excellent common sense.** I definitely would like to say one day that common sense kept me from making bad decisions. I see so many academically smart kids at Stanton that seem to lack common sense.
18. **I am very happy and have no regrets**. I don't want to do anything that I'll regret in twenty years. The next

time I come to a fork in the road, or I am about to make a bad decision, I will have to ask myself if this is something that I will regret one day.

I looked at the list I had just written. I had just described a life opposite to my father's. It encompassed who I wanted to be. I wasn't sure if Mr. Zoose would approve of it.

I went to English class and showed my life map to him. I was not nervous about him looking it over. He's not the kind of teacher that ever made students anxious or nervous. He looked at it, smiled, and said it was very good. This is how Mr. Zoose reacted to anything anyone ever wrote. Mr. Zoose was the master of positive feedback and made me feel at ease. Mr. Zoose then handed it back to me.

"It's your map, not mine. Keep it in your wallet, and make decisions in your life based on the map and it will lead to where you want to be in twenty years." I folded it and placed it in my wallet.

Sal Carus was in the hallway. I knew of him, but really couldn't say that I knew him well. He was very smart, and a bit of nerd. Sal did well in his classes, but did not have many friends. He took his academic life very seriously and was ranked in the top ten.

"What's up, Sal?" I said. With angst, Sal said he was done with high school. I asked if he was dropping out and he laughed. His science research project had led to a scholarship to Pratt University. This would be his last month in high school. He would start college full time in January.

Maybe there was something wrong with me; first, for not having a scholarship, second, for not starting college early, and third, for wanting to finish my senior year in high school. I was not jealous of Sal; clearly I was just not as smart as he was. He had a gift for academics that I did not. I was looking forward to the ski trip, the prom, and just seeing my friends everyday. After speaking with Sal, I felt like I was lagging behind, like I was at the bottom of the barrel. But I would not want to trade places with Sal. He was awkward, had no friends, no social life, and dressed funny as well.

I shook his hand and congratulated him. Mr. Mash, our principal was making his rounds. Jubilant, with a large grin, he proudly placed his arm around Sal. "It is a remarkable achievement, Ignacio," said Mr. Mash.

"Ignacio?" I asked.

"That's my real name. Everyone just calls me Sal because I'm Italian."

Sal proclaimed that he couldn't wait; his goal was to finish college in three years, and start graduate school.

Mr. Mash and Sal exited the hallways. I was about to head to my next class, when Mr. Zoose approached with a strange look of confusion.

"Did I hear that correctly?" he asked with arms crossed.

"Sal is starting college in January; he has a scholarship to Pratt University for his science research," I replied.

Mr. Zoose shook his head. "That's terrible. He's already a year younger than he should be because he skipped a grade. Ignacio's definitely not emotionally or mentally ready for college. This is a disaster."

"He's really excited about going, and he's ready to start. Sal's planning on graduating college in three years and starting grad school," I said.

The next thing Mr. Zoose said was like a shotgun going off.

"I've had to talk Ignacio out of suicide twice. Ms. Carus, his mother, has been through a lot. He's even seen a psychiatrist for depression. It is best not to be in a hurry to finish or skip important years of your life. You can never get them back." Mr. Zoose walked back to his class.

I was in a state of complete mental suspension. Sal was at the top of the class, and was revered as a true genius. His projects in engineering were the best in the school. I never would've guessed that he was suicidal. He was the typical Stanton type A personality.

At lunch, I told Sam and John that Sal would be starting college in a few weeks. Sam was furious. He wondered out loud how Sal was getting all this success and attention.

"How could a guy named Sal get such a scholarship and such an opportunity?" Sam asked. "Shouldn't he be making pizza somewhere?"

"His name is really Ignacio," I said.

"That's even worse than Sal," Sam said.

John decided to play along, just to raise Sam's ire. "The Italians have always been famous for scientific breakthroughs. Look at Copernicus, Galileo, Volta, Marconi, etc. The list goes on and on. He's probably the descendant of one of those guys."

Sam's face was turning red. We had pushed the right buttons.

John continued, "Not to mention the greatness of the Roman Empire, the greatest empire of all time."

Sam yelled expletives at the long defunct Roman Empire, and spewed an angry diatribe denouncing the "euro-centric education that had brainwashed all of us." John and I were laughing until tears came out of our eyes. Sam continued on his verbal rampage, explaining the greatness, magnitude, and contributions of the Persian Empire. He could not hear us laughing over his anger. Our insolence was making his blood boil. Next he decried the poor American education system that had somehow left out the Persian Empire in its high school curriculum. Sam was almost in tears when he cursed how we had to study Greek mythology, European history, the Roman Empire, and Julius Cesar, but none of us knew of the Persian Empire or had heard of Xerxes.

John asked, "Who's Xerxes?" and that's when Sam stood, composed himself, and said we were "still chimps swinging on vines." He took a deep breath, looked at both of us, and said "I'm all that's left of the Persian Empire. And how do I spend my time? Talking to monkeys." Then he left.

In reality, Sam was not angry with the Roman Empire, or Italians. He was very proud if his Persian heritage, and did not like the fact that it was left out of our American history books.

"I don't get along with Sal. He thinks I'm an idiot," John smirked.

"Why's that?" I asked.

"We were lab partners freshman year. I did not have the Periodic table of elements memorized. For God's sake, it was only the first day of school."

I looked over and saw Sal eating alone in the corner.

"Let's fix the past," I said to John.

"Huh?" John looked confused.

I motioned Sal over to our table with a hand gesture. John rolled his eyes. Carlos just joined us and looked perplexed. Sal walked over with his tray and sat down.

"I was just telling these guys about your good news," I said to Sal. There was a long, awkward pause. John did not make an effort to speak to Sal. I kicked John in the shin.

"So, Sal, what will you major in?" asked John.

"Well, more than likely engineering of some sort. But it's not really what I am most interested in." Sal was in a good mood, perhaps the result of human contact.

"What are you interested in? If not finishing high school?" John said with a wry smile.

"I'm going to major in engineering, only because I know I can get a good job in that field. But I prefer the older sciences," Sal said and kept eating.

"Older sciences?" I asked.

"Today we study physics, astronomy, and chemistry. But I'm more interested in metaphysics, cosmology, ontology, and alchemy," he said and stopped eating. He looked up with a serious look on his face.

"Explanation?" I asked.

"Well, there is more out there than what the science books are explaining. I have studied the old alchemy ways, and the principles of mysticism that are centered in metaphysics." Sal looked at us, and probably could see that we really had no idea what he was talking about.

"Okay, let me say this. I committed suicide twice...."

John interrupted, "Sorry...huh? What do you mean you committed suicide twice?

You are still here."

"Yes, but I was legally dead for a few minutes each time. See, using alchemy, I was able to stop my heart, and leave my body." Sal started eating again, apparently not the least bit concerned about sounding out of this planet.

"You left your body? What does that even mean?" I asked.

Sal leaned in, and whispered, "My spirit left my body and walked around. Like astral projection. Then I came back."

John and I looked at each other in silence. Sal kept eating. Carlos finally spoke.

"It's not so unheard of. This sort of thing is practiced in the eastern religions, and some Native American tribes have been doing this for centuries, but it takes years of meditation to accomplish these feats." Carlos made a hand gesture indicating that Sal was out of his mind. John rolled his eyes.

"Normally it would take years of spiritual practice, but I have designed and produced a machine that does it in seconds. Isn't that the goal of science anyway ?"

"What did you see?" I asked, playing along.

"I saw the spirits of the deceased around me. There are several planes in the netherworld, and I did not get very far. It was a little scary," Sal said, then started heading to class. "But it all comes back to Newtonian laws of physics. Remember—energy cannot be destroyed, but transferred. So I wondered where does the energy go when someone dies? I can explain it to you later," he said walking away from the table.

"You mean the soul?" asked John.

"Religious beliefs call it the soul, but it's still energy. The body produces energy, runs on energy, and one can say that the body is, in fact, energy. Electrochemical, biochemical, etc. but still energy."

I wasn't a big believer in metaphysics, astral projections, or even spirits. But Sal was the most scientific of students and one of the smartest kids in Stanton, and I'm sure there was much more behind his story than he was telling.

"So what did you come up with?" John asked Sal.

"It was quite an experience, an out of body experience."

John giggled at Sal, but I was more concerned with his mental state of mind.

"Sal, what you are saying seems a little far fetched. Have you considered Achem's razor?" I asked carefully.

"If you are wondering...if the simpler explanation is that I was delusional...the thought has crossed my mind. That's why I did it a second time." Sal stormed out, insulted.

The whole thing sounded ridiculous, but Sal was a genius. I wasn't sure about an afterlife, who really knew for sure? John believed that there was an after life, because his religion tells him so, and he accused me of lacking faith. It was a bizarre conversation, but I did not place too much stock in it.

Later that week, I approached Delancey. "Are you going to lunch?" I asked her.

"No, I have to leave early. My mother and I are going away for the weekend," she said.

"Where are you headed?"

"Miami."

I had a feeling that I should ask her out again. My life map included a life with regrets and hesitation. "Maybe when you get back, we can hangout?" I said playing it cool. The second that the words left my lips, my heart started to pound like a drum. I could feel anxiety building in my stomach. Delancey didn't answer. She slowly looked at me. The she blushed, and glanced downwards. Her head and body swiveled.

"It's no big deal," I said. "I just thought that maybe you'd like to see the tree at Rockefeller Center or something. I'll even buy you hot chocolate. But it's...."

"Okay," she said. "It's not like this is a date or something? I mean, are you asking me out?"

"Honestly, I just want to get to know you better. Before it's too late, that's all."

A warm smile slowly emerged, and her eyes shined with new energy.

"When I get back on Monday we'll talk about it. I haven't seen the tree yet."

She walked away, and I was very excited. I had a smile on my face that I could not suppress if I tried.

Several days passed, and I eagerly waited for Delancey to return. Finally, she was at lunch on Monday, sporting a new tan. "How was Miami?" I asked her.

"Hot, and a lot of fun."

I walked her out of the cafeteria, making it a point to escape Sam's line of vision.

"So how about we hang out on Thursday?" I suggested, trying to look calm although I was nervous and sweating.

"Thursday's not good. How about Wednesday? After school?" she said.

Wednesday was my day to make dinner for my family. I hesitated, thinking about my responsibilities. "Sounds good, I'll meet you after school at the newspaper office, and we'll go from there."

The solution to my problem was to make two dinners on Tuesday, and place one in the refrigerator. We'll eat pasta and baked chicken twice this week. By the time he came home, my father was so tired, he probably wouldn't notice anyway.

That night I couldn't sleep so I went to the basement and practiced guitar. I kept thinking about Delancey, and couldn't help but imagine us at Rockefeller Centre. I thought about what I would say, and what I should do, but decided just to play it by ear. When I finally did fall asleep, I had a dream about her. We were ice skating together, and holding hands. I was leading, then her hand broke from mine, and when I turned back, she was gone. That's when I woke up.

The next day the guys noticed I was a little dressed up. I kept quiet about my plans with Delancey. However, at lunch, she walked up to me, and Sam flashed an angry glance.

"David, I'm going to be a little late this afternoon; just wait for me." The words spilled out of her lips as she walked by. I could imagine Sam's heartbeat pulsating a little faster, and the blood pressure rising in his veins as he glowered at me.

"You have plans with Delancey?" asked John.

I didn't want to say too much. Actually, I did not want to say anything. John quickly glanced at Sam, and didn't mention anything further on the subject. Sam continued to stare, like a wolf when something enters its territory. The awkward silence continued for a few moments. The last thing I needed was Sam having an emotional implosion in the cafeteria.

"You have a big problem here," said Sam.

"What would that be?" I asked.

"Delancey is mine and she is off limits to you," he said.

"I don't think Delancey would agree," said John.

"You must have a death wish," said Sam.

"I'm not afraid of Death, and I'm not afraid of you." I began heading to my next class.

"You know what your problem is? You lack loyalty. You don't even know the meaning of the word. You are a back stabber!" Sam's face was bright red.

"I'm the loyal one here. You are the one that needs to wake up. She is not interested in you and she is not yours or anyone else's; if you knew her at all, you would know that." I left the cafeteria agitated.

After school, I was working on the newspaper when Delancey arrived. She instantly smiled when she saw me. I smiled back, which was no small feat, since I never smile. We exited the school together and headed to the subway.

The psychic was in her store window as we passed by on Dekalb Avenue, and when she saw us together, she got a pained expression on her face. Delancey walked, and I sauntered. We discussed the upcoming holidays. It was so cold that I was shivering. Delancey seemed fine.

"I'll be in Long Island with my mother and stepfather for the holidays, before the ski trip; what about you?" she asked. There were no false intentions or ulterior motives with Delancey. When it came to Delancey, what you saw was always what you got.

"Other than the ski trip, I'm going to try to work at the café. Earn some extra money," I said as we boarded the F-Train.

"I haven't heard you play the guitar since last year. Play something for me sometime," said Delancey. The cold in my body turned to instant warmth. I loved the fact that she liked my guitar playing.

"For you, anytime."

The train went over the Manhattan Bridge, and we both looked out the window in silence as we peered down below to the East River, and lower Manhattan's skyline.

"The prom is going to be held at the World Trade Center, at Windows on the World," she remarked.

Gazing at the towers, I felt that there would be no better location for a prom. We talked about school, our teachers, and I told her about my job at the café. She seemed genuinely intrigued.

"What about your family?" she asked.

"What about yours?" I asked.

"Don't answer a question with a question."

"Well. . .you already know, it's just my father, my brother and I."

"Yes, your mom. . ."

"My mother passed away when I was 11."

"What was she like?" Delancey looked genuinely curious.

No one had ever asked me that question before. "Her name was Maria. She taught music, and vocal lessons. She was a great singer, but never really pursued it. She taught me to sing. She was really great."

"It must be difficult." Her expression changed to one of remorse. We were both silent, as the train entered the tunnel again. No more daylight.

"So what about your family?" I asked.

"You know my parents are divorced. I live with my father in the city during the week and with my mother and stepfather on the weekends, in Long Island." She seemed more than okay with the arrangement, but I found it odd that she did not live full time with her mother.

"Whose decision was it that you live with your mother on the weekends?"

"Actually, it was mine. My dad needed me." Her countenance changed again, seemingly expressing empathy for her father. Mentioning her father caused her face, gait, and overall energy to shift.

"I think you feel every strongly about your father. Is he all right?" I asked.

"He's fine. You know, he has no one else in his life. It's just me, and his work. He would be physically fine, and could live without me, but I worry about him. I worry he would be lonely and just work all the time. Besides, my mother has her new husband, and she is very happy."

I thought about my own father's happiness, and loneliness. He has me and Harry, but I wondered if that was enough. We arrived at Rockefeller Center and marveled at the monumental Christmas tree in front of us. The frigid winds whipped around in all directions, and both of us shivered in the cold. Below, several ice skaters maneuvered with style and grace, oblivious to the cold. Delancey commented on how much she liked the decorations. I noticed the resplendence of the red ribbons, green wreaths, different lights, and ornaments everywhere.

"I love New York during the holiday season. People just seem so much happier, and the whole city seems much more alive. We put our tree up two weeks ago, and I already finished my Christmas shopping. What about you, are you fully decorated?" she asked.

"The truth is we are not fully decorated. Actually, we are not decorated at all. We used to celebrate Christmas in a big way with a tree, and presents, and lots of decorations. But my mother passed away just before Christmas Eve, and we have not celebrated since." I glanced downwards, and thought that I was probably coming across as a sad case. I did not want to give her that impression, and I immediately looked up and changed the topic.

"Look at the golden sculpture below, near the rink." I pointed to the stunning gold statue and she smiled.

"That's Prometheus, from Greek mythology. Do you remember what he is famous for?" she asked.

I laughed. "I am going to impress you with this one! Prometheus was famous for giving fire to the humans. He really angered the gods by doing this, and was severely punished. I think that he was chained and attacked by a bird."

"Not bad, David. Not bad. But, his punishment was to have his liver eaten by a large eagle every day. A slow and painful punishment."

"So what happened to him?" I asked.

"Eventually, a hero came along, killed the eagle, and broke the chains," she giggled. "That's mythology for you...a hero always comes along." We gazed down at the grace of the ice skaters. "I'm still waiting for my hero to come along," Delancey caught herself daydreaming. "It almost looks like the ice skaters are dancing specifically for Prometheus, like in his honor."

"I wonder how much the sculpture is worth. You know, because of the gold? I hear its 24 carat," I remarked casually.

"I think it's priceless, and not because of the gold, but because of what it means to millions of people and tourists that see it every year. Could you imagine how empty Rockefeller Center would be without it?" she asked.

"You're right, but you can't pay the bills with sentimentality. I think it must be worth at least 10 million dollars." We walked closer to the tree. Several large crows gathered, eating scraps off the floor.

"How about some hot chocolate? You look so cold!" I said with a smile.

Delancey's hand reached across my face and wiped a tear from my eye. Her hand was so warm.

"That's from the cold winds," I said.

She smiled. "I would love some hot chocolate."

I ordered two hot chocolates, and we sat in a nearby coffee shop and warmed up.

"I think you should bring Christmas back to your house," Delancey suggested.

I looked at her, and kept drinking my hot chocolate.

"If it was me, I would do it. Decorate, and all. I bet it would bring cheer to your father and brother." When she spoke I felt assured by her words.

"It's different. YOU could do it. But, and don't take this the wrong way, but that's one of the advantages of being a girl and a daughter. It's perfectly normal for you to do things like that. If I did it, I'm not sure how my father would perceive me. He's a real tough guy, and he probably would think it's feminine for his oldest son to decorate."

"Don't give me that crap. You are such a sexist! You think its woman's work." She hit me on the shoulder.

"I'm not a sexist, but you don't know what it's like to be a boy. It's not that easy, to bring Christmas back, and to decorate. Things are not that festive in my house." I sipped my hot chocolate, ignoring the fact that it burned the insides of my mouth.

"I guess you don't have the courage to try to bring a little happiness back into your family's life. I wonder what your mother would have wanted." Delancey stared at me as she finished her hot chocolate. We were warming up.

"You know, if it was me, I would want that...someone to go the distance to do what it takes. I think every girl is looking for a guy like that no matter where or what the circumstances," Delancey smiled.

I accompanied her home, although she insisted that it was not necessary. We took the subway cross-town and to the Upper West Side. We walked to her building. A uniformed doorman greeted her. The doorman told her that her father was already home.

"I had a really great time," I said smiling uncontrollably.

"So did I."

"Let's do something again soon," I belted out eagerly. She handed me a sheet of paper, with her phone number on it. We embraced and I headed home.

I was on cloud nine, distracted from my studies and my homework. I heated dinner up, and we sat down and ate. Harry noticed it was the same meal as yesterday. My father said, "When you're hungry, everything tastes good."

After dinner, my father walked over to the wooden cabinet and pulled out a bottle of Wild Turkey Bourbon. This always had an immediate relaxing effect on him, and he looked at us, and asked about school. Harry spoke for a few minutes about his high school band and about his football team. Harry was athletic.

"Don't waste your time on music; study something where you'll be able to find a decent job," my father bellowed at Harry. I wondered if Harry remembered that my father was once a talented guitarist, many, many years ago. It was my father who had taught me to play guitar. Harry seemed saddened and sullen.

I thought about bringing up holiday decorations, but decided not to. My father was never in a good mood this time of year. The holidays changed his personality dramatically for the worse.

It had been six years since my mother passed, and my father had never been out with another woman. I once heard my grandmother asking him if he would remarry, and he answered that it wouldn't be fair to "the boys." He always called us "the boys." We had a small house with thin walls, and I always overheard everything said. My grandmother sometimes told him that "the boys" needed a mother and that he needed to move on with his life. My father always said, "Later, when the boys are older." The holidays were always tough on us, but for the first time, I realized it must be tougher on my father.

When I went to work, I noticed that The World Financial Center was decorated like a holiday gem. Christmas trees were everywhere. Large, fully decorated wreaths hung from the ceilings. Bright red and yellow poinsettias lined the lengthy marble staircase in the

Winter Garden. Holiday music was playing throughout the building. It caused my mood to change, and I felt festive.

After my shift at the café, I saw Reggie the security guard talking to a woman. Reggie was holding a box. The woman was the head of events for the World Financial Center, and she was throwing out a box of Christmas decorations. She had tried to give it to Reggie, but he could not use it. He asked if I wanted it, and I hesitated.

I thought about Delancey, and about what my father would say. What would my mother have wanted? I decided to take the box home with me.

It was not easy carrying such a large box on the trains, and up the subway stairs. I carried the box a few blocks from the subway to my home, stopping intermittently for a break. The box was heavy.

Harry was already home and his face lit up when he saw the Christmas decorations. We pulled all the items from the large box including small artificial wreaths, ribbons, bells, garlands, and more, and decorated the house. After we were done, we both looked at each other in awe. This was truly something different for us, and we felt the same uneasiness when both of us wondered how my father would react. The hours passed in silent anticipation.

My father came home and looked around in silence. He managed a forced smile. He went into his room, and did not come back out, except once, for the bottle of bourbon. The decorations made an impact, and he looked sad and happy at the same time.

The next morning, he surprisingly made us an early breakfast. I ate the pancakes before I went to work. As I was leaving the house, my father walked me out, and said, "Sometimes you have nothing and everything...at the same time." His demeanor had changed to one a little brighter.

Mike was also late, as usual. The work day went fast. Many tourists stormed the World Financial Center. Christine suggested that I go with her to buy presents for my family. I was in the holiday spirit, making money, and felt like spending.

I went with Christine to Hester Street, in Chinatown, and met Eddie Lo there. Eddie was quite the salesman, showing me many different items and offering me a special discount. Here I was hanging out with Eddie Lo, the coolest guy I knew. I was exhilarated.

I bought gifts for my family. They had designer labels in them from famous brands, brands I could not afford. I wondered if they were fakes, but Eddie said they were the real thing. Eddie gave me a big discount on top of the incredibly low price, and I went home and wrapped all the presents the best I could.

Christmas finally arrived. In the past, my father gave us cash, a modest amount that he could afford. But this year was different. We had presents to open for the first time in a long time. Harry was impressed with the new leather jacket I bought for him. My father reluctantly opened his gift, asking how I could afford these presents. I explained about Eddie Lo's discount. He and Harry were very happy. It was a new experience to watch my father's face as he opened his new coat. His face lit up when he tried it on. My father remarked that it was likely stolen merchandise. "I paid for it at a store and have receipts to prove it," I blurted.

At the end of the evening, I called Delancey, but her answering machine picked up. I left a message wishing her a Merry Christmas.

chapter 9

THE NEXT DAY was the Senior Ski Trip in upstate New York. I stayed awake the entire night, nervous about being away from home for the first time, but also eager to try skiing. I had packed my underwear, sweatshirts, and jeans. I did not own any ski clothing, and wouldn't even know where to buy it.

My father was asleep when I left the house on a freezing cold Sunday morning. It was a rare day that he slept in.

I carried a large, overstuffed duffle bag as I boarded the subway from Astoria. I bought the *Daily News* at five am. December mornings were painfully cold, and I felt a shiver in my bones. Subway service was slow. Hardly anyone else was on the platform. In the newspaper, there were several articles about a Pan Am plane that had gone down over Lockerbie, Scotland. There was a bomb on the plane. This made me think about the bus trip, and my imagination took over and wondered what would happen if there was a bomb on the ski trip. For a moment I had second thoughts about going, but I shook it off and told myself that I was just being silly. This was not the occasion to be pensive.

At the Queensboro Plaza station, two hoodlums entered the train car from the morning darkness. Although the subway car was empty, they decided to sit directly in front of me. They weren't looking for conversation. Sometimes the nervous energy in my stomach goes into over drive in a bad situation. This was one of those situations.

The men had hoods covering their faces, and large, puffy, extra long goose down coats. The doors closed and the train starting moving into the tunnel. I was in the car with the conductor. I'm not sure if they knew that, but I'm guessing they probably didn't care. One of them raised his head, exposing his silver-capped teeth and a large scar on his face.

"You going somewhere?" he asked.

"School," I said. My voice was firm, my tone was even. I wasn't afraid.

The other one looked up and said, "You must be dumb to have to go to school on Sunday." They both started laughing. Then they moved and sat on either side of me.

My duffle bag was heavy, maybe 30 lbs. I wasn't going anywhere without it; I needed this bag for the ski trip. The guy on the left grabbed my arm. The other one said, "Gimme your wallet."

I tried to stand up, but they pulled my arm down. No sign of the conductor.

Both thugs started laughing. I did not know what was so funny. Did they have a gun?

"Gimme your wallet!" he shouted.

"All I have is my train pass and student ID." My tone was now best described as nervous. I also had fifty dollars for the trip, hidden in my shoe.

They burst into more laughter. They were laughing so hard, I started laughing too.

When they saw me laughing, they fell on the floor and rolled over in uncontrollable laughter. I was laughing so hard watching them laugh, that tears were coming out of my eyes. The three of us kept laughing for a few more seconds.

"We're just playing with you," one of them said. "Why aren't you scared, we could have killed you. But I guess it's not your time." They got off at the next stop, and said, "Stay in school young man, or you'll end up like us." They kept laughing as they exited the train.

One of them dropped a large jagged edged knife and bent down to pick it up. He looked up and smiled, and then the doors closed.

I breathed a sigh of relief. I wasn't afraid of death, but that was stressful.

The conductor came in, looked at me and said nothing. I'm not sure what just didn't happen, but I was glad that it was over. I was lucky after a lifetime of not being lucky in similar situations. Maybe my luck was changing. I sat on the careening train in the same seat for the rest of the ride. It was still very early on a Sunday morning; the hoodlums were probably high on crack.

I arrived at school and boarded the bus. The bus headed north on a three hour drive. Most of the kids were talking, goofing off, or listening to music on their walkman. One kid had head phones that looked like he may use them for earmuffs. I closed my eyes and thought about how lucky I had been this morning. I could not figure out why I laughed, but was glad that I did, because it made a big difference.

When the bus left Brooklyn, I was skeptical that we would find snow. I had never been to upstate New York, and didn't know what to expect. The kids on the bus were rowdy, and boisterous. I could not sleep. Some of the kids started singing songs. The singing, clapping, and cheering grew louder with every song. Someone handed me a ukulele. I played while some of the girls sang. Everyone seemed to be taken back by how well I could play the ukelele. It really wasn't much different from the guitar. Delancey was not on my bus.

About two hours into the drive, there was plenty of snow on the ground. We arrived at the Valdis Ski Resort surrounded by snow and mountains. I had never seen mountains before, and the Catskill Mountains were covered in evergreen fir trees, snow, and ski trails.

The trip advisor was Ms. Bulzer, my health class teacher. We were met outside by the other buses and two chaperones. It would be three boys to a room.

Mr. Bulzer called out three names at a time, and said to go to the front desk to get room keys. I waited a while for her to call my name. One of my roommates was Eddie Lo, my friendly neighborhood Chinese gangster. The other was Maurice, the religious Jewish kid.

We went to our rooms to settle in. Maurice unpacked his clothes, a bible, which he called a Torah, and some religious garb, snacks, and toiletries. He had a second suitcase with food. Maurice only ate kosher food and brought his own with him. I unpacked just clothes and toiletries, no snacks, and no religious items of any kind.

Eddie was unpacking as well. He unpacked his underwear, toiletries, socks, boots, ski mask. He pulled out a silver .22 caliber pistol, nunchucks, a butterfly knife, ninja stars, and a red rope.

Maurice and I glanced at each other. It was easy to take Eddie out of the city, but harder to take the city out of Eddie. Maurice asked Eddie why he brought the weapons.

"These days you can't trust anyone. Besides, you've got your religion, and I've got mine," said Eddie, holding up his gun.

"Do you really think the Deceptors would come all the way up here to cause trouble?" Maurice asked.

"No one knows who the Deceptors really are. They could have arrived here by bus with the rest of us," commented Eddie.

"But this is a vacation from school. I think you are too paranoid; even if they did come up here, they would be out of their element," said Maurice.

"Look, I've fought the Deceptors before, on the subways, in Brooklyn, and in Queens. These guys are dangerous, and they will strike whenever and wherever. Death does not take a vacation. I'm going to be prepared for anything on this trip. As far as I know, you guys could be one of the Deceptors," Eddie grinned at us in silence.

"BOO!" yelled Maurice, and we all laughed.

"Besides, this is a good opportunity for the Deceptors. They can rob our rooms while we are skiing." Eddie continued to unpack. I was confused about his red rope. Eddie was being overly concerned, but there was a possibility that he could be right. I grew angry with the thought of the Deceptors robbing and stealing from us during the trip. I decided to stay alert and keep my guard up. I'd rather be safe than sorry. I decided to play it down a bit.

"I think you are on the wrong senior trip, Eddie" I said. "The trip to Armageddon is not this week. This is the ski trip."

"I know. That's why I brought my ear muffs," joked Eddie.

"What's the rope for?" I asked.

"In case I ever need a way out," he remarked casually.

A way out of what? A tunnel? A mountain? He didn't make sense. Eddie Lo was the most famous or perhaps infamous student on the trip. It was hard to believe that he was my roommate. I was glad that I was on his good side, thanks to Christine.

I peered out the window. Snow covered tree branches complimented moonlit white ski trails, and a family of raccoons scurried across the parking lot. The scenery appeared to have been tinted blue. On the far right side, there was a pond, appearing frozen over. The snow fell in slow motion. The image was beautiful and surreal, as if I had fallen into an Ansel Adams photo.

Students gathered in the main dining hall for lunch. There was a large stone fireplace at the far end of the dining hall. Several kids stood in front of the roaring fire to warm up. The ski lodge was closed to outsiders. Its guests were our school, and another school from Staten Island. We joked around that the other school didn't stand a chance against us on the slopes, even though most of us had never been skiing before.

There were many students from school that I did not know. But I also saw faces that I did recognize. Natalie was there. Jacob was there with Sandra. And Delancey was also there, dressed up like a professional Olympic skier. Most of us did not own ski clothes, and wore denim jeans. Not Delancey, she looked like an Olympic pro.

Eddie Lo was in his usual Chinese Gangster uniform—tapered jeans, black leather jacket, t-shirt, and spiked hair. Eddie was not going to be the coolest guy; he was going to be the coldest guy. He could freeze to death on the slopes by wearing such thin clothing.

Delancey and I sat down at a table with her two roommates. I did not them know from school, but they were friendly enough. The ski lodge had a buffet lunch, consisting of baked chicken and French fries, and at least ten other items. Maurice joined us and ate a sandwich that he had brought from home.

"Who's your other roommate?" asked Delancey.

"Eddie Lo," I said proudly. The table went silent.

"Eddie the Chinese Gangster?" asked Delancey. Maurice made it a point to take a large bite of his sandwich so that he wouldn't be able to comment.

"Yes, that Eddie Lo," I said. I didn't want to speak too much on the subject, and I certainly did not feel comfortable divulging Eddie's packing list.

"I hear there's a party tonight," Delancey said eagerly.

"Oh really? Should be fun," I replied as the knots in my stomach tightened.

"It's a dance party," said Delancey, staring at me with wondrous eyes.

This made me sick to my stomach. I could live with a Chinese Gangster for a few days, but the thought of dancing in public was scary. Dancing was never my thing.

Delancey and I were walking after lunch when we were approached by Juan Perez, the class president. Juan seemed like a typical politician, formally shaking my hand, saying and doing all the right things. Juan was in formal attire, suit and tie, despite the fact that we were on a vacation. He wore his trademark long black leather trench coat. Juan always wore a suit, as if perpetually campaigning.

"Where's your room Delancey?" Juan asked.

"I'm the last room in the West Wing where are all the girls are staying," she said.

"I'm in the South wing, first room on the right if you want to come by later. We're planning an after hours party," said Juan.

"I'll think about it," replied Delancey.

"I hope you have a great time and remember that it was at my urging that this was put this together......at my constant requests," said Juan. The guy was a constant self promoter. Delancey told me that Juan had asked her to the prom.

"Did you say yes?" I asked.

"He's a lot to take. I can deal with him for about five minutes, but no more than that. I get the feeling that he only wants to go with me so that he can tell all his friends that we are going out. Juan is very self absorbed. I guess I'm looking for someone not like Juan....some one that would go the extra mile for me, someone that isn't afraid or too busy to really go the distance for me. He's not that guy." Delancey looked out the window.

"Hey...there isn't anything I wouldn't do or anywhere I wouldn't go for you," I said.

"Thanks, David."

Juan Perez was also a highly ranked senior student, at the top of the class. I did not know much else about him, other than the fact that I didn't care for him or his political antics. When he left, I saw him glower at me.

Delancey seemed lost in thought, staring in silence out the window at slowly falling snow flakes. It was cold where we were standing. I was about a foot from her, and I could feel the heat and warmth radiating from her body.

"What's on your mind?" I asked.

"Well, it's just that I wish it didn't have to end. I'm not ready to leave high school. I sometimes think that life is over after high school. At least life as I know it. I have a lot of expectation and demands from my family, and once I get into college, the expectations will increase." She kept staring out the window.

"It's the opposite for me. I can't wait for high school to end. I really don't want to be a kid anymore. I just want to live my life, my way. I want to leave and never look back." I was feeling very confident in the way I said things. The more I said it, the better it sounded.

"That's because you have nothing holding you back. For me I am constantly getting pulled in different directions," her eyes were melancholic as she spoke.

"I guess that's true," I agreed, never before considering that there was really nothing holding me back.

"I have a lot here. I'm very close to my father, and my mother, and just my whole life in New York. We go to restaurants and Broadway shows, and high society parties. It's really a wonderful way to spend my teenage years."

Delancey had a great life, and she was attached to her high society soirees, and her night life. Delancey was a good friend, and I was very attracted to her. Nonetheless, I was hesitant to jeopardize our friendship by trying to take things a step further. I still felt that she was out of my league. For now, I was happy just to be in her company.

I rented boots and skis and joined a group of kids taking a lesson. It was helpful, but I realized you just have to do it, and no lesson was really going to prepare me for actual skiing.

I stood waiting for the handheld lift to take me up the beginner's hill. Natalie was going up the bunny trails. I was still staring at Natalie as the lift was coming my way. I reached out and grabbed it, distracted, not realizing the force with which it would pull me up the hill. It pulled my arm very fast and very sharply. I felt a twinge in my shoulder. I tried to let go, but my sleeve was caught in the lift, and I found myself getting dragged to the top of the bunny slopes. My skis were being dragged with me, and my ankles were twisting. I was struggling to free my wrist from the lift strap.

I continued to be dragged up the hill, and could see the faces of my fellow students pointing and laughing. I finally managed to straighten up and at least look like I knew what I was doing. I freed my sleeve at the top of the hill. If I wasn't cold and wet, I probably would've been warm enough to feel embarrassed.

From the top of the hill I felt frozen with fear. Everyone was going down the hill so fast. "Its now or never" I shouted, and quickly jumped down the hill. The wind was whipping across my face, and I was exhilarated. Other people were waving to me, and it felt like I was flying. It was so much fun, until I tried to stop, and could not slow down. At the very end, I twisted my legs, and came to a stop by violently tumbling down. My legs and knees twisted, and my face rubbed against the ice like sandpaper. I couldn't wait to do it again.

By the end of the day I was ready for a bigger slope, which I figured I could do the next day.

I changed out of my wet clothing. Maurice entered the room and his skin was bright red from ski burn, matching his red hair. We both sat in our beds completely exhausted. No sign of Eddie. I took a hot shower and got ready for dinner. My shoulder stiffened, and I had aches and pains all over. I had bruises on my ribs and back as well. I really didn't mind; I had a high tolerance for pain.

I ate dinner with Maurice and a few other kids that I did not know too well.

Maurice was eating *shwarma*, his meal brought from home. It looked like a gyro.

"One man's gyro is another man's *shwarma*, you say tomato and I say *shwarma*," he said. The others seemed like normal kids; many were involved in various organizations throughout the school. Their personalities were much easier to deal with than Sam's.

There were kids from the yearbook committee, from the band, from the chorus, and the last thing we spoke about was Stanton or colleges. I felt like I chose the wrong friends, and missed out on knowing a lot of cool people. This was my opportunity to remedy that notion before high school was over.

The food was pretty good, but, like my father always says, all food is great when you are hungry. I had worked up quite an appetite skiing.

I went back to the room and took a nap. When I awoke, I could barely move my shoulder. I was in tremendous pain. Maurice said my shoulder was completely swollen. I took another hot shower to loosen it up.

At the dance party, I grabbed a Coke and watched the kids dance. It turned into a great party quickly. The music was loud, and the ski lodge provided flashing strobe lights and a smoke machine.

I was the only one not dancing. It looked worse that I was not dancing than it would if I was a bad dancer. In addition to being a terrible dancer, I could barely move my shoulder. On the life map, I wrote that I would never be intimidated by any situation or person and so I started dancing with some friends. Delancey and her friends joined in.

A student fell down while dancing. Laughter followed. I thought nothing of it and kept dancing. At least no one was laughing at me. After the second song, I was less nervous. I danced five songs and went to the table to get my soda.

There were two identical cups of soda on the table. Unsure of which was mine, I took a sip from one of the cups and realized there was a lot of liquor in it. I grabbed the other soda. It was just coke. This one was actually mine. On the dance floor, the kids continued dancing and laughing. Another kid fell down. More outbursts of laughter followed. Most of the kids were drunk.

Jacob noticed that I was favoring my shoulder. He offered me a shot of whiskey, saying it would numb the pain. Jacob held out the plastic cup inches from my mouth. I didn't want to seem like an unsociable loser. I sipped it slowly, and he complained that I was doing it all wrong. He said "Drink it quickly, like a shot." I swallowed it fast and it burned my throat. Jacob laughed.

The school chaperones were dancing as well, oblivious to the inebriated situation. The Life Map was in my thoughts. This really didn't fit in with not having any regrets, because if I got drunk and made a fool of myself, I would definitely have regrets. It was easy to not have another drink because the whiskey tasted awful. If they had beer, it probably would've been a tougher decision. That was the last drink I had.

I continued dancing. Ms. Bulzer was also dancing. Some kids were entering and exiting the back of the dance hall. I went to see what the activity was about and as I exited, I smelled pot. Twenty kids were smoking pot outside. Juan was walking back into the dance party. He glowered at me again, this time with red, watery, glazed eyes.

I thought about my options. I wasn't planning on smoking pot and didn't come this close to graduating and getting out of New York, only to be suspended, expelled or arrested for smoking pot or hanging around kids that were. One of my goals on the Life Map was not to be arrested. I immediately went back to the dance floor. The one shot of whiskey had kicked in and I was buzzed.

Maurice had joined the party by this time. I asked him if he was going to dance, and he said, "There are no laws against it" with a big smile on his face. He said he was Sephardic, not Hasidic. "The rumors of my Hasidim have been greatly exaggerated." And then he spoke of god, religion and his point of views for the next few minutes.

"We're at a party. Maybe we should dance," I said, quickly getting bored by the conversation. Maurice was quite the dancer. He moved like Michael Jackson—and ended every song with a moonwalk. He even did the moonwalk during slow love ballads. I danced a few songs with Delancey before Juan Perez rudely cut in.

Delancey was giggling non-stop with Juan, as I watched from across the room. It was obvious that they were both stoned. When Delancey fell down, I realized she was completely drunk as well. Juan was all over her as he tried to help her up. I walked over, stepped in front of Juan, and helped Delancey up.

"She's fine," Juan said. Delancey nodded.

I asked her to walk off the dance floor with me.

"Delancey—it's obvious that you are not your self and I really don't like Juan all over you like that."

"I know. What's with that guy? He's all touchy feely. Typical politician. But I'll be fine. Walk me to my room." I took Delancey to her room, and then went to my own room.

It was after midnight, and I was completely exhausted from the skiing, and also from waking up so early. My shoulder felt more than swollen and I was in tremendous pain. Maurice arrived back at the room shortly thereafter. Eddie was already in the room when we arrived. The party was still going strong. My shoulder was stiff and throbbing. I intended to try to sleep it off.

Eddie had been night skiing.

He talked on and on about the skiing he had done, and boasted that he was the best skier in our high school. Then he left the room and went to the party. I went to sleep. So did Maurice.

At three in the morning, I awoke to a rumble outside of the room. There was shouting and loud thumps, sounding like a fight had broken out. Maurice turned on the light. Eddie came inside panting, and locked the door behind him; he went to his suitcase, and pulled out the gun, placed it in his pocket, and then placed the nun-chucks in his hand. I asked what was happening.

"It's getting pretty bad out there. It's us versus them. The Deceptors are here. Are you coming?" Eddie said.

"Don't go out there," Maurice said.

Eddie described how he had been ambushed and punched in the face. I could see a bruise on his face.

"Eddie, if you're going back out there, leave the gun here," I said, smelling alcohol and marijuana. That wasn't exactly a winning combination considering he had a suitcase full of weapons. Eddie didn't reply. He had completely lost all self control.

Maurice shouted at him, "Eddie if you take a gun out there, your life is over!" It's not easy trying to talk sense into an inebriated, oversized Chinese gangster. If he didn't have the gun, it would have been easier to reason with him. A gun changes everything.

I've been around people with guns my whole life. If Eddie didn't have a gun, he would have just been angry and somewhat dangerous considering his enormous size. But since he had the gun, it was like he was on steroids. He was practically salivating to go out there and show his gun off. Eddie wanted to be the kid with the most power. There was no long term thinking in his mind.

"I'm going out there, with or without you," Eddie said.

Maurice yelled, "We're not in a gang, and this isn't a gang fight!"

"One of them could have a gun, and this would even the playing field," said

Eddie. "I'm only going to use it for self defense. How's it going to look if I don't strike back? People will talk. They'll say that I'm a wimp."

That's how most people justify carrying a gun. They think it's only for an extreme situation or for self defense. In reality, Eddie was building up bravado, and he aimed to brandish his weapon to let everyone know that he had it. Eddie wanted to be the big gangster tonight. He headed for the door.

Maurice shouted, "It's all over—no college, just jail if you go out there."

"You are not thinking straight; just put the gun back into your suit case," I pleaded. Eddie walked out, gun in one pocket, and nunchucks in one hand. Maurice and I stared at each other.

"This is not good, and it's going to get ugly," Maurice sighed. "We should tell Ms. Bulzer."

"I don't think we have that much time." I was getting dressed to go after Eddie, when Maurice tackled me to the ground. My shoulder hit the floor hard, and I screamed in agony.

"You're not going anywhere. That's world war three out there, and you'r unarmed. Stay in the room; there's nothing you can do." Maurice sat on my legs, and I could not move. I tried to push him off, explaining that Delancey might be out there.

"Do you have a death wish?" he asked.

There was a loud commotion and then two gun shots. People were screaming and we heard the rumbling of a stampede.

Maurice hit the ground next to me. "Something happened!" he screamed. I ran out of the room to find Delancey. Flashing police lights could be seen out the windows. I thought it that was the last time I would see Eddie, that he might be dead. There was no sign of Delancey. The police ordered everyone to their rooms. Minutes later, Ms. Bulzer and the police removed all of Eddie's belongings.

The police found the butterfly knife, the ninja stars, and the red rope. One of the cops held the rope and remarked, "If you give a man enough rope...well, you know the saying."

They searched our drawers as well, but did not find any more weapons. Ms. Bulzer, in disbelief, mentioned that Eddie had been accepted to St. John's University.

The ski lodge announced they were throwing us out. Everyone had to pack their belongings. At seven a.m. we boarded the buses and headed back to Brooklyn. I sat next to Delancey on the bus. She said she had returned to the party after I dropped her off at her room, but was very confused about the events. She remembered someone falling on top of someone else and a fight breaking out.

It was a long, silent bus ride home, and Delancey was clearly upset.

"I had to sit on David to keep him from running after you," Maurice said to Delancey. "He was willing to risk getting shot to make sure you were safe."

I was embarrassed when Maurice blurted this out.

"Is that true?" she asked. I nodded. "Why would you risk your own life to find me?"

"I was just worried that something could've happened to you. I'd go the distance for you Delancey." She smiled and said "I know."

Three hours later the buses arrived back at Brooklyn. Delancey and I went to Junior's restaurant on Flatbush Avenue.

"I took your advice," I said to her, with a wry smile.

"What advice was that?" she wondered.

"I decorated my home for Christmas."

"What did your father think?"

"He didn't say much, but the next morning he made us breakfast. I guess there's a first time for everything."

We took the subway to the West Side of Manhattan and I carried her bag the entire way. She insisted that she could carry her own bag, but I wouldn't let her. My shoulder was still stiff, still swollen, and it was a struggle. To my relief, one of the doormen took it from me when we arrived at her building. She gave me a warm embrace and a kiss on the cheek as we parted.

chapter 10

MY GRANDMOTHER WAS cooking a feast. She noticed I was favoring my shoulder and gave me an ice pack to reduce the swelling. Harry was at his job, and my father was at work. Drained from the lack of sleep and the long bus ride home, my grandmother's hot soup was just what I needed. I just sat and vegged.

"David, how are you doing with your grandfather's passing?" she asked.

"Fine. But I do miss him."

"I know you were close with him. Lake talked about you all the time. Are you sure you are okay with everything?" Now she sounded concerned.

"It's going to take time to get used to him being gone," I replied somberly.

"I know that you have a hard time letting go. At least you did when your mother passed. Your father is the same way. You get it from him."

"I'll be fine, don't worry about me." The year following my mother's death was hard on all of us, and my grandmother said she heard me crying in my sleep, although I never grieved when I was awake.

My grandmother made enough food for three days. We talked about school, and I told her my desire to leave home and go off to college.

The topic of my father came up, and I asked if she thought that my father was lonely. She paused, put her hand on her hip, and said, "He must be. That's probably why he doesn't want you to go away to college."

She was silent for a while. The silence was broken when she said, "You know he lost your mother twice." A month before my mother passed for good, she was in the hospital. We were all there with her. My mother was very sick, and at one point, her heart monitor went flat, indicating that her heart had stopped beating. My father was devastated, and he crumbled to the floor like a mudslide.

We all thought she had passed, but the doctors and nurses came in and brought her back with a defibrillator. She flatlined for more than a minute, and the doctors revived her. But we got her back for only a month. My father did lose her twice.

Following New Year's day, gossip spread about the maelstrom of events during the ski trip as the day wore on. By lunchtime, everyone knew about the party, the drinking, the pot smoking, the pills, the fight, and of course, Eddie's involvement.

I told Sam, Carlos, and John my version of the story. Sam rolled his eyes when I told him that Maurice was one of my roommates. Sam was not only in the habit of making ethnic slurs against Italians, but every other ethnicity as well. It would be fair to say that he hated just about everyone. Finally, unable to stay quiet, he said, "Did he convert you to hasidim?"

"Actually he's Sephardic. And I had a great time with him and he did me a big favor," I said.

Carlos was very interested in the party. "What kind of liquor?" he asked nonchalantly. I did not feel the need to answer.

"Man...I really should've gone. If I was there, I would've had a lot to drink, and probably would've smoked something. It's a ski trip; you're there to have fun," Carlos said smiling.

"You know, Carlos, that's always the story with you. Shoulda, coulda, woulda...besides there were chaperones, and I really didn't want to do anything that I may regret in the future."

Carlos looked a little annoyed. "When are you going to live a little? You're gonna graduate high school as a little prissy girl." Sam laughed out loud.

John shouted "Smoking pot and getting drunk doesn't mean you're living. Look at Eddie; I bet he thought he was really living."

Carlos continued, "And you sold out Eddie. Why didn't you hide his stuff?"

Sam mentioned that people in the school were saying that Maurice and I did nothing to help Eddie, or the students involved in the fight. "They are saying that you and Maurice were hiding in your rooms, on the floor, rolling around on top of each other," Sam smirked.

"I have bigger things like college to worry about. I didn't need to get into a fight just months before graduation." I was getting angry with the tone of the conversation. The reality was that no one else was there, and their judgment was based totally on hearsay.

The table was quiet for a while.

"So our boy Sam here has a new girlfriend and...carnal knowledge of her," Carlos laughed.

Sam explained that he had been intimate with his neighbor's daughter. He said that she was good looking, her family was from Afghanistan, and they were trying to set them up for marriage.

"Marriage?" I asked.

"After college.... It's common for Persians, Afghanis, and most people from the Middle East to marry at our age. I'm just getting as much action as I can." Carlos jokingly punched him in the shoulder.

"She goes to school here at Stanton," Carlos said.

"Who is she?" John inquired.

Sam said he wasn't telling. The four of us left for our next class.

I was annoyed about the assertion that I was a coward. I wondered if other students at school were thinking the same thing or if Sam was just pushing my buttons again.

When I left school at 5pm, I saw Maurice on my way out. I asked if he had heard about any rumors that we were cowards for not helping Eddie Lo. Maurice said he did not care what anyone thought of him, only what God thought of him. "Besides, no one will remember any of this after high school." I asked if it was difficult to be the only religious Jew around.

"Are you crazy? This is Brooklyn. There are more of us in Brooklyn than anywhere else outside of Israel."

"I meant at Stanton."

"To tell you the truth, I never even think about it. After all, *Ehyeh asher ehyeh*...I am what I am," Maurice grinned.

I told Maurice that he sounded like Popeye the Sailor. He said, "You're kidding right?" and walked off.

Maurice was right. No one would remember the ski trip in twenty years, or even in a year. Besides, there was only six months to go before graduation and I decided not to pay any more attention to the rumors about me at school. If I was a weaker person, the kind who placed enormous weight on the present and not the future, then I would need to make sure everyone knew that I was not a sellout. There was life after graduation, and I could not pay any more attention to an undeserved reputation.

I went home to study for upcoming exams, but I was still thinking about what Maurice had said, and I pulled out the Life Plan from my wallet. I wrote in #19:

I only care what God thinks of me, and not other people. I have to do what I know to be right in the future and not get carried away by allegiances or my sense of loyalty.

I was not religious, but did believe in God controlling things here on earth, maybe not for everybody, but certainly for me. Perhaps I was more superstitious than religious.

I called Delancey later that night. Her father picked up the phone, and asked me who I was.

"Tell her it's David."

"David who?"

"David from school."

"From what school?"

"From Stanton."

"What school?"

"Stanton."

"Oh. Well what do you want?" Her father sounded frustrated.

Delancey finally got on the phone, clearly annoyed with her father.

"I just wanted to talk, but not about school or tests or anything like that," I said.

"That's fine, I'm a little tired from all the studying as well," she said.

We made small talk for a little while until there was an awkward pause on the phone.

"Delancey? Are you still there?"

"I'm still here."

"Why are you so quiet?" I asked.

"I don't get it," she said.

"Get what?"

"We've known each other for such a long time and we finally go out. I thought we had a great time, we danced together at the ski trip, and you don't ask me out again. Am I missing something here?" She sounded dejected.

I remained silent.

"Are you still there?" she said.

"I'm here," I said, confused. "I thought that you made it clear that you did not want to date."

Another long silence.

"Well, Delancey?"

"Well, you shouldn't take no for an answer. Maybe I'm more open-minded now than I was before." I could feel the warmth of her smile on the other end of the phone. "Besides if you really like me, you would want to spend more time together whether it was dating or not. Now tell me the truth...how do you really feel about me?" she asked.

"The truth is that I like you; I like you a lot. I've always liked you, and I think you are absolutely gorgeous, and for some reason whenever I'm around you, or I spend time with you, I can't sleep. I stay up thinking about you. But I don't know what to do. We are graduating in less than six months, and we are both going off to college, and I'm not sure about the long distance thing. I don't know if I want to start something now and put us both through that. I think about you all the time. I wish we could really be together." I sighed. This was a lot to get off my chest. I really did not like exposing myself like this. But I was so tired that I let my guard down.

"David…I like you as well. But I want you to know that I'm not girlfriend material. I'm not the kind of girl that's going to follow you to college or wherever you go. I'm really focused on school, my eventual career, and making my family proud. But I can't help but see that you have been reaching out to me, and I think that I'd like to know if we have something here," she said.

I breathed a sigh of relief. It felt magical, the way she said it, like we were in a dream or another realm of some sort. She spoke the truth, and I knew it when I heard it.

"You're in an entirely different league, when it comes to girls. And you are so beautiful, everything about you." I could see her clear as day in my mind. I could feel her blushing, and pictured the dimples on her face, her smile at full crescendo. "You know, I don't have a lot to offer you. You could go out with anybody at school." My insecurities kicked in.

"David, you have to live for the moment, and for the present. If we have six months to go, fine. If it continues then so be it. I'd rather have something now, than nothing forever. Besides, I'm not sure if this will even work out; my father will not approve."

"Look, I'm just a guy trying to make it out of high school. But if you want to start dating, I would really like that," I said smiling.

"Well…let's just try hanging out more and see how that goes," she said. "I'm not looking for a boyfriend. I have too much going on in my life to get involved with anyone seriously. I'm really afraid to get attached. And I'm not about to throw away my plans for the future for you or any other boy in high school."

"Fine. I'll see you tomorrow."

I hung up the phone, and stared at the wall in front of me. I stayed up the entire night, unable to sleep. My exuberance was like caffeine.

The next day at school, I walked into the cafeteria, glancing at my usual table, and noticed Sam, Carlos, and John. I smiled and walked right by them, and sat next to Delancey at another table. She gave me a kiss on the cheek.

Sam was boiling over in jealous rage. As we were leaving the cafeteria and heading to our next class, I saw Juan in the far distance in his usual black business suit. Juan was staring us down with sinister eyes. If looks could kill, I would be a dead man.

Delancey and I planned to go out tomorrow after school, but she insisted that it was not a date. We were just hanging out, maybe as friends, maybe as something more than friends. For the rest of the day I was on cloud nine. I didn't care about Juan or Sam. I did not care for anything. Being with Delancey was, as Sal would say, like an out of body experience.

The next day, Delancey wore a worn and faded pair of denim jeans to our first non-date. She had a gray sweatshirt with "Haverford" in bold letters. She was a sight to behold that day, and it was obvious she tried to look ordinary and unpretentious. However, in my opinion, she had never looked better; and I have a photographic memory. Her extraordinary attempts to dress down made her look all the more radiant. Delancey's worn out blue jeans didn't hide the shape of her hips, or the curves of her thighs. The over-sized gray sweatshirt could not conceal the outline of her breasts or her tender shoulders. Her attempts to make this a non-date had the opposite effect on me.

She smiled warmly, and asked me, "How do I look? I hope I'm not too dressed down for wherever we are going."

"Delancey, you've never looked better." I laughed out loud. She feigned disappointment as we headed to the streets.

We walked past the multicolored attached brownstone buildings, each a different shade of brown slab, each with newly windswept concrete front steps. The tree-lined Brooklyn streets were teeming with pedestrians heading home. I walked slower than usual, though not on purpose. Time seemed to slow down. The hurried pedestrians pushed past us on the way to their apartments. It was a cold January day, but when I grabbed her hand, I could feel her warmth through her mittens. She retracted her hand, reminding me that we were not dating.

We arrived shortly on Fulton Street. A blue awning with white lettering revealed the name Academy Café. As we stepped inside, I held up two fingers to the owner, who placed us in a booth by the window. The waitress walked over to take our order, and I chose minestrone soup, while Delancey ordered the Pluto burger, which was the biggest meal on the menu. It was a hamburger the size of a small planet.

"That's another thing about me that you probably didn't count on. I like to eat, and I'm not ashamed of it. I'm not dainty, and I'm not going to hide my un-girly appetite." Delancey folded her arms and looked at me.

"Fine," I replied, holding back a grin. Her notions of eating were amusing. Why should I care how much she ate or didn't eat?

"And I'm not insecure about my weight either. I feel really good at this weight and I don't care if you or anyone else think I need to lose 20 pounds."

"Fine. I think you look great."

"You know I'm not one of those ultra-skinny girls."

"I know."

"And don't ask me to lose any weight."

"You really don't need to."

Delancey then relaxed and we both stared out the window. She seemed to breathe a little easier now that this was out of the way. She remained silent, as did I, but not for much longer.

"My mother and I will be going away for the winter break. We're headed to London for a few days. Her sister, my aunt, lives in London, and I can't wait." Delancey spoke about how much she loved London for the next few minutes. The waitress brought over our order. She took a massive bite of her Pluto burger, which was so humungous it could barely fit on the plate. "Delicious!" she commented. Some of the melted cheese had dripped onto her lower lip, toward her chin, and I reached over and wiped it. Delancey beamed heartily, and her eyes lit up as if I had done something that had delighted her.

It seemed as if she spoke without taking a breath for a while. But, she still seemed to have her guard up. I wanted to get to know the real Delancey.

"Did your parents' divorce really upset you?" I asked.

She placed her cheeseburger down, and took a sip of coffee. Her magnificent eyes glanced out the restaurant window, and the sunlight softened her intensity, adding a celestial glow to her eyes and her face.

"You know, David, it did not bother me for too long. I guess initially I blamed myself, thinking that if I had been a better child, a better daughter, it wouldn't have happened. But right away, I noticed that my father was so much more pleasant to be around without my mother. And my mother was initially morose and somber, but a few months later she started dating Bruce, my stepfather, and she is much happier and easier to be around as well. I really have to say...I think the divorce was the best thing for them.

They were such stark opposites of each other. My mother was definitely a child of the 60's generation, and was proud of it. She was a Broadway actress. That's how they met. She was starring in a play on Broadway and my father went to see the show and arranged to meet her afterwards. She always wanted to be a free spirit and a flower child. My father on the other hand was very controlling. I guess the question is, how does someone possessive, materialistic, and controlling, like my father, go about trying to control a free spirit, like my mother. I am as rebellious as I am because my father is so controlling."

Delancey continued to eat her cheeseburger, and we both remained silent. The subject of her parents' divorce opened her up to real conversation, but at the same time she had less she wanted to talk about.

"So, David, why do you want to go to a state college?"

"A lot of it has to do with affordability. I really can't afford a private school. And even if I could, I would feel bad about having to call my father and ask him for money. I will need to work through college, so I need to go to a school somewhere, where I'd have a good chance of finding a job. But you know…even if I had a scholarship, I'm not sure how it would be at a private school where I would have nothing in common with a lot of those kids. I don't have a car. I've never really been around rich kids." I was nervous to discuss this topic with her.

"David, that being said, you did befriend me, and without sounding too full of myself, you know that I come from a wealthy family and you seem okay with it."

"I am trying to be comfortable with you. But it's not like I'm surrounded at Stanton by wealthy kids, who are all going to Europe while I stay at home." I glanced down, and could feel that the topic had stirred up some emotion. "I'm not the kind of guy that would want to be washing dishes at the college dining hall while everyone else is having dessert or going to a party."

"Rich people aren't that bad; they don't bite, you know. Well, just my father," Delancey giggled. "Seriously David, a private college can offer you so much more. It's smaller, more intimate, you get to know more people, the reputation is often better, the alumni associations are better, and there is financial aid."

"Delancey, I don't want to be in debt for the next twenty years either. Besides, what could I learn in a private college that I couldn't learn in a public college? I know that the brand name means something, but having money to pay tuition means even more. My goal is to not be poor, and having all the debt from a private college just seems to undermine that goal."

"David, you can be anything you want to be, and you can do anything you want to do. The sky is the limit, especially here in New York. But you only go to college once, as a true freshman. I checked out Haverford over last weekend. It's so beautiful and quaint, and it seems so much better than what I've seen elsewhere." Delancey pointed to her sweatshirt.

"It's easy for you to say. Sure, you can be anything you want, and do whatever you want, but my goal is to get a career and not end up poor for the rest of my life. Look, Delancey, I've already been poor, and now I'd like to see the other side."

Her face motioned downward as she sipped her coffee, and her beaming eyes looked upwards at me. Her high cheekbones revealed a cordial smirk, and then she said, "See you on the other side." She had a great sense of humor.

"Don't think I have it easy. There are so many expectations for me. There is so much pressure. From everyone, even my grandparents. Everyone pulls at me from different directions." Then she suggested that I talk to her father about money, careers, and colleges.

"Doesn't he hate me?" I asked.

"Oh...don't be so insecure. Once he knows you, then he'll hate you." Delancey's devilish grin appeared once more. The waitress brought the check, and I pulled out my wallet.

"No, you don't," she said. "It's my turn; remember, it's not a date." She paid the check and we walked to back to Stanton. Her father was picking her up today, and they were going to a Broadway show.

"Which one?" I asked.

"Cats. It's my favorite," Delancey beamed. "What's your favorite?"

"I'll get back to you on that one." I smiled, hands in pockets and shrugged my shoulders. I had never seen a Broadway show.

A fancy black car was stopped in front of the school, and Delancey tapped on its window. Her father was in the back seat, and the driver came around and opened the door for her. The car pulled away, and I walked to the subway, trying my best not to get mugged.

The next day at school, Delancey and I agreed that I would walk her home every day after school, as much as possible. It was a good way to spend time together, since I worked Saturdays and Sundays. This agreement came with much argument; after all, we were not dating, and she didn't want me to cramp her freedom or independence.

We took the subway to the upper west side, and stopped off for hot chocolate at a café near the subway station. Her smoldering eyes were drawing me in deeper and deeper. Delancey couldn't stop smiling, and neither could I. There was such a genuine innocence in her character; no malevolence toward anyone, and not an ill word from her mouth on any subject at all.

"Aren't you concerned about Sam or Juan?" she finally asked. "I did see them staring us down in the cafeteria today. What is Sam's problem?"

"Sam is kind of obsessed with you."

"In a really creepy way, so I've noticed. Juan and I used to be good friends. I turned him down a few times. He really isn't my type at all. But he is very possessive, and has told everyone that he's going to the prom with me this year."

"Well, I'm not concerned with either of them," I said.

I would rather forget about Juan and Sam completely. But I wasn't afraid of them or anyone else. If their jealousy ever led to a fight, if they ever wanted to get violent, I was prepared. But I didn't think that would happen. Juan was the class president, and a natural born politician, with big aspirations, and likely bound for the Ivy League. But he was a fake, always smiling and shaking hands, and you never really knew what he thought. He was the kind of kid that had a thousand people that he called friend and but no one in particular.

As for Sam, one minute he was my friend and the next he was spreading rumors about me. If we ever got into it, so be it, but I planned on staying out of their way if they stayed out of mine. I wasn't some kind of great fighter or anything, but I wasn't the kind to back down either. Juan had an entourage with him at all times. I could see trouble coming from his friends, but not from him directly.

"What if Juan and his friends start something?" Delancey asked.

"I'll cross that bridge when I come to it," I said.

chapter 11

AT THE CAFÉ that weekend, I was no longer fascinated with the details of Christine's gangster life and stories. Christine's stories really didn't seem that interesting.

Christine explained that Eddie was expelled from Stanton. She was angry about his punishment and did not see any harm in Eddie firing a shot in the air.

"I didn't know you and Eddie were so close," I said.

"You're the one that was his roommate on your little senior ski trip. Maybe you are closer to him than you think."

She appeared different. I could see bags under her eyes from the lack of sleep. It was hard to believe she was just a teenager; she looked much older today.

Mike the manager awoke, and did his routine, drank coffee, ate a muffin, splashed cold water on his face. He walked around, trying to manage the employees who actually did the work, and then realized it was nearly one o'clock. He had overslept at work.

Mike asked about school, and I told him about the events of the ski trip, without mentioning Eddie by name.

"You don't drink?" Mike asked.

"I did have a taste, one drink, but didn't like it. It wasn't tempting because it tasted awful. My father's side of the family are alcoholics, so I've been around drunks my whole life. Sometimes I have a drink with my uncles, and my close group of friends. I am just not accustomed to drinking with everyone from school."

"Were you tempted to smoke pot?" Mike asked.

"I was not really tempted. I have a cousin that sells pot all over the city and I can't stand him, and there are people on my block that smoke pot on the corner all hours of the night. I'm really not into smoking anything. Besides the ski trip was not the time or the place," I said.

"Most kids your age are eager to do things to seem cool, but you seem to have been desensitized to these vices. That's probably a good thing," Mike said. "When I was your age, I just wanted to drink and try whatever I could. I didn't grow up where it was always around me. It was a cool thing to do with my friends. But you have a negative association with drinking and pot, so it's the uncool thing for you."

Mike asked if I was tempted to get into the fight. I shook my head no. The truth was I was tired of fighting. Every week of my life there was a fight, from bullies and muggers, kids from school, my father, my brother, etc. I really did not want to fight any more. "The people that like to fight don't really know anything about fighting," I said. "It's a way of survival for me, fighting to defend myself, or fighting not to get robbed. Fighting to get home in once piece. But other people just fight to fight, and that's not me."

During my lunch break, I went outside and walked onto the brick-paved esplanade. I leaned over the metal railing with the Hudson River underneath it. I had a sandwich with me, and a cup of coffee. I could see the Jersey City skyline, along with a sign for the Colgate factory. A ferry was bringing people across the river from New Jersey. A building called The Winter Garden was in the back drop, and the lack of sunlight made its glass and steel beam construction seem dim.

In the offices above, people were hard at work making millions, just for the sake of making millions. I wondered if I'd ever be one of these people. Some of them were very wealthy, and had high paying jobs. I was a poor high school student from a poor family. My grandparents had been poor, and so were my great grandparents. We were probably poor before that as well. Adults do not have to deal with the uncertainty about the future that I had at seventeen. Adults may have their own set of problems, but they didn't have school, college applications, and the prom.

A large sail boat pulled into the North Cove Yacht Harbor, just a few yards from where I was standing. The winds picked up, and I shivered. On board was a family, dressed for winter boating, with designer nautical jackets and shoes. They were blonde, blue eyed, and had perfect skin. There wasn't a trace of wrinkles on the wife's face, or bags under her eyes. She stood on the bow, and I watched as the wind whipped around, lashing her hair. They lowered their anchor and tied their boat. They had a daughter, a beautiful teenaged girl, with the most extraordinary blue eyes I had ever seen. The women disembarked, and were heading inside to the shops. They walked right past me, but the daughter looked up and smiled. People in Manhattan don't usually walk by complete strangers smiling. I guess they were not from the city. She was gorgeous, and she reminded me of Delancey. She didn't look anything like Delancey, but there was an energy about her that was similar. The daughter was my age, and looked it, unlike Christine.

The father then disembarked, and left the son, a teenager, to tie the boat and lower the sails. The father wore brown leather boat shoes, blue jeans, and a thick white wool turtleneck, like a fisherman's sweater. The father walked by, the wind blowing through his long salt and pepper colored hair. He was a distinguished looking man, with a jaw line made of steel. The father nodded his head to me and smiled as well. Now I was certain they were not from Manhattan. The son was still on the boat. He finished up anchoring, docking, and tying the boat a few minutes later and walked off the dock to join his family.

"That's a beautiful boat. How long is it?" I asked. I wasn't sure if he would answer the question. If he was from Manhattan, he would probably ignore me and keep walking.

"Thanks. It is quite beautiful. It's my Dad's new toy, a 42-foot Pearson," he said. He stopped right in front of me, as if he wanted to have a conversation. This was odd, because people from the city usually keep walking away even when they are talking to you. He had decent manners.

"Is it new?"

"My dad bought it a couple of years ago. Usually we sail around Long Island or up to the Cape, but he wanted to see the World Financial Center this weekend."

The Cape of what? Maybe he meant Cape Cod. The boy had a strange accent. He pronounced every letter, and spoke softly, and with proper grammar. He sounded confident and smart.

"I can't believe he let you do everything yourself. You're just a kid."

"I've been sailing since I was 8 years old. I already have a captain's license."

I paused and thought about what to ask next. "How many people can sleep in there?"

"It's got a master cabin and 2 others, so probably 6 people comfortably."

"If you don't mind me asking, how old are you that you are a captain?" He said he was going to be eighteen soon. We talked for a few minutes. He was from Cold Spring Harbor, and was attending Boston College in the fall. The boy said he was going to major in history, and probably go to law school. Then he left, shaking my hand. I told him I would keep an eye on the boat, and he laughed.

"It doesn't have a car alarm, so that's probably a good thing."

I liked this rich kid. He had good manners, and I could probably learn more from him than I could from my own friends. I had once thought about majoring in history, and up until now figured that people that majored in history became history professors. It didn't occur to me that you could also become a lawyer. There's so much that I didn't know, but I did not have anyone to answer these questions. My father did not know much about college, or careers.

I went back to work, feeling a little refreshed.

Mike said to me that he had an answer.

"What's the question?" I asked.

"The question you asked me a few weeks ago. What was the difference between me and my roommate—why I got messed up and partied so much, and my roommate didn't."

"So what's the answer?" I asked.

"It wasn't in his plan," Mike responded.

"Was it in your plan to party your way out of school?" I asked.

Mike looked at me in silence, appearing to have a revelation unfolding. "You know what, I think that the partying was definitely in the plan, but I didn't have a plan for anything else. When you don't have a plan, you go along with the situation and other people's plans. Circumstances become your plan. My roommate had a plan for success. He was committed to graduating and doing well in school. He had goals for his grades and his college career. He had a plan that he would only party on Fridays and Saturdays. He had a plan to get good internships. He planned for studying, and he planned for success. He also planned to only have a few drinks and never drink too much. And he stuck to his plan. I never went in with a plan. I drank what came my way. I tried pot because it came my way. I tried other drugs, because they came my way. People offered it, and I said yes, because I wasn't planning on anything else."

Mike paused, took a gulp of black coffee, and said, "If you don't have a plan for your life, then someone else will."

Christine asked if I wanted to go to Eddie's store. She said Eddie was getting new merchandise. I said, "Sure, I'll take a look."

As I was leaving the café, Christine mentioned that Eddie Lo was picking her up and that I could ride with them. Eddie pulled up on Vesey Street. He and Christine got into a full blown argument in Cantonese. I didn't have to speak Cantonese to know that they were arguing over my presence in the car. I felt uncomfortable.

Christine paused, smiled, and sarcastically said, "Eddie's really glad you can join us." Eddie was about to explode in rage.

I suggested that I could come to his store some other day. Eddie said tomorrow would be fine. We parted ways and I headed to lower Broadway by foot. They drove away in his Oldsmobile Cutlass.

I walked several blocks to the South Street Seaport, in an effort to find Delancey a gift.

It was a fifteen minute walk to the Seaport. The Seaport was converted to a shopping mall, with restaurants, and bars, and sometimes I hung out there with the guys from school. It was hard to imagine that this was once the gateway to America from New York by ship. Dutch and English colonists had used this Pier for trade and for shipping. Now it was a tourist attraction and a mall replacing history.

Shadows covered the streets as the sun was sinking fast. One thing I did not like about the Seaport was how the frigid winds picked up as I got closer, ripping through my hair and stinging my ears.

In the main entrance, I heard alarms going off. Security guards were running around like crazed chickens. My first reaction was that there might be a fire. The security guards were running out the west corridor. I followed them and saw a car outside that I recognized instantly. It was Eddie Lo's car, and Christine was in the driver's seat. Eddie Lo jumped into the car after dumping an entire rack of clothing in the backseat. I stood peering from a distance, behind a stone column. The car drove off; I wasn't sure if Christine or Eddie saw me.

The police soon arrived and the security guards described a robbery by Chinese gangsters. I was a little stunned. I knew Eddie Lo was a gangster, but I didn't realize he and Christine were common thieves. The coolest guy I knew in school was a common criminal. I had a sick feeling in my stomach. A cop told the manager of the store that the goods were likely to end up in Chinatown stores. I had heard enough, and left the South Street Seaport.

The subway ride home was long and lonely. I did not know what direction to take with Christine or Eddie. I certainly wasn't going to turn them in but I was in danger of placing loyalty in the wrong place. I thought about the Christmas presents I had bought from Eddie's store.

The next day I did not go to Eddie Lo's store. I wasn't sure if Christine or Eddie had seen me. At the café, I rolled my eyes when Mike said Christine had called out sick with the flu.

On Monday, I heard more of Sam's sexual escapades with his neighbor's daughter. At this point, he was just gloating about having a sex life.

Sam received a letter from Harvard acknowledging that his application was under review and indicating there would be an interview. We were all sure Sam would be admitted. He had very high grades, a strong family background in medicine, and the rest he was going to exaggerate, elaborate, and fudge.

I wondered if Harvard could uncover Sam's true personality in a 20 minute interview. The college application process did not require an emotional or psychological evaluation. There was no section for ethical and moral behavior. Colleges only cared about what was on paper. This worked to Sam's advantage. I wondered if Harvard had any idea about Sam's short temper, immaturity, or his ability to fabricate letters of recommendation. Did Harvard even care?

In my mind, and perhaps in my imagination, Harvard was a college for the best of the best, the extra special, and the most elite. It was disappointing that someone like Sam was being considered. I expected better from the best college in the nation.

"How's it going with Delancey?" asked Sam.

"Fine."

"Are you going to walk her home today?" he asked.

"No. I've got work to do on the school paper." This wasn't a topic I wanted to discuss with Sam.

"Listen, David, everyone knows that you two are dating. Word has spread like wildfire. Juan is furious. He is keeping a close eye on you." Sam tried his best to look genuinely concerned, but his insincerity was obvious.

"I'm not worried about Juan or about you."

Carlos decided to chime in. "Juan is not someone to joke around with. Everyone says he's a got a temper and even worse. There are rumors that he orders his enemies to get jumped. You don't even have a posse."

"Carlos, I don't need a posse," I laughed at the notion.

"Neither does Juan, but you ever see him alone? There are always two or three guys around him. How are you going to fight that many guys?" Carlos looked at me as though he was confused.

"I'm not going to fight anyone."

In the newspaper office, I asked Doreen if she heard back from any colleges. She said she had been accepted to a few schools, but had not heard from Harvard. I asked if she had received a confirmation letter from Harvard. She had not. This was a little odd. She was going to check with her guidance counselor.

"So I heard a rumor that you and Delancey are going out," she said. I was astonished that the rumor had reached Doreen. "Just be careful...its no secret that Juan is obsessed with Delancey."

"Thanks for the heads up," I said smirking

"I'm serious. I know that Delancey is a great girl, and that she's really pretty and all. But have you ever wondered why she isn't at some private school in the city? With her family money and she lives much closer to prep schools...but she goes to school in Brooklyn? Juan has put it out there that only someone looking for death would go out with her." Doreen crossed her arms, and tilted her head.

"I'm not dating Juan Perez. I am dating Delancey. And what are you trying to say? Maybe she would prefer to go to Stanton." I kept working, and Doreen came back a few minutes later.

"David, how much do you know about Delancey?" Doreen asked.

"Why? Is there something that you know?" I asked.

"Delancey tends to rebel against her father, just to cope. That's why she was drunk and high at the ski trip. That's why she was asked to leave two private schools. Don't get caught in the middle of their crossfire."

She had no reason to lie. Doreen went back to working on the paper, and I sat there distracted for the next hour.

When I left school at 5 o'clock, Eddie Lo was outside smiling as he walked up to me. This was the strangest sight, only because Eddie Lo, and Chinese gangsters in general, never smile. He was wearing new clothes, undoubtedly stolen over the weekend.

"Sorry about Saturday, I didn't know you were coming and had to pick something up," he said.

"Not a problem. I didn't want to be a burden. Are you back at Stanton?" I tried to decipher any signals he may give indicating he knew that I witnessed his crime.

"No...still expelled." There was a moment of awkward silence.

"So are you and Christine...together?" I asked.

"We dated a long time ago, nothing serious...and now we're just friends. Everyone needs friends, David." Eddie was wearing sun glasses but was staring at me, trying to read my expression. He needed to find out how much I saw, and how much I knew. It was important that I didn't give anything away.

"Yeah, things got a little crazy at the ski trip. I appreciate you trying to stop me, but that's not who I am—I never back down. I'm burnt out from high school, and college was not going to work out for me anyway. I've got too many obligations, if you know what I mean. Why don't you come over to the store today, and I'll show you the new stuff we just got in over the weekend," he said with a huge grin. At the park across the street, and the usual Chinese gangsters were watching Eddie and I talk. Gangsters don't talk to a non-gang member in public. It just wasn't done. I could feel the weight of his eyes through the sunglasses. He knew I had seen him at the Seaport commit his robbery.

"You know...I really don't need anymore clothes. I have to save my money for the prom, and college," I firmly replied.

"No problem, I understand. You're more than welcome to stop by the store whenever you want...I can always make you a good deal. We can keep it discreet," Eddie said.

"Discreet." I nodded. Eddie walked to the gangsters hanging out in the park.

As I approached the subway, I saw Delancey walking into Junior's Restaurant with Juan Perez. They did not see me. At first, I thought my eyes were playing tricks on me, and then I felt some anger, and some jealousy. But it was definitely Delancey walking in with Juan. I decided not to approach them, but rather I would call Delancey later and ask her about it.

I studied on the subway ride home for my State Spanish test, and planned to study until midnight. I'm not sure why I cared so much about my grades, but I always believed in giving 100%. It's ingrained in me, probably from watching my father work two jobs my entire life. When I was younger, I thought it was because we really needed the money, but now, that my brother and I had jobs, I wondered if my father worked so much to avoid being home. Did he not want to be reminded of my mother's death? The last thing I wanted to do was let him down by doing anything halfheartedly.

I called Delancey at nine. She picked up the phone. Much to my relief, I avoided being grilled by her father.

"Hey there, I was wondering if you were going to call," she sounded happy. I pictured her smiling, with exposed dimples, and playing with her hair. We made small talk about school.

"I think I saw you after school," I said.

"I went to Junior's after school," she said.

"For cheesecake with the girls?"

There was dead silence. I couldn't even hear her breathe.

"Delancey?" I asked.

"I'm here." Her voice cracked.

"Well, I went to Junior's with Juan." She paused.

"Oh, I know, I saw the two of you. What was that about?" I asked.

"Actually, it was mostly about you," she said.

"Me? I find it hard to believe that Juan wanted to talk to you about me." I laughed out loud.

"Just the opposite. I wanted to talk to him about you."

"That's unusual. What does he have to do with anything?" I was confused.

"I wanted to make sure that he was not going to do something out of anger or jealousy." She was biting her nails.

"I'm not worried about Juan; I can take care of myself."

"David, I know that. I want to make sure Juan does not cause any trouble and he won't. I still think something is seriously wrong with you for wanting to go out with me." Delancey was unnecessarily apologetic and seemed to be fishing for compliments. I really didn't mind reassuring her.

"Delancey, every guy I know would want to go out with you. You're sexy, you're beautiful, and you're smart, funny, and great to be around. If I'm crazy, then all the guys at school are crazy too." I heard her giggle.

We spoke for a while, changing the topic eventually to her father.

"I've been arguing a lot with my father," she confessed. "He's really stressing me out."

"Well, I think that all kids our age go through the same thing," I tried to reassure her.

"He does not want me dating or hanging out. He says boys will just ruin my future."

"I take it he's referring to me specifically."

"My father's just very over protective. He even got me a licensed handgun for my birthday. He said that I needed it for safety, especially on the subways."

"A gun? Delancey, it's impossible to get a pistol license in New York City." I was shocked.

"My father knows Governor Cuomo. I didn't want the gun, but he said that New York was really dangerous and I should carry one with me. It was a small gun with jewels on it, customized to look feminine. It doesn't even matter, because the gun was stolen from my bag right after my birthday. Its fine because I don't want it."

It was strange that a man would buy his daughter a gun for her birthday. Carlos had Delancey's gun.

The next day, Doreen found out through her guidance counselor that Harvard did not receive her application. I could barely understand anything Doreen said. She was hysterical. One of her friends tried to console her. When she calmed down, she said that she mailed the Harvard application on Dekalb Avenue.

I remembered the day I saw the mailbox fire. Sam and Doreen had broken up right about then. I could never figure out why Sam was being so friendly to a girl he was not interested in, but now the thought occurred to me that the whole relationship was a ruse. All Sam wanted was to make sure that Doreen's application never reached Harvard.

But could he have done it? Was he that diabolical? I was pretty sure that he had something to do with Doreen's missing Harvard application, but there was a small part of me that wanted to give him the benefit of the doubt. I had to tread carefully. Facts were more important than my intuition.

"Doreen, there was a mail box fire on Dekalb Avenue. It was a couple of months ago."

"No, I did not hear about that. What the hell is a mail box fire anyway? There's no spontaneous combustion in mail boxes. When did this happen?" She was starting to suspect why I brought this to her attention.

"A few weeks ago, just before Thanksgiving."

Harvard would not accept a late application from Doreen. If anyone was to be accepted to Harvard, it would have been Doreen. She was ranked in the top five of all seniors.

I told John my suspicions about Doreen's Harvard application. He thought it wrong to assume something so egregious without having any facts to back it up.

"I have to admit, with Sam's blind ambitions, I wouldn't put it past him." Then John told me that Sam's girlfriend was thirteen years old.

"How do you know this?" I asked.

"Carlos told me this morning," he said. "She's a freshman here at Stanton."

I was appalled that Sam was with someone so young. I'm sure that in his mind, Sam thought he was doing nothing wrong. This was just another act for his personal gratification. I would never date someone that young and would have had a hard time being with a sophomore.

At lunch, I asked Sam if his girlfriend was really thirteen. He laughed and said that she had just turned fourteen the day before. I called him a child molester.

"I am not a pedophile. She is in high school, here at Stanton, and it's my business and not yours...so stay out of it!" He began shouting expletives, and I shouted back. He threw his lunch tray at me, covering me in food.

Sam shouted, "I'm seventeen, and it was her parents' idea for us to get together. All they wanted was to trap me into an arranged marriage. It's customary in their culture for girls to marry and have babies at a very young age. They know I'm going to be a big success, and they want to cash in early."

"First, you are almost eighteen. Second, there's a big difference between an eighteen-year-old boy and a thirteen-year-old girl," I said. "Where are your morals and ethics? You really disgust me. You are practically a sex fiend. And just because it's their culture doesn't mean you should be so willing to adopt it." I left the cafeteria with everyone staring at my food covered clothes.

"You're just jealous because you're virgin!" Sam shouted across the cafeteria. Many people laughed.

"At least I didn't set fire to a mailbox to make sure Doreen's application never reached Harvard!" I yelled back. The crowd gasped. More than a hundred students heard this heated exchange between us.

Sam's face turned bright red. He slammed his fists down onto the table. Carlos was also bright red. I had hit the nail on the head. They were clearly guilty. Sam was in tears when I left, crying like child. But it wasn't the first time I had seen this. Sam's anger and emotional outbursts always led to tears. His temper and emotional problems seemed to be getting worse.

I marched into the boys' bathroom to wash my clothes. I took off my tee-shirt and pants, and threw them on the large hot metal radiator to dry. It wasn't easy walking around with wet clothing on a cold January day.

John and I walked together to the subway. The psychic was outside her storefront, trying to get us to go inside with her usual tactics. We kept walking. She waved me in. The look on her face gave way to a luring, evil smile.

John explained that some kids were calling Sam a pyromaniac and a pedophile.

"I think he'll get into Harvard. With Doreen's application missing, Sam is a sure bet."

"It's what he wanted all along. He knew with Doreen's application gone, he'd be a cinch," I said.

"I think you were too hard on him about his girlfriend. She is fourteen, and there are lots of young girls that are sexually active. And it is their culture. In the old days that was marrying age for women," John said.

"In the old days, slavery was normal. So were five-year-old chimney sweepers. It's not right. We are not living in the old days. I don't buy the excuse that it's their culture. What if human sacrifices were their culture? Would he do it?" I said.

"You know, I think he would," John smiled.

"I think you're right. He probably would do it. All I'm saying is that he's seventeen, she's now fourteen and there's a big difference." We both slowed down as we approached the mail box on Dekalb Avenue that we had seen on fire.

"Sam must have had Carlos do it," John said. "It's a federal crime."

"Its just speculation until we have the facts...or until we have a confession," I said. "But I know that they did it; the look on Sam's face gave it away."

I asked John if he would ever be so desperate to go to a psychic.

"Why, are you thinking of going to that woman?" asked John.

"I'd be lying to you if I said that the thought never crossed my mind."

John stopped me in the middle of the sidewalk, just a few yards from the subway station. He placed his hand on my shoulder and said, "Psychics are for people that don't believe in God. If you really trusted God with your life, going to a psychic would be a violation of this trust." John explained his strong beliefs that psychics were not only after your money, but they were after your soul as well. "Psychics will try to get you to believe that they will pray for you, that others are trying to do you harm and that you have to participate in some strange rituals that involve your money."

"How do you know so much about psychics?" I asked.

"My mother lost a lot of money, and maybe more to a psychic. That's why we are always in church on Sundays."

I didn't believe in black magic or the occult. But I felt bad for John's mother. "It sounds like your family only goes to church out of fear for the devil, and not from devotion to God," I said.

"You may be partially right, but church is church, and we're still going," John said. "I can't say the same about you."

"Well, even though I'm not religious, I know God exists, and I do believe that he has a plan for me."

John was skeptical. "You know what your problem is? You lost faith when your mother died." He said it as if he was stating a fact. He was my closest friend, and knew my family well enough.

"I may not be the most religious person in the world, but I know better than to mess with my soul." I cringed for no reason when I said this.

"David, you need someone in your life to steer you in the right direction when you're not capable of doing it yourself. I have God, who do you have? "

"I have myself."

We walked to the subway, and boarded the F-Train.

Evan, an acquaintance from Stanton, was also boarding the train; I noticed his face was bright red and peeling.

Evan explained that he had thrown a piece of candy in Sam's chemistry project, causing the solution to change color and ultimately not work. This sounded like Evan, because, from the little that I knew of him, he was a goofball. Sam saw Evan laughing and eating candy, and then threw the solution into his face, causing some minor burns.

They both went to the principal's office after Evan left the infirmary. The principal lectured them and suspended Evan for 2 days. Sam said that Evan tried to sabotage him, knowing that he was close to being valedictorian.

This is a good example of how justice gets served at Stanton High School. Mr. Mash did not take kindly to attempts to thwart important school projects. Mash did not care that Evan's face had nearly burned off. Stanton wasn't the type of school where individual safety came before academic success. Our train arrived, and Evan waited for another train, as John and I boarded.

I asked John about his Regents exams, and he said he was going to ace them because of his superior intellect. I laughed, because John seemed to have a lot of confidence in his "Superior Intellect." His grades were not that great, and he was no intellectual. I suppose his confidence was a good thing.

My father came home from work around seven or so, and we ate around half past eight. I was still wearing my dry but stained clothing from earlier. My father asked if there was a food fight at school. Harry chuckled. I explained that Sam had a meltdown at school and threw his lunch tray at me. My father said that just because someone is smart doesn't mean they have any self control.

"My boss has a son, who has a master's degree in business, but he can't stay out of trouble. Here's a kid who had it all, looks, money, a good education, but when his girlfriend left him, be had to be committed to Belleview Hospital," my father said.

It was the third week of January and I was in Mr. Zoose's English Class, when there was a knock on the door. Mr. Mash was in the hallway, and motioned for Mr. Zoose to come outside. There was a lot of whispering. Mr. Zoose then closed the door, and continued to talk to Mash. A few minutes later, Mr. Zoose came back inside.

The expression on his face indicated there was bad news. Mr. Zoose spoke in a solemn tone, and was very calm.

"Class, there's some bad news. About an hour ago, a student, a senior at this school, jumped off the Brooklyn Bridge. We really don't know much about it at this time. I don't want anyone here to be in that kind of a situation, where you feel a strong sense of hopelessness and despair and think that taking your life is a solution."

Delancey asked who had committed suicide. Mr. Zoose said that it was Wilson. Everyone gasped. Delancey started crying. Other students followed. I was quiet. Someone wondered out loud if they would move up in the rankings as a result of Wilson's death. This may seem callous, cold, and opportunistic, but this was Stanton, and I'm sure more people wondered silently about the impact on the rankings.

I did not know Wilson well, but I did have classes with him a few years ago. Wilson was a very high strung person, very emotionally charged, and seemed a little off kilter. He wasn't just another Type A personality, he was a Type A+. School was his life, and academics were everything to him. Wilson tried very hard to get the best grades possible. I had last spoken to him about a year before, when he wanted to be a sports reporter for the paper. He later changed his mind, and dropped off the newspaper staff. He didn't have many friends, and spent most of his lunch hour studying. Wilson once said that there was enormous pressure for him to do well in school and get a scholarship, because his parents did not have the money to pay for college.

This was a typical of many of the students at Stanton. Stanton not only pulled together the brightest students, the best math, reading and science scores in New York City, but also many of the kids came from the poorest backgrounds. Wilson was one of many kids that had to bring home high grades and ultimately a scholarship, or else disappoint their families and themselves. I thought about Sal, and wondered how he was making out in college.

Stanton always had nine student deaths a year in the Senior Class. I can't explain it, but as long as anyone could remember, it had been true. Wilson was near the top five percent academically, but this meant nothing at Stanton. If you are not ranked in the top ten of students academically, and you are not an athlete, then a full scholarship to an Ivy League school was not likely. Some got partial scholarships; most got financial aid. I always said Stanton was a very competitive school, but, the truth was the competition was in our heads.

In other schools, students often care about social acceptance, or how many friends they had. At Stanton your grade point average determines your social acceptance and who your friends were. The smart kids hang with the smart kids. The B students eat lunch with the B students.

High School is not easy. At the time of your life when you are most insecure, the least confident, the most vulnerable, the most impressionable, and the most confused, you are thrust into a situation where the vultures come out to prey. High school is great at amplifying your problems. If you are most insecure about not being smart, then you constantly focus on the kids doing well in school, and that's what you pay attention to. If you are insecure about your body, you tend to notice the fully developed boys and girls. This isn't going to help you feel better. If you're insecure about your family being poor, then you tend to keep an eye on the kids with the fancy clothes from wealthy backgrounds, or the kids that are attending the fancy private colleges without financial aid. There's always something to remind you about your insecurities in high school.

People develop at different times in their lives. Some get over their insecurities during high school, some take ten years afterwards. Some kids blossom after high school, and show up to their ten year reunion full of pride and confidence. Others peak in high school. It's hard to imagine that the best years of someone's life may occur before they turn eighteen, but it happens.

Some student athletes find out after high school that the real world doesn't care if you were the quarterback or a cheerleader. In high school, everyone knows who the captain of the team is, or who the best pitcher is, but it's all over when you graduate. Some have to find a new identity and a new self concept. The real world can be unkind to kids who were popular in high school.

For those who are beautiful in high school, their armor may start to lose its luster a few years later. Other kids who are not physically attractive in high school can become a knock out in their thirties. Some kids are mentally strong at a young age, and others, although physically developed, are mentally still developing, and these are the ones that suffer the most emotionally.

Wilson was the first Stanton suicide that year and the second death. Most of the school's suicides occurred between January and May, when college acceptance and denial letters are mailed to students. This is the time that scholarships are awarded, rankings are established permanently, and social awkwardness and loneliness are highest. This is also the time when the kids start thinking about Valentine's Day, the spring dance, the prom, and the pressure builds.

After school, Delancey and I went to the city for Indian food. We went to Sixth Street, an entire block of Indian restaurants. She picked out a restaurant on the lower end of the street, called Yama. It was her favorite. Delancey was very upset about Wilson's death. She confessed that he had asked her out on a date, and she had turned him down. Guilt was deep in her teary eyes.

"Delancey, it is not your responsibility to follow every boy that calls out your name. If Wilson was headed down this path, it would've happened anyway."

I ate the naan bread with curried chicken. Delancey hardly touched her tandoori chicken. We were somber for the entire meal.

"The last thing he said to me was that he was afraid to fail in high school, and in life," Delancey said.

"How long ago was that?"

"Before Christmas."

We left the restaurant and headed uptown to her neighborhood.

We held hands as we walked to her building. The doorman greeted her, and ignored me, as usual. The doorman said that her father wanted her to call him right away. I went up the elevator with her, to the top floor. We walked into her apartment, and I was immediately blown away by the views, and the size. Awestruck would be an understatement.

The apartment appeared designed by an interior decorator. I glanced around and saw Central Park from the windows. My reflection shimmered in the polished beige marble floors. The apartment had rich mahogany doors with furniture to match. Her kitchen was out of *Architectural Digest.*

A feeling of anxiety overtook me. The apartment was a reminder that Delancey and I came from two different worlds. She was still out of my league, even though we were friends. If I ever brought her home, it would be the end of our friendship. The stark reality of my lifestyle would painfully remind her of how poor I was.

She was on the phone with her father, and my feelings of inferiority increased. I looked at the dining area, and marveled at the fancy china with gold accents. I felt poorer and poorer with every glance. I started walking backwards, toward the door, as Delancey hung up the phone.

"My dad wants me to meet him later." She noticed that I was heading out the door.

"I have to leave...I'll see you tomorrow." I walked out and shut the door as she called out my name. I bolted the stairs all the way down. I ran out of the building, and into Central Park. I walked south, trying to breathe the cold air. I thought that maybe the whole thing was a mistake and I should just end our friendship then. We were just so different. This relationship was just going to end badly. I never should've asked her out to begin with. But I was happiest whenever I was near her. I was falling for her, more and more each day. I sat for an hour on a park bench. It was too cold to sit in Central Park, and contemplate how different we were. I finally headed home.

The next day, there was a lot of talk about Wilson. The students were talking, but the school officials and teachers were silent. I went through it every year at Stanton, and I never got comfortable with it. Student deaths, especially suicides, were always a shock.

Doreen knew Wilson well, and explained that he had been rejected from his top five choices for colleges. She said Wilson did not interview well, and his essay displayed lack of a well-rounded character. He had been accepted to all the state colleges, and second tier private colleges. But his goal, like all Stanton students, was to be accepted at a top Ivy League school.

Rumor spread that his father had lashed out at him, and his mother had expressed extreme disappointment. Wilson left a suicide note in the school library, apologizing for the shame he had brought to his family and his school. The note said he could not go on shaming anymore in this life. The school, under pressure from the teachers and Wilson's friends, finally made an announcement. Mash announced over the PA that Wilson was a fine student, that they were very proud of him, that he would be missed, and that he was ranked number 97 of the graduating class out of seven hundred. I moved up to #299 and it felt awful.

I carefully assessed every kid in the hallway, trying to detect anything about them that would give some indication of emotional fragility. Everyone had the same indistinguishable dismal look. Anybody could be the next Wilson.

Sam was disturbed by Wilson's suicide. He'd had a conversation with Wilson the previous week. Sam told Wilson that if he wasn't accepted into Harvard, his future was over. Sam thought that this may have influenced Wilson's decision. I remained silent, unwilling to rekindle my friendship with Sam, or alleviate his guilt.

At lunch, Delancey asked if we could hang out together after school. As much as I wanted to, I told her that I could not. I didn't want to be reminded how different we were, and how hopeless our future together was.

Instead, the boys and I were going to the movies in Astoria. Six of us went by subway to a movie theater on Steinway Street. There was a Greek diner next door where I ordered a spinach pie, one of my favorite dishes. The waitress served us beer. This was a good situation for me because it was a short walk from home. I never had more than one beer anyway. It was very different from being on a ski trip with people that I didn't know, in a place that I was not familiar with. My father always said there was a time and place for everything. Fridays at the diner with my close friends were good times for a beer.

Sam came to the movies, and so did Carlos. I was planning on ignoring Sam. John rarely came out; he had to work most Fridays, but this week he joined us. He explained that January was a slow month for their store, and his father gave him all Fridays off. Two other boys came, acquaintances from school—Steven, and William.

I ate a gyro and drank my beer, with a side of spinach pie. I was stuffed. Carlos had three beers in the same time that I finished one. As usual, we bought a ticket for one movie. Sneaking in to see a second movie was always a bonus.

All I could think about was Delancey. She lived in a palace on Central Park West. I lived in a small house in Astoria. She was out of my league. We were worlds apart.

John left early. Although he had the entire month of January off, he felt guilty about it. We left the theater at about 9:30, and started walking. We were joking around about girls we knew in school, and the subject of the prom came up. William said that he was going with Cherry, a girl that I vaguely knew. Steven mentioned that there was a school dance in April and that he was taking Vivian.

Sam thought his parents would give him a hard time about it attending the dance. Sam's parents did not want him to assimilate and end up with an American girl. This was their biggest nightmare.

Outside the subway on Steinway Street, four hoodlums stood blocking the entrance. One approached us and started taunting and pushing William, who was the smallest of our group. William was black, and extremely dark complexioned. His parents were from Africa, and his complexion often got him teased, especially by African Americans hoodlums. This was the case on this day.

The thugs covered their faces with bandanas. All I could see were the whites of their eyes. One of them had a belt buckle with the letter "D" on it. These weren't ordinary hoodlums; they were Deceptors.

They grabbed Sam and William and demanded our money. I yanked William away by his sleeve, and things got interesting. One of the Deceptors pulled a knife and lunged toward me. It was four inches in length, with a jagged edge, and red handle. I kicked him in the hip. He stabbed toward my leg. I fell down, feeling a sharp pain shooting from my shin, and immediately jumped back onto my feet, fully prepared for a fight. When I stood up, no one was moving.

The Deceptors stepped back, slowly retreating and shouting at us. They turned around and walked away. Sam asked if my leg was all right. I told him I was fine, but the stinging continued. I didn't understand why they had backed off, until I turned around. Carlos was holding a gun. I assumed it was the gun from Halloween.

"You still have that thing?" I said in disbelief.

"I usually do. This thing just saved your life." Carlos laughed and put it away, revealing its jeweled handle. It was Delancey's gun. I couldn't mention the gun to her; it would make me look like I hung around delinquents.

My shin was bleeding, but the actual cut was superficial. The rest of the guys took the subway, and I walked home. I went into the kitchen and put rubbing alcohol my leg, and wrapped it with a bandage. My father asked what happened and I said that I banged it into a tree. I couldn't tell him the truth; it would mean the end of my Fridays with the guys.

I wondered if Carlos would've used the gun. I really wasn't sure. A part of me was glad that he had it tonight.

I told John about the Deceptors. John reminded me that Carlos had said that he did not have bullets.

"That was months ago, after Halloween. He could've bought bullets by now."

chapter 12

THAT WEEKEND AT the café, I worked with a sore leg. Christine wasn't forth coming with conversation. She was probably aware that I knew about her and Eddie stealing merchandise and gave me the cold shoulder.

Mike finally awoke at lunch time. Mike asked about school and I mentioned Wilson's suicide.

"Some kids are entirely too wrapped up in high school. They live in a very small world, and their self worth is determined by their high school success. Whether it's academic, or athletic, or social, they don't realize that high school is not the real world. They don't live long enough to realize how much better life is after high school," he said. Mike might have been lazy, but he was definitely a smart guy.

On my way out of the café, Mike wanted to talk to me. We went into the lobby of the World Financial Center, and stood near the entryway.

"Don't worry about college. There are lots of benefits to going to a state school. Listen, I had a friend in high school from a poor family that was accepted to a private school. He received some scholarship, some financial aid, work study, and washed dishes at college for four years. In the end, he had thousands of dollars in loans to repay, graduated in the middle of the pack, and never really fit in socially or within any student groups. College gave him an inferiority complex, and he was broke with a fancy degree. That was just his experience. Go to a college where you are comfortable and where you will fit in. These expensive private schools are ideal for the wealthy. No wealthy kid at a private college is gonna invite the dishwasher from the dining hall to a party or even to study with. If you want to go to an expensive private school, go there for grad school."

"Mike, I'm not going to commit suicide, and I'm perfectly happy with my choice," I said guessing Mike's true concerns.

"Are you sure? Because we really need you to bake on the weekends." Mike and I both laughed.

"Colleges are a modern day caste system. The whole convoluted acceptance process is a throw back to the feudal system. They break people down into social hierarchies. The kids with rich families go to the best colleges, not because they are smarter than anyone else, but because they do not need financial aid. The middle class go to the public colleges. The elite schools maintain tradition with nepotism and donations. Do you know what a Legend is?" he asked. I shook my head no.

"If your father went to an elite college, you would likely get in as well. These elite schools are supposed to be for the best of the best, and yet they admit kids that have mental breakdowns, and sell drugs to pay tuition. It's a lot of nonsense. Something else bothering you?" Mike asked.

"I've been spending a lot of time with a girl from Stanton."

"So what's the problem?" Mike asked.

"What makes you think there's a problem?" Mike crossed his arms, as if to suggest that I was insulting his intelligence.

"She's rich, and I'm...not," I confessed.

"Oh, I see. Look, that's tough. If the situation was reversed and you were rich and she was poor, would it matter to you?"

"I don't think it would." I felt a little better as Mike had a point.

"David, at your twenty year high school reunion, you don't want to look back and regret anything. So many people do. So many people spend the next twenty years wishing they could've done things differently in high school. You can't go back in time and fix things twenty years from now. Do it now. Go out with her now, and don't look back. Whatever happens. . .happens."

I thanked Mike for his advice. I went home and called Delancey. We spoke for a while, I apologized for my recent behavior, and we made plans to hang out after my upcoming Spanish test.

John called and asked me if I could do him a favor. "I think I like Natalie Morales," he confessed.

"What's not to like, she's beautiful," I said.

"I know that she's friendly with Delancey." John was beating around the bush.

"Spit it out John."

"Could you poke around and find out if she's going out with anyone? Especially to the April dance?"

"Sure," I said. "I'll do what I can."

The next week at school was Regents week. I was sick of all the studying, and was running out of gas. During the State Spanish Exam, Natalie Morales sat next to me. I'd never seen anyone look so good to take a test. She smelled like she just took a shower. The smell of bath oil was intoxicating. She was wearing tight black pants. I could see the outline of her thighs and was thinking that Natalie could easily be the most physically attractive girl at Stanton.

"Natalie, this should be a breeze for you. . .don't you speak Spanish at home?" I said.

"I speak Spanglish at home. . .which is like Puerto Rican Spanish and English mixed. This test is like a Spanish grammar test and it is probably easier for you than for me."

"What are you doing after the test?" I asked Natalie.

She paused, and it seemed like a month went by.

"Nothing. Why?"

"How about we go to Junior's and get some cheesecake and coffee." I waited for a response.

Natalie smiled and twirled her hair, dimples on full display. She glanced down, and didn't say anything.

"Aren't you dating Delancey?" she asked.

I laughed out loud. "I'm not asking you out; Delancey will be there too." Natalie laughed as well, but I still didn't get an answer.

"Don't be the kind of girl who twenty years from now regrets not having tasted the best cheesecake in Brooklyn. After you graduate, it will be too late; the cheesecake won't taste as good!" I blurted out with a sheepish smile. She still hesitated.

"Natalie, if you turn me down, then you'll be responsible for why I fail this test, and you'll have to carry that with you for the rest of your life."

"Sure…why not? I do like cheese cake," she finally agreed, with a cheek to cheek smile. "Just don't give me a guilt trip again."

"Life is so good," I said out loud, placing my hands in a folded prayer position, and silently thanking God for my good fortune. I wouldn't let John down. Natalie asked if I was nervous about the test.

"What test? I get to go to Junior's with the two most beautiful girls in school."

I spent the entire hour daydreaming what it would be like if John married Natalie and I married Delancey. I pictured us on double dates, hugging, and kissing. I envisioned us on the beach, and in restaurants, holding hands and drinking wine. I heard romantic music playing in my head, and in my daydreams everything moved in slow motion.

There was a last minutes change of plans. Delancey had to meet with her guidance counselor, and could not join us, but insisted that we go without her. Delancey was very comfortable with this; other girls would have been jealous.

Natalie and I walked to Junior's Restaurant. We talked about school and our teachers. Natalie was not looking forward to graduating. She was having a great time in high school, even though at times she was overwhelmed.

I asked her about her plans after graduation. Her parents were insisting that she stay home for college, and become a nurse. Natalie was great to talk to. She had a lot questions and a general curiosity about my life.

"You know, I know very little about you," she said. "It's so strange that I've known who you are for four years and we only been acquaintances. High school is so odd that way. It's like we're fish in an aquarium, swimming around each other and never really stopping off to have cheesecake."

"I hear fish love cheesecake," I said.

"The one thing I do know about you is that you are funny and sarcastic. This was really nice; thanks for inviting me for cheesecake," Natalie said. "How are things with you and Delancey?"

"Great." I smiled.

"What about her father?"

"Haven't really met him yet," I said in a firm tone.

"Her dad can be a really scary dude. He has intimidated every other guy in school that has thought about asking her out. Why aren't you afraid of him, given his reputation?"

"I've got nothing to lose," I smirked.

I paid the bill like a real gentleman, like the characters played by Bogart or Cary Grant in those old movies. On our way out, I blurted, "I have to tell you, you look really different lately. Much better than before."

"Is that a compliment…or…are you saying that I looked terrible before?" she asked with a confused expression.

"That did not come out right. I meant that you look beautiful." I really had to be more careful. "Are you going to the April dance with anyone?" It sounded as if I was asking her to the dance.

"I think you are a really nice guy, and we could be friends but I don't think that would be a good idea," said Natalie.

"Natalie, I wasn't asking you to the dance for me. I was asking for my friend John."

She glanced down, obviously realizing the reason we had cheesecake was so that I could bring up John.

"Is there another guy?" I asked.

"No, not exactly." She sighed, and her eyes peered o the left, and then to the right. "I just joined the GLBU and..."

"Did you just say the GLBU? Why would you join that club, everyone is going to think you're a lesbian," I said.

There was a new club at school called the Gay Lesbian Bisexual Union. There were a plenty of jokes about the club. I didn't know anyone in the club, but I did laugh at many of the jokes that were going around school.

"Well, that's the thing. I think that I am a lesbian."

"Wow...all this time I thought you were Puerto Rican." We both laughed. She seemed nervous, and I was in shock, but I didn't want her to feel awkward.

"Well...good for you..." I playfully punched her on the arm, like I would with one of my guy friends. I was stunned and speechless.

"I hope you don't think of me differently," she said.

I had new visions of our future together. I daydreamed about us playing basketball, and arm wrestling, and fixing cars together. I snapped out of it.

"Well, you're the first lesbian I've ever met. But I'd still like to be friends," I said.

"I'd like that too."

"Natalie, how do you know that you are a lesbian? You're so young and it's a big statement. Have you ever dated a boy?" I asked.

"I have dated boys before, though nothing serious. I just feel attracted to girls. My parents are freaking out; we're Catholic and they want me to talk to a priest."

"If you change your mind about John, let me know," I said.

We walked to the subway, and took different trains. I gave her a hug good-bye.

"David..."

"I won't say anything to anyone. That's your business."

January had come to a shocking conclusion. Later that night, John called.

"She's not interested," I said.

"Why not?" John asked.

"She's out of your league, man. . .way out of your league."

The next day, Delancey and I were walking toward the Subway. The psychic was standing outside and invited us for a palm reading.

"No thanks," I was replying when Delancey interrupted.

"Sure! Let's see how good you are."

Reluctantly, I entered the psychic's storefront. Delancey had already sat down. The psychic introduced herself as Delfina. Delancey's face was full of hope and amazement, even before Delfina said anything.

Delancey placed her open right palm into Delfina's hands. The curtains were closed; very little daylight entered the room. Several candles flickered. I sat skeptical.

"First I will tell you what I see about you. Then you may ask three questions," said Delfina, in a low voice, just above a whisper, with a foreign accent.

The dim room was replete with statues from a myriad of religions, and small pictures of saints and demigods. The flickering candle light created hard to ignore shadows on the walls. An ominous feeling overtook the room. Delfina stared fixedly into Delancey's palms.

"Listen, I don't want to do this; its better if you leave," Delfina said, releasing Delancey's right hand.

"Why, is it bad?" Delancey asked. I rolled my eyes, but held my tongue. I figured this was how Delfina lured someone for more money.

"I really don't want to do this. . .please just take your money and go home." Delfina looked seriously frightened.

Delancey was unwilling to leave. She offered an extra twenty dollars. Delfina turned it down, and remarked that it would be better if Delancey did not know her future. Delancey offered more money, which Delfina rejected again.

"Listen, if you don't read my palm, I will just find someone else who can. I know a very good clairvoyant in the East Village." Delancey folded her arms, and stared at Delfina.

"Okay...have it your way," Delfina replied.

Once again, Delancey placed her right hand in Delfina's hands, and opened her palm.

"I see that you are a very head strong person, maybe even a feminist. You are independent, and you want to remain an independent person. I see lots of sadness in your life...are your parents divorced?" asked Delfina.

"Yes they are."

"You are depressed...for a long time. You are very close to your father, but he is overbearing. He loves you very much, but he is very controlling and you don't handle this well. You are more like your mother...you want to be free...There is pressure in your life, and you stay up late unable to handle it....tell me, what kind of pressure do you feel?"

A tear rolled down Delancey's face, and her eyes welled up.

"I just...can't deal....I mean.... my father is very controlling, and he tries to make every decision in my life for me. I can't choose the colleges I want to apply to, or even what I want to major in. I can't choose what I want to eat for dinner....he's worried I'm going to get fat so he orders a salad for me whenever we are out. It's really a lot to deal with." Delancey was crying. I remained silent, feeling her pain.

"You have a digestive problem?" Delfina asked.

"I was bulimic last year."

Delfina asked if she should continue, and Delancey nodded.

"You are unable to sleep, and even when you do, you don't sleep well. I see that you are afraid to disappoint your father; his expectations are very high for you. You come from a wealthy family, but you are not happy. I see that you are looking for an escape, and you drink or do drugs when you can't handle the pressure anymore. You rebel by letting yourself get out of control...it's how you cope with a controlling father."

Delancey wiped her face, but tears continued to fall silently.

"You try to portray yourself as strong willed, an overachiever... but that's not who you really are...you want to be a normal teenaged girl...more than anything else. You would rather be a normal woman, wife, mother, kids, married. You really don't want to be an overachiever. Now you may ask three questions."

"Will I get married? I'm just so worried that with all I have to accomplish in life, I won't meet someone," said Delancey, trying to compose herself.

"Yes, you will, sooner than you plan."

"Tell something about the man I'm going to marry..." Delancey giggled, seeming much relieved.

"He's someone who will go to great lengths to find you, and to bring you home. Someone that is not afraid to go anywhere just to see you." Delfina glanced at me, just for a split second.

"Last question...what do you see becoming of my friendship with David?" Delancey glanced at me with a smile.

"It won't last...you will leave after high school. And he is crazy in love with you, but he is not mentally strong enough to hold on to you." We left the psychic's storefront.

On the subway ride home we hardly spoke. I was disappointed and pessimistic...about my future with Delancey, and insulted that Delfina called me mentally weak. I decided not to bring up her bulimia or anything from the reading. There was no evidence that the psychic had any special abilities. It was just rubbish.

chapter 13

I'D NEVER LIKED the month of February—too much going on in too short a time period. February in New York is too cold for the gangs and street thugs. They don't hang around in plain sight. Instead, they lurk like shadows in alleyways, housing projects, and of course the subways. February is also split in half—by Valentine's Day, a much feared high school holiday.

The month began on a cold Wednesday, the weather calm; the real storm was brewing in school. By third period, news was circulating of two suicides. One was a girl name Amy. The other was a boy named Albert. It was disturbing, although I did not know either student personally.

It was rumored that Amy ingested the contents of an entire bottle of Tylenol. She left a note stating her life had not turned out the way she had intended, that she felt like a major disappointment to her family and school. Albert did not leave a note. Instead, he jumped in front of a subway car on his way to school.

At lunch, Sam was still bragging about all the fun he was having with his young girlfriend. The look on Carlos's face was classic—he was fascinated and at the same time envious. I wondered if Carlos had his own brain. Still disgusted, I told Sam to end it. He refused.

"You don't get it. I'm not like you, and I have no intentions of being like you, with your high brow, condescending attitude. Her parents are okay with it, and I'm having a lot of fun. Worry about your own girlfriend and mind your own beeswax," Sam said.

A flyer was distributed throughout the cafeteria about Valentine's Day. A student organization was arranging to have a rose delivered to the person of your choice for one dollar. Around the cafeteria, there was both giddiness and despair. Panic spread like the creeping death, from girls and boys, who felt the pressure to both send and receive roses. This would be normal at any other high school, but at Stanton, the kids are academically smart and emotionally underdeveloped.

John said, "I'm going to send some roses to a handful of girls."

"Oh yeah, like who, John?" said Sam.

"There are five girls that I kind of like. Nothing serious, but now they will know."

"I think I'll send one to Doreen," Sam joked. I glowered at him.

While ordering a few roses for Delancey, I saw Sal out of the corner of my eye. He had been there all along, completely unnoticeable, standing and watching, sipping coffee, studying all of us in the high school cafeteria. I approached him from the left, catching him off guard.

"Sal what's going on?" I asked.

"Happiness in intelligent people is the rarest thing I know. Hemingway said that, and it's truer at Stanton than anywhere else," Sal said.

"You can't quote Hemingway, not now, not here. You're not qualified yet," I remarked, impressed with my own wit.

"Qualified? What would make one qualified to quote Hemingway?" Sal didn't look my way, but kept observing the students in the cafeteria.

"About twenty years of hard drinking and womanizing. Then we'll know if you mean it."

"Very funny, David. Why aren't you eating with your cafeteria friends?"

"I saw you out of the corner of my eye, and wondered what you were doing here. I thought you had started college."

He held his hand up signaling that I should remain quiet. I stood next him trying to see what he found so interesting. But, after several minutes, I had no idea what he was doing. Finally, he lowered his hand, and faced me.

"I had the day off and decided to come here. High school has a collective consciousness. It's the mood, emotions and minds of the students. It changes from day to day, emitting energy that cannot be seen, but can be measured. There is a considerable amount of negative energy today. Look at my device." I glanced at a device in David's hand. "It is connected to diodes in the heating system. The mood of the school changes the charge of the water in the heating system. When the kids are really stressed out, they give off negative energy, collectively." Another of Sal's crazy assertions.

"I'm observing the students because I believe I can predict the next student death." I peered out the window, searching for a padded wagon going to Belleview.

"It sounds nuts. But it's true. I've been studying the patterns for sometime. The pressure is really building; I can feel it...like steam in a pipe, about to burst. Someone is going to crack." I shook my head in disbelief and left.

I was distracted by the Valentine's Day flower delivery. It was nice to have someone to send flowers to on Valentine's Day. I thought about asking Delancey to the April dance or the prom. Then I grew nervous, reminding myself how different we were.

She was on my mind every waking moment of the day. We were good friends, but she had made it clear that we are not dating. Perhaps if I had money, or a fancy car, or if I was attending a fancy private college in the fall, maybe she would want to be more than friends.

Mr. Zoose saw me in the newspaper office. He asked if I was all right.

"Well, Mr. Zoose, I'm not really dating Delancey, although we spend a lot of time together. I really like her, and I think she likes me, but I'm from a poor family, and well, you know she has money and lives a fancy ridiculous life. And I'm having a hard time with it."

"How so? Is Delancey giving you a hard time?" Mr. Zoose wondered.

"No. I was at her place a little while ago, and it was apparent how mismatched we are."

"David, high school is a short period in your life. Don't waste time on things that you can't change. So what if her family is wealthy. It doesn't mean that they are better or smarter or kinder or nicer people. If she's okay with it, you should be too."

Sal was in the hallway.

"Sal, what are you still doing here?"

"I heard about Amy and I wanted to stick around." Sal seemed distracted and was fidgeting.

"Amy? Were you too very close?" I asked.

"I'm not close to anyone by design, but I did have a few classes with her. I liked her a lot." Sal sighed. "Besides, I was working on a project in the basement, and needed to make some notes."

I didn't ask. I knew better. Sal went into a lengthy explanation about his experiments into the Astral Plane. He claimed to have developed a scientific device that was able to transport him back and forth and bring him closer to understanding the spirit world. He seemed genuine and honest, but he also seemed crazy. Despite the strong conviction in his voice, I remained unconvinced.

"I can tell that you don't believe me. But I can prove it to you."

Sal asked for my home address, and phone number, and reluctantly, I gave it to him.

"You'll see what I mean. Soon enough."

I had an appointment with Ms. Eris, the psychologist, at her request.

"David, have a seat," she said.

"I can't stay long."

"I just wanted to check in with you, make sure that things were going smoothly." She smiled her plastic smile, and spoke very slowly, as if I was a preschooler.

"Everything is fine, Ms. Eris."

"Have you heard back from any colleges yet?" she asked.

"Not yet. I only applied to one, a state school up North."

"Have you received your SAT scores yet?" she asked.

"No, I haven't."

"Well, you should be getting your scores very soon. Albert and Amy had just received SAT scores prior to their passing." She gazed intently into my eyes.

I understood why I was here. She was concerned that I might be disastrously disappointed with my scores.

"I am not suicidal."

"No one thinks that you are. My job is to talk to all the kids that I am assigned to. This is a tough time of year. There is a lot happening all at the same time. Lots of kids start to feel depressed. Some of it is hormonal, some if it has to do with an overwhelming feeling that things are spiraling out of control. The SATs do not define your success in life or your happiness. Don't place too much emphasis on them."

"Are you saying that I did poorly on the SATs?" I asked.

"I'm not saying that at all. I have no idea what your score is. I am saying that many kids think that the SATs define their lives and they do not. It's not like anybody walks around with their SAT scores in their wallets for the rest of their lives. The score is just a number, nothing more. That may have been part of the problem with Albert, who felt like he was a failure and jumped in front of the train."

The more I thought about it, the more I realized that she was suicide prevention at Stanton.

"Was there something else?" I asked.

"Feel free to talk to me at anytime...about anything. I can offer advice sometimes, and sometimes I can be a good listener. How's your guitar playing coming along?" she asked.

"I haven't really been practicing. I'm getting more serious and more focused about life."

"If playing the guitar makes you happy then do it. Remember that happiness is the goal. Don't deny your own happiness." This was in stark contrast to the school's opinion of me when I played guitar in the cafeteria. They had thought that I had cracked. Now she was telling me to play guitar if it made me happy. I left her office and went to hang out with Delancey.

Delancey and I went to Ray's Famous Pizza in the East Village. I stared at her face while we ate. She had angelic features, and I loved the way her eyes smiled along with her lips. She was more than beautiful, in the traditional sense of the word. There was something special about her, something that not only invited me to be open and honest with her, but also something that made me very possessive toward her. She talked about school, college, and Valentine's Day…and I just sat staring, my eyes fixated on her eyes, and the movement of her lips. I leaned over and kissed her. I didn't think about it, and I didn't overanalyze it. I wasn't worried about what her reaction was going to be. It was something that I had wanted to do for a long time, since the first time that I saw her, nearly three years ago.

Delancey blushed. I placed my arm around her. She didn't resist. We spent an hour laughing and talking. It was cold outside, and the other customers still had their coats and hats on. But I felt warm and comfortable. The smile on my face grew like an illuminating candle flame. In close proximity, she was intoxicating. I couldn't concentrate on her dialogue. I was thinking about how much I really liked her, and how great she smelled. I asked if she was wearing perfume, but she was not.

We were about to leave, when I noticed an old gray haired woman smiling at me. Delancey was in front of me, and exited first. The woman said something, and it sounded like she said, "You are so in love." I kept walking, astonished by her statement. I wondered if it was true, if I was in love with Delancey.

We walked to Washington Square Park. NYU college students were hanging out, along with an eclectic crowd of hippies, vagabonds, and the usual village crowd. The park was deserted in comparison to how congested it is in the spring and summer. We walked under the large, white stone arch. I gazed up, marveling at its detail and height, feeling small in comparison.

"How high do you think it is?" asked Delancey.

"Maybe 70 or 80 feet."

"Have you seen the one in Paris?" she asked.

"There's one in Paris too?" I asked astonished.

"You're so funny." She giggled out loud. "This arch is modeled after the one in Paris."

"You've been to Paris?" I asked.

"We used to go every year, but I haven't been there in about three years. The last couple of summers we went to London and Frankfurt." She stopped herself from carrying on, realizing that I was not a fellow world traveler. We strolled to the statue of George Washington.

"How did you spend last summer?" Delancey asked.

"I was actually a few blocks away from here, working at a bar on Bleeker Street. I cleaned spilled beer, changed kegs; it was a pretty good job. What about you?"

"I spent the summer on Long Island. My stepfather, Bruce, has a house in Florida that we visit from time to time. But I would really like to go back to Paris. It's the best city in the whole world. It is my mother's favorite city as well." Her face enlivened when she recalled Paris.

"It can't be better than New York. There's an old saying...there's no place like home. And I love New York!" We both laughed and twirled around with arms wide open, heads leaned back, and eyes to the sky. We embraced and kissed, and I no longer felt the chilly air. I might as well have been on a warm beach. The physical affection that we were starting to share made my spirit jubilant.

A folk singer was playing guitar in the center of Washington Square Park. I gave her a dollar, and asked her "sing New York, New York for my Parisian loving friend!'

"I don't know how to play it on guitar," the folk singer said.

"I do." I picked up her acoustic guitar, and played while the folk singer sang the lyrics. She was really belting it out and I joined in on the vocals. A crowd huddled around us and the folk singer stopped singing. I kept the song going. Dozens of people now gathered, and the singer walked around with her hat to collect change and dollar bills. I couldn't see Delancey, but kept singing and playing the guitar to New York, New York. The singer pulled a tambourine out of her coat. The crowd cheered and applauded. It was a real New York moment.

Delancey was difficult to spot. The song came to an end with an over the top crescendo, much to the delight of the crowd. I bowed to their applause, and the folk singer offered half the money in her hat. I declined, but thanked her for the opportunity. The crowd dispersed, but I did not see Delancey. I walked around the fountain, and called out her name twice. In the distance, three large figures in familiar black leather trench coats huddled around Delancey. The large figure in the middle turned around. It was Juan Perez.

The two boys that were with him immediately turned their attention to me. Juan held his hand up, to call off his goons. He leaned over, and gave Delancey a rather long embrace and a kiss on the cheek. Then a second kiss on the cheek. Juan flashed me a devious grin. She walked away from him, and he playfully held her back. Delancey was a little embarrassed. Juan and his friends finally walked away, laughing at me.

"What were those guys doing here?" I asked.

"I don't know. They said that they were in the area getting a hair cut," Delancey explained.

"You are on very good terms with Juan," I said.

"He thinks more of it than I do. We're friendly but there is nothing else." She wrinkled her forehead as she emphasized the word nothing.

"It means nothing for you, but I wouldn't bet he felt the same way."

We rode the subways to the upper west side and walked to Delancey's apartment building. A black Cadillac pulled up in front of her building. A tall, middle aged man in a dark business suit stepped out of the car.

The first thing I noticed was his soft brown leather shoes, then his finely tailored pants and suit jacket. The man's hair was slicked back, and he held a dark brown leather briefcase in his hand. The man approached us, staring disapprovingly.

Delancey's hand broke away from mine. The man glowered, perhaps even growled, and I started to feel intimidated.

"Hi, Dad," she said. My heart sank, like an anchor hoisted into an ocean. Knots in my stomach were pulling at each other.

"This is my friend David," Delancey said. "David, this is my father, Peter Kenmare."

I held out my hand to shake his, but Mr. Kenmare did not reciprocate. "It's nice to meet you, Mr. Kenmare," was all I could stutter.

He stood in front of me, looked me up and down, and smirked. He glanced at Delancey, and took her by the hand. Snug around his thick hairy wrists, his Rolex reflected a flash of light from the street lamp.

"Lets go eat something, honey. I made reservations at the Russian Tea Room."

"That sounds great, Dad."

They walked into the building, and Delancey turned around to wave goodbye. I stood in the cold, sweating. The doorman said I was lucky that Mr. Kenmare didn't run me over with his cab.

"Thanks," I said wryly, "that makes me feel so much better now."

I was angry for being intimidated by him, and affronted that he was such a cold hearted snob.

For the rest of the week, I didn't see Delancey after school. She was busy with extracurricular activities. I only saw her at lunch and in the hallways. She didn't mention her father and did I not feel the need to bring it up.

Friday night arrived, and the guys were going to the movies. I backed out; my funds were too low. I had spent all my money going out with Delancey and this was not a pay week.

My brother and I rented a video. My father came home with Chinese takeout. Harry and I talked about Delancey, and I mentioned that I had bumped into her disapproving father. Harry said the best thing was to avoid her father since the relationship wouldn't last forever.

"What do you mean?" I asked.

"It's likely over when you graduate or when you both go off to college."

It was hard to believe that I was getting advice from my younger brother. I felt saddened by the reality that my relationship with Delancey probably had an expiration date.

The phone rang and to my surprise, it was Sal. He was really jazzed up.

"David, what time are you going to sleep tonight and what time do you plan on waking up?" Sal asked.

"In about an hour...I'll get up about six for work."

"Would you do me a favor, and take a pen and paper with you to bed." Sal wasn't asking, he was instructing.

"Why?"

"I'm going to prove it to you. Keep the pen in your writing hand, and the paper in the other hand. And remember which hand has which. Sleep on your back, not on your side or stomach." Sal hung up.

Harry and I watched a little more TV, and then I went to sleep, taking a small note pad and pen with me. The whole thing seemed bizarre, but then again, this was Sal.

The alarm clock rang at six am. I had a difficult time waking up, and felt exhausted, like I had worked all night. As I was heading out the door, the phone rang.

"Sal? Why are you calling me so early?" I was still barely awake.

"Never mind that, when is my birthday?" He was giddy.

"What?" I asked, confused.

"When is my birthday?"

"I have no idea."

"Are you sure? What's my home address?" Sal asked.

"How should I know?" I said, still confused. "Sal, I have no idea, and I have to go to work now." I was annoyed.

"Check the paper you took with you to bed."

I went back to my room and saw the note pad. In my handwriting it said "Sal 9-30." It also had an address written on it. "Sal, is your birthday September 30?" I asked.

Sal burst out laughing and said, "Yes, it is!" I remained silent.

"The dream world is the beginning of the astral plane. We'll talk in school this week. I have to come by anyway."

I arrived at work, still perplexed by Sal's trick. Mike was more than an hour late. To my surprise, I heard a tapping inside the café. The lights were off, and the glass doors were locked. Mike had spent the night sleeping in the café.

Christine asked me six times to grab a bite after work. Reluctantly, I agreed. At the end of the day, we walked outside and found Eddie Lo in his car. He popped his head out and shouted, "Get in, we're going for Dim Sum."

"I don't know," I said. I really did not want to get in the car. Christine insisted that I get into the car, and then pushed me in.

I was in Eddie's black Cutlass, the same car from the Seaport robbery. I sat up front with him. He asked if I knew how to drive. I did not have a license, but explained that I could drive my father's station wagon just fine.

The three of us ate Dim Sum at a restaurant on Grand Street. Everyone knew Eddie at the restaurant. The service was prompt, and always with a smile. The manager seemed nervous around Eddie. She brought the Dim Sum carts as quickly as possible.

We spent an hour there, and Eddie picked up the tab and promptly threw it in the garbage. The manager, trembling with fear, apologized for handing Eddie a bill. The manager at the restaurant treated him like a VIP, out of fear. We left the restaurant.

Eddie was driving when he said, "Let's see you drive," and pulled over on Water Street. I was anxiety stricken. I had never driven in Manhattan. Christine remained silent in the back seat. Eddie stepped out of the car, walked over to the passenger side, and opened the door.

"Let's see what you can do, if you can really drive or you are all talk." He laughed.

Then he leaned into the car, and said "I'll be right back." He took a box from Christine and walked into a nearby store. The box looked like fireworks. This did not seem to be anything out of the ordinary. Chinese New Year was that week. Suddenly, there was a loud bang, and Christine ducked down. Firecrackers exploded on the street.

There were 28 seconds from the time I saw Eddie leave the car, to when I saw him hit the ground after three loud bangs. I incorrectly assumed the louder bangs were just bigger fire crackers. The fireworks exploded outside of the clothing store Eddie had entered. Smoke covered the sidewalk, making it difficult to see. The store's alarm went off; its glass front shattered. I knew why Christine had ducked down.

Gun shots were being fired, muffled and disguised in the smoke and clangor of fireworks. Eddie ran back to the car and jumped into the passenger seat. Christine handed him a metal object from the back of the car. Eddie screamed, "Drive! Drive! Fast! Now! NOW! GO! GO!"

As I slammed my foot down on the gas pedal, in the mirror I could see Chinese gangsters chasing after us. Eddie fired his gun, temporarily deafening me in the process. An enormous cloud of thick smoke was behind us.

My heart was racing, and my stomach cramped up. Another loud bang, and the driver's side mirror shattered. The bullet missed me by inches. I floored the accelerator, going 70 miles per hour on Water Street. This was Manhattan, and no one ever did 70 miles an hour.

"Make a left here!" Eddie shouted. I turned sharply left, nearly hitting two oncoming taxi cabs. My heart continued to pound fast, my ears still ringing from the gun shots. I kept driving fast, and thirty seconds later, I was on the Brooklyn Bridge. Eddie kept shouting to go faster. I entered the Bridge at 90 miles an hour, and crossed the divider onto on coming traffic to pass three cars in front of me. I switched back to my side of the divider, my heart racing faster than the car.

I started to slow down at Christine's insistence. I made a sharp left at a traffic light on Tillary Street, drove another block, and then pulled over in front of a subway station. I stormed out of the car.

"Where do you think you're going?" Eddie shouted.

"What the hell just happened?" I demanded.

Eddie was frustrated that I had stopped the car.

Christine said it was a rival gang attack. "We were in their territory." Eddie yelled back in Cantonese.

I ran to the nearest subway station, angry with them and with myself. Christine chased after me, insisting that they would give me a ride home. The last thing I wanted was a ride home from those two.

Why had I driven the car? Why did I even get in the car to begin with? Why did Eddie want me to drive his car? I was mixed up with a Chinese gang, and I wasn't even Chinese. I didn't think things could get worse, but I was wrong.

My criminal cousin, Brass, was at my house, the last person I wanted to see. His deceased father was my father's cousin, and as a result, we kept in touch with him.

Brass earned his nickname when he was expelled from junior high school for fighting with brass knuckles. He eventually went to three different high schools, and was expelled from all three, before he finally dropped out in the eleventh grade.

Brass was a thirty year old marijuana dealer. But officially, he was a welder. Brass always bragged that he was in the iron worker's union, and had a union membership card to prove it.

We ate dinner, he exchanged pleasantries with my father, and then we went to check out his new car. It was a Cadillac Sedan Deville, with black leather seats and a polished wood interior. The sound system was pretty impressive, and the engine sounded powerful.

"I just got it last week. Turn up the stereo and check under the seat," said Brass.

My hand pulled a chrome colored Magnum 44 pistol from under the driver's seat.

"It'll blow a hole in someone like a cannon ball," Brass said, proudly showing off his latest weapon.

He was a big talker, and really never let anyone get a word in. It was better not to speak anyway, because Brass had a short fuse and anything you'd say...and I do mean anything, could set him off. I once saw him punch and kick a guy for making a remark about the weather.

Brass boasted that business was booming, and he was making thousands of dollars a week. His customers were bodegas throughout Queens, and Brass explained that he needed to hire more people. He asked how much I was earning working at the café.

"Minimum wage," I said.

Brass offered me ten times minimum wage if I worked for him. I turned him down. He said that I could make enough to buy my own car and pay for a fancy private college.

"Come on, it's not because you go to Stanton is it? Get off your high horse and do something to help your family. Where's your loyalty to your family? Look, I'll make it easy for you; all you have to do is sell at school. You go to school anyway, why not make some money while you're there. I'm already losing money in schools because of the Deceptors. All you have to do is collect ten dollars per bag. You'll be helping out your father," Brass said.

"I'm not going to work for you." I could find a way to pay for college without selling weed.

"Look around. Your family in is financial hot water, and you're doing nothing to help out around here. David, you are the smartest kid in this family and deserve to go to a great college. Wake up, will you. There are plenty of kids that sell dope to pay their high tuition."

"I don't believe you. Stanton kids get scholarships and financial aid," I said.

"Yeah—scholarships. There's the Weed Fund Scholarship. There's the Crack America Scholarship. There's even the Cocaine Club Scholarship." Brass was having a good time with this. "College doesn't care where the money comes from, as long as you pay your tuition on time. There are no questions on the application about selling marijuana to pay the bills, and they don't ask you for the source of your funds, and if you don't believe me, go to the Marcy Projects in Bed-Stuy and see who's dealing from the roof tops."

I started walking away.

"Your mother would've wanted better for you than an ordinary school. Think about your future. This money can open so many doors for you." Brass glared at a police car driving by. The cops stared him down, but kept driving.

"Okay fine, if you don't want to sell weed, there's other products. There is a high demand for steroids and speed. You'd be helping football players get scholarships and helping smart kids stay up later to study." Brass moved to within six inches away from me. "All you have to do is supply. They're already buying from someone else—its just business."

I knew every athlete at Stanton, and could easily sell these guys steroids; it would be no big deal. But I thought about my grandfather, and my promise to him, and my life map, and turned Brass down again.

Agitated, he drove off in his fancy Cadillac.

My father didn't care much for Brass and his antics. Brass had brought him a bottle of Johnnie Walker Gold scotch, which he placed in the liquor cabinet. "All that glitters isn't gold," he said.

The mail was on the table. Two envelopes were addressed to me. One was from the College Board, with my SAT scores. The second envelope was from the state college I had applied to. My father had already opened both letters.

My SAT score was close to my scores on the practice tests. The second envelope was better news.

"What IS this?" My father asked.

I was accepted to state college. Predictably, my father was not thrilled. He asked how much it would cost. I explained that between the financial aid, my earnings from work this year, and with part time work during college, I was ok for the first year. A heated argument ensued. He insisted that I stay home and go to college in the city.

"I'm an adult, and I can make my own decisions," I shouted.

"Adult? You're still a kid. And you are still my kid and I say no."

We continued to shout at each other, my father's volume steadily increasing with the length of the conversation. He insisted that he could use my help financially as a working adult. Just to irritate him, I threatened to join the Army. My father was now really angry. One of his brothers had died in Vietnam.

He left the room nearly in tears. Then he left the house, slamming the door behind him. I hadn't seen him this angry in a long time.

What an awful day. I looked at the bottle of scotch in the China cabinet. If I took a swig now to solve my problems at seventeen, what would I be like at thirty? We didn't need another alcoholic in the family.

chapter 14

IN HIGH SCHOOL, the scariest holiday is not Halloween. Valentine's Day was on full display at the cafeteria. Sam had sent Delancey roses. She thanked him and walked away. It was clear that she wasn't interested, but knowing Delancey, she probably didn't want to be rude. This irked Sam; all he could do was watch as she went to a few other tables thanking other boys for their roses as well. "Serves Sam right," I mumbled to John. I had sent Delancey a dozen roses. She sat next to me holding about four dozen red roses. She was diplomatic, and it drove me nuts. I wished she had just rejected the other roses.

John was watching his plan in effect. He had sent five roses to five different girls, and all five were sitting with him at lunch. He was blushing, laughing, and giddy. I'd never seen him happier. Sam and Carlos were watching John and the all attention he had garnered. They looked like hyenas waiting for the lion to leave so they could attack the pride. There are only two types of friends—those who can be happy for you, and those who view your success as their own failures. Sam was the latter.

John had also sent Natalie a rose, and she came over and thanked him with a firm handshake, the kind you get at a job interview.

I tried to kiss Delancey, so everyone would see us together and hopefully take notice, but all I could get was her cheek. We made plans for after school.

Sal sat down with a big grin on his face.

"Sal, how did you do that?" I asked.

"If I told, you probably would not believe me."

"Tell me anyway."

Sal spoke in a loud whisper, claiming that he left his body, and traveled through the astral plane. He described the astral plane as colorful, and busy, and a bit scary. His said his spirit was in my house and spoke to me while I was dreaming.

"It's easy to get lost and never return to your body." Sal spoke enthusiastically, as if he had been to an undiscovered country or rather THE undiscovered country.

"How long have you been doing this, and how do you do it?" I asked, still skeptical.

"Just a couple of weeks. It's why everyone thought I attempted suicide. I invented a machine that works the opposite of a defibrillator. I climbed inside and the magnetic force pulls your energy out of your body. The first time, I was gone for five minutes. The second time was a little longer. I have to admit...every time I come back, I feel different, as if I'm losing it...mentally."

"I'm not sure I know what to say. Obviously you did it. But I don't know what to say. What did you see?" I asked.

"Different beings and energies, it's hard to explain. But I'm not going far, so I don't see much. Getting to you was easy. While you slept. I told you what to write." I left Sal to go to class.

In global history class, and for the first time in my life, but certainly not the last, I heard the name Salman Rushdie. My teacher was Mrs. Moynihan, a child of the sixties. She was usually very laid back, and a total flower power girl. Today, she was not so easy going.

She was a petite woman, with graying waist length hair. She wore an ankle length peasant skirt, a tee-shirt with some sort of political statement about women's rights, and a brown leather vest. Her wrists held a myriad of metallic, canvas, and leather bracelets. She always wore sandals, even in winter. The sandals were a reminder how she had danced in Woodstock. Today, the peaceful flower power child was nowhere to be found. Mrs. Moynihan was red in the face, and breathing unusually fast.

"A *fatwa* was issued by the Ayatollah calling for the death of a writer named Salman Rushdie. Rushie has written a book called *The Satanic Verses*, a parody of the Koran. Anyone who kills Salman Rushdie collects a bounty," said Mrs. Moynihan. The Arabic world felt that it insulted had their religion.

"And this man's life is now in danger, because the rest of the world does not respect freedom of speech or expression," she said, tears welling up in her emerald green eyes. Mrs. Moynihan was not the only one angry or in tears. A student named Zahra slowly raised her hand.

"You know, Mrs. Moynihan, if the writer is going to insult an entire religion, and a holy book, then he should suffer the consequences," she said, her face matching her quivering voice. She was angry, but also nervous.

"Zahra, we should not have to live in a world where writing a book gets a person murdered. We have rights in this country and it is disappointing that you think it is justifiable to order someone killed for writing a book."

Zahra took a series of deep breaths to gather her composure. Her ire was raised, her anger positively more pronounced. Zahra's nostrils flared when she said, "No one has the right to denounce other religions. How would you feel if someone wrote a book maligning Jesus or the bible?"

"I wouldn't think that the person should be killed. If you disagree with the book or don't like it, then don't buy it, don't read it, or protest!" Mrs. Moynihan was almost shouting.

"There has to be consequences. If Rushdie has the right to freedom of expression, then the Ayatollah had the right to issue the *fatwa*!" Zahra shouted.

"The question is whether someone should die for writing a book. Civilized people don't issue *fatwas* calling for murder!" Mrs. Moynihan retaliated.

Zahra stormed out of the class. When it comes to political debates in Brooklyn, someone always gets offended.

A hand went up slowly. A student said, "The rest of the world does not share American views and values on basic rights such as freedom of speech." Everyone agreed with the fact that freedom of speech had to be protected, but they acknowledged that it was primarily an American right and concept.

Mrs. Moynihan disagreed, and said, "Freedom of speech is a human right and a not a political right." The bell rang, and class was dismissed.

I agreed with freedom of speech, but knew that this was an American freedom, and probably a freedom in most other democratic nations. Everyone on the planet did not have this right, as much as I would like them to. The universe chooses where you are born, and on the back of your birth certificate, written in invisible ink, are the rights you have or don't have.

I tried to ignore Sam after school. Our friendship was still strained. He asked if I had heard what Salman Rushdie had done.

"What Salman Rushdie has done? You mean what the Ayatollah has done issuing the *fatwa*?" I said.

Sam was furious. "Don't tell me you're one of these bleeding heart liberals! What if someone had done that to the bible or burned the American flag?"

"They burn American flags all the time in the foreign countries but Congress is not calling for someone to be murdered."

"Let them burn it here and see what happens. It's different. This is about our religion. What if it was about your religion?"

"It's not about a religion, so don't make this a religious debate. It's about freedom of speech and issuing a *fatwa*. It's about a writer getting killed for something he wrote. And besides, now you're a Muslim? I saw you eat a ham sandwich last week. I know your dad brews beer at home. Salman Rushdie writes a book called *The Satanic Verses* but you complete an evil ritual with a woman just for sexual satisfaction. You are the last one who should talk. Hypocrite."

"Maybe I'm not religious, but I would be equally offended if someone wrote a book defiling your religion. What exactly is your religion anyway?" he asked.

"I'm a musician," I said.

"No wonder you're not getting it. My people were creating civilizations, societies, and cities with law and order, while your people were trying to string guitars!" he shouted.

I laughed. Sam laughed. "For a guy who's close to getting into Harvard and perhaps valedictorian of the finest public high school in the state of New York, you are an ignorant bastard," I said with a big smile.

"I guess I am. Let's go to my house and get some beers. My dad made a fresh batch and no one is home." Delancey and I had plans after school, but I agreed to stop at his house afterwards.

Delancey and I went to Junior's restaurant. We had cheesecake, and I gave her a gift and a box of chocolates. It was an album from her favorite band, Journey.

"This is awesome. I only have this album on cassette, and now I have the record. This is so cool!" Delancey was grinning from cheek to cheek.

"I think your favorite song, Separate Ways, is on there," I said.

"Yes it is, but it's really called Worlds Apart," she said. "I just have a weird personal connection to that song; I can't explain it."

"So, did your dad ever mention anything to you about bumping into me?" I asked. She had never brought up that day. I needed to know if my instincts were right about him not liking me.

"Oh...that's not a good subject to talk about. Talk about something else," she said forcing a smile.

"I got the feeling he didn't like me very much." I was intent on pressing the issue. Delancey glanced down, and took a deep breath. I could see her facial expression changing, tightening and frowning.

"My dad is not easy to impress. It's not you or anything you did, because you guys didn't even speak. My father has very high expectations for me. I'm expected to go to college, have good grades, a great career, and date a certain type of guy." She no longer had a pleasant look on her face, and I could tell the conversation made her uneasy.

"What type of guy?" I asked.

"One that meets his approval and from his circle of high society. Look, it's no secret he's rich, and he has very high....expectations. He didn't even want me to go to Stanton. My father had enrolled me in a fancy private school in the city."

"I'm guessing he wanted you to date someone like...rich," I blurted out.

"Yeah, you can say that. But don't worry about it," she smiled, easing the intense conversation. "Even if you were rich, it wouldn't matter. My father considers the new rich a certain class below him. He is very proud of his bloodlines, all the way back to England."

"Delancey, how did you end up at Stanton and not at an elite private school?" I asked.

"David, it's a long story."

"I have time."

She sighed. Her silence spoke volumes.

"I used to attend a couple of the elite Manhattan private schools. Where I'm from, money is a double edged sword. It opens doors, like to fancy parties, private schools, and a great education. And money also provides access to drugs, booze, and parties at the best night clubs in the city. With money, there is pressure and expectations. I constantly worried about failure and fitting in. A lot of wealthy kids have access to things that normal kids do not. It's a very different lifestyle. It's so competitive. There's always someone wealthier, someone with a bigger home, a better business, a fancier car, a faster boat. The questions are always there about college and grades. Stanton is much easier socially. I had a hard time with the drugs and booze and couldn't really be around the private school kids."

Her eyes filled with tears. I didn't press further.

I walked back to the subway alone and saw Doreen. She was without roses on Valentine's Day. "Doreen, shouldn't you be working all night on the school paper?" I joked. She shrugged.

"I found out why Delancey is not at a private school in Manhattan."

"What did she tell you?" asked Doreen.

"About the social pressures, and the drugs, and booze."

"Aren't you glad you're poor?" said Doreen.

I took the 7 train to Sam's house in Jackson Heights. The homemade beer was cold upon my arrival.

Sam heated up some leftover lamb kabobs and *pulow*, a seasoned rice dish. We went to his backyard. It was a cool day, but not cold. Good for February in New York by any standards.

"I could care less about this *fatwa* and Salman Rushdie, but the Ayatollah should get all the credit for making this unknown writer an international superstar. I'm sure his agent would agree. Besides, how much credence can you give a nation run by religious fanatics?" said Sam.

"So then why were you angry about the whole thing?" I asked him.

"Knee jerk reaction, I guess. But the reality is—I really don't care anymore. I am a nomad, a man without a country. How do you like the beer?" Sam asked.

"It's the best beer I've had. I can't believe your father made this from scratch. I guess he missed his calling. Have you considered becoming an American?" I asked.

"I could never be an American. I wouldn't know where to begin, and as big as this country is, I don't fit in anywhere, never have...never will. I don't share your values. I don't get your jokes. It's not for me. As soon as medical school is over, I plan on leaving for good."

"Sam, you are a teenager, and at some point in everyone's life, we all feel the same way." I had two beers and a lamb kabob before Sam's mother arrived and threw me out. She thought that I was a bad influence on her perfect, college bound son.

Later that night, John called with news of a date for the prom. One of the girls he had sent flowers to was Helen; she agreed to go with him to the prom.

"I am interested in Helen; I always have been. Natalie is great but like you said, she is out of my league." Some people never fall in love and some people fall in love only once. John Moon falls in love every day.

I tried to understand the world Delancey lived in. I couldn't afford drugs even if I wanted to try them. Expectations for her were so different than they were for me. There were no expectations for me, beyond graduating high school. My expectations were self created. I could not imagine what her world must be like.

At the café, Mike was late, but he did not go to sleep. Christine and Kenny arrived at 9 am. I did my job and avoided any interaction with Christine. I was still furious with her and Eddie.

Mike brought up the topic of Salman Rushdie. "Maybe I need a *fatwa* to launch my career as writer," he joked. "You know, I didn't have a clue as to what Rushdie looked like before, but he's on the front cover of every newspaper and magazine. The media is crying outrage, but they are helping the Ayatollah get his *fatwa* by printing Rushdie's picture everywhere," said Mike. "It should probably be a photo editor at a news magazine that collects on the *fatwa*!"

In the afternoon, Christine approached me.

"I didn't mean for you to get involved. Its not like you are one of us," she said.

She apologized with regretful eyes. I decided not to hold anything against her.

I took my break on the promenade overlooking the choppy waters of the Hudson River. The Statue of Liberty stood in the distance. Ellis Island was visible as well. A ferry unloaded passengers, and then headed back to New Jersey.

Maybe I would be better off going to college in the city and living at home. I was second guessing state college. I had my share of self doubt, but sometimes I think I received someone else's share as well.

I stood overlooking the Hudson River, holding on to the black metal railing, silently contemplating my life. If I told you that I was feeling overwhelmed, it would be an understatement. I was nervous about so many things. Every decision regarding my entire future had to be made very quickly. At the top of the list, I needed a date for the April dance, and I was not sure Delancey would say yes. Was I really ready to go away to college? I had never been away from home before, other than the ski trip, and look how that turned out. Then there was Brass. The money he was offering was good, too good. It's not easy deciding your entire future before you graduate high school, but that's exactly what I felt I needed to do.

I looked down into the gray, choppy, chilly waters of the Hudson River, and thought about the kids at school that had committed suicide. If it was me, I think I would jump into the river and drown myself. I would probably freeze to death before I drowned anyway. I took a second look into the dark, murky waters again. If I jumped in right now, who would even notice? No one else was there. I needed a change of scenery. I never had these thoughts before, and I needed some coffee or something to wake me up.

"Don't even think about jumping in; you're the only weekend baker we have!" yelled Mike. He was standing right behind me. Mike leaned over the rail.

"I suffered from a weird teenage depression thing until I was about twenty-nine years old. It's normal, but some kids take it too far. That's the reason there are so many suicides at Stanton. The kids there are high strung to begin with, and when the moody blues take over they have no control over their emotions. Now get back to work!" Mike had the uncanny ability to read my thoughts.

My shift flew by quickly and I was out by five pm. When I left the cafe, Eddie Lo was talking to Christine on Vesey Street. He sarcastically asked if I needed a ride. They both laughed. I just kept walking

The April dance was on my mind. If I asked Delancey, she probably wouldn't say yes, for it would imply that we were dating. It drove me nuts that we spent so much time together, but she didn't want it out there that we were dating. Either she wanted to keep her options open, or she didn't like me the same way that I liked her.

I sat on the steps of a pale brownstone, waiting for her. I wondered if these were the best days of my youth, or my entire life for that matter. Would I ever have a girl like Delancey in my life again? It's almost a shame to leave high school now that Delancey was in my life.

From the distance she looked like a faint vision, hair blowing in the breeze, walking slowly with Juan. I could see him smiling, teeth like razors. She didn't see me. I was almost invisible on the steps, hidden by the large stone hand rail and balustrades. Juan put his arm around her.

Behind Juan were three other large boys, part of his entourage. I waved to Delancey, and she waved back. Juan walked in the opposite direction, and she quickly approached me with a friendly smile. I felt very possessive about her.

She placed her left hand in mine. I pulled her body gently toward me. Juan watched in the distance. He swung his arm around in a mock punch. That was undoubtedly for my benefit.

We walked to a local café on Fulton Street, and ordered coffee.

I held Delancey's hand in mine and our fingers briefly interlocked. I felt close to her, closer than ever. There was some sort of strange physical presence in the space between us, like an electromagnetic field. She was all dimples and smiles. Everything I said made her laugh. We talked about the future and for the first time, I told her my dreams and desires and a weight lifted off my shoulders and chest.

I told her how much I would really love to play guitar professionally, and she encouraged me to pursue my dreams. I shared that I needed a career to fall back on. Delancey brushed the hair on my forehead to the side, and explained that in order for my dreams to succeed, I needed to pursue them with zeal. "One hundred and fifty percent, full steam ahead. If it doesn't work out then you can always get a job."

"Delancey…it's easy for you to say. You have a tremendous amount of financial support from your family."

"Well, if you came from a well to do family, what would you do differently?" she asked.

My life would have been very different if I was from a wealthy family. My choices for life and college would have been different.

"I would probably pursue a career in music, and singing, and maybe go to a college that specializes in the arts. But the reality is that I need to go to a college that I can afford. I also need to get a job one day. I don't have the luxury of daydreaming about what could have been."

"That reminds me, a friend of mine in the city has a Journey cover band and their guitar player is sick. They need someone to fill in on Friday night. I told them that you were really good and they are desperate. What do you say?" Delancey had a hopeful look in her eyes.

"I have to work early Saturday morning."

"Its pays a lot of money for a one hour set."

"Tell them I'm in."

"Great, just bring your guitar to Kettle of Fish Friday night at 11pm. I won't be there. I'll be with my mom on Long Island."

I was beaming at the prospect of making some extra cash, going to a college bar, and playing in front of a live audience.

We hung out for a little longer and I rode the subway with her, holding her hand the entire way. Then I went home to practice songs by Journey.

That week, Doreen was out sick with the flu, but rumors circulated that she had been turned down by another Ivy League school. I had to help out and do some of Doreen's assignments. I was assigned to interview Juan Perez. I asked if anyone else could do this interview, and but the faculty advisor said I was the man for the job.

In Global History, we discussed the Soviets leaving Afghanistan. Mrs. Moynihan said that this was in America's best interest, as the United States had supported the *mujahideen* fighters in Afghanistan. She called them freedom fighters against the Soviets. Svetlana Ionikov was in class that day, one of the few Russian students at Stanton. She laughed out loud. Mrs. Moynihan was annoyed and asked her to elaborate on the humor.

"One man's freedom fighter is another man's terrorist. Now that the *mujahideen* have US weapons, and no war to fight, they will become America's problem," Svetlana said.

Mrs. Moynihan explained how freedom won against oppression, and said it was a good thing that the *mujahideen* had held off the Soviets. Mrs. Moynihan said, "This is a great day for Afghanistan. A few cave dwelling rebels can hold off the Soviet Army. When a war is fought, the people fighting for their homeland tend to fight to the death, until every last blood is spilled, and there is no strategy against this."

Svetlana smiled, which was a rarity for her. I had assumed that it was not a cultural practice for a Russian to smile naturally in public. "You are correct, Mrs. Moynihan, which is why the Americans could not win in Vietnam or Korea, " Svetlana remarked acrimoniously.

Svetlana was a tall girl, with blue eyes, and light brown hair. She was a fully developed woman, the most voluptuous girl in school. Usually soft spoken, it was not in her character to test Mrs. Moynihan. Everyone was growing up fast senior year.

I thought about people fighting to the death for their home, even if it was just a cave. I wondered if there was a place that I would fight to the death for, and decided that it was New York. I hadn't been to the other states, and if they were invaded, I would fight, but wouldn't want to die. But I loved Manhattan, and would fight to the death to protect it.

After school, I went to the student government office to interview Juan. There was not a lot to like about an obvious politician.

Juan had a bulky build, wore heavy glasses, and was considered a smart student.

He always said the right things, shook hands with everyone, and kissed up to the teachers and faculty. He never hid his dreams of running for political office one day. Juan had a mullet hair style and as always, wore a suit. We sat for the interview in the student government office. He went on for ten minutes about how great it was to be class president, and how he would miss Stanton and all that the

Stanton means to him. I asked him where he was going to college, and he said Harvard.

I asked if his SAT scores were very high. Juan was annoyed by my question.

"I did well on the SATs, though not great. I am senior class president, and that goes a long way."

"What else?" I asked.

"I had a letter of recommendation from a Brooklyn congressman who is a Harvard alum."

"How did you get it?" I was genuinely inquisitive.

"Mr. Mash arranged for an internship in the congressman's office last summer," Juan said.

I guess that's what I was looking for—to find out where I had gone wrong. I was working with Chinese gangsters baking breakfast for the hungry tourists and earning minimum wage. Juan was working for a brighter future.

"That's really great. I'm happy for your accomplishments Juan. Harvard is really expensive. I couldn't even afford the application fee," I said.

"It is expensive, but my family is paying for it, with some financial aid. My folks own a few restaurants in Queens and some apartment buildings. I have to do well, otherwise I've wasted my parents' hard earned money," Juan said.

He asked where I was going to college.

"State college," I said.

"Jeez...sorry man. I guess you'll end up working in the garment industry or for the government." Juan laughed.

I closed my notebook, and Juan moved closer. The interview was over; I had done my part, and now he wanted to get to down to business. His entourage closed the door.

"Delancey is a great girl," Juan said. "I would hate for you not to understand this," he spoke calmly, placing his hand on my shoulder and leaning in.

"She's a good friend of mine, too," I said without fear or anger in my voice. "Look, David, I have no quarrels with you, and you are a great guitar player and singer, with such nice long fingers that I am sure you will need one day. But Delancey should not be with you. She should be with a winner, like me; after all, I'm Harvard bound and I am the senior class president."

"The only person who has less power than a class president is the General Secretary of the United Nations, and I don't appreciate you threatening me," I said. I could feel Juan's blood pressure rising.

"David, you are being selfish. Brooklyn is dangerous. How could you protect Delancey? You have no posse. You can't fight, and you have no money. Be reasonable here. You can't give her anything. If she sticks with you, she'll become a loser girlfriend to a loser guitar player."

"I am not a loser, and it's her choice anyway," I said, disgusted.

"High school is nearly over. We have a handful of months to go. I am going to take Delancey to the prom. I will buy her a ticket, and arrange for a limo. We will go to the best after party in the city. I will buy her an expensive present. The prom is a special night in a girl's life. Don't ruin the prom for her, David. You can be friends with her, all you want. But...she deserves a memorable evening, and you can't provide that for her."

His words were daggers in my heart.

I wrote a nice article about Juan. I thought about his career choices for me, in the garment industry or working for the government. I know he was kidding, but neither of these really appealed to me. I grew sullen and depressed. He was right about Delancey, about the prom and the fact that I did not have the money.

Juan Cabeza de La Vaca Perez was smart and confident. Harvard was a school for the cream of the crop. I felt like a lost sheep. I did not have a job that reflected well on college applications. Juan Perez wanted a career in politics, and was able to get a job in a congressman's office. Sam wanted to be a doctor, and wrote on his applications that he worked in a hospital. These guys planned well, and I had failed to plan.

I had insomnia. Did I jeopardize my future? Was it really better to go to a private college? Should I have applied to an expensive school? I truly believed it was up to the student to take advantage and make the most of their education. But, at the same time, I knew that having a degree from an elite school made a difference.

I grew more depressed thinking about wasted opportunities. I wished I had completed an internship, but I didn't because internships didn't pay. I needed money, and worked at the café. As usual, I was upset about my family's financial situation. I wished it had been better. I considered making money selling drugs, and shrugged it off. What's the point of going to college to become a criminal?

About an hour later, my biggest fear hit me. I saw myself as a balding, middle aged guy disinterested in life and my career, working at a boring job, and not living up to my potential.

It's worse to be indecisive than to make a bad decision. My grandfather knew what he was talking about. It was better to be on some course in life than to be stagnant like a moored boat. This was a revelation. I needed to go full speed in the direction of my choosing, which was state college. No more looking back with self doubts.

I was going to State college and I was going to make the most of it. I didn't have Sam's emotional problems, and I wasn't a political opportunist like Juan. I was just as good as those guys.

I went to school that week, feeling like a million bucks. The entire week was a joy. John asked if I was on drugs, and I said that I had a new philosophy for my life.

"I call it never look back. It's basically that I am going full speed ahead in my choices in life, without second guessing myself. I'm no longer going to be a sitting duck, or a moored boat, or Hamlet," I proclaimed to John.

"Hamlet?" he said.

"Yeah, Hamlet. His biggest problem was that he couldn't make a decision. That's not me," I said.

"You sound like you didn't get any sleep last night. I really don't follow."

"Okay, say that I decide to go to state college. Then I go there with the purpose of giving it my all. I go and do everything to get ready for state college. Choosing a dorm, finding out about classes, etc. I've been sitting around and questioning my decisions. I've been full of regret instead of going full speed ahead. It doesn't do any good to be indecisive or regretful. I've been too careful, and too cautious, second guessing everything that I do. Imagine that I am a captain of a ship. Imagine if I needed to bring that ship to the North Pole. I could spend months deciding if it's a worthwhile trip. I can sit around moored or docked and debate the entire thing. Or I could get some food, some clothes, and start heading north."

"But what if you get there and decide that the North Pole is too cold, too dangerous, and there is nothing there. What if you spent all that time and energy and decided it was a mistake?" John stared at me, waiting for an answer.

"There are no mistakes, because I would have accomplished the task of making it to the North Pole. For the rest of my life, I can say that I have seen the icy waters of the North Pole. I can turn around and head in a different direction. The point is that once I choose a destination and direction, then I will go there full speed ahead!"

John sighed. "I guess I'm guilty of the same thing. I still don't have an answer from my father about whether I can go to college next year. Right now, I'm in one of those indecisive ruts. Man, I hate that everything is up in the air. My entire future is waiting on my father to make a decision." John was clearly dejected.

Friday night arrived and I went to the Kettle of Fish to play guitar for the Grim Reapers Band. The bar was packed. The band was a group of college kids. I had practiced Journey songs all week. Their manager's advice was "just go out there and cut loose."

I was grateful Delancey was able to get me this gig. The first set of six songs was greeted with cheers from the audience. At the end of the second set, I sang parts of one song. The band played until midnight, but I would've played until sunrise. I was having a great time and made the equivalent of three weeks worth of pay at the café.

The college crowd loved the band. The band's manager took my phone number and said he would call me again. The lead singer was dropping out of college to pursue his musical career.

The bar gave us free drinks, but I only had two beers, because it was long subway ride home. I called Delancey the next day to thank her, but she was in Long Island with her mother.

The school holidays came the last week of February. I was looking forward to having a few days off of school, and I had arranged to make some extra money working at my regular part time job. I went to work at the café at six in the morning on a Monday, my first time working on a weekday. The café was the busiest I had ever seen it. There was no time to chat or to think. I think I made four hundred cups of coffee.

A café worker named Shesha approached me and introduced himself. He was from Pakistan and I had a hard time deciphering his accent. I left the café at 4pm, weary from a very busy day. Shesha left at the same time, and we took the subway home together.

I was starting to understand Shesha's accent better. He told me that he had been in New York for less than a year, and had previously worked as a cab driver. He was thirty years old, and left Pakistan because his family had chosen the wrong candidate to support in the last rigged election. Every other word he muttered was an expletive, and I was surprised at how much profanity he had learned in the short time he was in New York.

I told Shesha that I was a student, and this opened up a new topic of conversation for my loquacious coworker. Shesha described his days as a student in Pakistan as the happiest time of his life. He played a lot of cricket and soccer, although he insisted it was proper to call it football. He described himself as a good student, but not good enough to have a real career in Pakistan. Only the top 10% of students had a real shot at getting a further education in Pakistan. The rest of the students in Pakistan fall into the category of having to fend for themselves.

I disclosed that I was accepted to a college upstate. Shesha thought I must be some kind of a genius, but I told him that things worked a little differently in America.

"Everyone can go to college here," I said.

"Even the rotten apples?" he asked.

"There are many different tiers of colleges, but if a student with poor grades wants to, they can find a college somewhere that would accept them," I said.

"That doesn't make any sense. It might better be that they learn a business or a trade and not waste their time and money." Shesha seemed perplexed.

"America is the land of opportunity," I remarked. "Everyone is entitled to an education."

Shesha smiled sarcastically. "I've had the opportunity to become educated as a cab driver and a coffee boy."

"Well, you just got here. Who knows where you will be in ten years or twenty years?"

"I have a plan," Shesha said as he pulled out a folded piece of paper.

He had written down a plan for his life in America, and it started with him working at the cafe, and becoming the manager. The plan called for Shesha to open his own coffee shop, and buy buildings where he would open a coffee shop in each building.

"This is a good plan. When did you write this plan?" I asked.

"The night before I left Karachi. College is not necessary for owning fifty coffee shops."

Shesha asked if I had a girlfriend. I told him I did not and said he did not either. "I guess we're both bachelors!" he shouted. He asked if I went to prostitutes. I was not interested in prostitutes, and said I was looking for the right girl.

"The right girl for what?" he asked.

"The right girl for everything."

"I think I knew one in Pakistan," he said. "And she was expensive."

At home I called Delancey but learned that she was on vacation in Florida with her mom and stepfather.

I made plans to visit John at his family's store in Forest Hills. I took the F-Train to Forest Hills, and walked a few blocks to Austin Street, off of Continental Avenue.

Forest Hills was a fancy neighborhood with plenty of senior citizens. High rise apartment buildings were on every other block. It was a busy commercial district, with various retail stores, cafes, restaurants, and office buildings. I walked to the Four Moons Mini Market. His mother, who spoke little English, angrily asked what I wanted. She was was suspicious of me because I was not Korean.

"Mrs. Moon, I am here to meet John." I explained myself for ten minutes while she stared with disapproving eyes. Finally John came out of the back area of the store covered in dirt and sweat. John's father also walked out of the back area of the store, yelling at him in Korean. John looked embarrassed.

"Don't worry, I don't speak Korean," I said.

Mr. Moon pointed toward the basement. John said "wait here" and he went back into the basement. His father walked outside, his face still red from the yelling, and lit a cigarette. In a thick Korean accent, Mr. Moon said "Stupid. My son is very stupid."

I no longer wondered why John was always telling us how smart he was. I think he was reminding himself.

About fifteen minutes later, John emerged from the basement, and we walked to his family's apartment. It was on the second floor, above a hair salon. John took a quick shower and changed his clothes, while I waited in the living room. Hardly any furniture was in the apartment. I saw a kitchen table, with two chairs. There were Korean silk blankets on the floor, and large overstuffed pillows. I surmised that the Moon Family all slept on the floor. The apartment smelled like *kimchee.*

An old lady emerged, and started yelling at me in Korean. She was about 4 feet tall, with white hair, and a wrinkled face. I could not understand what she was yelling about, but tried to explain that I was with John.

She briskly walked into the kitchen, brought out a broom, and started sweeping me out of the apartment. She backed me into the doorway, unable to understand me. She kept yelling and sweeping me out of the apartment with her traditional Korean straw broom.

John came out of one of the bedrooms horrified. They spoke in Korean for a couple of minutes. She paused, looked at me, and smiled.

"So nice to meet you," she said, and then offered me some *kimchee*. It burned my throat going down, but it was very tasty. I bowed to John's grandmother at least a half a dozen times.

We went to Beefsteak Charlie's, a local low priced steak house restaurant chain, which had an unbelievable buffet for only ten dollars. We ate steaks, baked potatoes, and drank a few beers.

"From what you told me, I have to ask, why didn't you have drinks on the ski trip?" John asked.

"You know, I really wasn't comfortable having drinks on a school trip with kids that I didn't know well. It's different with you and Sam and Carlos. You guys are my friends, and I trust you guys... well, I trust you. There's a time and place for everything."

"I think you are right. There are certain things that you allow yourself to partake in, but it should be in the right setting." John said as he finished his beer.

"Its amazing how certain behaviors are inappropriate and appropriate, depending on the location." I signaled the waitress for two more beers. The drinking age was changing to twenty at the end of the year, and we enjoyed it while we could.

I was a lightweight, and drinking three beers had me very buzzed. John and I split the bill and headed out. I said goodbye to the waitress, and without thinking twice, I told her that she was beautiful. She laughed and said that I had drank too much beer.

"John, you are almost an adult, and you have to make these decisions for yourself," I said.

"It's not that easy. If I leave my family, it can lead to their financial collapse, or at least leave them in a bad situation. My father will never forgive me for that. Korean families are different than American families. I can't go against his orders."

"You can, but you won't. You are just afraid to cut the cord."

"What cord?" asked John.

"The umbilical cord."

"The Korean umbilical cord cannot be cut."

We went our separate ways at the train station.

That weekend at the café, Mike was late and Shesha, and his cousin Amin, had been waiting twenty minutes when I arrived. I literally couldn't understand a single word out of Amin's mouth. The regular crew did not come in that day.

We served customers for two hours before Mike woke up. Shesha and Amin were laughing at Mike the entire morning. Amin pointed to Mike and said "Bum!" and this I clearly understood.

Mike informed me that Christine, Kenny, and the others had been fired. I knew Mike got rid of them to flex his managerial muscles. He did not like them challenging his authority.

When I was leaving work, I noticed Shesha was staring at Mike with eyes bright with anticipation. I shook Mike's hand before I left, and told him that I would always appreciate his advice. I had a strange feeling that would be the last time I would see Mike, and I was right.

chapter 15

Carlos was always Sam's friend, and through osmosis, became part of my hang out buddies in high school. Osmosis can be a dangerous thing, as you tend to forget that permeability includes those in your life you want, and those you do not. I always believed that certain basic principles of science could be interloped into life. For example, Newton's law that says for every action there is an equal and opposite reaction. Whenever the Deceptors were on the prowl, I'd always felt that their actions were met with fear, which was the opposite reaction to their intimidation. Carlos was the type of guy that believed this as well, and generally tried to create an equal and similar reaction to every action, not an opposite one.

I met Carlos in June of the previous year, eleventh grade. I had been on the subway with Sam and John. We were laughing, telling jokes, and goofing off. Hoodlums on the train took exception to our laughter, and demanded our wallets as compensation. Carlos stood on the sidelines watching, and shouted to Sam, "These guys are cowards. Don't give them a penny."

The three hoodlums looked at Carlos, as he pulled out a large knife. It looked like something he borrowed from a sugar cane plantation—a long, rusty machete. Carlos pulled it out of his pants from the waist, and brandished it toward the three hoodlums who proceeded to exit the train shouting expletives. Carlos was right; they were cowards when faced with a bigger weapon.

That day, Carlos joined our group of friends. Carlos was wearing the same outfit he always wore, a black tee-shirt with a heavy metal rock band on the front, and old, faded Levis jeans. In the winter he wore an old black leather motorcycle jacket. Carlos wasn't into sports, and rarely joined us after school for basketball, or baseball or football. He had a very quiet nature, was never one to lose his temper, and had long black hair, and light brown, rough skin.

Carlos and Sam had an odd connection from the beginning. Sam was a scholar, with high grades and a bright future. Carlos had low grades, and no future plans. Ever hear the expression that opposites attract? This was the case with Sam and Carlos. I knew Carlos smoked pot, drank beer after school in the park. Carlos was very bright his freshman year, but had run out of patience for school and studying. He was visited by social workers at school. There had been several domestic disturbances at his home.

It is often said that March comes in like a lion and leaves like lamb. That was certainly true of this March, as heavy winds and cold rains swept through the city. It was gloomy, miserable, and the winds blew garbage cans and debris all over the streets

Doreen was back at the helm at the school paper. She was recovered from the flu, but felt burnt out from all the AP classes.

"You take Advanced Placement classes?" I asked.

Doreen laughed and said, "Don't you? Don't you want college credit now?" I did not like her condescending attitude. I needed to work and could not dedicate the time towards AP classes.

Doreen had a weird smile and was twirling her long, curly hair. In my limited experience with girls, I recognized that this was flirting, though at an amateurish level. The April Dance was a month away. Doreen must be getting desperate.

When I completed my sports assignments for the week, my digital plastic watch with the Yankees logo indicated that it was five o'clock. The school was more or less deserted at this time, and students that remained were practicing for a sport, working on the school newspaper or the yearbook. Most of the teachers and faculty were gone, and the school custodians were busy cleaning and mopping. It bugged me that I did not take AP classes and Doreen had. I decided to check if Mr. Zoose was still around. I would ask him if taking AP classes in high school made a difference.

The custodian was giving me a dirty look as I traipsed through the hallways leaving a track of footprints behind. I apologized, and removed my sneakers, and walked the rest of the way in my socks alone. The custodian's hard work would not be in vain. He appreciated this and gave me a nod of approval.

Walking the hallways with just my socks made me silent like death. As I approached Mr. Zoose's classroom, I noticed that the lights were off. I thought I was too late. I was about to leave, but, for some inexplicable reason, I decided to have a look, just in case he was still there.

I peered through the glass on the upper portion of the door. The door's handle was locked. Something stirred in the back of the class room. It was Mr. Zoose embracing someone, a female. Her head was in his chest. His hands were much lower than they needed to be.

I wanted to leave, to run down the stairs, but the girl's hair looked familiar, and I froze where I stood. I could not discern her face and did not want to get caught. The last thing I needed was to make my favorite teacher my enemy.

Darting into the corner of the hallway, I hid in the stairwell. I quietly put my sneakers on, and peered through the small space created by the stairwell door. My heart was pounding. Perspiration accumulated as I waited for ten minutes in silence.

Mr. Zoose stuck his head out the door and looked in both directions. He could not see me; the hallway lights were off, and it was getting darker by the minute. I crouched down in the stairwell, trying not to breathe too loud.

Mr. Zoose and Svetlana walked out together, a few seconds apart, heading in my direction. I bolted down several flights of stairs, all the way to the exit and raced out of the building in a hurry.

I darted out the main doors of the school, as fast as I could, looking back to make sure they were not behind me. I never saw the Deceptors outside the school's exit. A clenched fist pounded the side of my head and I hit the ground like a falling tree.

My head thumping, I was disoriented and seeing stars. Quickly, I rose to my feet, and was punched again, though not as bad as the first punch. The goons pushed me, but I did not fall down. There were two of them, in dark coats and masks. They grabbed and pushed me against the wall of the school building. My heart felt like it was going to jump right out of my chest.

In a street fight, whoever lands the first punch wins the fight. Street fights last fifteen to twenty seconds, and rarely does anyone get to land a second punch. The Deceptors had already landed the first punch and the second punch. I had already lost.

I kicked one in the midsection; you could say it was a knee jerk reaction. I had no fear that I could make things worse. These were Deceptors, and things were already worse. The bigger one took another swing, I moved back, avoiding getting punched a third time. I suspected they were carrying weapons. I swung back at him, and missed, falling on the ground after losing my footing.

The bigger Deceptor kicked me twice. He pulled a butterfly knife out of his jacket's sleeve. The smaller Deceptor walked away, indicating that he was keeping watch. The bigger Deceptor demanded my wallet. I remained on the cold concrete ground, unwilling to hand over so much as a penny.

Mr. Zoose traipsed out of the school and saw me getting attacked. He approached my assailant from behind without realizing the Deceptor had a knife. The big Deceptor was startled, and swung at full speed ahead. The knife slashed downwards with full force across Mr. Zoose's shoulder. Svetlana was a few feet behind him and let out a loud scream. Now there were two of us on the ground.

A gun shot was fired from the park across the street. The Deceptors took off in hurry. I raised myself off the ground, and asked Mr. Zoose if he was all right.

"Call an ambulance," he said. I yelled out to Svetlana, "Go back into the school and call 911." Mr. Zoose was trembling. Blood dripped from his shoulder. I was grateful to Mr. Zoose for stepping in, but felt guilty that he was injured. Several teachers remained inside, afraid for their own safety.

The police and ambulance arrived a few minutes later. Paramedics attended to Mr. Zoose who was now pale, with blue lips and shivering from the loss of blood. Svetlana was crying, but they would not let her in the ambulance. The police had some questions for us, and took Svetlana and me into the back of their police car to the nearest precinct. Svetlana could not stop crying the entire way. I noticed the missing door handles in the back seat, making it impossible for someone to exit.

The police car veered quickly toward Classon Avenue, sirens flashing all the way to the 88th precinct in the Clinton Hill section of Brooklyn. My first impression of the precinct was that it was chaotic. People were yelling and screaming at each other, and police were yelling and screaming at civilians.

Svetlana and I waited for what seemed like an eternity, until a detective was available to see us. It was almost seven p.m. Svetlana was still sobbing. It was my first time at a precinct, and I hoped it would be my last. I wondered who fired the gunshot.

"Mr. Zoose is going to be fine," I whispered in her ear. "If they ask, tell them you were with me at the school." She realized instantly that I knew about her illicit affair. She nodded and stopped crying.

Sitting in a police station is worse than sitting in the waiting area of an emergency room. I thought about what to say; I did not want to lie, but I had to protect Mr. Zoose. I had always prided myself on being loyal, and Mr. Zoose had intervened to save me. I owed him one.

A detective finally spoke to us. I explained that Svetlana had arrived late, and didn't see anything. Svetlana nodded. The detective asked her, "What were you doing at school so late?"

"I was with him." She looked at me, took a deep breath, and said, "He's my boyfriend." She kissed me on the lips, a slow, soft kiss, and when I opened my eyes, the detective told her she could leave.

I sat in a chair next to a desk piled high with files and papers. The detective's name was Ganz, and he pulled out a notepad and shouted that I had better tell him everything, "Or else you'll spend the night here."

"I was walking out of school, and a couple of guys attacked me. One punched me in the head, and pulled out a knife. They were Deceptors, and wanted my wallet. Mr. Zoose came out of nowhere to help me, and the Deceptor stabbed him," I said.

"And what did this perp look like?"

"He was tall, had a dark jacket on, and wore a black bandana as a mask," I said.

"Was he black, white, or indifferent?" said Ganz, laughing at his own joke.

"They were Deceptors," I said.

"Are you in a gang?" Detective Ganz slammed his notepad down, and yelled out loud.

"No, sir. I'm still in high school, accepted to state college in the fall, and I'm sports editor of the school paper."

"Come with me, Mr. State College." We walked down a hallway, and made a left. I was in a room with another police officer and a guy in a suit. Ganz picked up the black phone next to the one way mirror, and yelled to bring them in.

Five guys walked into a police lineup. Four of them looked like thugs, and the other was Eddie Lo.

"Take a careful look. Are any of these the perp that stabbed your teacher?" Ganz looked at me carefully, trying to read my facial expressions. He was a middle aged man of medium height with lots of gray hair. Ganz looked like he hadn't slept in ten years; he had dark circles around his eyes. He held a cup of coffee in his left hand, as he blew smoke in my face.

Eddie had fired the gunshot that scared off the Deceptors.

"No," I said. "What's with the Chinese gangster?"

"We found him in the park across the street loitering. If I were you, I'd have a second look. Do you know him?"

"His name is Eddie and he's on the basketball team at Stanton."

"Well, for your information, your good friend Eddie Lo is a real bad guy in Chinatown, and if I were you, I'd stay away from him. Now take a second look."

Ganz stared at me, and I could feel him breathing down my neck, literally. His breath smelled like coffee, cigarettes, and tuna fish.

I tried to picture the attackers. When I had hit the ground, I saw another person down the block, watching, wearing a bandana over his face and a dark business suit.

"I can't tell; it was dark, and the guys had masks covering most of their faces," I said.

Ganz said I was free to go. I was stressed out, and felt like vomiting.

It was a long ride home. I wondered if Juan was behind this, if he was coming after me because of his obsession with Delancey. Was he the person in the dark suit?

Would Juan ever attack Delancey? The thought of something happening to her turned my stomach. But maybe Juan had nothing to do with it; maybe it was just speculation.

My father asked why I was home so late. I hesitated, because I knew I couldn't tell him the truth. I did not want him to have more to worry about in his life. The last thing he needed to hear about were my problems.

I explained that I had witnessed a crime against a teacher at school, and was at the police station giving a statement. That's the best I could do without lying.

"Be glad you did it; whenever you do the right thing, there's no need to look back." My father went to sleep.

I ate half of my dinner, while doing my homework. Well after midnight I was still awake in bed staring at the ceiling. I was stressing out about the attack. Mr. Zoose was in the wrong, but so was Svetlana. There was too much on my plate and I didn't want to get involved in their situation.

At lunch, and to my dismay, Delancey was sitting with Juan. Her back was facing me. Juan smiled at me before he threw his arm around her.

In the far corner of the cafeteria, Svetlana sat alone at an empty table. Sam, Carlos, and John looked confused when I sat with her. She was not eating. Delancey stared at us.

"How did you know?" Svetlana asked.

"I saw the two of you in the classroom with the lights off. How is Mr. Zoose?"

"He is going to be released tomorrow. I'm going to the hospital today after school to see him," she said.

"I'll go with you," I replied. Svetlana looked disappointed.

"It's better that you are not alone with Mr. Zoose." After a long pause, she agreed.

"How long have the two of you been…" I asked.

"A few months. I'm almost 18 you know; it should be okay after I graduate." It was obvious that she was in love with Mr. Zoose.

"It could cost him his job and land him in jail. You should really cool things off."

She started sobbing and I nervously looked around to make sure no one was watching. To my chagrin, everyone was watching; it was a high school cafeteria after all.

"Please don't say anything to anyone," she said.

"I won't. I owe Mr. Zoose for stepping in when he did, and I feel really bad that he was stabbed and is in the hospital," I said.

Svetlana commented that I was right to feel bad.

"How did the whole thing even start?" I asked. I couldn't conceive of how a seventeen-year-old girl would even approach a teacher about having an affair, or vice versa.

"Well...like all the other girls, I was fascinated with him. Mr. Zoose is good looking, charismatic, well spoken, mesmerizing on romantic literature. I don't know what I was thinking. I was drawn to him. I often sat in the front of his class, and he has a sort of magnetism that lured me in. So many of girls feel the same way. One day, I was the last person to leave his classroom. I walked up to his desk, and I looked at him, deep into his lovely eyes. Mr. Zoose smiled back at me. I picked up the apple off his desk and took a bite. The rest, well you know."

Detective Ganz entered the cafeteria. To my shock, Svetlana kissed me, on the lips, for a more than a few seconds. Ganz saw us kissing. But so did Delancey and she angrily stormed off. I wanted to chase after her, but Detective Ganz called out my name.

Ganz asked me if I remembered anything else.

"Like what?"

"Like a gunshot being fired." He glowered at me, but kept looking around the cafeteria.

"I head a loud boom. I forgot about that," I said.

"Yeah, you did. I wonder what else you forgot." Ganz raised his voice, bellowing instead of talking. I became nervous.

"I don't think I forgot anything else."

"We'll see." Ganz left the cafeteria.

I went back to the table with Sam, Carlos, and John. "You and Svetlana? Wow!" said Sam. "When did that happen?"

"Look, it's not what it looks like. Yesterday I was attacked by the Deceptors. Mr. Zoose tried to help me but was stabbed and now he's in the hospital."

"And what about Svetlana?" John asked.

"She saw the whole thing; she's the one that called 911." I didn't want anyone knowing the truth.

I tried to find Delancey, but discovered that she had left school. I had to straighten things out with her. The last thing I wanted was to hurt her feelings.

After school, Svetlana and I headed to Brooklyn hospital. Mr. Zoose had a visitor in his room, so we waited in the hallway. The visitor came and greeted us. She was a tall, regal figure, wearing a white wool coat.

"It's really nice of you to come. He's going to be fine and they will release him tomorrow. I'm his wife, Juliana."

Svetlana squeezed my hand tightly as she held back tears. I could feel her gasping for air and then she had a coughing fit. I did not know that Mr. Zoose was married. I had never seen him with a wedding band, and he had never mentioned a wife.

Juliana went to grab a bite to eat, and we were alone outside Mr. Zoose's room.

"I didn't know he was married," I said to Svetlana.

"Neither did I and I feel awful…and like a fool," Svetlana said. Mr. Zoose had an I.V. in one arm, and bandages around his shoulder. A tattoo of a cobra was on his arm.

"I guess you met my wife," was the first thing he said. He grimaced, but I don't think it was from the pain in his shoulder.

Svetlana started crying. She put her head on my chest, and I placed my arm around her.

"Mr. Zoose," I said, "I wanted to thank you for helping me out…and getting involved."

"What's the story between you and those thugs?" he asked.

"It's complicated. Someone may not like the fact that I'm friends with Delancey."

He looked at Svetlana, unable to take his eyes off of her. "Detective Ganz is on his way over here now. Can I have a moment alone with Svetlana?" he asked.

I waited in the hallway. Outside his room the patient name tag read "Zewsyzski." That was his real name. Zoose was just a nickname.

Ganz was walking toward me from far down the hallway. I followed the detective as he marched into Mr. Zoose's room.

Mr. Zoose told Ganz that the person responsible wore a mask. Ganz demanded to know who the assailant was, and called me a coward for not telling him. I remained silent; Mr. Zoose's eyes weighed heavily on me, commanding me to give a name. I took a deep breath, Svetlana moved closer to me, and now everyone in the room was awaiting an answer.

"It was the Deceptors. That's all I know for sure. I think that I may have seen Juan Perez in the distance. "

"Where can I find this Juan Perez?" asked Ganz.

"He's the class president. But he wasn't the one that actually attacked. I saw someone that looked like him watching the whole thing. I think he sent the Deceptors."

"What else?" said Ganz.

"I don't know for sure if he was responsible. I only think I saw him. "

"Detective Ganz," said Mr. Zoose. "I can vouch that David is good student, and that he is not a gangster or into criminal mischief."

Ganz indicated he would try to determine if Juan was involved. Then he stormed out of the hospital room.

"Please take Svetlana home," Mr. Zoose said. "Before Juno gets back."

"Juno?" I asked.

"My wife, Juliana."

"I will, Mr. Zoose."

"And whatever you know stays between us." He had a desperate look on his face.

"Of course, don't worry about it. "

We left Brooklyn Hospital, and took the subway. She lived in Brighton Beach, Brooklyn, a neighborhood with a growing Russian population. I figured that the U.S. was winning the Cold War because I had never heard of an American family moving to Russia, but Russians were coming to Brooklyn in droves.

Svetlana was a beautiful girl, and used to remind me of a movie called "From Russia with Love." Now she reminded me of a book by Nabokov.

I didn't have much to say, and neither did she. She stared at the floor the entire trip. Finally she said, "What must you think of me? I'm not a little Lolita. I'm seventeen. I did not know that he was married. If I had known, I never would have had an affair with him."

I really did not know the right thing to say. But she seemed to be honest. Her brown eyes were wet with tears and red with scorn. I was less than a foot away from her, and I could feel electricity between us. I felt nervous and anxious. She was taking very deep breaths, and I could see her breasts heaving up and down. Svetlana did not look or behave like a high school girl. In so many ways I was still a boy, and in so many ways she was already a woman. I was a late bloomer and maybe in Russia they are used to an early harvest. She was a fully blossomed woman at seventeen. There was a part of me that could not blame Mr. Zoose. I didn't know what to say, and I couldn't stop staring at her big, pouty lips. Her stop was next on the N-Train. Unable to fight my urges, I placed my hand on top of hers. I squeezed her hand, feeling her soft skin, and she squeezed back. She raised her head, face covered in salty tears, eyes filled with sorrow and regret. I leaned toward her, and kissed her, first on the cheek, then on her forehead, and then on her big, luscious lips.

She kissed back, placed her hand on my neck, and pulled me closer. My chest touched hers. She pulled away, stood up and walked out of the train. I stood watching her as the train pulled out of the station. She was standing on the platform waving goodbye. A coy smile emerged on her face.

Delancey's answering machine picked up each time that I called. Either she wasn't home or she wasn't taking my calls. I was annoyed at her immaturity. She was the one that did not want to date. I thought about Svetlana the entire evening.

The next day, I anxiously went to school early and stood outside the entrance for a half hour. There was no sign of Svetlana. I was unable to focus on anything other than the kiss we had shared the day before. I roamed the cafeteria, but she was not at lunch. I felt dejected and disappointed. Maybe the kiss was no good.

Sam and Carlos remarked that I was acting weird. They were going to the billiards hall after school, and I agreed to join them.

Later that afternoon, Delancey walked past me in the hallway without saying hello. She gave me the cold shoulder. It felt more like the cold war.

"How's it going?" I asked, catching up to her several yards away.

"Fine."

"So why are you giving me the cold shoulder?"

"Why don't you go back to kissing Svetlana. Isn't that how you prefer to spend lunch?"

"Freedom of Lunch," I said.

"What?"

"It's in the Bill of Rights after freedom of speech and freedom of religion."

"Don't be such a wise guy." Delancey was not amused, and clearly jealous. "Look, I can't stand Svetlana, and her pouty personality. I can't believe you are even friends with her."

"Well, it's not like I can stop you from having lunch with Juan."

"I wasn't having lunch with Juan. He just happened to stop by my table at lunch. It's not the same thing." She stormed off. "And stop calling me!" she yelled.

And just like that, Delancey and I were over before we ever began.

After school, we went to the pool hall, our usual place off West Fourth Street in the village. Tekk Billiards was an underground billiards hall, well known for nefarious characters, and a daytime hangout for high school players. There was gambling at Tekk Billiards, and at night, only the best of the best came to play pool there.

Sam and Carlos were talking to someone, a rather large figure. The pool hall was dimly lit, and at first I couldn't make out who it was. As I drew closer, I realized it was Eddie Lo, my friendly neighborhood gangster.

Eddie seemed happy to see me. I was less enthusiastic. Christine popped out of the ladies room a few minutes later. Fluorescent lamps hung above the billiards tables and smoke filled the room. Sam was puffing away, adding to the fog. Eddie bought us some beers. As usual, Eddie knew the manager, and it was no problem. Eddie knew everyone.

We played a few games of eight ball. Sam and Carlos were missing some pretty easy shots, shots they would typically make. They didn't want Eddie to lose. They feared his reputation, and after all, he was buying beer.

I leaned over to take a shot, and Eddie was standing at the opposite end of the table. I was focused on the shot, my back bent toward the table and the pool stick in my hands. I pulled off a double bank shot into the corner pocket. Christine clapped.

We continued to play for an hour, when Eddie and Christine asked to talk to me in private.

"What's going on?" I asked.

Eddie and Christine apologized for the incident with his car. He said he made it up to me by firing a shot that scared off my attackers.

"We're even," he chuckled.

Suddenly there was a commotion and a scuffle at the entrance of the pool hall. Eddie yelled out in Cantonese, and Christine grabbed my arm, and whisked me to the far end of the room.

The shouting had to do with Eddie and a group of rival gangsters that had just entered the pool hall.

The situation escalated, at times profane, and in English. Christine shouted back, her face turning red with anger. Eddie drew his gun in response to his rivals drawing theirs. I was standing between them, in the line of fire. So much for the apology.

I stepped back into a corner. It was an argument amongst Chinese gangsters, and I didn't want to get involved. But Carlos wasn't like me. He failed to remain neutral, stood next to Eddie, and brandished his jeweled gun. I could see Carlos's thoughts in his posture, in his eyes, and in his stone face. He saw Eddie as a friend. Carlos was loyal to a fault.

The manager came out from his office, shotgun in hand, yelling at everyone to get out of his pool hall. Sam and I walked out first, through the side exit. We stood on a side street, waiting for Carlos.

The shouting grew louder, and shots were fired a minute later. A stampede of people rushed out. The rival gang ran out. Carlos ran out as well; Christine followed, but there was no sign of Eddie.

Christine and I went back inside, and found Eddie standing over a dead body. Christine tried to revive the man without success.

Eddie looked panicked. Christine yelled at him and Eddie took her by the arm and bolted out of the pool hall. I ran out and headed to the subway.

When I reached home, I threw up in my bathroom, sickened by the smell of death in the pool hall. The sight of a dead gangster bleeding on the floor was etched in my memory.

Svetlana was at lunch the next day.

"I didn't see you yesterday," I said.

"I was home. Felt sick, threw up. Maybe I'm just sick of all the nonsense."

Maybe we both had the same virus. She smiled and thanked me for taking her home. She kissed me on the cheek.

"It must be going around; I was sick as well. What are you doing after school?" I asked.

"Nothing," she said.

"Do you like cheesecake?"

"I love cheesecake." She left the cafeteria.

I was intrigued by Svetlana, and if Delancey didn't want to speak anymore, then so be it. I was now guilt free and able to hang out with Svetlana.

Sam and Carlos approached me as she walked away. Sam said, "I guess the Cold War is getting warmer."

Carlos placed his hand on my shoulder and sang "From Russia with Love." We all watched Svetlana walk away. It was the highlight of my day.

"Carlos," I said, "Why did you get involved in Eddie's argument?"

"You know, for some reason, it was like an involuntary reaction. I couldn't just watch. I don't know Eddie that well, but I had a gun on me, the same one from Halloween, and I chose sides. It's like a loyalty thing; you wouldn't understand."

"I know all about loyalty, Carlos. Trust me. I'm loyal to people who deserve my loyalty." My loyalty to Mr. Zoose might have cost me Delancey.

"Never fight a land war in Asia," Sam said, quoting General MacArthur.

Junior's Restaurant was not a national landmark, but it definitely was a Brooklyn landmark. Svetlana was waiting for me inside when I arrived and seemed genuinely happy to see me. She smiled and we embraced. I ordered a couple of cheesecakes, and some coffee.

"I'm glad you took me home the other day," she said. I assumed she was referring to the kiss.

"Me too. It was great, and I would like to do it again," I replied.

"Do what again?" she asked coyly.

"Take you home."

"You can take me home any time you want," she said, causing me to blush. "I'm done with him; I'm moving on."

She preferred to be called Lana. She didn't look like a Lana. The waitress came over with our cheesecakes.

"Lana, how long have you lived in Brighton Beach?" I inquired.

"About five years. My family came here about six years ago. For a year we lived in Bensonhurst. Where do you live?" she asked.

"In Astoria. I've been there my whole life."

I learned that her family had left Russia for Brooklyn, and had lived in France for a short time. Her father had been an engineer in Russia, but now worked a mover for a large moving company in Brooklyn. Her mother had been a teacher in Russia, and now worked as a receptionist in a doctor's office.

I had never really noticed her beauty in school, although we were in the same history class. She was hard to miss, because of her slight Russian accent, and also because she was so voluptuous. I must have been blind until now.

"What are you going to do after graduation?" I asked.

"I'm going to Long Island University to study pharmacy." Why couldn't I be this decisive with my future, and why couldn't I just commit to a career choice instead of going back and forth. But I didn't want to seem confused or lacking direction when she asked, "What about you?"

"I've been accepted to State College. Probably major in business." I hesitated, and then said, "But who knows, I may join the Navy."

Smiling, she said, "America doesn't need any more soldiers to fight the Russians. Things are changing fast in Russia. Why business? You go to Stanton; why not study engineering or become a doctor?"

"You mean like everyone else? Well, I really can't see myself in medical school or dental school or pharmacy school. And engineering is...not exactly my cup of tea. I plan on making a lot of money, and I think the business field is probably going to get me there."

"You go to Stanton, the best public high school in New York. This school produces more doctors than any other public high school in the nation. This school produces more physicists, astronomers, dentists, engineers, than any other school in the country. Why not go into the sciences?" Svetlana had drunk the Stanton Kool Aid.

"I don't want to be locked into a future and twenty years from now, I'm miserable and feel that I wasted my entire life in a career in the sciences or engineering. That's not for me. Just because I go to Stanton, doesn't mean I have to be like everyone else."

Svetlana laughed. I asked her what was so funny.

"You know what you are? You are a dreamer, a naive dreamer. You probably day dream about your future and see yourself making all this money in business. Business is risky...but if you go to medical school or engineering school, then you are almost guaranteed a good job with a good salary in the future. Why take all this risk and end up with nothing? Why go to Stanton to be a round peg in a square hole?" She looked at me expectantly.

"You know, this is America, and not Russia. We don't have to play it safe, because risks can be taken with great rewards. If I wanted to have no opportunity to make it big, then I would move to Russia."

"You're all talk. If you mean what you say, then you would pursue a career in music. You have talent; you just don't have courage," she smirked.

"Like the courage you had to pursue Mr. Zoose," I smirked back.

I wasn't sure how she would react, but when she stormed off, I knew she did not take it well. I may have come across a bit condescending. I may have come across as another product of the American propaganda machine, and another patriot during the Cold War. But I probably came across as a jerk. She walked to the exit, looked back at me, and seemed surprised that I wasn't following.

I paid the bill, and walked toward her. She had tears in her eyes. I had never made a girl cry before. I apologized twice. She took my hand, and we embraced. Svetlana leaned in and kissed me. When I opened my eyes, the entire restaurant was staring. We had created a scene.

I was astonished to see Delancey sitting nearby with her friends. Tears welled up in her big, sad eyes. She had been there the entire time. I felt awful; the last thing I wanted was to hurt her. Later that night I tried calling Delancey, but there was no answer.

High school baseball season would soon be underway, and I needed to interview the coach and some of the players. I liked to write about how they trained, and what hours they kept. The academic workload at Stanton was challenging for everyone, but especially for the school's athletes.

Julio Sease (or Yulee, as he was known) was taking batting practice. Not only was he the best hitter on the team, he was also the best pitcher on the team. Everyone knew who Yulee was, and everyone knew that his girlfriend was Penny, a gorgeous senior.

Yulee stood six feet six inches tall. His forearms were thick; veins popped up when he squeezed the bat. His wrists were twice as thick as mine, and ball after ball seemed to fly effortlessly into the outfield. A machine pitched baseballs at 90 miles per hour. Swing after swing was like watching perfection at work. Yulee's stance was perfect; his follow through was exact, and the way he turned his waist so that his navel rotated with his enormous swing, generated more torque than any baseball player I had ever seen. The baseballs ricocheted deep into the outfield each time he connected. I was in awe.

"Yulee, any decision on college?" He had gotten the nickname Yulee in freshman year when his poor handwriting led a teacher to read his name that way. Everyone laughed, and the nickname stuck.

"I've been accepted at Annapolis and State schools. I have a visit scheduled for Annapolis this weekend. I should make a decision soon." He spoke without missing a single pitch. His concentration was flawless, and I could see the reflection of the baseball in his eyes as his pupils dilated. I wondered if he was taking steroids or if he was the real deal.

John approached me; we were going to take the subway home together. Yulee took a break and John picked up the bat. John stepped into the batter's box, and missed the first two pitches. By the third pitch, he was hitting the ball further than Yulee had. Pitch after pitch went flying into the outfield and beyond. I was amazed at John's natural ability. After two dozen hits, John gave the bat back to Yulee and walked away.

"Who was that guy?" asked Yulee.

"That's John, he's a friend of mine."

Yulee was planning to major in history.

"How do you know you want to be a historian?" I asked.

"Actually I don't. I'd like to be a high ranking member of the Navy. Your friend is a pretty good hitter."

I looked at the bulging veins in his biceps, his muscular build, and enormous calves, again wondering if Yulee was natural.

"What's your point of view on the growing number of high school athletes taking pills to make them better?" I asked.

"I know why they do it. They want to get scouted; they want to look good. They want to get scholarships. Off the record, it's mostly the football guys, but I've seen guys on the baseball team using the juice. It's not something I would do. I don't need it." I believed him. I ended the interview and thanked him.

John and I walked toward the subway. There were more Chinese gangsters than usual today. They were watching the students of Stanton leave the building.

John asked about Svetlana. I told him that she was not my girlfriend.

"That was some scene, kissing her in the restaurant. I think Sam is a little jealous," John said.

"John, how did you know that I kissed her at Junior's?"

"People talk. High school is a magnetic field for rumors." John was right.

"That sounds like Sam; he's not really capable of being happy for other people. He just wants whatever I have." I had come to expect it from Sam.

"Did you ever play baseball?" I asked.

"Just some pick up games in elementary school." John shrugged.

"I think you really missed an opportunity there. You could've been better than Yulee."

"So what? What'll it get you anyway? Baseball is for the birds. If Yulee doesn't get a scholarship, then what? The chances of making the pros' are slim. My dad says it's a waste of time," John said with a tone of regret. "It's too late anyway. I'm graduating soon."

If John had had supportive parents his life would've been so different. If he'd had parents that didn't call him stupid, his life would've been so much better. He may have earned an athletic scholarship. He would have had a lifetime of high school memories, made new friends, and his development would have been shaped differently. I wasn't physically gifted, but John was, and it was a shame for him to not utilize that potential.

Yulee was right to ask who John was, because he was an unknown. I would hate to come back for my twenty year reunion and not have anyone remember who I was. I would hate to be an unrecognizable loser.

chapter 16

ON THE SUBWAY, a disheveled was person sleeping in the corner seat. His face was obscured, but his hair and clothing looked familiar. It was Sal. I shook him. He did not wake immediately, but I kept shaking him until he came to.

"Sal, what are you doing here?" I asked. He smelled like a homeless person.

"David. Where am I?"

"You are on the subway."

"What day is it?"

Sal was completely out of it. I asked where he lived, but he did not know. I told him to check his wallet. His home address was in Brooklyn. I took him home by subway. Sal provided no answers explaining his condition.

His mother opened the door, elated to see him. She explained that he had left home a week ago and no one had heard from him. She felt that he may have had a mental breakdown.

She gave Sal soup; it looked like minestrone. He ate as fast as he could. He had not eaten in many days. Then he went to shower.

"Why do you call him Sal?" his mother asked me.

"That's his nickname because he looks very Italian. Speaking of which, Carus doesn't sound like an Italian last name," I said.

"It was originally Carusonelli. Our family's last name was abbreviated and Anglo-sized when they came over from Italy. My grandparents were held at Ellis Island for a few days and the name change occurred then. Many immigrants from other countries experienced something similar." I thought about my grandfather's name and was glad I had filed the name change.

Sal seemed more alert after the shower, but was still confused.

"David, I've been exploring the astral plane, and went much further, and got lost. It's so dangerous, David. I think I was over there for maybe a day."

When he said, "over there," he was not referring to anything of this world. Sal appeared ten years older, gaunt, and perhaps ill. I followed him into the basement where I saw a lot of scientific and medical equipment. He explained that he'd found broken equipment, fixed it, and used it for his experiments.

Some of his equipment was sophisticated. He removed several key components, and placed everything in a large duffle bag.

"Take this, and hide it somewhere. I get the feeling my mother is going to have me committed. I need to stop going to the other side. I have to try to regain my mental faculties. All the important stuff is hidden at Stanton. They will never find it." Sal handed me two duffle bags and ten notebooks.

"Hide these." One of the pages had flipped open, and I saw one of Sal's design specifications for a large electromagnetic coil with a large metal extension attached to a copper headpiece. Sal had labeled it "The Leviathon." The contraption was serpentine in design, configuration, and appearance.

I carried his oversized duffle bags home with me, and threw them in my basement.

Harry had made dinner. Old mail was on the table, including the results of the SAT scores.

I continued to second guess going to state college. I thought about my father, and how much easier things would be if I stayed home. I was full of self doubt.

John had scored higher than I did. Carlos said he did not receive his scores yet. I dreaded calling Sam, but I did anyway. Sam had a near perfect score, as expected. I started feeling like a loser. I needed to stop comparing myself to others. Sam had a different education system in England, and his parents were both doctors and had sent him to an expensive SAT prep course. I didn't have those benefits.

My father handed me a phone message. The message said to call back tonight, no matter how late; it was urgent. I did not recognize the number, but called it nonetheless.

"Hi, this is David, I'm returning your call from earlier today."

"Are you the same David who played guitar for the Grim Reapers at the Kettle of Fish?" the voice on the other end said.

"Yes."

It was Woody; the manager for the Grim Reapers. Woody explained that they had lost the band's guitar player to a drug overdose. He wanted me to go to a studio in the city the next day. The band was recording a demo and they were really in a bind. He gave me the address.

"No problem," I said. "I'll be there."

Maybe my SAT scores were not up to par, but my guitar playing certainly was.

chapter 17

THE APRIL RAINS fell like a monsoon. The tree-lined streets of downtown Brooklyn were now soaked in water, and the street corners quickly flooded. Puddles grew into ponds. The brownstones were a darker color that day. Water changes everything, even the color of stone. In New York, the rain doesn't keep people away.

I was anxious about recording the demo, and as soon as school was over, I rushed over to the subway, guitar in hand, and headed to the westside of midtown. The rest of the band was already there.

I reviewed the music and the lyrics, and practiced for about 15 minutes. That's all I needed and I was ready to go. Woody said I was a natural. We had to do the song over and over again, and I sang back up. Finally, at nearly eight o'clock, we cut the demo. It sounded great.

On my way out, Woody asked if I would like to join their band.

"I was planning on going to college," I said.

"We play colleges also. This may not go anywhere, and if it doesn't no problem. But you are very talented and you should give it a shot. If you want to quit at anytime, it's no problem."

"I'll think it over," I said.

Woody gave me three hundred dollars and his business card. I was thrilled.

I went to work at the café that weekend. Christine came back to work that weekend, and surprisingly, Shesha was the new manager, arriving a half hour early, and preheating all the ovens prior to my arrival. Shesha arranged for Mike to be fired.

"What's happening to Eddie?" I asked Christine.

"He's in trouble and hiding out. That rival gang from the pool hall is looking for him."

The weekends were getting busier. There were more tourists and workers visiting the World Financial Center. More investment bankers were working Saturdays, and they were drinking more coffee.

At the end of the day, Detective Ganz was waiting for me.

"How did you know that I worked here?" I asked.

"I'm a detective, remember?" Ganz snorted. "When was the last time you saw Eddie Lo?"

"Why, did something happen to Eddie Lo?" I asked.

"You tell me." Ganz glared.

"I haven't seen Eddie Lo in a week," I said. I was careful with the words I chose, because I did not want to give too much information, and at the same time, I did not know how much Ganz already knew about Eddie Lo.

"And where did you last see him?" Ganz shouted, poking me with his cold fingers. Ganz used intimidation and various tones of voice, shouting, staring, or speaking softly. It was effective, until I realized what he was doing.

"Why are you asking me about Eddie Lo?" I yelled back.

"We cannot find him. He's been hiding out....likely in Queens, with some relatives. I'm just trying to get some information here. Now where was the last place you saw Eddie Lo?"

"I saw Eddie Lo at a pool hall, last Tuesday." I looked Ganz right in the eyes. He seemed to be reading my every motion and gesture.

"Your friend Eddie Lo is very popular, especially with rival Chinese gangs. It's for his own good that we find him, before some one kills him. Call me if he turns up."

"What about Juan Perez?" I asked.

"Nothing, he's a model citizen and he's been accepted to Harvard. You should be more like him." Ganz drove off in a hurry.

I went home and told Sam that a detective was asking questions about Eddie Lo. No one had contacted Sam, but he agreed to call Carlos to warn him. Carlos became an integral part of the shooting in the pool hall that day when he chose Eddie's side.

Sam and Carlos wanted to talk in person. We agreed to meet at my house and then go to Central Park.

I wondered if Eddie thought I was a coward for not standing by him, like Carlos had done. I replayed the event in my head, and I could see Eddie pulling out his gun, and Carlos next to him. I felt disloyal; I felt cowardly. I did not have a gun, but I should have done something.

Ganz knew that Eddie Lo was in the pool hall. Maybe he also knew that someone fitting my description had been there playing pool.

By the time I walked out of the shower and got dressed, Sam was already in my living room. Sam was very polite and respectful toward my father. Sam always let it be known to everyone that he intended to go to medical school and practice medicine just like his father and grandfather. This never impressed me, but it always impressed my father. Not many kids at our age were as decisive as Sam.

My father was sitting on the couch, looking a little banged up. He had been assaulted and robbed early that morning while he was driving his cab. A few teenaged boys came out of nowhere and pulled him out of his cab. He was punched, kicked, and robbed of every dollar he had made that day.

My father would not be able to work a few days. Harry had a sullen look on his face. I wondered how close my father might have come to getting shot or stabbed. The thought of losing our father was unbearable. New York was the murder capital of the world, with more than twenty two hundred murders the year before, and close to one hundred thousand robberies. My father was part of a statistic. I was just sick and tired of things like this happening. My father worked very hard, did things the right way, and just deserved better. Money was tight and now it would be scarce.

Sam was in the room, when my father said, "This is why I'd like you to stay home for college. If something happens to me, you are the oldest son and you will be the man of the house. If something happens to me, you and Harry will need each other." I was angry that his statement made sense. Harry was crying. My father was bruised and cut in several spots.

I asked Sam where Carlos was.

"He's outside, talking to someone," Sam said. "Someone with a fancy blue car."

It was like Lewis met Clark, or maybe a little more like when Smith met Wesson. Carlos was outside talking to Brass. Carlos was wearing his Stanton gym tee-shirt, and they were smiling and shaking hands. The sky blue Cadillac was parked on the sidewalk. Brass looked like the cat that had just swallowed the canary.

He approached me, and we walked a few feet away to have a private conversation.

"I came here because I know you don't want to sell weed or steroids or speed. But what about guns? You can make a lot of money, and you would be helping your fellow students and teachers keep from getting killed. What do you say?" Brass had his arm wrapped around my shoulders.

"I'm not interested."

"No problem, I completely understand. I like your friend Carlos for the job anyway."

Brass insisted he would find the guys who had assaulted my father and get revenge. He said that I didn't have the guts to find the guys myself.

Sam, Carlos, and I took the subway to Central Park and entered on 60th street. We'd been to Central Park many times, but this day would be different. The year before, Sam had tried feeding the ducks Alka-Seltzer tablets to test whether the duck's head would explode from the gas created by them. However, the ducks never came close enough to eat the tablets. Sam said it was done in the name of science, but I knew otherwise.

The park was dirty. Garbage cans overflowed, and the sweeping Manhattan winds blew trash throughout the park. There were not many people in Central Park that day. The April rains had left the park muddy with puddles the size of small ponds. We could not find a decent spot to talk. The three of us made our way far north to an area of Central Park we had never entered before. We found ourselves at the theatre. Like I said, water changes everything.

"What should I tell the detective asking all the questions about Eddie?" I asked.

"I'm not about to lose any part of my future over Eddie Lo and Chinese gangsters. I've just been accepted to Harvard. All we did was witness a gang shooting. Forget that we were playing pool with Eddie. Forget that Carlos came to his side." Sam spoke in a highly emotional tone and flashed us his new Harvard tee-shirt. Carlos as usual, remained silent.

"All I'm saying is that this detective is asking me questions. He probably does not know about Carlos yet." I looked at both of them. Sam nodded, while Carlos remained silent. "Congratulations on Harvard."

"I'm not volunteering information, but if I'm approached, I will spill the beans. I'll do it. I'm not here to make friends with gangsters, Chinese, dead, alive, or in between. I have no fear of these gangs or what they represent. I've seen worse. Where I come from, the police are worse than the criminals. I'm going to Harvard, and nothing is going to hold me back." Sam was definitely using a more aggressive tone of voice.

"Look, let's be reasonable here," Carlos said. "None of us pulled the trigger. We did not go there with the intention of meeting Eddie Lo. If a cop asks me what I saw, I'd have to say that a gang war broke out in the middle of eight-ball. It's that simple."

"It's not that simple for me. The detective knows that I know Eddie Lo," I said.

We were quiet for a while. "I'm sorry about your dad," Sam said. "If it was me, I would be angry and want to find those guys." Sam sounded like he was questioning my family loyalty.

"I am angry," I replied, resenting Sam's insinuations.

We headed to the north end of Central Park, trying to find an exit on the west side, near a subway. I needed to go home and help my father. I had a few hundred bucks saved up that I would give to my father to pay the bills while he was unable to work.

I gazed upward, and in the distance, towering above the trees, was Delancey's apartment building. I couldn't help but miss her.

We kept walking, and I felt the presence of others behind us. "I think we are being followed." The three of us glanced over our shoulders.

There were five teenaged hoodlums lurking behind us. I didn't want to get into a fight, and neither did Sam, so we ignored them. Carlos was a different story. The hoodlums quickly moved closer to us. As they moved closer, I noticed their clothing, and the bandanas tied around their faces. They were Deceptors.

They teased Sam about his crimson Harvard t-shirt. One of them kept shouting "How do I get to Harvard?" while the others laughed.

They moved closer, more methodical, in Delta formation: one in the lead, two behind, and the other two on the perimeter. The park was desolate, rare for a Sunday in April; the rains were to blame. I didn't see any policemen.

One of the thugs asked Sam if he was smart. Sam ignored the question and kept walking. Carlos remained silent. The five of them quickly surrounded us and I prepared for a fight, clenching my fists. The adrenaline was rushing throughout my body; my heart was pounding faster and faster. My breathing was quick and short.

"I asked you if you were smart," their leader shouted to Sam.

"Smart enough," Sam said.

"What do you want?" I said.

"That Harvard T-shirt," one of them shouted back, "And your tuition money." They were guffawing. Carlos started laughing as well. The Deceptors found Carlos amusing.

Carlos was laughing louder than everyone. The Deceptors smelled like pot, and their eyes were red. The five thugs stared at

Carlos as he continued to laugh long after they had stopped. Carlos sounded maniacal. I wondered how long he had spent with Brass outside my house. Maybe Carlos was high as well. The thugs were no longer amused. One of them pulled out a knife. Sam stepped back, and was pushed to the ground.

"These Harvard boys can't seem to fight," said one of the Deceptors hovering over Sam.

Carlos glanced at me. In these situations, it's better to be decisive. I recalled the rules about street fights; the guy that lands the first punch wins the fight. I nodded at Carlos, and then clenched my right fist, and took a deep breath. My goal was to be swift and powerful, and if I broke every bone in my hand, so be it. I widened my stance, shifting all the weight to my right side. I took a full swing at the hoodlum hovering over Sam.

I hit him in the jaw, as hard as I could, and he fell down, stunned and delirious. I turned to pick up Sam and a punch landed on my head. I swung back but missed. I braced myself for a maelstrom.

All I could think about was my father being attacked and robbed. Anger grew inside of me, my blood boiling. But when I looked around, no one was moving or throwing any punches.

Carlos had pulled out a big gun from his backpack. Carlos pointed the gun at one of the hoodlums, the one who demanded the money and the tee-shirt. The hoodlum was pointing his gun back at Carlos. I recognized the gun that Carlos was holding, it was Brass's gun. I walked to Carlos's side, and Sam followed. The five thugs stood next to their leader with the gun. He was holding a .22 caliber, a much smaller gun, but at such a close range, equally deadly.

Carlos stared at the lead Deceptor in the eye, and with his other hand, threw me his backpack. Carlos motioned to the backpack, and I opened it. I pulled out another gun and handed it to Sam. Sam declined, and I held the jeweled gun in my hand. This was likely Delancey's gun, the one her father had bought her, the one that was stolen from her bag. This was the gun that Sam had bought after exchanging a bottle of perfume for cash. One of the Deceptors pulled out a gun from his oversized black coat.

Now, although they outnumbered us, we were even, two guns each.

I was breathing heavy, and beads of sweat formed on my forehead. I continued to hold the gun, standing next to Carlos.

The next few seconds felt like Chernobyl's nuclear reactor about to meltdown. No one moved; no one back down. I was breathing harder. Sam was sweating. One whole minute went by, seeming like an hour. The five of them stood across from us, staring us down. No one spoke, no one moved a muscle. My heart was pounding; my throat was out of air. Carlos had a devious grin on his face. I was nervous and afraid, but not Carlos. He looked like he wanted to pull that trigger. Sam's hands were shaking.

I held my gun out with both hands, my arms fully extended. I had never fired a weapon before, and felt scared, but also I had mixed emotions.

Sam shouted, "Shoot 'em! Shoot 'em before they shoot you! These are probably the same guys that assaulted your father. They robbed him, took his money. Do the world a favor and kill these bastards. Avenge your father. Where's your family loyalty? Where's your honor?"

Could Sam be correct? Is this the same group that robbed and assaulted my father? I looked at their dirty fingernails, their dirty eyes, and could even feel their dirty hearts. How many other people had they had robbed this week? How many more people would be better off if I pulled the trigger? My heart pounded louder, and my throat became drier.

I would have loved to blast one, right in the chest. I pictured his friends running away and I pictured myself shooting them in the back as they tried to run off. I was so angry about my father. I was angry about so many things, including not helping Eddie Lo in the pool hall or the ski trip. I was angry about not helping Mr. Zoose who had come to my defense. I was breathing heavy, and couldn't get enough air. My hands were trembling, but they were tight around the handle of the gun.

When you are in a gun fight, the guy who fires first could also fire last. Would they shoot first? Would Carlos shoot first? Would I shoot first or would I be lying dead with Carlos. I wanted to shoot first. I could not afford to miss; I might only get one shot. My hand was starting to dip, from the weight of the gun, and from holding my arm extended for as long as I had. At least three minutes had now passed.

I was pumped up with adrenaline and had a lot of crazy thoughts in my head. I thought about college, and going away. I thought about Svetlana, and how beautiful she was. I thought about Delancey, and how I was such an idiot to ruin our friendship by kissing Svetlana in front of her. I thought about my father, and how he was barely able to walk. I thought about my mother, and pictured myself crying at her funeral. I thought about my grandfather, and remembered that he said to make good decisions. By holding this gun, by shooting one of these thugs, would I be making a good decision? The life map was in my wallet. By shooting first, would I stick to my plan? What if I was arrested? Instead of going off to college, I would be going off to Sing Sing.

Then I had another thought. After Halloween, Carlos had said that the gun that I was now holding did not have any bullets. But that was five months ago, I'm sure he must have bought bullets by now. I looked at the gun. Here I was in Central Park, surrounded by thugs, two of them with guns, Carlos with his gun, and I may not have had any bullets. How dumb would it look if I pulled out the cartridge to check for bullets? How dead would I be if there were no bullets in the gun I was holding?

I had to look confident. I had to remain looking like I could pull the trigger and think nothing of it.

"You don't have the guts...come on, pull that trigger boy," said one of the thugs holding a gun. His voice broke the silence, and I instantly knew he was from the Bronx, by the nasally way he spoke.

"You have Stanton and Harvard to think about, and tests, and graduation," the lead Deceptor said. "We have nothing to think about, nothing to lose."

"I'll pull this trigger five times and never look back," I replied, my voice full of anger. "There's no one around. I'll be on the subway in ten seconds, and I won't leave any witnesses."

"You won't do it, because you've never shot anyone before. You don't have the *cajones*," said another Deceptor.

"I'll be doing the world a favor if I shoot the five of you today, right here in Central Park," I said grinding my teeth.

"You're no Bernie Goetz," he said. The reference was to a famous subway vigilante.

"This is what it comes to," said Carlos. "Manhattan isn't big enough for the both of us. Your group and my group. Criminals and regular people. We are high school students, in New York City, the center of the universe. We go to the best high school in the state, and we have to put up with animals like you guys everyday of the week. On the subways, in our neighborhoods, everywhere. We go to school, study hard, trying to make it to college. Our parents try to make a decent living, and you jerks do the opposite. You drop out of school and expect us to pay for your welfare, your food stamps, your prison stays, even your rent. And how do you thank us? By robbing us, assaulting our parents, and holding us at gunpoint. And my friend is right; we'd be doing the world a favor." Carlos remained cool; his voice never quivered.

"If you want to do the world a favor, go ahead. Shoot me right now," said the smaller Deceptor with a gun. "I'm not asking you to do me any favors. I don't need your handouts. I'm not going on welfare or public assistance. I'll shoot you in the head. And I'm not going to prison. It's people like you, that act that you're entitled to everything, that you own the entire city, and only your kind matters. You think you can look down on the rest of us. Maybe I'm the one doing the world a favor, by just pulling this trigger. It's the haves versus the have-nots, and I'm tired of being on the short end of that equation.

You guys think you're so cool, so privileged. You think you're the golden boys, but all you ever do is ruin life for everyone else. This could be payback time."

Another minute went by, absent of dialogue, and one of the hoodlums started walking backwards. Then another followed. We took a few steps back, not turning our backs on them for a second. The Deceptors were retreating, and I was relieved when their leader put his gun down. They continued to walk backwards, staring us down, and yelling expletives. I put my gun down, but Carlos still held the Magnum. He finally put it down a few minutes later after the Deceptors were gone.

Carlos took a deep breath, gave a sigh of relief, and put both guns in his backpack. We walked in silence to the subway station, and entered the A-Train. No one said a word.

Carlos smiled. "I like your cousin Brass. I think we reached an agreement today."

"Be careful with Brass—he's got a very short fuse." The least I could do was to warn him. Carlos was not concerned.

"Did my gun have bullets?" I asked.

"It doesn't matter. Maybe it did, and maybe it didn't. The question is whether or not you would've pulled the trigger," Carlos said. "Well?"

"I came pretty close to pulling the trigger. After what happened to my father, and Eddie Lo, I came pretty close," I said.

"That's why I gave you the gun," Sam said.

"Because you wouldn't have pulled the trigger?" I said.

"No, because I would've pulled the trigger the second I had the gun in my hand," Sam confessed. "I'm not into the think first and shoot after thing; I'm the opposite."

"Did it have bullets?" I asked Carlos.

"No, it didn't. Neither did my gun. Brass took the bullets out before he gave it to me." I looked at Carlos's Stanton gym tee-shirt, wondering if he had given something away and if the Deceptors would come looking for us.

chapter 18

THE NEXT DAY at school, Svetlana said that it was urgent that we have lunch together. Delancey sat nearby, glancing at us every few seconds. I felt terrible doing this to her, but I needed to continue the cover up for Mr. Zoose.

Svetlana was amazing. Everyday that I grew to know her, I grew to like her, and I was being hypnotized by her Russian accent.

"The cops have been asking about you and me, if we are really dating," she said. "I don't want anyone to know about me and Mr. Zoose."

"Everyone thinks we are dating. Don't worry about that."

Svetlana did not seem to have many friends, especially female friends. While we were eating, I noticed that hardly anyone came over and said hello to her. It was the opposite of sitting with Delancey. She ate in a hurry, hardly chewing her food. She placed her hand gently on my leg. It caught me off guard, but I reciprocated. I placed my hand on her thigh, then pulled away realizing that Delancey might see.

After lunch, we saw a flyer posted for the April dance. It was being called the Coca-Cola Dance, sponsored by the famous soft drink company. Svetlana read the flyer.

"Well…what do you think?" she asked.

"About the dance?" I asked. I thought about Delancey. I hated dancing, but I wondered if Delancey would want to go.

"Yes, the dance. I would really like to go. I studied dance my whole life." She smiled.

"You want to go to the dance?" I asked, regretting I said it before I could finish the sentence. I was asking her if she was intimating that, and not actually asking her to go with me.

"I thought you'd never ask. The answer is yes!" She laughed and headed to her next class.

Now I was really stressed out. I was a terrible dancer, and had never been to a school dance before. What would Delancey think? Would she be angry? I was breathing…no…I was panting. I inadvertently had made a date with Svetlana.

I stood in the hallway, oblivious to the fact that I was late to class, and frozen by the idea of dancing in front of the entire school. The events of the past few weeks, like watching Eddie Lo standing over a rival lying in a pool of blood, being grilled by Ganz, and nearly getting killed in Central Park, seemed to pale in comparison to the school dance.

A school dance was something out my element. Violence, shootings, etc., had always been part of my life. But, dancing in front of the senior class, in full view of all my friends, and teachers…there really should be a law against school dances.

Mr. Zoose saw me having a panic attack and asked me if I was all right. He looked just about back to normal.

"Can't breathe! Can't breathe!" I gasped for air.

Mr. Zoose said to calm down, and gave me a cup of water. I took a deep breath, and he asked what happened. I wasn't sure if I could tell him; after all, he had intimate knowledge of my "problem."

"Mr. Zoose, I'm going to the Coca Cola dance with Svetlana, but I don't know how to dance, and she's some kind of expert…I'm going to make a fool out myself."

Mr. Zoose held back a laugh. "Look, you have time to practice…go watch some people dance on television and practice at home. Just have fun. I'm glad I bumped into you. Svetlana and I are over. It's for the best; after all, I am married and want to stay married. I thank you for your help. I really don't know what I was thinking." He went into his classroom.

Sam approached and asked if I was having an asthma attack. I told him about the dance, and that I was going with Svetlana.

"All I could teach you is how we dance Persian Style!" He placed his hands in the air, and started twirling in a circle. Sam clapped his hands in a wide circular motion, and moved his hips. A dumb smile sprung across his face. Sam wanted to go to the dance, but was afraid his parents would freak out and suspect him of trying to become an American. "It's different, the men dance with the men where my parents come from. And the women get excited."

"You could take your girlfriend, the freshman," I said.

"Oh that. Well, I called it off when she asked if we were going to the prom together. Ridiculous! Why would I go the prom with a freshman?" Sam smirked. "Besides now that I have been accepted to Harvard, I can probably get any girl in the school."

"Maybe even a sophomore," I said sarcastically.

Delancey walked toward us. She wondered if there was something wrong with my appendix, since I was still hunched over. Sam blurted out, "He's nervous because he doesn't know how to dance and he's going to the Coca Cola dance with Svetlana."

Delancey looked shocked. "I didn't realize you two were still together."

"We're not...we are not together. We're just friends," I said quickly.

"Wow," Delancey said, with flushed cheeks. She appeared devastated. I was livid with Sam for telling her about my situation.

"Are you going to the dance?" I asked her.

"I'm no longer sure. I thought I might have had a date, and now that doesn't seem to be the case," Delancey replied.

"Well maybe you and I could go together. I'm a real good dancer," Sam said. I was in disbelief. One minute he wasn't going, and the next he was asking out Delancey, right in front of me.

"I don't think so," Delancey said curtly. She looked at me and said, "By the way, there is a fundraiser this Friday night in Long Island…my mom is part of the group hosting. I came by to invite you; you should come, it will be a lot of fun, and I'll get you in for free. You…can…bring who…ever."

Before I could answer, Sam said, "We'll be there, just give me the details."

Delancey gave us an invitation and left. Sam was pleased with himself.

"First of all…I don't know where to even begin! Why did you tell Delancey about me going to the April Dance with Svetlana? Second of all, you said you could not go to the dance…and third of all, you ask her out, right in front of me, and fourth of all, I don't want to go to some stuffy fundraiser. We'll be completely out of place. Those are rich Long Island people and two boys from Queens are going to stick out like a sore thumb."

"Listen to me carefully….this is a good opportunity for you to see the other side. Rich people are great, very friendly, and it will do you some good. Besides you owe it to Delancey after stomping on her heart. You agreed to take Svetlana to the dance, not me. Also, it's for a good cause, it's a fundraiser. Charity is a good thing. Now, I will be going to the dance…to dance with Delancey. I'll find a way," Sam said.

The address on the invitation read Oyster Bay. It sounded so far away. A few things in life made me uncomfortable; being held at gunpoint in Central Park was one of them. Dancing in public was another. But the thing that made me most uncomfortable was being around rich people. I wasn't ashamed that my father was one of the hardest working poor people on the planet. But I was not willing to be scrutinized by the rich. The last thing I needed was to go to this fundraiser, but Sam would not let me out of it, and now Delancey was expecting me.

I went shopping for clothes to wear to Delancey's fundraiser and the dance. I ended up on Steinway Street in Astoria, a busy shopping area with stores run by mostly Greeks. I told the clerk my dilemma, that I needed an outfit for two occasions, and he sold me something that he said would be perfect. I was a little hesitant; after all, the guy dressed like a night club owner in Athens, with gold chains covering his hairy chest. I paid for it with the money I made from the café last weekend.

On Thursday, I went to the Ziegfield movie theater in the city, with Svetlana. She wore a leather skirt and white sweater. Her hair was made up nicely, but she had a strange expression on her face. She was not her usual self, and seemed aloof. We sat and watched the movie. Let me repeat that...we sat and watched the movie, in its entirety. There was no physical contact between us. She didn't want to hold hands. She didn't want to sit close, nothing at all. I wondered if it was this cold in Siberia. When the date ended, I looked at her as she walked away, and knew that my friendship with Svetlana was just about over.

On Friday, I was dreading the entire fundraiser ordeal. At lunch, Delancey confirmed our attendance. Sam asked her what to wear, and she said it was a dressy event.

"I don't own a dress," Sam said and then chuckled. Delancey seemed annoyed that Sam would be accompanying me. We would have to take the Long Island Railroad to Oyster Bay and then take a cab.

"My dad is going to pick us up at eleven. So going back won't be that bad." For all the trouble he's worth, Sam always had a plan.

We decided to meet at the Nathan's Hot Dog stand in Penn Station at seven o'clock. I wore my new suit and my father said I looked very European.

Sam was wearing a gray suit, white shirt, and skinny leather tie. His black shiny shoes matched his tie. He looked preppy and even wore a Harvard lapel pin. If Sam could carry a large flag that read "I'm going to Harvard" he would.

Sam laughed when he saw me. He said that I looked "like a Greek night club owner," and then asked me for a souvlaki. It was going to be a long night.

We took the long ride on the Long Island Railroad. Through the dusty windows of the train, the congested streets of Queens flashed by. I had butterflies in my stomach; I had never been to Long Island before, and I didn't know what to expect. I pictured myself in my strange outfit, and my Queens accent, trying to fit in.

We had to take a cab from the station to the house. When the cab pulled up in front of the house on Crescent Moon Drive, Sam told me to close my lower jaw. It was the biggest house I had ever seen, a contemporary design, on a dark, tree lined street with no other homes visible. The mansion was white, with a stucco and glass exterior. There were lots of windows, and a large circular driveway preceded it. It was built to be intimidating, and I sat frozen in the cab.

The cab driver was as astounded as I was. "This is some house," he said. "Wow." He took the words right out of my mouth. I paid the fare. Sam, as usual, did not have any money.

"How much bigger than my house do you think this is?" I asked Sam.

"At least six or seven times your house, and that's just the first floor."

We walked up the long cobble stone driveway. A man asked if we were the valets. Sam replied, "Not us, not tonight."

When we arrived at the oversized entry doors, a butler in a black tuxedo immediately asked our names, and a man with a clip-board checked us in. The party was in the back. Sam and I walked through the house to find the back door. The floor was granite, and the ceilings were at least twelve feet high. The front stairs were marble, with dark wrought iron railings. There were several fireplaces. One was made of flat gray stones, stacked one on top of the other, all the way to the ceiling of the second floor. The kitchen was as big as my entire house, complete with cabinets made of shiny white metal. Sam and I stepped out of the kitchen by opening an oversized sliding glass door. We stepped onto a large wraparound limestone patio. The back-yard looked as big as the Great Lawn in Central Park, which no longer seemed so great from where I was standing. There were lamp posts in the yard, but it was mostly dark.

Delancey gave me a big hug. She was dressed like a model from an upscale fashion catalog, wearing a blue dress and a matching scarf around her shoulders. It was made of silk, with a jeweled clip in the middle. She introduced us to her mother, who shook our hands, and thanked us for coming. There were no other young people; everyone else was an adult.

The deck was lit by torches, and several tables were set up with hot foods. The caterers walked around with serving trays and napkins. On the far left was a kidney shaped swimming pool, complete with a diving board and a swim up bar. The yard was enclosed by large old trees, some as high as fifty to sixty feet. Sam and I ate appetizers, but here on Long Island, the waiters referred to them as hors'doeuvres.

I felt uncomfortable, and completely out of place. I walked into the backyard, alone, as Sam stayed back and kept kissing up to Delancey's mother. I now understood that Sam would fit in at the Ivy League. I lacked his social graces. Sam was a smooth talker. I guess that's what happens when you're a doctor's son.

A waiter offered me a glass of white wine, and I took two glasses and walked deep into the sprawling backyard, into its darkest corner, hoping that no one would see me or follow me. I wanted this evening to be over, as my level of anxiety and social awkwardness increased with every person that said hello to me. I just wanted to be alone, away from their smiles and pleasantries.

In the corner of the backyard was a small house, with a sign that read "Cabana." I peered in and saw some adults snorting lines of cocaine off a glass coffee table. They were laughing. Some had drinks in their hands. Brass needed to find his way to the suburbs if he was serious about making money.

The people in the cabana were friendly, and even offered me some of the white stuff. I declined, explaining that I was cutting back due to the recession. They roared with laughter. I slipped into the darkest portion of the yard, a corner dark as an abyss, behind the pool house, and slowly drank the wine. In this moment of social awkwardness, I knew that it wasn't the party that was the problem, it was me. I stood under the shadows of a weeping willow tree with long leaves and dipping branches, and became an observer. I was far enough not to be seen. I watched in silence.

Sam, was talking to Delancey, and telling jokes to Delancey's mother and her friends. He had them laughing non-stop. Delancey's mother looked just liked her, tall, with regal features. When Sam told jokes, he couldn't stop laughing. Sometimes he could barely get the punch line out.

The ladies laughed, and one reached over and held the Harvard pin on Sam's lapel. She then moved her fingers slowly up and down his arm and shoulder. Sam looked very comfortable in this situation. On the other hand, I was insecure about my outfit, my hair, my shoes, my looks, and my family's lack of money. Even my wallet was feeling insecure.

Sam told the ladies that he had been accepted to Harvard, and that his father was a doctor at New York Hospital. He was a really big hit, more so here than in high school. He was meant for parties outside of school. Delancey was glancing around, looking for someone. She leaned in and asked Sam a question, to which he shrugged and pointed in my general direction.

Sam was having a great time, talking to everyone he could. One of the pleasant things about acceptance o Harvard is that it happens to be a great conversation starter. Acceptance to a state college was really not much of a conversation piece. I finished my wine and gazed at the stars. It was a clear night, slightly cool, and there were more stars in the wealthy Long Island night sky than there ever was in all of Queens. You get a lot for your taxes out here. I was only about 30 miles away from home, but it felt like I was in another country. The Pinot Grigio was good, sweet, but dry.

I stared up at the heavens, noticing Orion's belt, and the Big Dipper, and wondered if I would ever live in a house like this, if it was in my stars. I thought about my family, and how poor we were, and how my mother had worked long hours for such little pay before she passed. My father was good, hard working and honest. I wondered if we had some sort of family curse that prevented us from living a better life. I remembered a quote from last year's English class. I said it out loud, "the fault lies not in our stars but in ourselves."

"Hamlet, right?" said Delancey.

I was startled by her voice, and didn't realize she was standing right behind me.

"That's right," I said. "Nice party. Thank you for inviting us."

"It's my pleasure, thank you for coming. If it wasn't for you guys, I'd have no one here to talk to, no one here to quote Hamlet." Delancey glanced at the party, and seemed lonely to be apart from the crowd.

"It's for a good cause....I'm sure we are really helping out someone by being here, even though we can't contribute much. What exactly is the fundraiser for?" I inquired.

"It's a fundraiser to restore Ellis Island and make it into a museum," Delancey said proudly.

"Ellis Island has been closed for so long, why not leave it closed or why doesn't the federal government restore it?"

"Ellis Island opened in 1892 and has been closed since 1954. Twenty million passed through Ellis Island as immigrants. Millions of people in America, that is if they are of European decent, can trace their roots to an ancestor coming and stopping off at Ellis Island. Imagine, you get on a ship across the world, and you are waiting to get to America at Ellis Island. Diseases, death, poor conditions, medical inspections, all kinds of stuff, and then you were either sent back or allowed to come ashore to New York. It is too important a place to forget and ignore. If we wanted it screwed up completely, then yes, we would let the government handle it." She laughed, exposing the fire behind her eyes, and a passion for making things right. She really would make an excellent lawyer. "Actually, the president asked for this to be completed with private donations. Lee Iacocca, the chairman of Chrysler, is heading up the fundraising across the country. This is just a party to thank some of the donors. Ellis Island is going to open next year, and a great museum will open to the public."

I rolled my eyes and said, "Museums are for the deceased. Do we really need another museum in New York?"

"It's too much a part of the world's history not to make it into a museum."

I decided to change the topic. The last thing I wanted was an argument.

"Who's house is this?"

"It's my mother and stepfather's. They were married about four years ago. This is where I live on the weekends."

"It's a beautiful house, some property."

"Don't be intimidated by it. It's just a house, although it's nice to have ten acres," she said genuinely.

Delancey summarized that her stepfather was a Wall Street money manager for mutual funds. She offered to have her stepfather, Bruce, tell me more. Awkward silence filled the air between us. We both glanced down at the grass.

"I don't have many friends at Stanton," she said.

"I find that hard to believe; you seem so popular."

"It's true, there's no one that I really hang out with or can feel comfortable with. Except for you. I can't seem to relate to other teenagers...but for some reason, I feel I can have a real conversation with you." She looked down, feeling shy, or maybe just being coy.

"So why are you hanging out by yourself behind the cabana? In the dark?" she asked.

"You know, I really like it back here. I'm actually a big fan, an aficionado of cabanas. It's going to be my major in college—I will major in the design of cabanas." We both giggled at my sarcastic joke.

"You don't have to feel uncomfortable or awkward. These are really nice people. I know it's probably not your scene; it's not my scene either, but they are harmless." I couldn't help but stare at her lips.

"What gave it away, was it my suit?" I asked.

"I like your suit; it reminds me of my trip to Greece a few years ago. We had a bartender that had a similar one." We both laughed again. She drank my wine as I held the glass.

"So what's the deal with you and Svetlana? Is she here? Did you bring her? Its funny…but she doesn't really strike me as your type."

"No. I told you she, there is nothing between us. And what exactly is my type?" I asked.

"You are more cerebral, more bohemian, and I think you would like someone…uh…a little less developed, less busty, more demure… with an American accent." She was holding back her laughter, her eyes gleaming.

"How come you know so much about me?" I was astonished at her assessment.

"I always thought that you were interesting, and I guess I just paid attention. But, now that you are with Svetlana, I guess I really don't know anything about you." She glanced down.

"There's really nothing going on between Svetlana and me. We were friendly, but nothing serious. Its…well I can't get into it, but there is really nothing. I never even asked her to the dance, she just kind of invited herself to go with me. Don't believe Sam. She and I recently became friendly over the incident with Mr. Zoose," I tried to reassure her.

"I did hear about that. I thought her Russian accent turned you on, as opposed to my American accent. But I have to admit, I was a little jealous, I may even have thought that I had lost the cold war," Delancey was grinning.

"Well you didn't. And you don't have an American accent Delancey…you have a Long Island accent….everything west of us is America…this is different, you're different….." The wine was kicking in, and I was feeling much more at ease.

Delancey hit me on the shoulder and said, "Don't tease me about my Long Island accent."

"I wouldn't dare. I love your Long Island accent."

"You lllovvve my acccentt?" she said, slurring her speech. She didn't need any more wine. Our eyes met and she held my hand. She looked beautiful in the moonlight. We were alone, behind the cabana, in the dark, and I leaned in, put my other hand on her neck, and kissed her softly. She responded in kind, and we kissed for several minutes. I felt electricity between us, and the warmth of her skin against mine, through our clothing. I moved my hand softly up and down, caressing the curvature of her back. She was awesome to touch.

She looked at me and smiled. "I've wanted to do that for so long."

"You're a great kisser," I said, "and great to kiss."

She said that she really needed someone to be close to. I would have liked to be that someone, but reminded her our time was limited since we were graduating in a few months. She said that it was fine, for as long or as short a time period as we had. "There is life after high school, you know," she whispered in my ear. "We can be friends for all eternity."

"Is that what you want, just to be friends?" I asked.

"I don't want to think about the future or about categories of friendship. I just want to spend some time with you here, under the stars."

I kissed her again and we embraced. If there was ever a moment in my life that wished I could freeze forever, if there was ever an instance that I hoped could endure until the end of time, this would be that moment. I held her closer, feeling every breath she took. I didn't want to let go, and we stayed in the embrace for a minute or two.

"What about Svetlana?" she asked.

"What about her? Are you jealous?"

"Mr. Gorbachev, tear down that wall," she said, giggling like a little girl.

"It's done. But I am probably still going to the dance with her. I might be obligated," I told her.

"You still have to dance with me," she said eagerly.

"Absolutely!" I shouted.

We went back to the party, and I felt more comfortable. And it wasn't just from the wine. I shook hands with a few people, even saw an artist's rendering of Ellis Island depicting its restored appearance. The building still seemed eerie, even in the painting, which was an optimistic vision. I met Delancey's step dad, by way formal introduction, and she told him that I had some questions on his line of work.

"Well, what can I answer for you, besides how much money I make?" Bruce Yuridis laughed, shaking my hand.

"Don't worry sir, I would never ask anything like that. I'm curious...what did you study in college, and how did you end up in your field?" I asked as politely as I could.

"I went to a state college, and studied English and history. It's a long story. After graduating, a friend told me about an opening at his financial firm. They needed someone to write brochures, and draft and edit letters and prospectuses to clients. I signed on, and gradually learned more about the financial side of the business. When an opening came up in finance, I interviewed and got the job." Bruce seemed happy to tell the story.

"Wow, I would've guessed that you majored in economics or finance or something business related," I said.

Bruce had dark hair, and a stocky build. He wore a blue blazer, white shirt, camel colored dress pants, and no tie. He walked away, and motioned for me to follow, greeting various people along the way. He led me into the house. We made a left off the kitchen, and headed down a long hallway filled with pictures of Bruce with famous people. We arrived in his office, a medium sized room, with marble floors, and dark mahogany finished walls. The shelves held old leather bound books. On the far wall was a refinished English shield, the kind that knights took into battle. Near to the window was a large antique desk, and some pictures from his college days.

Bruce sat down in a hunter green leather chair that had an unusually high back. He swiveled around, removed a cigar from his humidor, and lit up. He offered me a Cohiba, but I declined. Bruce poured two glasses of scotch, and placed one in my hand. This time I could not decline. We clicked glasses, and he said "Salute."

I drank the scotch, not thinking twice. The scotch was smooth, and did not have an after burn.

"How do you like it?" Bruce asked.

"It's good. I'm not much of a scotch drinker," I said.

"I should hope so, its $200 a bottle. Single malt, 25 year old scotch that I brought over from Scotland."

"Its the best drink I'd ever had." I remarked gratefully.

"That's more like it. So...you are a Stanton man?" he asked.

"Yes sir, I am. I'll be graduating in June," I said proudly.

"I grew up on Long Island, but I know the Stanton reputation. My father went there." Bruce paused, taking another sip. "I grew up in Massapequa, in a middle class neighborhood. Where are you from?"

"Astoria, Queens."

"Sure...I know Astoria, lots of great Greek cafes and restaurants. Gotta love that souvlaki. Now I understand your outfit." We both laughed.

I sipped more of the scotch and it went down smoother. My posture was relaxing, and I was feeling intoxicated and was slouching in my chair. I glanced around the room. He had various antiquities. I saw an antique Grecian urn on a pedestal, and a marble bust, as well old paintings of mythological scenes. On the far right corner, he had a statue of a man's body with a bull's head on it.

"You buzzed yet?" he asked.

"Maybe a little."

"I know you never actually asked, but I'm willing to offer you my advice. Believe it or not, people pay plenty of money for my advice. "

Bruce took a long sip of scotch, and I remained silent, contemplating my luck tonight. There was no chance for a poor kid like me to ever get advice from a person at Bruce's level. My ears perked up.

"Go to any college you want, and major in anything you like, and it could lead you down a career path that may seem unlikely and completely unexpected. I have friends from college that majored in liberal arts, or history, and they are bankers, and stockbrokers. Of course, they had to pass the series 7, but your major in college shouldn't determine anything. Keep in mind that this is America, the land of the capricious and it's becoming normal to have three or four career changes in one's life time. Success boils down to how hard you work, whether you are good at a certain field, or if you interview well or make an impression on people. I see that your friend Sam is going to Harvard."

"Yes. He's practically been accepted to all the top schools in the country and he's graduating at the top of our class." I wasn't certain why I needed to paint an accolade filled picture for Sam.

"Harvard is one of the best schools in the country, and probably the world. A lot of people here are impressed with that stuff, but I listened to and watched Sam, and I wasn't impressed. Sure he says the rights things, but he seems like a real suck up."

I laughed. "Bruce, I guess you can really read people."

"I've been around a long time. Look here's the deal. Harvard is as good as it gets, but not everyone that goes to Harvard excels in life. Some become very good in their respective fields, but Harvard is filled with legacy, nepotism, and political favors. The kids that attend the elite prep schools are destined for Harvard, and they have the ability to pay without financial aid, which is a big deal. Keep in mind, its harder to work your way up from nothing. I personally would have never felt comfortable at Harvard when I was your age. I come from a blue collared background, my father was a cop, my mother was a housewife. I loved state college. There were more kids like us there, and it was a lot of fun. But, whether it's a state school, or an ivy league school, you gotta make the most of it. You gotta try everything, do everything, meet everybody, and just live it up. It'll be the most important four years of your life as far as personal development. The academics are important but not as important as your personal development. The last thing you want is to leave college the same as when you entered. That would mean that you did not develop." Bruce puffed his cigar, and drank a more scotch.

"I have friends with kids in the Ivy League and other private schools, and they really abuse the alcohol and drugs, like the kids do in the state colleges. Its bad stuff and it doesn't discriminate. The Ivy League is for the cream of the crop, but a regular college is for rest of the crop. Go to any college, into any field you want, just make sure its something you are good at and you will find a way to make money. Any questions?"

"I'm not sure about the public school versus the private school thing." I took another sip, and the room starting to swing.

"Listen…if you can afford private then go, and if you can't then don't. That's a decision that your family's circumstances make for you. Real people, in the real world, would never judge people by where they went to college. That's something that only ivy leaguers do. They like to feel good about themselves by hiring other ivy leaguers, and socializing with people from the same college, but it's a lot of non sense. Elitist crap. These blowhards jog with tee shirts that read Yale. What a load of crap. How would they like it if I jogged around wearing a tee shirt with my net worth in bold numbers?"

Bruce leaned back in his chair, cigar in hand. His hair was thick and slicked back, his skin tanned, and he looked the very essence of success.

"This is going to sound silly," my guard was down from all the booze. "I play guitar, I actually play it very well, and I'm not sure if I should pursue a career in music or go to college."

"David, why not do both? Why limit yourself? I've never heard you play guitar, so I really do not know if you have any talent. But why not audition, write music, join a band, and still take come classes. Nothing has to be one or the other. Any other questions?" Bruce placed is hands behind his head, and propped his feet up on the desk.

"Any advice on women?"

"Don't marry an actress, too much drama." Bruce chuckled to himself. "Women get a little crazier every year you spend with them. Men get more boring in return." He poured us both another scotch, and then glanced out the window, his back toward me.

"I'll tell you this in all seriousness. Be careful who you date, and who you have a long term relationship with. Women, and some men, are changed by everyone they are with. Whenever a woman is with a man, whether it's for one night or for ten years, her soul changes, her emotional stability changes. It's like watching a flower being pollinated by insects. Like an asteroid colliding with another asteroid. There are some impacts that last forever. When I was younger, I met a woman and we had one date, just a single cup of coffee. She was gorgeous, and nothing else ever transpired, but I can still remember every word she uttered, every time she looked at me, and what she wore, and even her smell. I can remember every freckle, and every time her eyes lit up. I can't recall anything about what happened last week, but this woman, thirty years ago, Wow! Her image is embedded in my soul. I've known a lot of women and I'm not saying this to brag. I can see it on their faces. Women keep secrets, but it's always the same secret. They never stop thinking about the men they've been with, and they always wonder what if things had been different. You can always find a woman sipping a cup of hot tea while picturing her life differently. I don't want to lump all women in that category; I would never do that. I am speaking generally. For example, if a woman is quiet and lost in deep thought, I guarantee you she's thinking about a man from her past or a decision that she wishes she could reverse. Women are complicated and their complications get more complex each year."

I drank the rest of my scotch, not really having any input into the conversation. It wasn't exactly my area of expertise.

"Your best bet is to find a woman with as much experience in love as you have. Someone a lot more experienced will tie a harness around your neck and steer you like a mule." Bruce became lost in thought for a minute, and then returned to the conversation.

"The world is changing faster now than ever before. Look at the protests in China and in Georgia, Russia. There is outrage at oppressive governments. Something like that probably would never have surfaced ten years ago. Governments are unable to keep how they treat their citizens a secret. Communism is slowly changing to capitalism, but the real change is how unacceptable it is becoming for a government to repress and massacre its own people. There's probably going to be a lot of jobs created by the changes, for Americans, to either go overseas to work or something similar. The American economy is bleeding, David. Manufacturing jobs are going overseas, and I don't see that changing. Engineering jobs are vanishing. Once America starts bleeding, it may not stop. And it's not just the economy that's changing. Look at this Exxon Valdez spill. Its an outrage—fifteen years ago, people wouldn't have cared as much about the wildlife and the environmental impact of anything like this. The environment's going to be important in the future. We're just starting to discuss Global Warming, but this issue is not about to go away. It's going to impact everything. And in the business world, things are changing fast with computers. The way we do things is outdated and being replaced by new technology. Look at my desk, I have three phones on it, and I have a beeper. I fax things now that I would've waited for in the mail. It's really unbelievable. I just bought something called a cellular phone, take a look." Bruce handed me a rather large gray phone, it was about eighteen inches long and weighed nearly three pounds.

"With this phone, I will be able to call anyone from anywhere. It's going to be the next big fad." Bruce reached out for the cellular phone.

"I'm sure that's just for rich people," I said.

"That's what everyone said about television and now every house has one. Some people even have two." Bruce was having another scotch, and suggested that I have one as well. I declined, I was already feeling drunk.

"Try not to pick a career based on what will be hot in ten years, because things change fast. Look, if you're interested in something, and good at it, there's probably a future in it worth researching. Like your guitar playing. If you love playing the guitar, then pursue it." There was a long pause of silence when Bruce stopped talking.

"This is some office," I said.

"You probably think that I have the best life and you would love to trade places with me?" Bruce spoke in a strange tone.

"Yes, I have to admit, it has crossed my mind."

"Fine. Let's trade seats." Bruce stood up and walked over to me, and I then sat in his big hunter green leather chair behind his desk. It was luxurious; the leather was soft as butter, and I definitely liked the view from his side of the room. I felt powerful. I felt strong.

"How does it feel?" he asked.

"Really great," I said.

"Look up."

In the ceiling directly above my head was a large, sharp, metal sword that I had not previously noticed. It seemed to be held up by nothing, just air, and I gulped, thinking that if this sword fell on top of me, it would slice me in half like an orange.

"What's holding it up?" I asked.

"Ten pound fishing line...It's an 11 pound sword," Bruce said.

"You mean it's barely being held up?"

"That's right. It could fall at any time. Beware the sword of Damocles."

We shook hands and he thanked me for coming. I thanked him for the advice, and the scotch. I went back to the party thinking that I just had the most important conversation of my life. Delancey was looking for me and waved in my direction. Sam was jealous that I had a closed door conversation with Bruce.

"How did it go?" Delancey asked.

"Awesome. Just awesome. He's quite a guy, with great advice, and a lot of knowledge and insight. I think it was the best conversation I've ever had with anyone about my future."

"Bruce is really great. I keep threatening my father than I am going to change my last name to Bruce's last name, Yuridis. It keeps my father in line." We held hands and strolled in the back yard for a few minutes.

Sam's father was waiting outside. I said goodbye to Delancey and Bruce. Her mother waved goodbye from a distance. I didn't say more than two words to her mother all night. Sam was annoyed when I gave Delancey a warm embrace and a kiss on the lips.

On the way back home, I talked non-stop about what a great party it was. Sam was speaking Farsi to his father, although his father's English was flawless from what I remembered.

"My father doesn't want us going back to Central Park. He says it's too dangerous," Sam relayed back to me. "He wants us to promise that we will not go back."

"A woman was beaten and raped by a gang of thugs in Central Park this week. New York is very dangerous, and you have a bright future. Don't ever go back." Sam's father was adamant about it.

Sam's father did not know about last weekend's events in Central Park, and how close we came to getting our heads blown off. He would be greatly alarmed and probably lock Sam in the house if he'd known.

That night, I stayed awake for a few minutes thinking about Delancey and my conversation with Bruce. Sam was always jealous and annoyed when anything good happened in my life. What kind of a friend was that anyway? I thought about the woman that had been attacked in Central Park, and I wondered if she was attacked by the same thugs we confronted last weekend. If my gun had bullets, and I had shot these hoodlums, would that woman have been left alone?

chapter 19

I WENT TO work at the café the next morning with a terrible headache. Scotch and wine are not a good mix. Shesha and I talked while we worked. Shesha loved American women. I told him that I was at a party with a really nice American girl the night before in Long Island. I explained that she was just a friend.

"I don't understand this American concept of having a female friend. In Pakistan, there is no reason to have female friends. If you like a girl, you sneak into her house and try to have sex with her. Here in America, sex is allowed, and all you do is talk on the phone, go out in public, but remain friends. I just don't understand this country. In this country, the women like to have sex, and everything is in the open, and you are still a virgin. Explain that to me!" Shesha yelled. Christine had just arrived and started laughing.

Shesha saw that I was embarrassed and he yelled at her to get back to work.

"In Pakistan, when men are talking, the women know better than to interrupt."

There were many tourists and the day moved quickly with dozens of customers coming in every hour. Finally a lull came around eleven o'clock. Shesha told us to clean up and restock. Christine turned on the radio and started dancing. Shesha was watching with baited breath and biting his lower lip. It became embarrassingly apparent that he was aroused by Christine's dancing.

I asked Christine to show me some dance moves for the April Dance. Shesha threw wet sponges at us and yelled "Get back to work!" We were all laughing. It was a lot of fun working at the café that day.

At quitting time, I walked to the subway with Christine. "Have you heard from Eddie Lo?" I asked.

"I did. He is in hiding, but he is okay," she said. "The rival gang from the pool hall wants him dead."

I practiced some dance moves at home, and Harry laughed at how bad I was. He gave me some pointers.

The day of the April Dance came, and I decided not to wear my Greek night club outfit. I went casual, as nervous as could be. Svetlana and I agreed to meet at the gym after school. Sam was planning on attending the dance against his parents' wishes. He had a rough weekend after letting it slip about the situation in Central Park. His parents freaked out and wanted him home immediately after school, without delay.

I stopped by the school's newspaper office to check on whether the writers had turned in their assignments. Doreen was working on the paper, disheveled as usual, and not dressed for the dance.

"Are you going to the dance?" I asked.

"Why would I go to the dance? I have too much work to do." She looked down, and although her long scraggly hair covered her face, I could tell by the tone of her voice that she was unhappy.

"Is every thing okay?" I asked.

Doreen never lifted her head, never raised her eyes, but when she said "fine" I instantly knew she was upset.

I remained silent, pretending to look over the articles, while waiting for more of a response from Doreen. A few minutes went by; she lifted her head. She had stopped crying.

"David, I don't know what's wrong with me. No one asked me to the dance. No one asks me to anything. I feel like I'm invisible in this school. It's just a stupid dance, but it sums up four years of high school for me. Invisible. I'm not part of the in crowd, and I'm not even part of the out crowd. I'm part of no crowd." She wiped her tears, and walked out of the room.

Part of me felt that she was to blame for not trying to be more social, for being too engulfed in the school paper. I also knew that it wasn't her fault. High school is a strange time in a person's life. It was difficult to be friends with someone as intense and tightly wound as Doreen. At an elite college, with type A personalities, she would likely make a lot of friends.

Mr. Mash made an announcement warning against inappropriate dancing. Everyone in the hallways that heard the message laughed and gyrated their hips.

I had never seen so many girls doing their hair and make up. The dance started at four o'clock, and lasted until half past six. No one had the time to take the subway home, get dressed, and come back to school, unless you lived close by in Brooklyn. Svetlana said that she was going home to change, and that she would be back by five o'clock.

This struck me as odd because Svetlana seemed already dressed to go to the dance. I asked her why she needed to change.

"I feel underdressed compared to some of the other girls," she said. Her face cast a genuine look of worry.

Compared to what the other guys were wearing, my Greek Night Club outfit would've been perfect. Something that isn't appropriate at a party in Oyster Bay can be just fine at a party in Brooklyn. Lesson learned.

The dance was at the gym. Maurice was there wearing a white shirt with a skimpy leather tie and a fancy jeweled buckle. He wore leather pants.

"You look like a Jewish pop star," I said.

"Neil Diamond is my hero," said Maurice.

We drank Coke. There was plenty to go around since the world's largest beverage company was sponsoring the dance.

There were fifty television monitors stacked on top of each other, showing music videos and ads for Coca Cola. Shiny disco balls hung from the ceilings, large speakers were stacked on top of each other, and multi colored balloons filled the gymnasium. Banners hung from the ceiling with advertisements. The gym looked very cool. I asked Maurice if he came with anyone and he said that he was meeting a girl named Rachel here later.

"What about you?" Maurice asked.

"I'm waiting for Svetlana," I said.

"Svetlana Kalishnikov?" he asked.

"Her name is Ionakov" I said. Kalishnikov was her nickname, after the Russian assault rifle used in combat. The nickname meant that she was dangerous, because of her gorgeous physical appearance.

A smile lit up Maurice's face. He held out his hand to shake mine. "I have to say, that is very good news my friend. She's a beautiful girl, and I would've thought she was out of your league. But, I am very happy for you," said Maurice.

I was pretty sure that was a back-handed compliment. But I knew what he meant.. Maurice's shirt was unbuttoned revealing his chest hairs and gold necklace.

"Thank you, but we are just friends, nothing serious," I said to Maurice.

"Nothing serious yet, but just wait my friend, God has big things in store for you," said Maurice laughing, and using hand gestures, made a reference to Svetlana's breasts.

The gym quickly filled up, and the music was loud. The deejay played a lot of British Rock and new wave music. There was pop and dance music thrown in as well. Mr. Mash stood behind the deejay, supervising the music play list. Sam was standing next to Carlos.

The dance brought out the hairstyles and the clothing iconic of the decade. Everyone had big hair, tons of hairspray, and wore things that we would now consider bizarre.

Delancey was in one corner of the gym, with some of her friends, as Sam approached. I couldn't hear their conversation, but saw Delancey shake her head "no" twice. Sam walked away. Delancey waved to me, and I walked over.

"So are you going to ask me to dance or what?" she said.

There was no sign of Svetlana. "Sure, would you like to dance?"

"Love to," she said as she grabbed my hand and we started dancing. I moved as best as I could. Sam was in the distance watching with a grimace.

Delancey was a pretty good dancer, and she looked stunning. Her hair was blown out, and she wore a blue denim skirt, with boots, and a white shirt. We danced a few songs, and I became more relaxed and comfortable on the dance floor.

"I had a good time at the fundraiser, and no regrets," she remarked.

"I had a great time too, and have been thinking about you ever since." She blushed and giggled.

Juan Perez was watching with envious eyes. The dance floor was now nearly full. Sam was still trying to find a girl to dance with. Acceptance to Harvard doesn't mean social acceptance in high school.

I was having a lot of fun, and almost forgot about Svetlana. It was after five o'clock, and Delancey and I finally took a break. I went to fetch us two cans of Coke. Free soda was a big deal. I walked over to Sam. He didn't say anything or look my way. Carlos said that I was quite the dancer. He had his backpack on, and I wondered if there was a gun in it.

"You know, I think that the jeweled gun is the same gun that Delancey's father had given to her for her birthday." I had to shout into Carlos's ear because the music was so loud.

"I have it on me, in the backpack. It still doesn't have bullets. It's no good to me."

Sam overheard our conversation and grabbed Carlos's backpack. Sam said that he was going to sell the gun to get some money back.

John was not at the dance; he had to work. Carlos said that he meets with Brass everyday for work. It was amazing that Carlos referred to drug dealing as work. Carlos's outfit was very sharp, dress pants, dress shoes, and a silk shirt. Working for Brass was paying well.

I figured Svetlana must be running late because of the train. Yulee was dancing with Penny. Jacob and Sandra were dancing together. Sandra looked beautiful as always, and Jacob kept looking around the room at all the other girls. Jacob motioned for me to come over.

"Are you here with anybody?" he asked.

"Svetlana," I replied. "But she's not here yet."

"I saw you dancing with Delancey. Be nice to her," Jacob said.

"We're just friends."

"I think she really likes you," remarked Sandra.

"Why do you think that?" I asked, blushing.

"She talks about you constantly. She turned down all the guys that asked her to the dance so that she can dance with you as much as she could," Sandra replied.

Wow! I was speechless. I regretted agreeing to take Svetlana to the dance. She wasn't even there.

Carlos said that Sam's mother came to get him and she was right outside the gym doors. This was not going to be good, I thought to myself.

I went over to say hello to Sam's mother, and saw that they were yelling at each other. She saw me and said, "This is your fault. Sam is not allowed to go to the dance. Why did you bring him here?"

"I didn't bring him here...," I said. They continued to yell in Farsi.

Sam's mother demanded that he leave the dance and go home. Sam insisted he was staying. Several other students gathered to watch their display of family love. I wasn't sure if Sam was aware that Delancey was watching.

Sam's mother grabbed him by the hand, and he pulled away. She grabbed him by the shirt and he pulled away again. Sam yelled expletives at her. I knew because he had taught us the vulgar words in Farsi. To most, it would appear that Sam then spit at his own mother, but Carlos and I knew that in fact Sam spat on the floor as an insult to her. She then slapped him across the left cheek, and threw her shoes at his head. Sam was red faced embarrassed. The public humiliation was too much and he started crying. Sam noticed everyone was watching, and he glanced at Delancey. His mother grabbed him by the ear and then dragged him out of school.

This was typical of Sam and his mother. We had seen similar exchanges at his house over the years, but now, everyone at school saw their relationship.

A tall, elegant woman with dark curly hair had entered the gym. She was wearing an off the shoulder white dress and looked like a goddess. She recognized me and said hello. It was Mrs. Zoose's wife, Juliana.

"Have you seen my husband?" she asked.

"I'm sure he's around; there are a lot of people here. I'll go take a look," I said.

I asked several if people if they had seen Mr. Zoose. No one had. Svetlana was also still missing in action.

A sick feeling started settling in my midsection. It was nearly six o'clock. There was no sign of Svetlana and no sign of Mr. Zoose. I was a good math student and had no problem adding up this simple equation. I quickly ran out of the gym. Down the dimly lit deserted hallway, Juliana was waiting for the elevator. I quickly ran up several flights of stairs, and headed for Mr. Zoose's classroom as fast as I could.

The door was locked, but I could see Mr. Zoose and Svetlana alone in the back of the classroom. I banged on the door and yelled, "Your wife is almost here!" I still felt obligated to him.

"It's almost six o'clock!" he yelled. He opened the door. Svetlana would not look at me. The sound of high heels was coming down the hall.

Mr. Zoose told Svetlana to hide under a large cowhide-print fabric that was in the corner labeled "Materials for School Play." I darted around the corner into an empty corridor. I knelt down on the floor and remained still. My heart was pounding and my panting was loud. Juliana was talking to her husband, my favorite English teacher, and

Svetlana's lover. Their conversation went on for a few minutes. They stepped outside the classroom, and she said, "Aren't you going to lock the door?"

"There's no need, the janitors have to mop the room," said Mr. Zoose.

"I like that cow fabric; maybe after the play I could use it to reupholster the chairs in the basement," Juliana said.

"Juno, sure, that's fine. I have a ton of it donated by one of the parents."

"You mind if take a closer look at it?" she said, her tone was curious, maybe even suspicious.

"Now? We are so late, Juno," he said.

I ran over to them. "Oh, there you are, Mr. Zoose, I ran up here to tell you that your wife is looking for you. But I see that she has already found you."

"Yes, I found him, but thank you anyway," said Juliana.

"Are you guys going to the dance? It's almost over," I said.

"Let's go to the dance, Juno, right away. I wouldn't want to miss it." Having said this, Mr. Zoose took her by the arm and down the stairs.

Svetlana emerged from the cow fabric. She was wearing the same clothes that she had arrived to school with that day. She had never intended to go home to change.

I recalled Bruce's advice about finding someone that had as much experience as I did.

"Svetlana, I do not want to be friends anymore." I walked away angry and more emotional that I wanted to appear.

"It's not what you think. I'm pregnant," she blurted.

I stopped in my tracks and did an about-face. "Does he know?" I asked.

"I told him, and he said that it wasn't his. But it's his. He's the only one." She started to cry, but I had seen these tears before, and they lacked the impact they originally had on me.

"So what are you going to do?" I asked.

"I don't know. I'm more worried about what my father is going to do. He's a little crazy and short tempered."

"I think you have a lot of decisions to make." I headed back to the dance disgusted with Svetlana and her lies, and also with Mr. Zoose.

This was their problem, their relationship, and they were not part of the plan I had for my life. I planned on graduating, leaving home, and never looking back. I felt like a fool for helping Mr. Zoose with his wife.

Mr. Mash was in the hallway outside the gym. He was waving goodbye to Mr. Zoose. "Are they leaving?" I asked.

"Yes. He's a fine teacher and will likely be promoted to Assistant Principal," said Mr. Mash proudly.

I was disappointed to hear this, but held my tongue.

"And Sam, of course, we are so proud of your friend despite the incident today. He revealed that students were cheating the day of the SATs."

My heart almost stopped when he said this. If anyone cheated it had been orchestrated by Sam. That is why he was so curious about whether I had seen anything in the bathrooms the day of the SATs.

"Sam is a fine student, the best of the best, and has made us all proud. You should be very proud of your friend," said Mr. Mash.

"Mr. Mash, there is so much that you do not know, I would hate to be the one to tell you."

"If there is something of evidence, something concrete, something that you need to say, come forward with it," said Mr. Mash.

"I will think about that, Sir."

"David. I wanted to talk to you about graduation," he said.

"Graduation, sir?"

"Yes. This year we would like to do something different. You know spice it up a little. The students are always complaining that graduation is too boring. Imagine how I feel; I have to sit there every year. I would like you to do a performance—guitar, vocals, whatever, with the school's band and chorus. You are musically the most talented in the senior class. The song choice is yours." He seemed eager.

"Any song!" I beamed.

"Yes."

"Then I would like to do Separate Ways by Journey!" After all, it was Delancey's favorite song.

"Well, fine. I will let the music teacher know. Keep this a secret. We want to surprise them at graduation."

Delancey was on her way to Manhattan. She said that her dad was taking her out to a new restaurant called the Osiris Steakhouse.

"I can walk you home," I said.

"I'd like that; it's not safe, especially for women." She was referring to the attack on the woman in Central Park. It wasn't safe for men or boys either.

We walked toward the subway. Delancey commented that there were a lot of Chinese gangsters hanging outside the school that day. She was right; they lined the sidewalks, and watched everyone leaving the school carefully.

"If you are not Chinese, don't worry about it," I said.

"It looks like they are looking for someone," she added.

There were about forty of them. They stood on top of cars, mailboxes, and the rest were on the streets. The gang formed a perimeter around the school. There was no sign of Eddie Lo. I surmised he was the target.

Delancey and I took the subway to Manhattan's upper west side. We talked about the dance and about Sam's obsession with her. We talked about her dad, and about Bruce. Delancey was genuinely the best girl I had ever known. She was real, honest, and open about her life. There were no secrets, no affairs with teachers, nothing to hide. I really liked this about her. We arrived at her building and I kissed her goodbye. We shared a warm embrace.

I didn't notice her menacing father nearby. He put his heavy hand on my shoulder and said, "That's enough." If looks could kill I'd be in a grave somewhere.

On the subway ride home, I deliberated telling Mr. Mash about Mr. Zoose, Svetlana, or Sam. I didn't want to be disloyal to anyone, especially to Mr. Zoose.

I pulled out a sheet of paper from my backpack and a pen, and started writing an anonymous letter to Mr. Mash. Maybe I wrote it because I was angry and felt betrayed. I'd prefer to think that my intentions were noble, and that I was doing the right thing, but I wasn't sure. I thought about Sam, and even felt guilty about being disloyal to him. I despised Sam for burning Doreen's college application. Was it my place to tell Mr. Mash about Sam? Was I doing the right thing or was I jealous that he was accepted to Harvard?

I wrote two paragraphs. The first was everything I suspected about Sam cheating on the SATs, as well as burning Doreen's application. I did not mention Carlos. In the second paragraph, I wrote all that I knew about Mr. Zoose and Svetlana. I signed the letter "Anonymous." I stopped by the post office and mailed it. There was no looking back; the letter would get to Mr. Mash that week.

Delancey was on my mind. A voice inside tried to talk me out of asking her to the prom. I could not afford to show her the good time she deserved. Juan was right; I could not afford a limousine. She might be embarrassed to be with me. I could hear Juan and Sam's voices in my head, but the more I listened, the more I realized they were all my own voice. We were from such different worlds, and I was too embarrassed to ask her to the prom. I had to be practical. I really couldn't afford to buy her ticket, a limo, and take her to the after party. I talked myself out of asking her to the prom.

chapter 20

IN MAY, THE news of Tiananmen Square and the photos that followed were the topic of conversation in history class. The image of a Chinese student protestor standing in front of a military tank could be seen in every magazine and newspaper, on every newsstand. Classroom discussions centered on freedom of expression and freedom to demonstrate one's opinion against the government. Mrs. Moynihan routinely showed the photos. A student from China explained a few things to the class about the Chinese government.

Wing King had arrived in America from China less than three years before, and felt the need to defend his native country. Wing was intelligent, a top student, and very proud of his Chinese background. Mrs. Moynihan was closed minded to Wing's nationalism. She explained that there were no human rights in China like there were in America.

"Mrs. Moynihan...American democracy is not a model for democracy for the entire world. China's government is not looking for 1960's American type protests and riots," Wing said.

"The 1960's protests were of the Vietnam war. Sometimes the police got carried away, but there were no official government tanks that tried to run over students," Mrs. Moynihan said. She proudly added that she was speaking from experience.

"I was referring to the treatments of blacks, and the Civil Rights movement. They protested against segregation. But the protests against the Vietnam War are a good example as well. America is not the model for human rights given what has occurred. China has been here for thousands of years, and changes are slow. The Chinese government will make changes, and if it takes one hundred to two hundred years, it is considered very quickly." The class laughed at Wing's time frame of quick change.

"Well, here in America things don't take that long. A change is voted upon and enacted by Congress and things change much more quickly," argued Mrs. Moynihan.

"The laws may change quickly, but the minds and memories of a nation change much slower. That's the real change. I am sure that black people and Native Indians do not feel the same way about the quickness of change," countered Wing.

"You really should say African Americans and Native Americans," said Mrs. Moynihan, impressed that Wing knew so much about American history.

"In thirty years, China will be the most powerful country in the world. Then the Chinese government will become the model for democracy that the United States is today," said Wing.

"In thirty years, China may be a powerful nation, but the United States is not going to disappear," I said. "The United States will still be a superpower and a model of democracy that will be on display to all nations. The United States will still be the most powerful country," I said.

"America is already bleeding—jobs, corruption, crime, diseases. Trust me, David, the bleeding can't be stopped." Wing held his chin up in the air.

"Why is that? Why would China become a model for democracy?" asked Mrs. Moynihan.

Wing remarked, "Because the most powerful nation on the planet has to set the example in order to become stronger in people's minds and not just on paper. Real superpowers are respected and feared without exercising their might."

"Well said," I replied to Wing. "But I think America will come back. We always do." I complimented Wing's knowledge of international politics and excellent English language skills. He had been in the states for such a short time.

"I studied English for ten years before I came to this country. Do you study Chinese here?" he asked.

"I think Chinese is only offered in colleges right now," I answered. "You must have also studied American history."

"Yes. I have seen the pictures of the protesters, the dogs, the hoses, and police brutality. You should not be so quick to condemn China based on pictures of Tiananmen Square, given your country's history."

"America has learned from its past, and continues to make changes and head in the right direction. Can you say the same about China?" I asked.

"Only time will tell, but yes, changes are occurring in China, and soon the Chinese Army will be the most powerful in the world," Wing said.

"But will communism survive or give way to democracy?"

"We have democracy in China, its just not American democracy," commented Wing.

I held up a picture from a magazine of the Chinese Student at Tiananmen Square standing in front of a tank and said, "Is this what you call Chinese Democracy?"

"It will get better," Wing said. The bell rang, ending our debate, and we walked out together in the hallway.

"If you don't mind, can I ask you to explain the difference between a Republican and a Democrat?" Wing asked me.

"There is a well known and simple way that a journalist once explained it. Let's say that you go out to dinner with four friends. Everyone orders something different—steak, lobster, a salad, and someone just has an appetizer. Everyone drinks something different—water, soda, scotch, and champagne. The bill comes. Now a republican wants everyone to pay for what they ordered. A democrat wants the bill split evenly in four ways."

"I see. Which one are you?" Wing asked.

"It depends." I answered smugly.

"Depends on what?"

"On what I ordered and how much I ate," I laughed. Wing laughed a moment later, but I wasn't sure if he understood the joke. "What about you?" I asked.

"I'm from the People's Republic of China...we eat family style and I like to taste what everyone else ordered." He catches on fast.

"Well then that makes you a communist," I said.

"Actually, that makes me full," Wing responded.

I was writing an article about the top athletes in school and where they were to attend college. Mino did not get a scholarship, but was accepted at a big ten school in the Midwest. I wondered how he could afford it. In my interview, Mino said all the right things about feeling honored, being excited, and the making the most of the opportunity. He looked depressed. I asked him if he was okay.

"I don't even like football. I'm sick of it. I lied to my mother and told her that I received a scholarship."

"What are you going to do? How can you pay for it?" I asked.

"Where there's a will, there's a way."

I interviewed Kenneth from the basketball team. He talked about his full scholarship. I quoted him in the paper "I have no regrets about high school; I did everything I wanted to."

Sandra from the swim team was able to get a half scholarship to a State school. Jacob was going off to a different college, and she was realistic about the future. She added that if Jacob really cared for her, he would go to any lengths to be with her.

Many seniors were staying in the state, as the national economy headed south and the best deals were within our own state college system.

The choice for me was made—I came from a poor family, and we could not afford an expensive private school. For middle class families, there was a real debate. The expense of private schools might be worth the reputation for them. A top private school could really open doors in the future. I went to see Ms. Eris. She was in her office and welcomed me in.

"What's on your mind?" she asked.

"I'm second guessing everything. I've been accepted to a state college, I can't afford a private college. I don't know if I'm making the right decision by even going to college...because...I want to pursue a career in music. I just don't know."

"This means that you are a normal high school senior. All your fears, all your concerns, all your second guessing...it all boils down to the same thing. You have a fear of the unknown, just like everyone else. Up to this point, your father has made all the decisions in your life. But now it's up to you. You fear the unknown world outside of high school. It will be fine no matter what direction you choose. There is life after high school. Just make sure that you accomplish all that you needed to while you are still here, because one day, ten years or twenty years from now, you don't want to look back and have regrets."

For the first time Ms. Eris made sense.

Carlos was waiting for me.

"What's up?" I asked.

"I have a problem. Someone told Mr. Mash that I was one of the students that cheated on the SATs. Mash knows all the details. Do you know who turned me in?" asked Carlos.

"Did you cheat on the SATs?" I asked. Carlos hesitated, but I stared at him, arms folded, waiting for answer.

"Several of us brought cheat sheets and dictionaries into the boys' bathroom that day. The SAT board is saying that our scoring was too similar and it indicates cheating, but they also know how we cheated, in detail, so someone told them."

"Carlos, did you ask Sam?" I said.

"I did. Sam said that I shouldn't blame him for cheating and getting caught. There were a few of us that cheated. Sam was one."

"I think that only someone involved could have given that information." Carlos had already figured this out before he came to meet me.

"I guess it was Sam," said Carlos. I didn't have to tell Carlos that it was Sam that ratted him out. Mr. Mash had obviously received my anonymous letter and what he did with it was his decision.

About an hour later, I finished my article and left Doreen and the rest of the newspaper editors for the last time. It was rewarding working on the school newspaper and although things took twice as long because of everyone's egos, it was still a valuable high school experience.

Carlos and Sam were walking to the subway. I caught up with them and John also joined us. The four of us had not been together in a few months. We walked by the psychic. She called out Sam's name. Sam looked at her and kept walking. She said, "Betrayal."

Sam had been staying at John's place. The incident with his mother at the dance did not end at school. Sam had shown up on John's doorstep at midnight looking for a place to stay. Sam had argued with both of his parents after the dance. He and his family exchanged various slaps, pushes, then objects flew, dishes were broken, and various people choked each other. Sam then locked himself in his parents' room, urinated on their bed, and was consequently thrown out of the house. John took him in. Sam asked persistently if he could spend a few nights at my place and I agreed reluctantly.

"Sam, did you hear that there was cheating on the SATs?" I asked.

"There is an investigation as well," John said. Sam remained quiet.

"Mr. Mash said that a student came forward to expose the cheaters," John added.

"Sam, what miserable student would've come forward to turn his friends in?" Carlos asked.

"It was me," said Sam.

"How could you turn me in!" shouted Carlos.

"I didn't. Mr. Mash started asking me all kinds of questions. I turned in the others and they must have mentioned your name to Mash."

"Why would you do that?" I asked.

"It's wrong for them to cheat," said Sam. "They would not have scored as high without cheating and it really ruins the rankings."

"But you cheated as well," said Carlos.

"I don't consider it cheating. I enabled you guys to have my answers in the bathroom, but I did not cheat," said Sam.

"But we could not have cheated without your help!" yelled Carlos.

"I helped you, but I did not cheat off your answers. Besides, I have a bright future at Harvard and you guys don't. The impact of your cheating is greater than the impact of mine," said Sam. "Your cheating caused you to score above what you normally would. Mine did not."

There was no reasoning with his logic, and I really did not want to see Sam go into an emotional tailspin, so we left it alone. Carlos was heated but he did not say more.

Changing the topic, I asked Sam if he would consider giving Delancey her gun.

"She's rich; her father can get her another gun. I need the money and I am trying to sell it." I argued that it wasn't his money to begin with, but Sam's logic didn't see it that way.

Sam came home with me and I made him a bed on the couch. John's parents no longer wanted the responsibility of having Sam at their home. My father was not happy with the situation and felt that Sam was still a child and should be home with his parents. I explained to my father that Sam was going to Harvard and that hardly made him a child. My father responded that anyone who urinates on their parents' bed is still a child.

During dinner, my father said to Sam, "I don't appreciate that Iran held fifty-three Americans hostage for more than a year."

"I don't either," said Sam.

"I'm not a big fan of the Shah," said my father.

"I don't like puppet governments set up by the CIA either," Sam smirked.

"Why can't Iran get its act together?" asked my father.

"Look, I'm Persian but I can't defend Iran. But I tell you this, the Persian Empire was all that an empire ever could be. Look around at the influence of the Persians in Europe, in mathematics, in architecture. We were once the greatest of all the empires. When the Persian Empire ruled India, it was the Persian ways that they brought with them. That's why the Taj Mahal still stands. That's why people from the northern part of India to the southern part of Europe, to the northern parts of Africa look a little Persian. Persian literature and architecture influenced...." My father interrupted Sam.

"The Mughals ruled India, not the Persians. They were Timurids, from the Mongols of Genghis Khan's army, not Persians," said my father. My father usually ate dinner in silence, and never discussed history and politics.

"They were Islamic, and not Zoroastrians like the Persians had been. They ruled Iran the same time they ruled Central Asia. And it was a Mughal king who built the Taj Mahal. It still stands because it is a symbol of his undying love for his wife who died. It still stands because when you create something out of all your love, all your pain, all your emotion, it tends to last forever."

My father had just blown my mind.

"How do you know all this?" asked Sam, stunned as I was, but only because it was the first time that anyone ever corrected his view of the Persian Empire.

"I didn't go to college, but that does not mean I'm not educated," said my father. "My father came from a British colony in South America. Half of the population were indentured servants from India."

"And what about the other half?" asked Sam.

"Mostly Africans, but some Portuguese, Dutch, British left over, and Chinese."

"Why such a mix?" asked Sam.

"Like most nations in the western hemisphere, its history was of a search for gold. Different parts of Europe colonized the Guyanas They all came searching for El Dorado. But when Europe abolished slavery in the early part of the 1800's, it really ended only the African slave trade. So they went to India for their labor, with the same slave boats from the African slave trade and brought indentured servants to the Caribbean. They packed the Indians in tight, as they did with the slaves. The trip was twice as long as a trip from Africa. The Chinese came as well. It was called Indentured Servitude but working without pay is called slavery." My father went back to eating.

I was really impressed with his knowledge.

"Some of the boats crashed due to storms. That is why so many people in the Caribbean look Indian. They may be Jamaican, or Dominican, or from Guadalupe, Trinidad, etc. but they have Indian blood of indentured servants."

"What happened to the gold?"

My father gave a deep sigh, leaned back and said, "All that glitters isn't gold."

"Your self education is very impressive, sir," said Sam.

"There's too much emphasis on a college degree, and not enough on real education," my father said.

We finished dinner, and watched television. At eleven o'clock, there was a knock on our front door. We never had visitors that late.

My father opened the front door and found Sam's mother. She threatened to call the police and report that Sam was being held against his will at my house. She sounded and looked the part of a raving lunatic. My father ordered Sam out of the house at once. Sam wasn't surprised by his mother's unexpected presence at our house. He quietly got dressed and left. He climbed into the back seat of his father's car, and they drove off. I've seen happier faces in the backseat of police cars.

"Never again," my father said.

That weekend at the café, everyone was on edge about the attack on the woman in Central Park. Christine told Shesha that she couldn't stay late anymore and would prefer to leave at three o'clock. Shesha refused her request and said that she had to stay until six o'clock.

"I found out about Eddie," Christine said to me at the end of the day. "He's in real trouble. The Tongs have ordered him dead; his own elders from his own gang. Eddie had gotten into a personal feud with the rival gangsters that he shot. Eddie dropped out of the Chinatown gang, and is going by a new name—The Serpent," said Christine.

"Have you heard from him? Why do they want him dead?" I asked, recalling Eddie's Stanton basketball uniform read Stanton Serpents across the top.

"No one has heard from him directly. He shot and killed a rival gang member on his own that day in the billiards hall. In order to avoid a war between the two gangs, the elders have ordered him killed for his actions. "

"Who did he kill?" I asked. "The son of a Tong from another gang, a guy named Johnny. He didn't mean to kill him in the pool hall; it was just self defense. It's very dangerous for Eddie, too dangerous," Christine said worried.

Eddie could have had a bright future in college, but now it really didn't matter. On the subway ride home, I thought about Eddie Lo's violent side, and Sam's emotional problems. These were two smart students at one of the most competitive and highly reputable high schools in the entire country. I thought about Eddie playing basketball, and how he'd been offered his dream, a scholarship to play at St. John's and how he had ruined this opportunity. Eddie was accustomed to a life of crime; it was all that he expected out of life. He could not consider life beyond his Chinatown Gang. It was hard to conceive that this was my roommate from the high school senior ski trip. It was hard to believe that this was the coolest guy that I knew. Now his days were probably numbered.

The next week there were many Chinese gangsters outside the school. These were not like any gangsters I had ever seen before. They were older, rougher looking, and looked like they had already done hard time. They must have thought Eddie was still going to school at Stanton.

Delancey and I were growing closer. I walked her home nearly every day that I could. We were both worried about crime. She was uncomfortable about the presence of Chinese gangs outside the school. At times, there were forty to fifty gang members. They surrounded the school.

"Why do you think they are here?" she asked me.

"Chinese democracy," I replied.

We went for cheesecake and coffee. Delancey expressed that her mother wanted her to go away to college in California. Her father preferred that she go to school in Boston. She explained that it had been an agonizing decision.

"So what did you decide?" I asked.

"I'm going to Vassar," she said.

"I guess we won't be that far away, maybe two and half hours by bus. Maybe I'll come and see you once in a while." We both knew that we probably wouldn't see each other at all after high school. We sipped coffee and ate cheesecake. The silence was deafening.

I was head over heels in love with Delancey. She was a beautiful girl, inside and out. We would both grow and develop into adults by going away to college, but it would also quell any chance we had of getting serious with each other.

My heart ached and my appetite receded. If I could do it all over again, I would've gotten close to her earlier, as early as the previous year. But I had lacked confidence, and always felt that she was out of my league. She looked up; her eyes were glazed over with tears.

"I wish we had more time," I said, as my voice choked on the words. "Here we are and it is already May of our senior year."

"I wish we had different circumstances for our futures," she said. "But if something is meant to be, then it will happen."

She meant that we were approaching a fork in the road. We were going to take different paths.

The ride to her father's apartment in the city was in silence. I held her hand, and threw my arm over her shoulder. We were both saddened, realizing how little time we had left. I walked her to her building on the West Side of Central Park. We were affectionate for a few minutes. Now that we knew that our friendship had a deadline, things were different. I went home, a little depressed.

We ate lunch together every day. I grew more and more in love with her as each day passed. Sam was jealous of our relationship, and made no secret about it. Sam's greatest flaw was his inability to conceal his emotions.

There was a big change in my English class. Mr. DeJesus, the woodshop teacher, was now in charge of the classroom. Mr. Zoose had been fired, much to the shock, anger, and dismay of many students. I was angry with myself for writing that letter. I had betrayed my favorite teacher, the man who had come to my defense. Someone asked what a carpenter would know about teaching English. Mr. Dejesus replied that he was just a teacher now, and carpentry was behind him.

John called me at home, and reminded me that we needed to rent tuxedos for the prom. He knew a place with a really good deal. The next day, on our way to the tuxedo store, Sam started complaining out loud about my friendship with Delancey.

"I can't believe she's interested in you," Sam smirked in a jealous fit. "She should be going out with me. You can offer her nothing."

"We are just good friends, Sam. Besides, she likes me and not you."

"You're not even going to Harvard, I am."

"If that was a requirement, then you would date every girl in the school," I laughed.

"You can't even afford to date her. Your family is so poor. You live in that dingy small house." Sam was trying to start a fight.

"You mean my poor family who took you in from your lunatic parents?" I countered. Sam's face was turning red.

"You can offer her nothing. You're not even graduating at the top of the senior class. You're not an athlete; you are nothing." He paused, then said "And you will always be nothing. Your future is dim. You're not going to be a doctor or an engineer or anything, just a worker at a dead end job. Don't embarrass yourself by asking her to the prom. She could never say yes to you and embarrass herself in public that way. You're too poor for a girl like that."

"If you want to fight, just say the word!" I shouted. We were outside the tuxedo store.

Sam was not a fighter. To my surprise, Sam took a swing at me. He missed by a mile, and I swung back hard, hitting him in the cheek. Fight over. His face was red, and his eyes welled with tears, not from the pain of my punch, but from the pain of defeat.

We went inside and ordered our tuxedos, trying on the shirts and shoes, as well as the trousers and jackets. I looked in the mirror. I had never worn a tuxedo before. It made me look like an adult. The salesman came and took measurements. He would have to adjust it a little.

Sam was quiet the entire time, and I hoped he was regretting some of the things he'd said to me. I did not regretting punching him in the face, but what good did that do? It didn't change who he was as a person. It did not change how he really felt about me and Delancey.

On the way home, Carlos and I went back to my house.

"I thought you handled that well without losing your cool," Carlos said.

"I should have hit him a second time," I said. We kept walking.

"You should've hit him months ago....Brass has a real short fuse. People that lose their temper easily are not going to last too long in any business." Carlos's face displayed regret. "Are you having second thoughts about going into business with Brass?" I asked.

"I am. The guy is nuts. He's paranoid, and has already threatened to shoot me in the head. I told him that I want to quit his job and go to college. I've saved up a lot."

"I think it's a good move, Carlos. Working for Brass is not going to get you anywhere."

"I'm really lost when it comes to a career choice or even a major in college," he confessed.

"You don't need to figure it all out now. Just see what you like and what interests you. That's the hold that Sam and Brass have on you. They can steer you in their directions because you have no direction of your own." We walked to the nearest subway station.

"What about the SATs and the investigation?" I asked him.

"No one cares that Sam was involved. He's at the top of the graduating class," Carlos said.

"You are probably right," I said. "Stanton is not about to let a Harvard guy and a potential valedictorian take any blame."

"The rest of us cheaters have to re-take the SATs. They already cancelled our scores. I'm okay with it, as long as I still get to graduate." Carlos headed into the subway.

"I don't know why you hang out with that guy!" I shouted.

"I could say the same about you," Carlos said as he left.

There was something about Sam that made it hard to end my friendship with him. He was a terrible friend, and an obvious user. But he was smarter; more sophisticated, and always found a way to hang around. It was too late to do anything about my friends. There were only a few weeks left until I graduated high school, and what would be the point in changing the people that I hung out with now?

At school, it was very difficult to focus. It was a perfect May spring day, and a percentage of students were not turning up for all their classes. This included Sam, who could be seen on the concrete steps of the neighborhood brownstones. He was hanging with Juan Perez, smoking, loitering, and doing nothing. Juan seemed to like smoking pot with Sam. They both hated the fact that I was close to

Delancey, and they were both attending Harvard in the fall, so I guess they had a lot to talk about.

The cafeteria was empty. I gazed out the window and saw many students at the park across the street. Some played Frisbee and hacky sack; others just sat on the grass relaxing. Stanton did not enforce too many rules on the senior class at this time. The school year was nearly over, and the students had little left in their gas tanks anyway.

I had two Regents exams in June, and four finals. I was in a lethargic mood, but was intent on not skipping any classes. After all, this was my last opportunity for the rest of my life to be in high school...why miss anything?

I decided to find Detective Ganz after school at the Brooklyn precinct. Eddie Lo was on my mind.

I waited at the precinct for an hour. Finally Ganz emerged carrying a box filled with his personal belongings. He wore an overly starched white shirt, making him look very stiff. He was wearing a loud tie, and overly pressed pants. His hair was grayer, and still slicked back. There was no mistaking this guy was cop. He even walked like one.

"Did you get fired?" I asked, referring to the box in his hands.

"Even worse, I got promoted," Ganz said smiling. He was moving to a new Special Task Force division in Manhattan called the Asian Gang Intelligence Unit. He would operate out of the Fifth Precinct in lower Manhattan. The police now knew that Chinese gangs were a big problem.

"What can I do for you?" he said.

"We have to talk about Eddie Lo."

"Who—The Serpent?" said Ganz.

"Yes. I wanted to tell you that he killed someone, and that in order to avoid an all out war between the Chinese gangs, he's been ordered dead by the Chinatown Gang elders."

"This part I already knew. Do you know where he is?" asked Ganz.

"I don't. But I would hate for him to get killed."

"Then find Eddie Lo and get him to come in for police protection," said Ganz while he chomped on a chocolate doughnut.

"Eddie Lo is not exactly into keeping the peace. Word on the street is that Eddie has a short fuse, and takes everything too personally. " Ganz poured himself a cup of coffee.

"There was an incident at Tekk Billiards; he shot another gangster. The whole thing was self defense." I figured I'd tell Ganz everything since it may save Eddie's life.

"Well, I already knew that...I'm a detective...remember? And now Johnny Chan's dead. But Johnny's father is the head of a very powerful family. You really need to play pool with different people," said Ganz. "Eddie Lo can't risk showing his face. You know the gangsters that hang out outside of your school?"

"Yeah," I said.

"Well they think that Eddie may show up to school eventually. And they are looking out for him there."

"Detective Ganz, where do you think he his?" I asked.

"It's hard to find a serpent in the Chinatown underworld. Call me if you hear anything." Ganz gave me his new phone number.

I called Christine and told her about my conversation with Ganz.

"I doubt Eddie would ever go to the cops for help. But we have to try to convince him. He's going to get killed," Christine sounded very scared.

The owner of the café needed part time help on Fridays. I volunteered because I needed extra money for the prom. The owner had leased extra space next to the café to open a bar. My job was to clean the bar, and wash beer mugs and wine glasses. The place was packed; more than fifty people in a very small space, each more inebriated than the next.

The bartender was named Steve. He was really busy and told me to take orders for beer only. I poured twenty mugs of beer in my first five minutes, and then tried to keep up with the mess the customers were making.

An hour later, the crowd grew larger. I was pouring more beer and wine as well. Steve was making drinks with hard liquor and a frozen margarita machine. It was really busy, and I kept working at a pace faster than I had ever worked before. Steve was doing tricks in the air with rum bottles. He was talking to all the customers at once, and kept them laughing and smiling with his jokes. Steve would take a shot of something or another, and keep working. He flirted with all the women at the bar, complimenting them, and bringing smiles to their faces. I was very impressed with his ability to connect with the customers.

After three hours, things cooled down. I finally caught my breath. Steve was exhausted, and soaked in alcohol. My sneakers were soaked with beer. I cleaned the counters and tables, emptied ten bags of garbage, and started mopping. Beer and booze had spilled all over the previously pristine marble floors of the bar. It took a full hour to have the bar looking neat and clean. Steve called me over.

"We were supposed to have live music tonight, but the guitar player is too drunk to function. Do you play guitar?" Steve seemed desperate and I agreed.

I played guitar with a small band, simple songs, nothing fancy. There was a woman singing, a keyboard player, and a drummer. They sang songs that everyone knew, the classics, and they had a guitar and sheet music with them. I even sang a little back up, and did a duet. It was a lot of fun, and when it came to an end, everyone cheered.

"Nicccee jobbb today." Steve slurred his words, and was unable to focus. He was exhausted, and also quite inebriated.

Steve pulled out the cash from all the tip jars, and counted it. "You get ten percent in addition to your regular pay." He handed me one hundred and twenty dollars. I was elated and asked him if it was always this busy. "Thursdays and Fridays are always this busy. I make out pretty good for the week just on those days alone."

Steve handed me a drink, and we started talking, while I cleaned. It was a margarita, and the salted glass rim made the tequila taste good. Steve looked like a California surfer type. He was an actor, auditioning during the day, and working as a bartender at night. He was from a small town in the Midwest and came to New York to try to make it as an actor. That was ten years before.

Steve had an incredible ability to make friends out of strangers. As some of the patrons walked by, Steve was quick with a joke and extended a warm handshake. People genuinely loved him. I supposed that this part of his personality was a necessity in his role as bartender. I had never known anyone with such charisma.

"So what are your plans after high school?" Steve asked. An attractive woman came over and sat next to him, rubbing his shoulders seductively.

I told Steve about state college, and although he could not speak or think clearly, he became quite passionate and animated about the topic.

"You are making a mistake. You are such a good guitar player and singer...definitely take a few years to pursue a career in music. You have talent, and not everyone has that." Steve was energized by the conversation. The woman agreed with Steve.

"Look, I'm gonna give the actin' bug ten years, and if it doesn't work out, I can go back to college, but I have to try to make it. I'm not gonna sit around in twenty years and regret not having taken a shot. If I don't make it as an actor, I'll live. So what...you know....The same applies to you. You got to give it a shot, so you don't look back. Just think...what if Babe Ruth had decided to be a bartender instead of going after baseball? What if Ronald Reagan decided to remain a B-actor instead of going into politics? What if Martin Luther King Jr. had remained a preacher and not become a civil rights leader? David, my boy...all I am saying is that you have to try, otherwise you will never know. There's an old saying...it's better to try and fail than to fail to try."

Steve closed up the bar and walked out with the female customer. I had spent a total of five hours with him and thought that he was the coolest guy I had ever met. Steve's words weighed heavily on my mind.

I would have liked nothing more than to make it in music, playing the guitar, and singing. Fear had been stopping me from pursuing my dream. As Ms. Eris said, fear of the unknown.

The next day at the café, Christine was panicking.

"Listen, everyone is thinking that Eddie is going to be at the Seaport this weekend. It's Memorial Day weekend and all the gangsters are coming to John street for some business. Maybe you should try to talk to him," said Christine.

"Do you think he would go into police protection?" I said.

"You have to convince him. Look, he doesn't want to get killed. He may think that you can help him up with the cops. Just talk to him and persuade him. Eddie can't walk the streets. The Dragons are harassing his family, and they burned down his store. It's a complicated situation between the Chinese gangs right now. I'm really worried about him. Everyone has become his enemy. He feels that there is no way out."

What would I even say to Eddie Lo?

Shesha handed me a note from the café owner. It read, "I need you to work Sunday night at the Seaport at my other store. Come around four pm. Work until two am."

That Sunday, Christine was a no show. I worked from seven a.m. until three p.m. at the café. Then I headed to the Seaport by foot, feeling anxious and nervous. The streets were narrow; and there were few street lights.

On holidays, the seaport attracted a few thousand people, until the late hours of the night. The owner's other cafe had sixteen flavors of ice cream, in addition to food. It was a hot Memorial Day weekend, and I probably scooped about a thousand ice cream cones. The ice cream was frozen, and it took tremendous effort to scoop the ice cream out of the bucket. My wrists were sore after the first hour.

There were three other guys working that evening, and one was Kenny. Kenny and I spoke for the first time in a long time. He told me that he was not going home afterwards but intended to sleep on the floor in the café. Kenny was terrified about a gang war at the Seaport that night. "I can't afford to get shot and killed; I'm the man of the house. My father's dead."

I asked if he knew anything about Eddie Lo, and Kenny said that Eddie was going to be "in play." I explained that I needed to speak to Eddie. Kenny said to wear a bullet proof vest. "Tonight is very dangerous. There's not going to be a lot of talking."

A nervous and unsettled feeling simmered in my stomach. Was I really going to risk my life in the middle of gang war to talk to Eddie Lo?

The Seaport was packed with several thousand people, mostly tourists. But there were quite a few Chinese gangsters lurking.

At the end of the evening, I could barely feel my hands. They were frozen and swollen from scooping ice cream. At two in the morning, and I cleaned up, but could not get the smell of ice cream out of my nose. I decided to take the safest way home—Gold Street, which was a two way street with bright lights.

There was hardly anyone on the streets. The Brooklyn Bridge was a monumental sight in the far corner. Closer to me was the Manhattan Bridge. The lights caused the bridge to glow, giving a resplendent view of the hundred-year-old bridge. I headed toward Gold Street, but was told to not cross by the police, who had closed it off for a parade in the morning. I went toward Water Street by way of John Street, but ran into the same road block. I had no choice but to go the way I came, up the narrow and winding corridors of Fulton and Ann Streets. This was a corridor of crime.

I walked up the cobblestone streets. It was very dark and the moon lit the way home. There were no street lights. No sign of Eddie Lo. A homeless man was in an alley. I kept walking. There were a few hoodlums at the end of the block. I was headed their way. Avoiding trouble, I crossed the street and noticed that the thugs were not looking my way. They were more focused on a tall shadowy figure in the middle of the street. I could hardly see. I held my hand out in front of me, and barely saw my fingers. The tall shadowy figure was getting closer.

I walked toward him, and could tell that he had high spiked hair, and a long black trench coat. My pace was slowing down.

As I drew closer, I started to think that this might be Eddie Lo. I walked off to the side of the street in case it wasn't him. Some commotion was coming from behind me. Four guys were about a hundred feet behind me. In a nearby side street, a small group of men sat in a parked black car smoking cigarettes. I kept walking, drawing ever closer to the tall shadowy figure.

My heart was pounding out of my chest, and I was sweating. My stomach had a sick feeling in it, and I felt like vomiting. If this wasn't Eddie Lo, there was a good chance I might be in the crossfire of Chinese Gang War.

The gangsters behind me started shouting in Cantonese. The three guys in front of me responded by shouting back. I looked over and the men in the car were heading over slowly. The shouting escalated. The hoodlums I had seen earlier were no longer there.

As I walked closer, a street lamp flickered, and I could see bright red and green Dragon tattoos on their arms. The other group was just a few yards from them. The men from the car were inching closer, but silently. The shouting continued. I kept walking, barely able to see in the dark. None of these gangsters was Eddie Lo. Instinctively, I dropped to the ground and tried to hide behind a parked car.

"Where is Eddie Lo?" one of the gangsters asked. There was no answer. "Where is EDDIE LO!" the man demanded. There was no answer. A shot was fired. The tall shadowy figure first slouched over, then dropped to the ground. Everyone dispersed.

I remained crouched down. The shadowy figure appeared to be dead. Police cars quickly arrived, sirens screaming, light flashing. Several police officers sprang out of two patrol cars, and asked what I saw. I told them that there was a shot fired, and that a black car had just driven away. Ganz arrived seconds later.

Ganz was drinking a cup of coffee and eating a sandwich. "So, is that your friend Eddie Lo on the ground?" he asked.

"It's not him."

Ganz finished his coffee and sandwich. "Then who's the stiff?" he asked. I did not reply. I told him everything I saw, the car, the gangsters, and everything that I had heard. An ambulance came and hauled off the body.

"It's a shame about these kids," said Ganz.

Ganz said he would call me if he needed any information. The streets were closed off, and by way of the headlights from the police cars, I could see blood on the streets.

I walked to the nearest subway station sickened from witnessing an execution. The corridor of crime was silent. All was dark once again.

A tall figure emerged from a side alley. Despite the lack of lighting, instantly I recognized Eddie Lo's silhouette.

"Hey," Eddie said. "I was hoping to find you here tonight. So what are my options?"

"There is a detective, the same guy from the Brooklyn precinct lineup. He wants you to go into police protection."

Eddie took a long sigh. "I don't know any way out of this. The Dragons burned my family's store down, and beat up my mother. If I step out into the streets and someone sees me, I'm dead. If I remain in hiding, they will continue to harass my family. It's a Gordian knot. In order to retaliate, I have to come out from hiding." Eddie glanced over his shoulders. "I'm at the end of my rope. I keep thinking that death is the only solution. I can't walk in daylight; I fear someone may see me. I can't go anywhere, and the longer I stay hidden the worse it gets for my family. There's no way out of this mess. I don't know what to do."

"Eddie, wait here. The detective is only a few blocks away. I'll go get him." He nodded. Eddie vanished into the dark alley. I ran back to the scene of the shooting. Ganz was still there. He was talking to another cop, but still managed to see me motioning for him to come over.

"What is it?" asked Ganz.

I told him that Eddie Lo was nearby. Immediately, we jumped into an unmarked police car, and drove to where I had seen Eddie Lo. Ganz pulled into the alley with his high beams on. There was no sign of Eddie. I came out of the car, as did Ganz with his gun drawn.

Ganz left the head lights on, and brought a flash light with him. The alley was empty.

"I guess Eddie didn't hang around," I said.

"On the contrary," replied Ganz, aiming the flashlight above us.

Eddie was on the second floor fire escape, hanging from a red rope. His body dangled in the cool morning breeze. Ganz walked back to his car, and made a call. An ambulance and several police cars arrived. I watched as they cut down Eddie's dangling body from the noose.

Eddie Lo had committed suicide. All the pressure had built up inside him. It was too much to handle. This was his solution to his Gordian Knot. I recognized the red rope from the ski trip. He carried it in case he needed a way out.

The sun was rising when I arrived home exhausted. I pictured Eddie playing basketball for Stanton, and how he had incredible game. He was fast, agile, and could shoot from the perimeter. Eddie not only had a short temper, but also a short life.

I fell asleep at eight in the morning. It was Memorial Day, a holiday, and there was no school. I slept like the dead and finally awoke at three p. m. I had a message from John, that he, Carlos, and Sam were headed to Rockaway Beach.

I called Delancey, but she did not answer. My brother and I hung around the house. I was mentally exhausted and emotionally spent. I picked up a newspaper. The Daily News had a small article about a gang war in lower Manhattan. They identified Eddie's real name as Yan, and said that he was one of the victims.

I told Harry everything that had happened that night. Harry was shocked. I tried to call Christine, but could not get her on the phone.

News had spread throughout the school of Eddie Lo's death. Students mourned in the hallways, and the cafeteria. The basketball team was called into a special meeting. The other students in Chinese gangs went about business as usual. Ironically, it was the non-gangster students that were most affected by the news of his death.

Yearbooks were distributed that day. The senior class had taken yearbook portraits at the end of Junior year. This was due to the large number of student deaths senior year. I flipped through the book, and found Eddie Lo's portrait. The coolest guy I knew in school was now dead. Eddie Lo could not sign my yearbook, or anyone else's yearbook. The photo was surreal, but another image was brandished across my mind. It was Eddie dangling from his own rope.

Flipping through the year book, I came across a picture of Carlos and me at the pool hall. It was the picture that Delancey had taken months ago. Sam was furious that he was omitted from the picture and slammed my yearbook onto the floor. I pushed Sam away, and he retreated.

Delancey was melancholic about Eddie passing.

"I had seen him play basketball many times. We were not good friends, but I feel a real sense of loss. He had a bright future. He is the eighth student death of the year. There's always nine."

I was not previously aware of the count.

"Eight?" I asked.

"Some kids were killed in a drinking and driving accident over Memorial Day weekend. It was Vivian and Grace. They were six and seven. They were at a party at a night club in the city." I did not know them personally.

There was a rumor that Sal was in a mental hospital. "We should go see him," John said.

By the end of the day, I kept think about how short life was, and how time was running out. Against all self doubt, I summoned enough will, enough courage, and tracked down Delancey.

"Delancey—we should go to the prom together," I said nervously.

"If you are asking me to the prom, you're too late. Sam told me that you managed to get Svetlana pregnant, and that's why you hadn't asked me to the prom yet. I'm going with someone else."

"I did not get Svetlana pregnant. She and I never had sex and we never came close. We aren't even friends anymore. Why would you believe Sam?" I pleaded to no avail.

"I know that you and Svetlana were close, hanging out all the time. I saw the two of you kissing twice. Everyone in school thinks that you got her pregnant. You were the only guy she was ever seen with. But you're too late. I'm going with someone else." Delancey stormed off in a huff.

I chased after her, grabbed her by the hand, and pulled her closer to me. I was aware that others were looking on, and I kept my voice down. "Sam lied to you, and you should have checked with me. He's obsessed with you, and he just didn't want to see me take you to the prom. Mr. Zoose is the father of Svetlana's baby." Tears welled up in her eyes. She was speechless.

"Is that why he was fired?"

I nodded.

"Why would you be friends with someone like that?" she said.

"Who? Sam or Svetlana?"

"Either. Both."

"I really don't know." I was angry with Sam and wanted to find him and strike him down with my fists. I really did not know why I was friends with him.

"You're too late; I've already said yes to go to the prom with Juan Perez. And I promised him that I wouldn't change my mind."

I was really bent out of shape. Not only did Sam, my so-called friend, betray me, but now Delancey was going to the prom with Juan. I went hunting for Sam.

I searched the cafeteria, and checked his usual hangout spots. Sam had set his trap; Delancey had fallen for it, and now he was nowhere to be found.

The rest of the week was miserable. Eddie Lo had a lot of friends at Stanton, and a lot of enemies as well. Different people had different ways of dealing with their emotions, and at times it included fist fights and throwing chairs. The basketball team was highly emotional over his death, and several members of the team were asked to leave the school as a result of fist fights. It was not clear why the fights started, but there were nearly a dozen of them. Chinese gangsters were no longer on the perimeter of the school. Their quest was over.

Delancey and I walked to the subway. She apologized for believing Sam.

"It's my own fault; I should've asked you to the prom earlier," I said.

"Why didn't you?" she asked.

I hesitated to tell her the truth, but she was standing on the subway platform waiting for an answer.

"I can't afford a limo or a fancy after party or nothing. I come from a poor family, and you are from a wealthy background. You never wanted to be my girlfriend and I thought it was for that reason. I can't provide the prom experience that Juan can or that you deserve. I've always felt that you are out of my league," I said.

"I don't want to be anyone's girlfriend, not just yours. I'm not that kind of person. I have so much ahead of me...the last thing I need is a boyfriend in high school. I invited you to my house, we had a great time together, and we were becoming friends. I never did anything to make you feel the way you feel. I think you are just too insecure. Besides, I can get a limo and I can get us into a fancy after party," she said.

"It's not something that you said, it's my mentality. I did not have the courage to ask you to the prom," I confessed.

Tear puddles were in her eyes. She boarded her train, and I watched it leave the platform. Then we went our separate ways.

I made a really big mistake. How could the girl I was completely crazy about go to the prom with someone else? I was devastated by my error. There were just a few weeks of school left, and I ruined a great ending to high school by not asking her sooner.

I walked a few blocks to the G-Train station. The train was late, and I waited and waited. Deceptors were everywhere. I couldn't tell for sure, because no one knew who they were, but I could feel it. The subway platform was packed, and a lot of my fellow Stanton students were there waiting.

The train finally arrived after a half hour, and we pushed and shoved our way in.

I stood in the crowded G-Train amidst the nefarious Deceptors. I looked over my shoulder frequently. Nearly a dozen of them were in the train car.

John walked over, and we both stood in the corner, backs against the wall. The graffiti-stained walls of the train trembled, and the lights flickered. John and I were expecting trouble and we were not to be disappointed.

The Deceptors demanded everyone's wallets. They pulled out their knives and weapons, punching and pushing the other straphangers. Some of the younger kids immediately handed their money over.

Old ladies were getting pushed around, and once they handed over their money they were kicked and slapped. The Deceptors neared John and me.

"John, I'm tired of this, and I'm carrying too much money to hand over." I had been paid in cash for working at the Seaport over the weekend.

"I'm with you all the way; let's just get one of these jerks," said John. This was not what I'd expected from John. He was usually more docile and laid back.

One of the Deceptors with a red bandana covering his face, approached with a knife pointed toward me.

"Gimme your money!" he demanded through the red bandana.

"No!" I shouted.

Red Bandana lunged toward mc. I swung a closed fist it landed on his left cheek. John kicked him from the back, only to be punched by another thug. John quickly punched each thug in the face. Red bandana thug fell to the ground. The train went dark for a few seconds. The lights came back on and John was on the floor wrestling two Deceptors. I kicked one in the ribs, and the thug turned his attention toward me.

The train stopped, and the doors opened. The Deceptors ran out. I helped John to his feet. John had a bloody lip, but seemed to be okay.

John pointed to blood stains on the floor. "One of them must have gotten hurt," he said. "Are you okay?"

"Just a little stinging in my arm," I responded. John pointed toward the blood on the floor.

"Is that your blood?" John asked.

The trail of blood seemed to be coming from me. I lifted my sleeve, and I was bleeding from the forearm.

"It's not that bad," I said. I honestly felt that it wasn't that bad at all, considering I wasn't in much pain. But a few minutes later, my arm was throbbing, and the bleeding wouldn't stop. John removed his gym tee-shirt from his bag, and wrapped it around my arm.

"You gotta get to a hospital fast," he said.

"Not here in Bed Stuy. I'll get killed on the way to the hospital," I said. Bedford Stuyvesant was not the safest neighborhood in Brooklyn to say the least.

"You're crazy! You can't wait until we get to Queens. Let's go now!" John said, as he pulled me off the train.

John and I exited the subway, and walked up to the street level. My arm was bleeding worse than before. John asked a pedestrian where the nearest hospital was, and the person replied that Wycoff Hospital in Bushwick was the closet. I was not happy to hear this, since Bushwick was too far to walk.

This is the most dangerous neighborhood in Brooklyn. People got shot here all the time. And there was no nearby hospital. We waited for the bus in front of a sign that read "Marcy Projects."

There was plenty of activity nearby. I looked up and saw someone on the roof. Cars were pulling up to the curb. A teenager in a green track suit approached the cars, and took money from the driver. Mr. Green track suit whistled loudly twice, and looked up. On the roof top, someone threw down a soda can, and it was given to the driver. We made eye contact with the roof top drug dealer. It was Mino Torres, Stanton's star running back.

John and I were shocked as the bus pulled up in front of us. We rode the bus to the hospital.

"Can you believe that was Mino up there?" John said. "I heard he was accepted to a great college."

"He's has to pay for college somehow," I said. "Mino didn't get a scholarship. He said where there's a will, there's a way."

At the hospital emergency room I gave the nurse a fake name. John looked at me puzzled. They sewed my arm and wrapped a bandage around me. The nurse said she'd be right back with some paperwork. I ran out, grabbing John by the arm. We ran non-stop to the subway.

"I don't understand...why did you run out? Why did you give them a fake name?" John asked me.

"My father does not have medical insurance and I can't stick him with this bill."

My grandmother was home when I arrived and asked what had happened. I told her that I fell on a broken glass. My father had been robbed last month and my grandmother didn't need more to worry about. This was New York, and this was normal. I really needed to leave New York City and never look back.

That night I couldn't sleep. I kept thinking about Delancey going to the prom with Juan. I was full of regret for not asking her earlier. Juan had talked me out of it with his comments. How could I let Delancey go to the prom with another boy? But what was I supposed to do anyway? She said it was too late.

chapter 21

THE FOLLOWING DAY, I sat down with Sam, Carlos, and John in the cafeteria. John yelled and berated Sam for telling Delancey that I had impregnated Svetlana. Sam exhibited no signs of regret or remorse. Carlos hurled an expletive-laced tirade at Sam. Sam and I were looking directly at each other. I was surprised at Carlos's outburst but Sam had betrayed him as well.

"I suppose you have every right to be angry. But I don't feel bad for what I did," said Sam.

I sat still, ate my lunch, and continued to stare at him.

"You know me by now, and you know what I'm about. I'm not into your little high school beliefs about friendship. Look around this cafeteria. Everyone has the same social beliefs...that high school friendships are important, and that I should play by the same rules. Not me. I'm here to try to be valedictorian and to go to Harvard, and I could not care less about the rest of you losers...I hope I never see you people again after high school is over." Sam looked at me for a response.

I said nothing, knowing that if I remained quiet, he would lose it.

"And as for you and Delancey...I don't know what she sees in you anyway. I did not force her to go to the prom with someone else. All I did was tell her that you were probably going with Svetlana and that Svetlana happened to be pregnant. The two of you are not a good fit anyway. I mean, I didn't want Delancey to be embarrassed showing up to the prom with a poor, unsocialized bottom feeder like yourself…I just could not have her go to the prom with you instead of me. I don't care who she goes with, but not you. Not while I'm still in this godforsaken school." Sam was nearly in tears.

"Sam, I feel sorry for you. If you graduate and leave without making any long term friends, then you have missed the best part of high school. High school is not only about graduating. Not everything in life is a stepping stone," I said disappointed.

"The purpose of high school is not the same for me as it is for you. I'll get friends later in life, from college, from medical school, from my career. I don't need you losers." Sam was really on edge, his voice was wavering.

"Later in life, people will befriend you for how much money you make, or what you do for a living, or if you are colleagues. But real friendships that last a lifetime are forged in high school. This is when you are still growing and people become friends with you because they like you. It's never gonna happen again in your life," Carlos said.

"High school is for losers and once it's over, it's over," Sam replied. "High school is not the real world. In the real world, people like me, winners, successful people, they are the ones that matter most. Not the people like you, who remain desperate for over-valued and phony, emotional childhood bonds."

"The funny thing is that high school will never be over for someone with emotional problems and no true friends. For the rest of your life, you'll wish you had forged better friendships while you were here, because once it's over, it's over. You'll look back and always wonder why you have no real friends. Your immaturity and emotional problems will be to blame. Sam, you will look back, hoping and wishing that you could've done some things differently," I said and then walked out. John and Carlos came with me, leaving Sam alone at the cafeteria table.

At graduation rehearsal, I sat with Delancey. She was happy to see me. She said that we had such little time left and that I should try harder not to botch things up. I told her I would do my best. Juan Perez stared at us angrily.

June was a three week month for school. The prom was next week, and graduation the day after.

After school, John and I went to visit Sal at the mental hospital. When we arrived at Belleview Hospital, the front desk told us that Sal, or rather Ignacio, was all the way at the top floor of the building. We took the elevator, and while walking to the farthest wing of the facility, John had to close his eyes. The patients in the hallways were disturbing to see. Some were in cuffs, and some were in helmets. All were in hospital gowns.

The very last room in the left wing had a name plate which read "I. Carus."

I knocked but there was no answer. I knocked again, and still nothing. John turned the lock and opened the door.

Sal was crouched in one corner of the padded room, wearing a straitjacket.

"Hi, Sal, do you remember me?" I said.

Sal tried to focus. He had a hard time recognizing me.

Sal looked terrible. He hadn't shaved in days, and looked like he had stopped eating and sleeping. He stood up, using the wall for leverage and support.

"David? John? It's so nice to see you both." Sal was a shell of who he used to be. His voice was weak. He'd been the smartest guy in all of Stanton, the most scientific, the greatest of all overachievers and here he was in a straitjacket in a padded cell.

"What happened to you?" asked John.

"I went to the other side...for too long. I did not make it back before sunrise. I was gone too long. The other side. The undiscovered country. Lucy was there. I saw Wilson. I saw Albert. Everyone was there. It was beautiful. Four moons. Lots of lights."

"Sal, what are you talking about? Wilson is dead, Lucy is dead, and Albert is dead. You could not have seen them." John was confused.

"The Leviathon. . .it can take you there. . .sunrise is the deadline. David, death is not final. You know what I can do. I need more time to get back to normal. My mind is a mess. I see things, I'm far from normal. More time."

"Graduation is coming up, Sal," I said.

"I know. I've been invited to graduation. I wouldn't miss it."

We left the facility, shocked by the remnants of Sal's mind. He looked crazy, he sounded crazy, but I knew first hand that maybe he was telling the truth. . ..if not all of the truth, then some of it. John was devastated to see what had become of Sal.

On the subway ride home, we were hardly able to speak.

chapter 22

SATURDAY MORNING AT the café, Christine was understandably very somber.

"I'm sorry about Eddie," I said. "I did talk to him that night."

She appeared emotionally bankrupt and the energetic glow that she carried with her was gone. "I was supposed to be Eddie's date to the prom. He bought two tickets."

"Well, I don't have a date. You want to be my date to the prom?" I said without hesitating.

"Sure. Why not," Christine replied.

"He had a talent for basketball, and good grades...why couldn't he just stay away from the gangs?" I asked her.

"It's impossible when you live in Chinatown. It's like a whole different world. Underworld activity is a way of life."

"More like a way of death," I sniped. She was from a subculture completely foreign to me.

Christine wanted to go for sushi, like we used to do. This was something that I had really missed. But I had plans with Delancey for that evening. Delancey was not spending the weekend in Long Island. Her mother was out of town, and her father was opening a new restaurant in Boston.

Christine cried while telling me stories of how Eddie had fought off those who tried to tease her for her mixed ethnicity. She really opened up for the first time. We were starting to become good friends again.

Later, Christine said she was renting a room on Broome Street. "I can't live at home anymore. My mother and I don't get along. She kicked me out of the house. I'm working full time and I'll be finished with high school in two weeks. I'd like to go to college part time, and try to find a better job. I like being out on my own." With Eddie gone, she was definitely on her own.

Upon arriving at Delancey's building, the doorman greeted me with a friendly smile. The doorman laughed and said, "Don't look so worried; her father already left."

Delancey was happy to see me. It was early for a Saturday night, and I wasn't sure how we were going to spend the evening. We had not planned anything. I was less intimidated by her luxurious apartment.

No one ever looked more stunning in just blue jeans and a tee-shirt. We drank wine and talked for an hour about everything from state college to my childhood in Queens. She spoke about her life and plans for college. She poured more red wine from her father's liquor cabinet.

Delancey felt detached from her life, from school, and from her lack of friends. Her home life was difficult, juggling between Long Island and Manhattan, between her mother and father. Their divorce had taken its toll on her. Her father was always overbearing and controlling, but now her mother had become equally overbearing. She felt that everyone was pulling at her from opposite directions. Her father and mother were trying to poison her mind against the other.

"High school is really the beginning of the end for me. My father is going to open more restaurants in Boston, and unless I go to college in Boston, it's going to be very difficult to see him. My mother and Bruce are talking about moving to Miami. There's a lot of change happening in such a short time period. I really don't know, David. I'm starting to feel like I'm sinking into an abyss. I think I'm developing some sort of depression." She poured a second glass of the Merlot for both of us.

I looked at her face, and behind the smooth skin of a beautiful teenaged girl, I could see anguish, pain, and the weight of family pressure pushing down on her.

"David, I wish I could stay in my own little world and not leave New York."

"You're just depressed, but it's going to get better."

"Everyone wants me to follow in their footsteps as far as college and a career. There are just so many expectations. It's too much to take. My life is not even in my own hands. My choices are not mine to make." A single tear rolled down her cheek.

There was an intimate energy in the room; a soft, delicate bond of closeness had formed, with an undercurrent of something more. I'd never felt such warmth toward anyone. I thought that I should leave. I really didn't want to, but it was late. She walked me to the door, and we embraced.

She seemed lonely. I wiped the tears from her cheek, and said life would be different after high school. Delancey squeezed my hand and we kissed. I wasn't expecting that. But it continued further. Her full lips tasted like saltwater. We took a step back into the room and closed the front door. We kept kissing, at times delicately, at times ravenous. We ended up on her bed. Through her mesmerizing eyes, I could feel the essence of her soul, her essential being. She emanated vibrations of an old soul. She was so alluring, so angelic, so irresistible, with thick brown hair, and a beautiful, womanly figure. My hands caressed her tender shoulders, rubbed her supple skin.

She undressed, removing her tee-shirt and her blue jeans. I stared like a deer caught in the headlights. Truly, in all my life, I had never seen a sight so beautiful, so vibrant, and so full of life. I removed my shirt. I wasn't sure if I was ready to lose my virginity, but it felt like it was a good time, and she was definitely the right girl. We laid next to each other on her bed. I was nervous; she looked anxious as well.

I awoke about three hours later, and was a little foggy. Delancey was in my arms, and it was very dark outside. She asked if I was okay.

"I'm better than okay," I said.

"You know, I think I really love you," she blushed. I could feel warm blood rushing to my heart, as it started to beat stronger, not faster, but louder and with full force. I gushed with sheer joy as I started to get dressed. She sat on her bed in her bra and panties. I couldn't help but stare; this was all so new to me.

"I love you too, maybe for a long time. We're both leaving for college soon," I said.

"Why don't you stay here in New York, and go to college in the city. I can do the same; this way we can see each other all the time," she said buttoning my shirt.

"I really want to get out of New York. I've been accepted to state college and everything. I don't want to live at home any longer. I have very little here. I was planning on leaving and never looking back," I replied. It was so tempting to agree to stay home and see her all the time.

Now fully dressed, I started heading out of the front door. I glanced back at Delancey; she was still in her beige underwear. She was an amazing sight to witness and I took a mental photograph, knowing that it was something that I would never forget. Losing my virginity that day was completely unexpected, and completely wonderful. I felt drawn to her. The first cut really is the deepest.

"David, come on. Stay here with me. New York has everything; there's no place like it. We could have a great time going to college here in the city." She was very convincing. I thought about changing my plans, and my entire future, just because she asked.

"New York is great for you, because you have money. Not so great for me; I live in the other New York, where it's mostly crime and anguish."

I tried her to give her one last kiss goodbye, and we couldn't stop kissing. The radio was playing. Actually, the radio had been on the entire evening. At that very second, something on the radio caught my attention. It was the song that was playing. It sounded so familiar...

"Delancey—the song that's on the radio!" I shouted.

"Yeah, it's a new song. I've been hearing it all day. Good song right? It's from my friend's band...."

"I know...I played guitar on the demo...that's me! That's me playing guitar on the radio! And singing backup!" I was elated. It was surreal...I was on the radio.

"When did you record the demo?"

"Weeks ago, one day after school. The manager said I could join the band!" I had to stop myself from jumping up and down.

The song ended, and we embraced. We kissed again; one thing led to another, and I decided to stay and live for the moment.

A few hours later, I needed to get dressed all over again.

I finally arrived home, in the wee hours of the morning, just as the sun was rising. My father, already dressed for work, asked where I had been. I told him that I had worked late and hung out with a friend. He was not happy that I was keeping such late hours. I told him about the song on the radio.

"Oh, that reminds me. Woody called for you yesterday. You may want to give him a call back at a decent hour; he said it was urgent." He left for work.

I took a shower, trying to wipe the smile off my face, but I was pretty happy. Harry asked what I was so happy about.

"I had a pretty good day after a long, long time," I said smiling. We had coffee together and I told him about the song, the band, and the radio. I told him that I had spent the night with Delancey. Harry was as excited as I was, about everything.

It was still too early to call Woody. I decided to call him from the café—I still had to go to work.

Shesha had baked half the muffins by the time I arrived, twenty minutes late for work. Quickly I picked up my own slack, and completed the rest of the baking. I could barely keep my eyes open from the lack of sleep. After twelve cups of coffee I was wired, and also consumed with nausea.

At nine a.m. I called Woody.

"David, have you heard the song? It's all over the radio!" Woody's excitement was uncontainable.

"Woody, I heard it last night. It was surreal."

"We need you to join the band. There are eleven more songs that need to be recorded in the studio for the album. This is your big chance, David! It's a once in a lifetime opportunity. We start recording the album in two weeks!"

The time frame would situate the day after graduation as the day we would be recording the album. I immediately called Delancey. First, I told her that I'd had a great time the night before. She said she had a wonderful time also. I said that her that I loved her, and then told her all about my conversation with Woody.

"What are you going to do?" she asked.

"I can't join the band and go away to college upstate. Maybe I won't even go to college. I really have to think about this."

"David? Are you serious? What do you have to think about? Why are you second guessing this opportunity? Just go for it!" Delancey was laughing. It was so simple to her, but not to me.

I mentioned that Christine was my date to the prom. Delancey was more than okay with it since Juan would not let her out of the date. He had bought her ticket, and rented a limo. She felt locked into the ordeal with Juan.

I worked the rest of the day with a lot on my mind. The band could flop; the whole thing might not even happen. Woody might be exaggerating the success of the song. The album could fail. If I was to forgo college, and the band went nowhere, what would I have?

The second guessing was wearing me down. Negative scenarios kept playing in my head. Maybe Delancey was right, there was nothing to think about. This could be a great opportunity for me. The whole thing might even work out...who knows? By the end of the day I decided to join the band and let state college know that I wouldn't be attending in the fall.

Before I left the café, Christine and I arranged that I would pick her up the night of the prom.

My first final exam was in history. I had studied on the subways for the past week. Svetlana was also taking the test. She had put on some weight and could not hide her pregnancy. I finished the test in a half hour, and then grabbed lunch. Carlos was also in the cafeteria.

"I'm not going to college. It's not going to work out," he said.

"What happened?" I asked.

"I quit working for Brass, and I had a few thousand dollars saved up."

"So you should have no problem paying for community college," I interjected.

"Well that's just the thing. Over the weekend, Sam called, we got together, and I made the mistake of telling him I had this money. We went to Beefsteak Charlie's, and had a lot to eat and drink. We rang up a large bill. I paid for it. Of course Sam didn't have any money. Then we went to Times Square to try to get fake ID for the prom after party and...well...the whole thing ended really bad; we were held up at gunpoint in Hell's Kitchen and now I have hardly any money left." Carlos was obviously disappointed in himself.

"Wow! Why didn't you stop at Beefsteak Charlie's?" I asked.

"You know how I get after a few drinks."

"And so does Sam," I said.

"It's not like he put a gun to my head; actually someone else did," Carlos said. "Sam has the uncanny ability to know what buttons to push. He convinced me that if I went to college I would be fed up with school in less than a year. Sam is a master manipulator. I really don't know why I hang around that guy. But I think it has to do with me and not him. I come from a pretty tough home life. My father is abusive to me, my siblings, and my mother. The good news is my father just left. I have not seen him in two weeks. I have to find a way to pay the bills and put food on the table. I can't work for minimum wage at a part time job—it's just not enough money. "

This was obviously very difficult for him to talk about. Choking back tears he said, "My home life is very difficult. It's not a normal situation. There is no money, no support. I have no guidance, no advice, no one looking out me. We fend for ourselves when it comes to finding something to eat. We're on food stamps, and maybe we'll be able to get some more assistance. I need to make some money and help out. I am not as smart as the other Stanton kids, or as athletic. I just don't think I'm good at anything." Carlos was starting to shiver. I didn't know what to say to him, but I knew I had to listen.

"Man, I don't even know where I fit in. I'm not sure if I'm Latino, Pakistani, or Indian. I barely understand Spanish, and I don't understand any Urdu. My parents didn't want me to forget about my roots, and I'm just lost. To be honest with you, I've been very depressed about my life. That's the reason I never bought bullets for that gun. I'm scared to have that option for myself. Sam sees this in me, and just brings the worst out in me. He emphasizes that I'm a loser. He knows what a loser family I come from. I know he is evil, but he goes out of his way to be my friend. Even if he is a user." Carlos could not go on speaking any further.

"If you can't fit in with any other nationality, well, that makes you an American. This is a country comprised of people whose ancestry didn't belong in their home country. Sam has no other talents. He seems to have a certain hold over people by just bringing out their worst fears and self doubts. He manipulates you and me and everyone else to his advantage," I said, understanding more about Sam.

"He gets a near perfect score on the SATs, and others have to pay the price. He gets you to start a mailbox fire, without any risk to himself. He is a smart student, but never participated in anything, zero extra curricular activities, but fabricates an entire student resume that gets him into Harvard. High school is not the real world, and I'll tell you this much; Sam can't fake it in the real world." We both digested our revelations about Sam.

"Look, Carlos, I know that you have a tough situation at home. But it's up to you to make it better. Once you leave high school, things will get better. High school is like a fish tank. You live in a limited environment and life on the other side of the glass is much better. I know you lost all your money. You needed it for your family, and for your future. We all know how you get after a few drinks, and I think Sam took advantage of that."

"College is out. Hey, it was probably never in. I want to try my luck at military life," Carlos said. "If I join the Marines, I'll get out of New York, and send my mother whatever I make. I can't take living here and seeing her situation every day. I think I'm better off and they'll be better off."

"You're pretty good with a gun, so I think it's a good move," I chimed in and we both smiled. Carlos actually would make a good Marine. He was smart and fearless in the face of danger. In all the time that I had known him, he'd never once fired a gun, although he almost always had one. College was not for him; he did not have the patience to sit in a classroom anymore.

"Besides, you like traveling, right?" I said.

"I'd love to see the world, and never look back," he said.

"Then join the Marines. It's a much better option than working for Brass."

"Brass was likely to lose his temper and blow my head off anyway," Carlos added.

"Who are you taking to the prom?" I asked, changing to a lighter subject.

"With my funds depleted, and the fact that I really don't know any girls at Stanton, I'm going solo. I bought my ticket when I still had money."

Svetlana was standing in the hallway outside the cafeteria.

"How are you?" she asked.

"I'm fine. How are you feeling?"

"I have some morning sickness but overall I'm okay."

She put her head down, and started fidgeting. She needed to say something more. Perhaps she wanted closure with this conversation.

We looked at each other in an awkward moment of silence. I thought about how much I liked being with her in the short time that we were friends.

"I'm still going to college to study pharmacy," she blurted out.

"I'm glad. You are very smart, and have a bright future ahead of you." I wanted to ask about the baby, but really didn't want to pry.

"I'm going to give the baby up for adoption."

"Have you heard from Mr. Zoose?" I asked.

"He called offering money. But my father nearly killed him. My dad confronted him and Mr. Mash. I have to move on. It was wrong, on so many levels." She started to tear.

She wiped the tears from her cheeks. "I know why I did it," she said. "I think that my relationship with Mr. Zoose was my way of coping with all the stress and pressure. It was wrong, and it has cost me dearly. But everyone in this school has problems and their own way of dealing. Some commit suicide, some are violent and join gangs. Some do stupid things. Some rebel against their families or situation. Maybe Mr. Zoose was my way."

I kissed her on the cheek and wished her the best of luck.

I went to rehearse for my special graduation performance. The music teacher, Ms. Virgil, had the sheet music for "Separate Ways." We ran through it ten times. It sounded good, but needed to be better. Members of the school band insisted the song was actually called "Worlds Apart."

Delancey and I had a bite to eat at Morana. The food was terrific, and it was free since her father owned the place. Mr. Kenmare was in Boston again. I smiled when she told me this, and Delancey smiled in return. We went back to her building afterwards.

The doorman flashed me a dirty smile as we stepped into the elevator. Delancey looked weary. We talked for a while about how close to the end of high school we were. She silently reached out and grabbed my hand. She pulled me toward her and we embraced. I loved being with her, in every way, in every shape and form. I grew more and more attached to her every minute that we spent together.

That weekend, we went to see a movie, but didn't see much of it. We were in the theater kissing the entire time. She was tender and warm. Being with Delancey made me happier than I had ever been in my entire life. After the movie, we went for dinner, at a Middle Eastern restaurant in midtown, Café Anubis. I ordered hummus, babaganoush and kababs, but Delancey hardly ate a thing.

On the way home, she had a hot dog from a street cart. "The works!" she shouted to the vendor. She was ravenous, and after gulping down the hot dog, she ordered another one.

"I guess you don't like Middle Eastern food," I remarked.

"Middle eastern affairs are better left to the middle east," Delancey said. Her father was still out of town.

We were intimate at her place, and I stayed until well past midnight. Whenever I was with her, it was like time standing still. I really didn't want to leave, but knew that if I wasn't home by a decent hour, my father would freak out. We drank tea, and ate desserts. She wore my shirt and nothing else when she walked around the apartment. "This will forever be my favorite shirt," I said.

There was a strong bond between us, and she easily made my heart melt. There were instances when I took the time to picture our future together, but I stopped myself, knowing that we were headed in two different paths.

When I was dressed, I kissed her goodbye. I looked back at her in the apartment. It was painful to leave her behind. As I rode the elevator down, my heart ached to be with her. I had never experienced anything like this feeling in my life. I was already so attached to her, so quickly, so deeply.

When I had arrived home, I apologized to my father. He was not amused and did not like the fact that I was home so late again. "My house, my rules," he said.

"I have good news for you. I will not be going away to college." My father smiled, looking happy for the first in a long time.

"I am joining a band. I recorded a demo with them some time back and the song is on the radio. I really want to give this a shot."

"David, I know. I spoke with Woody. Don't sign any contracts until we get a lawyer to read it. I hope it works out, and if doesn't then you can just stay home and go to college here."

Delancey and I went out for Chinese food. It was a hot summer afternoon, typical of June, and dark clouds started to gather.

We ate at a small restaurant called Yan Wang that only local Chinese immigrants frequented. It was dark, dingy, and without menus. Delancey knew Manhattan like she knew the back of her hand; otherwise it would have been impossible to find this place.

A waitress brought us dim sum, and Delancey spoke to her in broken Cantonese. I laughed out loud. Having heard Christine speak Cantonese, I knew that Delancey had butchered it. For sure it was the best Chinese food I had ever had. The waitress followed up with a big bowl of noodles with an unusually flavored meat. I asked what meat it was and Delancey replied that I should just eat and not ask too many questions.

Lightning flashed and a thunderstorm broke outside, quickly becoming a heavy summer squall. The restaurant's windows were battered with rain and wind. It seemed as if we had left New York and were caught in a monsoon in Asia.

The rains continued to come down hard, and Delancey and I raced through the streets of Chinatown hand in hand. We were getting soaked, and I grabbed her hand and pulled her forward. She screamed as the cold rain drenched us. We ran through the deserted streets, past roasted ducks hanging in store fronts. We were the only people caught in the torrential downpour. We took the train to the west side and ran to her building, still holding hands, getting wet all over again. Water dripped from our bodies into the lobby and elevator, all the way up to the top floor.

Delancey resembled a goddess from a painting I had once seen at the Museum of Art. Her make up and carefully brushed hair had been washed away, and her natural beauty was shining through. "You look more beautiful now than I have ever seen you."

We entered her room, and immediately took off our wet clothing. She threw me a towel, and put on a hot pot of tea. I was shivering. Although it was June, the thunderstorm had really cooled things off. Delancey changed into a tee-shirt, and threw me a pair of her father's sweat pants. They were huge, at least three sizes more than what I needed. I sat with my bare chest exposed.

She lit a handful of red candles, explaining that electricity was sometimes an unnecessary convenience. The room was visible by candlelight only, and the flickering flames made interesting shadows on the walls. Random flashes of lightning provided the only other light.

We sat on her bed and drank the tea. It was boiling hot, and it warmed my insides instantly. I placed my hand on her cheek, leaned in, and kissed her. Her skin was damp, as angelic as anything in this world. She glowed as her wet skin reflected the candlelight. She kissed me and removed her tee-shirt. We embraced and rolled in the bed for the rest of the afternoon. I don't think we ever stopped grinning, not even for a second.

She blew out the candles, causing white smoke to rise like swirling ghosts. We talked about our future. Delancey had sent her paperwork and deposit to Vassar. I told her that college was out, at least for now, and that I was going to join the band.

"I could drop out of college and tour with you and the band," she said.

It was a tempting offer. But I knew better.

"Your father would kill me if that happened!" I shouted. We stayed up talking for the rest of the night. It was an incredible feeling to have her so close, both physically and emotionally. It was early in the morning when I realized I had to be home before my father awoke at sunrise.

My clothes were still damp, but I could stay could no longer. The more I was around her, the stronger my feelings for her grew. She was like a magnet, pulling me in. I quickly dressed, and left her apartment, glancing back to see her sleeping face.

The subway ride home was desolate, providing introspection. Delancey and I had such a good thing, and it was coming to an end soon. I thought about long distance relationships. She would meet another guy, and I would meet other girls. We were both young and needed to live our lives. We needed to find ourselves, and not get tied up into a long term relationship at such a young age.

On Monday, the prom was the talk of the school. It was just a couple of days away. I needed to pick up my tuxedo and a corsage for Christine.

John and Carlos informed me that Sam was going to the prom.

We were eating lunch when Delancey walked into the cafeteria. I felt her presence the moment she entered, though my back was facing her and she didn't make a sound. It is difficult to explain, but I had developed a sixth sense when it came to her. She kissed me hello, and sat down at our table.

"Even though we have separate dates for the prom, I am planning on spending the entire evening with you and not my date."

"Me too," I said.

"I have some really bad news. My father is back in town but will be away on business after graduation. I'll be staying in Long Island. I don't have to come back to Stanton, I passed the swim test last week." Delancey was deflated. Our time was now cut short.

"I could come out to Long Island by train," I suggested.

"We'll work something out," she said sadly. She went to her next class.

John would be taking Helen to the prom, and Carlos was going solo. We decided to split the cost of a cab ride to the city. We would pick up Christine on the way. This would save us some money, and we would all be together the night of the prom. The three of us discussed picking up our tuxedos at the same time tomorrow. Sam would be on his own.

"Did she say swim test?" Carlos asked.

"Yes, she did," responded John. "Why? Are you worried?"

"I can swim; I'm not concerned about me," said Carlos.

Stanton had a strict rule. No one could graduate without swimming twenty-five yards in the school's pool.

"Does anyone know if Sam can swim?" I asked.

"I know for a fact he can't swim. When we went to the beach on Memorial Day weekend, he wouldn't go past knee deep into the water because he couldn't swim." Carlos smirked.

"How is he going to graduate without passing that test?" asked John.

"The rule is if you don't pass the swim test, you have to take the swimming instruction class in the fall, which would mean that he would not be able to go to Harvard," I said. "This was the one rule that was completely inflexible in the history of Stanton."

Sam never took the swimming instruction class. I remember seeing kids with asthma, the flu, and all kinds of medical excuses, taking the swim test in order to graduate.

Stanton was a school with a long history, and the swim test rule was definitely part of its history. The school instituted the rule as a result of the large number of graduating students that went into the Navy following World War II. There is a famous old photo of the graduating class of 1941, sitting on the steps of Stanton. That year, the boys were sent to WWII in the Pacific. Many Stanton alumni were on board the USS Indianapolis which sank during a submarine attack in the Phillipine Sea. The ship carried about twelve hundred crew and enlisted men, and three hundred went down immediately with the ship, upon a torpedo attack from the Japanese Navy. The remaining nine hundred waited in shark infested waters, without lifeboats, food, or water. Legend has it that six hundred seamen died, and of the three hundred survivors, all ten Stanton graduates on board had made it. All had passed the Stanton swim test with flying colors.

I wondered how Sam was going to get out of this one.

I practiced my song for graduation with the band. The music teacher decided to enhance the song, and she brought in back up singers from the chorus. We tried different approaches, including speeding up the tempo, and going heavy on percussion. The song sounded perfect.

I was concerned that my vocals would pale in comparison to the original song. The band Journey had Steve Perry as their lead singer and his voice was probably the most unique in all of rock history. Ms. Virgil, the music teacher said not to compare myself to the original because no one could sing with haunting pain and anguish like Steve Perry.

After school, Sam and Juan Perez were hanging out on the front stoop of a nearby brownstone. They practically hissed at me. I still couldn't believe Juan was taking the love of my life to the prom. I had no one to blame but myself.

I went to Delancey's building. She was packing for Long Island. We went to her balcony, overlooking Central Park, and had a cup of coffee together. As I held her in my arms, a warm feeling of happiness surrounded us like an invisible bubble.

The feeling wasn't just from the hot June heat. It was energy, a tangible, electric energy. We hardly spoke; rather we drank our coffee and smiled a lot. She went back to packing.

"I was in a huge fight with my Mom…we really got into it… about not staying in the city after the prom. But she really insists. She says it's not safe for me to be alone. I wish we had more time, David."

"As do I, Delancey." I kissed her goodbye as my insides were being torn apart.

My birthday was tomorrow, I was turning eighteen years old. I wondered if Delancey would remember. My father never remembered. Late that night, my home phone rang at just past midnight. I picked up immediately, sensing that it was Delancey.

"David," she said, "I really did something to tick off my father. I changed my last name to Yuridis. But that's not why I called. I have an idea. Can you meet me at City Hall tomorrow?" she asked. "Say about noon?"

"Why? What's at City hall?" I asked.

"It is your birthday tomorrow right? I have a present for you." I paused, and didn't say anything. It was weird that her present was at City Hall.

"Do you or do you not wish to see me tomorrow?" she asked.

"I do."

chapter 23

THE NEXT DAY at school was a half day and hardly any seniors were in attendance. Most students had taken the day off to get ready for the prom. Carlos, John, and I made plans to pick up our tuxedos later that day. But first, the three of us headed over to City Hall.

City Hall was just over the Brooklyn Bridge. We decided to walk, soaking in a beautiful summer day. Halfway across, I took a deep breath, and remembered Wilson, who had committed suicide off this very bridge. A dove sat on the guard rail of the bridge. "Wilson, you poor fellow, I wish you well in the afterlife," I said. John and Carlos shouted "Here, here."

Delancey stood on the steps of City Hall, looking giddy, and wearing a fancy white dress. She was a sight to behold. She smiled and gave me a big kiss. She said hello to John and Carlos.

"So what's going on?" I asked her.

"Oh, it's a good plan, David, a little crazy, but a really good plan," she giggled. "My father and I argued a lot yesterday. He enrolled me at Boston University without my knowledge. So I finally made good on my threat and changed my last name to Yuridis."

"Bruce will be proud," I said.

"But...last night I had the greatest idea!"

She took my hand, and led me inside. "I was here early, and filled out the paperwork."

"Paperwork for what?" I asked, completely confused. John tapped me on the shoulder and pointed to the sign on the wall, and my heart jumped out of my chest. The sign read "Marriage Bureau." I looked at it a second time, and it still read "Marriage Bureau." I stood there speechless. We were both 18, and didn't need parental approval.

"David. Will you marry me?" Delancey had a hopeful expression on her face. Everything stopped, and a deafening silence filled my ears. My heart pounded louder than ever before.

"Are you doing this to rebel against your father?" I asked.

"What if I am? Is it something that you don't want?" she asked. "Will you marry me?"

"Only if you marry me first," I said. John and Carlos were jumping up and down, as happy for me as I was for myself.

I signed the forms, and presented my I.D, and said I do. John and Carlos signed their name as witnesses. The entire event was surreal. A rush of adrenaline raced to my head. I felt like I was in dream. It was exhilarating. We were married at City Hall. I kissed her, and we walked out together, marriage license in her right hand. We wore two simple silver wedding bands that Delancey had brought with her. Carlos and John were laughing ecstatically, repeating that they could not believe we were just married.

"What now?" I asked, standing on the steps of City Hall.

"I don't know. I guess we will have to talk about this some more later."

We were dazed by what had just happened. I just married the girl of my dreams. Later that night was the prom. The next day was graduation. The day after, I would be recording an album. I made a decision and went full steam ahead. For this one instance, for this one moment in time, I was the happiest I had ever been in my entire life, and it is true even to this day.

A fancy black car pulled up. Before the driver could open the back door, Delancey's father, in a well tailored suit, stormed his way up to City Hall with all his anger and fury on open exhibit. I stood frozen in my stance, watching a hurricane charging towards me. I had forgotten about my new father-in-law.

"Tell me you didn't do something stupid today!" he shouted at Delancey. "Tell me that you didn't change your last name!"

"You're too late! I changed my last name twice. Yesterday it was changed to Yuridis while you were at work, and then today I married David, and changed it to Orpheus! And there is nothing that you can do about it. I love him!" Delancey yelled back to her father.

Mr. Kenmare stood directly in front of me, and grabbed her by the shoulders, his enormous fingers stopping the blood flow where they squeezed.

"You did WHAT!" he screamed. "Get it annulled now!" he demanded.

"I love him. I want to be married to him."

"I will disown you and you will lose everything—your allowance, your inheritance, everything! No college, no money, and for what? For whom? Some random boy from high school? Some indigent skinny guitar player! Over my dead body!"

"No, Dad, over my dead body will I reverse this marriage! I'm old enough and I just want to live my own life, without you controlling everything."

"Sir, I love Delancey..." I started to say, and before I could finish my sentence, he punched me in the face. I fell to the ground. I probably deserved it.

"I will crush you," Mr. Kenmare bellowed, standing over me.

The police arrived and told us to disperse. Her father grabbed her arm, and pulled her into the car. "I'll see you later, David, at the prom!" she yelled out to me.

Mr. Kenmare shouted, "Don't get used to being Delancey's husband."

John and Carlos picked me up off the ground and dusted me off. I was shaken up by everything, especially the part where my new father-in-law landed me on the ground with a single punch. He hit harder than the Deceptors.

The three of us walked back over the Brooklyn Bridge. Carlos commented on what a great punch Mr. Kenmare had landed. John said it was the best he had ever seen. My face didn't think it was so wonderful.

John had a flyer advertising a special price on corsages. The florist was a small shop on Atlantic Avenue. The three of us were experiencing a special kind of euphoria, the kind that kids near the completion of their high school senior year tend to have. My euphoria was even better, like nothing I had ever felt before, because I had just married the girl of my dreams and there was nothing her mean father could do about it.

We were laughing, talking about the prom, and about Delancey's father. Carlos said that Thanksgiving was going to be a hoot for me with my new father-in-law. We were loose, and relaxed, and our guard was down.

"That ring on your finger makes you look all serious," John remarked.

"You know, I guess it does," I said, analyzing the ring.

"But what about your future together?" asked John.

"We will have to talk about it some more, but I have no regrets. No matter what happens, I'm ending high school by marrying the girl of my dreams."

We paid for the corsages, and stepped outside the florist. Gathered outside were five familiar thugs. They were the Deceptors from Central Park, the ones we had confronted with our guns back in April. Carlos and I brought John up to speed.

We started heading for the subway, and two of the Deceptors stood in front of us blocking our path. They were wearing oversized coats and baggy pants. It was June, and unnecessary to wear a coat. Their leader shouted, "Well if it isn't the Harvard boys!"

Deceptors used the extra room in baggy clothing to conceal weapons. Carlos did not have his backpack today, and that was both a good thing and a bad thing.

"Where's your backpack, Carlos?" I asked, inquiring about the gun.

"I no longer carry it. I've turned a new leaf in my life," he said.

"Good for you!" I said sarcastically. "Bad timing, but good for you."

Carlos without a gun meant serious trouble for us.

"Let me guess, someone left their gun at home." The five Deceptors laughed out loud.

We needed to make a run for it. Carlos said we had to stick together. "No man gets left behind."

"Agreed," I said.

"Leave no man behind," John said.

We were surrounded by the Deceptors, and just hours away from the prom. They pulled out their guns. This was not going to be good.

The chief goon spoke up, "Are those corsages for me?" The others laughed. "I guess you fellas are going to the prom tonight. So here's what I'm going to do for you...we're gonna take your money, beat the crap out of you, and then you guys are free to go...OR we're gonna shoot all three of you, and you guys are not free to go to the prom tonight."

Carlos pulled us to the side and started to whisper.

"No problem, fellas; please take a minute to think it over," said the leader, while the other four jackals guffawed. "It's your life!" he shouted.

We could not fight these guys; they were bigger, stronger, hardened criminals, and had weapons. Our conversation took less than a second. We looked at each other, took a deep breath and ran for the subway as fast as we could.

John was the fastest of the three of us, and was outrunning the hoodlums without a problem. We ran across traffic on Atlantic Avenue, cutting across the honking and screeching cars and buses. I was right behind John, and Carlos was right behind me. They chased after us, as we turned toward the subway at full speed. A shot was fired, and I kept running, but looked back. Carlos was still running behind me. John made it to the subway steps and headed down the stairs. I was heading full speed down the steps, when I heard Carlos yell out. Three of the hoodlums had grabbed him. I ran back to help him. He was getting punched from all sides.

I pushed one of the hoodlums down the steps, and pulled Carlos away. Carlos entered the platform. The Deceptors were right behind us. I tried to make it over the turnstile, but I was too late.

They seized my legs, pulling me away from the turnstile. I fell to the floor, and the thugs grabbed onto my ankles, dragging me backwards. I was being kicked in the head, stomach and back. Sharp pains jetted in my midsection. They kept punching away; I kept kicking but to no avail. I struggled to get to my feet, but could not do it while getting stomped. The top of my body was halfway under the turnstile, and John and Carlos latched onto my arms and pulled me forward, leaving my sneakers in the hands of the thugs.

We ran across the platform, and jumped down onto the tracks. We quickly ran across to the opposite station. I could see the lights of a train approaching a few yards away. There was no time to stop and even less time to think. I made it to the other side of the station, just in my socks, climbed up onto the platform and quickly rose to my feet. We entered the train, ran to the front car, and made sure the hoodlums did not follow. John was unscathed. Carlos had a black eye and a fat lip.

They both stared at me. "How bad is it?" I asked.

"It's not bad at all," said Carlos.

"You look fine," said John. They were both lying.

I could taste blood in my mouth, and noticed blood on my shirt. When the adrenaline wore off, my face started to throb. It felt swollen, and lumpy, as did parts of my back. I was in tremendous pain. My knees were scraped, and my left quadricep was stiff. Carlos and John took me home. I was having a hard time walking. I went to the bathroom, and could barely see the mirror. My right eye was swollen, puffy, and cut. I removed my shirt, and could see bruises all over my body. My lip was cut. Carlos and John said I needed stitches.

They took me by cab to the hospital. Nearly two hours passed in the emergency room before a doctor saw me. I filled out a fake name and information, knowing that I could not burden my father with medical bills. A nurse sewed my lower lip, and the cut above my eye. We left the hospital, and I swallowed a couple of painkillers.

All I could think about was the prom. Delancey was on my mind. How could she be seen with me in this condition? I still had to pick up Christine. I looked like I was on the losing side of a 12 round boxing match. I would just embarrass myself if I showed up looking like this. I seriously considered not going, but Carlos and John talked me out of that.

"You can't let Delancey down. Or Christine. The prom is a big deal for girls. You get only one prom in your life," said John. "Besides, you never looked that good to begin with."

We still needed to pick up our tuxedos. The line at the tuxedo store was more than an hour long. We were very much behind schedule and would be late to the prom. Carlos and John kept yelling at the store clerk out of frustration.

By the time we left the store, we were running two hours late. The three of us got dressed at my place, and the cab service that John had arranged could wait no longer. He left. We did not have a ride. We had no choice but to try to call our dates and have them meet us at the prom. John was able to get a hold of Helen and explain the situation, and she agreed to meet us at the World Trade Center. I was unable to reach Christine.

We took the subway during rush hour. I still looked like a mess, but I was no longer bleeding. The painkillers from the hospital had kicked in, and I was feeling numb.

I always hated rush hour. John's and Carlos's tuxedos were getting crushed, but none of the straphangers came near me. They all took one look at my damaged face, and took four steps back. The homeless couldn't even look at me.

We finally arrived at eight o'clock, sweating in the sweltering June heat. John met Helen at the entrance. She was upset that John was late, and had left her to come to the prom alone. John pointed to my face, and Helen almost fainted. She apologized to John for being upset. Then she apologized to me for my face.

We were in the courtyard of the Word Trade Center's Twin Towers. I looked up at the large bronze sphere in the center of the fountain. I had walked by this sculpture so many times, and had even sat under the statue with Christine once. It was supposed to symbolize world peace, and resemble the Grand Mosque at Mecca. It was the best outdoor sculpture in all of New York City. I gazed upon it, in awe of its magnitude and perfection. But there was something eerie as well, and it felt as if the sphere was an omen of something bad to come.

I found a payphone, put a dime in, and tried calling Christine. There was no answer. I put another dime in the phone, and called again. Still no answer. I remembered Bruce's cellular phone and thought it may actually come in handy one day.

I decided to take the subway to Chinatown. I told Carlos and John that I would join them later. "Tell Delancey I'm running late." They took the elevator up to the Windows on the Worlds restaurant.

The subway ride was about ten minutes to Chinatown. I hurried, limping a few blocks to her place. Christine was all dressed up and waiting for me outside.

"What happened to you? I've been waiting here for two hours in the heat!" she asked.

"I'll explain on the way there."

"You look awful!" she shouted.

Our cab quickly became stuck in rush hour traffic, and by the time we arrived, it was almost nine o'clock. I told Christine my entire ordeal, and how, of all days, this had to be the day that I was attacked by the hoodlums. She was wearing a sexy red dress, with five metallic gold stars across the top.

"You look ravishing," I said. Christine did not answer. She sat as far away from me as she could.

"What? No corsage?" she asked.

"The Deceptors have it by now."

We went upstairs by elevator to the 107th floor. When I finally arrived to the prom, everyone had just finished eating. Christine and I sat down at a table with Carlos and John. I went into the kitchen and was able to get us two plates.

Carlos, John, and Helen were getting ready to go dance, and I introduced them to Christine.

"I have to find someone; I'll be back," I said. My pain medication was starting to wear off. I took a double dose of the painkillers from the hospital.

As I walked around looking for Delancey, everyone was staring at me. Some were pointing. A few were laughing. My appearance was worse than I had thought. I saw Jacob and Sandra; they were dancing and looked so happy and sad at the same time. Natalie was dancing with another girl. She waved hello.

I saw Mr. Mash, and still no sign of Delancey. Penny was dancing alone. I asked her if she had seen Delancey.

"She's in the ladies room."

I limped over to the ladies room, and waited outside for her.

Everyone was dancing. The girls looked really good, so different from how they looked at school. Even Doreen was having a good time. She was finally at a party.

Delancey walked out of the bathroom, and nearly fainted when she saw me. Sam laughed in the background.

"I bumped into some old friends. Are you ashamed of the way I look?" I asked her.

"I know you will heal. But you should get to a hospital."

"I've already been, and this is the best that they could do. How about that dance wife?" I asked her, smiling.

"I thought you'd never ask, hubby," she said.

"Where's your date?" I asked.

"Juan? Oh...he's around...letting everyone know he's here with me."

How many girls would have wanted to be seen with me tonight? I was grotesque, but she was still happy to be with me. We were married, I still couldn't believe it. I fought back tears of joy as we slow danced.

"I have a surprise for you at graduation." I wasn't sure if I should tell her about my performance.

"Oh! What is it? I love surprises."

"That's why I won't tell you," I laughed.

"Come on, give me a hint!" she demanded.

"Well, I am doing a special performance. And I selected a song with you in mind." I laughed again, having fun keeping the secret.

Sam interrupted to tell me that my hideous appearance was causing some people to vomit. He asked if he could cut in.

"No, you can't. I'll take my time dancing with my new wife."

Sam instantly noticed our wedding rings and his blood started to boil. Rage took over and the veins in his neck and forehead started to protrude. Sam ran back to Juan Perez and whispered in his ear. Juan, clearly inebriated, now shared the same infuriated expression as Sam.

Juan threw his glass to the floor, shattering it, and then overturned a table with engraved champagne glass party favors. Broken glass covered the dance floor. Juan yelled and screamed at me and Delancey. Sam stood by his side.

"So let me get this right! I chase after Delancey for a year; she agrees to go the prom with me, I buy her ticket, get a limo, get us into the after party, and you marry her? Are you trying to make me look like a fool?" Juan had lost all self control. He took a swing at me, missing. He was so drunk he slipped and fell to the ground, which only made him angrier.

"Mr. Zoose isn't here to save you this time!" Juan shouted. My suspicions had been correct. Juan was a Deceptor.

Juan, drunk, angry, and jealous, pulled a gun out of his pocket, a jeweled handgun. Delancey's gun. Sam had sold the gun to Juan the Deceptor.

The gun shimmered in the light. The senior class cleared out of the way trying not to be in the cross fire. He aimed it directly at me with a sinister look filling his eyes.

The music stopped. Everything went silent. I could only hear my heavy breathing and Juan's rapid heartbeat. "You have ruined everything!" shouted Juan. I was standing about ten feet away from him; Delancey was behind me. The pain medication was making me delirious and I laughed.

"What is so funny!" yelled Juan.

"You are. You have money, a family, Harvard, you're even the class president. You get to take the girl of my dreams to the prom, and now you want to shoot me. I have nothing. No mother. No money. Nothing, except for Delancey. You want to shoot me, go ahead."

I calmly walked up to Juan. My chest was inches away from the barrel of the gun; my heart pounded like a drum. I was close enough to feel Juan's panting, and could see the beads of perspiration forming on his forehead. Delancey pleaded with Juan not to shoot.

Juan pulled the trigger, as I knew that he would.

Nothing happened. The gun still did not have bullets.

Security immediately leaped on top of him and threw him out of the party.

I walked over to the far corner, and stood in the shadows, away from the crowd of seniors. I wiped the sweat from my face. I was drained and relieved.

Christine was in a corner talking to a well dressed young man. She was flirting with him. My medication was probably too strong, and I must have been delusional, because I thought the guy bore a strong resemblance to Eddie Lo. On further inspection, I saw it was Wing King.

Delancey was yelling at Sam. Sam furiously shouted back at her. Sam pushed her out of the way, and came charging towards me. I was focused on Sam, who held one of the iron table settings in his left hand, and barely saw Delancey falling on the floor, on the broken glass. I darted over to pick her up. Sam hit me on the head with the heavy metallic table setting, and I fell unconscious.

Several minutes later, Christine and Carlos were helping me up. I could barely walk. My legs and knees were stiff.

Maurice asked if I knew about Delancey. He reminded me that Delancey had fallen on broken glass and described how she was cut all over. "She was bleeding profusely. An ambulance took her to the hospital."

"Glass had entered deep into her heel, and torso," John said, "and she was bleeding pints of blood."

Carlos said, "Large shards of glass went into her foot, maybe four or five inches. She's at Downtown New York Hospital."

I had a sick feeling in my stomach. I needed to go to the hospital. I could barely walk.

"Where's Sam?" I asked.

"Sam was thrown out by Mr. Mash. He was gone before the police came. You were out a long time," John said.

Carlos agreed to take Christine home, and then meet me at the hospital. John also insisted on going to the hospital.

"Fine, let's go," I said.

"Count me in," said Helen.

This was so unbelievable. Worst case scenarios played through my head. Of all nights for this to happen, it happened the night of the prom, and the day we got married. As we headed toward the exit sign, I was handed a party favor. It was a tall champagne glass, one of the few that were unbroken, engraved with the words "Stanton Serpents." I was furious with Sam.

The five of us tried to hail a cab, but the entire senior class was doing the same thing. Cab after cab filled up with kids from the prom, all headed to an after party at the Limelight Club. We finally found a cab about a half hour later. "Downtown New York Hospital," I said to the cabdriver.

"Strange place for an after party," the driver said. I could only blame myself. I should've stopped Sam before he pushed Delancey. The entire evening was being second guessed in my head.

We arrived at the hospital nearly twenty minutes later, after midnight. We went to the emergency room and asked for Delancey. They didn't know who she was.

"A girl came in here from the prom, bleeding? With broken glass in her foot? She was probably dressed like she was at her prom," I said. "Like us." The person behind the desk finally found a record of her, and said she was having surgery in the emergency operating room downstairs.

When we exited the elevator, there was no one to point us in the right direction. We roamed the empty hallways for fifteen minutes. Finally, I saw a sign for "Emergency Operating Room."

Medical professionals wearing scrubs told us to wait until the surgery was complete. An hour passed. Helen had to go home, and John, being a gentleman, decided to take her back to Queens.

Carlos had arrived from dropping off Christine. He stayed, and waited with me for Delancey to come out of surgery. Another hour passed. A nurse commented that it had been nearly three hours. "It's pretty serious. Several veins and arteries in the foot were severed," the nurse said.

Another hour passed, and then Carlos left to go home. It was after three in the morning. A doctor came out of the operating room.

"How is she?" I asked. I could barely see out of my swollen eyes. Everything was blurry and dim. All I saw was a tall, shadowy figure in scrubs.

"Not good. Her main foot artery was severed, and so was her dorsalis pedis. She came by ambulance, but they could not treat the severed artery on the way here. I'm afraid she lost a lot of blood, and by the time we operated on the foot...well, I'm not sure we were successful. She fell on a lot of broken glass. We managed to pull all of the glass out of her body, including one that pierced into her stomach, but there was a lot of damage. I'm not sure she will make it. She's awake. You can talk to her for a few minutes."

That was as morbid a discussion as I'd ever had. I put on a set of scrubs, and a surgical mask, and went into the operating room. Delancey was barely lucid. She seemed ethereal.

"Hey, Delancey," I said. Her face was pale, tubes were in her arms and she could barely breathe. I now realized the severity of the situation. It was much worse than I had thought. She was barely in the room with me, her consciousness fading, hardly able to speak. I had hoped this was caused by the anesthesia. I started to cry, unable to find the words I wanted to say to her. I held her hand, and she tried to squeeze it.

"We didn't get to finish our dance," she said. Her voice was faint. She was speaking below a whisper. "I'm so glad we were married, if only for a few hours. I'll always love you, David. What was the surprise for me at graduation?"

"I'm doing a song, Separate Ways..."

"My favorite...you'll be great."

I told her she looked beautiful. She said she was embarrassed to be seen like that. A white sheet covered her legs. The heart monitor was beating slowly, with beats every other second. She turned her head and motioned for a nearby glass of water. The nurse placed a spoonful of water into her mouth.

"Don't remember me this way," she whispered.

"What? No honeymoon?" I mumbled. She coughed until she coughed up blood. I grew more fearful.

"You've never looked better," she said as she tried to smile.

"You're a sight for sore eyes."

"Very funny." She smiled.

"You're going to be fine," I pleaded as best as I could. "We'll walk out of this horrid place together. I'll gladly lead the way." She started to cry. Something was wrong, but I did not know what it was. The nurse told me that Delancey's right foot had been amputated.

Devastated, I tried to put a positive look on my face. Delancey sobbed uncontrollably. Her brown hair seemed darker, and tears trickled down her pale face. I didn't know what to say or what to do. My hand was still holding hers. I squeezed a little tighter.

I glanced at her feet, covered by the white sheet, and she winced. "I don't want you to see me this way," she said.

"It's okay. . .you're the most beautiful girl ever." I really meant it. I leaned over and kissed her purple lips.

The doctors came back into the room. They had to do one more surgery and demanded that I leave. The nurse explained that Delancey had glass in her kidneys. The doctor said Delancey needed more blood. The nurse explained that she had a rare blood type, and the hospital did not have enough of this blood.

"Just go and don't look back at me," Delancey said. "Promise that you won't look back and see me like this."

"I promise," I said.

"I wouldn't want you to remember me this way, with an amputated foot, and barely alive. Tell my parents I love them." I released her hand. As I left the room, they moved her onto the operating table. Out of the corner of my eye, I saw the sheet that was covering her fall to the floor.

I didn't want to look back, but she screamed in pain when they moved her. I tried my best not to glance back, not to break my promise to her, not to look at her amputated foot. But there was a round mirror in the corner ceiling of the operating room, and I saw her in the mirror. She knew that I had seen her amputated foot. She sobbed loudly, and my head turned. I saw her on the operating table. She cried louder.

The moment I walked out of the operating room, her heart monitor went flat. The doctors tried to revive her. I stood and watched as they used the defibrillator several times. In the end, nothing could be done.

The surgeon walked out, and said, "Sorry. She lost too much blood. There was really nothing more we could've done. "

The earth went silent. I could still feel her hand in mine. I heard them say, "time of death 5 a.m." It echoed in my head. Devastated and destroyed, I thought I was in a bad dream.

I sat on the steps outside the hospital in shock and disbelief. The sun started to rise. My vision was still blurred. A man was walking his dog. I was so disoriented that it appeared the dog had three heads.

Delancey's mother arrived, and so did Bruce. They asked how she was, and I couldn't answer. Bruce picked me up off the ground and shook me.

"She wanted you to know that she loved you." Her mother, decimated by my cruel words, fell to the ground. Delancey was the ninth student death that year.

My body ached, my lip was scabbed, my eyes bruised, and I could barely walk to the subway. But my physical pain did not compare to the depth of my strife and the torment of my grief.

I wondered if that night had just been a nightmare. But I knew it was real. How could this have happened? How could Death have cheated me yet again in my life? Every time an ounce of happiness came my way, any kind of love that entered my life, like with my mother, and grandfather, Death stole it away. I wished that there was a way to get her back. I had already lost so much in my life. Choking back more tears, I decided that I could not lose her.

The sunlight became brighter, and a thought entered my head. In the basement, was the bag from Sal's house. His books and equipment were still in the bag. Sal said he would be at graduation. He might be my only hope. What if everything Sal said was true? What if he wasn't completely crazy? I had to find him.

I needed to go to Stanton and bring everything he would need, the entire bag to graduation.

I was still a bloody mess, now wearing a destroyed tuxedo. but there was no time to change. John and Carlos arrived at my house just as I was walking out. They were on their way to graduation. I informed them of Delancey's passing. Grief stricken, they would come with me to graduation.

The news of Delancey's death had not reached the school. The graduating class was in the auditorium, cheering, smiling, and celebrating. No one knew. I walked in at the end of Doreen's valedictory speech, still in my bloodstained tuxedo.

Doreen ended her speech stating how we were all about to embark on a new journey. Not Delancey though.

John informed me that Sam was nowhere to be found because he was not allowed to graduate due to his inability to pass the swim test.

Carlos said Sam was probably distraught over the incident at the prom, not being named valedictorian, and not graduating, but was unsure of the order of his emotions. Harvard would consequently have to rescind its offer to Sam. Everything was moving in slow motion.

John stood next to me during the graduation march. He was not going to go to college in the fall. His father would not allow it that year. John deferred his college acceptance for another year. He was clearly disappointed, but had chosen to obey his father.

Mr. Mash called out the names, one after another. Delancey's name was called out. The audience applauded, whistled, and cheered on her behalf. No one knew that she had passed away. When she did not approach the stage, Mash skipped over her and called out the next student's name.

Painfully distracted, I could not remember why I was even there. And then I saw the bag in my hand, Sal's bag. I desperately needed him to help me. Mr. Mash continued calling the names of the graduates. I was inadvertently doing the graduation march and heading up to the stage, to shake Mr. Mash's hand, to get my sheepskin.

John accepted his diploma and shook hands with Mr. Mash. Carlos did the same. Sal sat on the stage, separated from the rest of the senior class. Sal looked lost in thought, his body slouching off the chair. He was my only hope, no matter his mental state.

Would the circumstances of Delancey's death have changed if I had asked her to be my date to the prom? If I'd had enough courage, and less insecurity, would she still be alive? I wondered if Sam was capable of feeling guilty.

"David Orpheus" called out Mr. Mash. I didn't really hear him, as I was deep in thought. "David Orpheus—class of 1989." Someone shook me by the shoulder and I started walking toward Mr. Mash. "Congratulations, young man," he said. He handed me my sheepskin, and I thanked him.

I stood staring at the audience. No one else understood my grief. Hardly anyone knew that we were married, that we were in love, and that everything was lost. I had not only received a diploma from high school, but also an education in death, pain, and grief.

Mash was distracted by my blood stained tuxedo. I looked like a complete disaster.

Mr. Mash spoke into the microphone. "And now, we are going to spice things up a little. Don't ever say your high school graduation was boring. With a very special performance of Separate Ways…also known as Worlds Apart…. here is David and the Stanton Serpents Band."

The curtains behind me rose high into the ceiling. The band assembled, and Ms. Virgil placed a guitar in my hand. I walked over to my microphone, stopping off and giving Sal his bag.

The intro started, heavy drums, just like we had practiced. Like a zombie, as if I was in a trance, I sang Separate Ways. I sang every word, with all the haunting pain that filled my heart. My vocals ricocheted of the walls of the auditorium. I wept as I sang; my fingers burned as I strummed and played every chord.

I felt lost when it was over. The audience, students, parents, and teachers alike, stood and cheered. The song was only a blur. I had almost no memory of performing. Everyone was patting me on the back and congratulating me. I spoke into the microphone. "That was for Delancey; it was her favorite song. She passed away a few hours ago."

The audience gasped. My announcement created havoc and commotion. The senior class was in grief. I walked down the stage, and Sal was waiting for me.

"Now I know why you brought the bag. Are you ready to do this?" he asked.

I could not answer. I could barely understand what he was saying. Every sound was muffled.

"There's no turning back, David, whatever happens. There is no turning back. If you go down this path, I really don't know." Sal was genuinely concerned. "You could end up like me."

Amidst the confusion, Sal and I walked out of the auditorium. He led me through a dark hallway in the basement. We went to a sublevel, and then through the boiler room and main plumbing room. We made several turns. I kept walking, unable to comprehend how my feet were moving. Sal led the way, talking fast, all kinds of nonsensical explanations coming out of his mouth. He talked about being homeless, living in the basement of the school, building the Leviathon with parts from the school's labs. Sal kept babbling on and on.

Minutes later we entered the school's electrical room. There was small door with a combination lock to the far left. I had no idea where I was anymore. Sal knew the combination, and opened the lock. We crawled through the small doorway into another dark room. Then Sal turned on the lights.

In the middle of the room was the design I had seen in Sal's book. It was the Leviathon, a monstrous set of copper wires coiled about six feet high. There were wires connected to electrical outlets, and a large looming structure at the top. It seemed different from the sketch in Sal's book, and I did not know why.

Sal lifted a series of switches on a panel, placing them in the upright position. The Leviathion lit up, and sparks flew from different sections. I didn't know how it worked, but I did know that it was using a lot of electricity. Sal was like a mad scientist from an old black and white science fiction movie. And so was the machine.

He opened the bag, pulled out all the missing parts, all the things he needed to make it function. At the very end, Sal removed a copper helmet from the bag, and using a stepping stool, connected it to the large looming contraption at the top of the machine. Now it looked exactly as it had in his sketch.

"Are you sure you want to do this?"

I needed to get Delancey back. I couldn't think straight; I was too consumed with grief. I had lost a lot in my life, and I couldn't lose her too. Losing her was too much to bear.

"I have no choice," I replied. "Full speed ahead."

It was hot outside, normal for June. It was even warmer standing next to the Leviathon. I was sweating from the heat, and thirsty, probably even dehydrated. The sweltering heat rose off the machine like poisonous gas. I walked around in circles, not knowing which direction to head into.

Sal took a while to set up the equipment. I watched in silence. He had never been the same since using the Leviathon. He explained how he had really messed up his last "journey to the underworld."

"David, I know how much Delancey meant to you. I really wish that you didn't need to do this. But I understand." He pointed to the stepping stool and told me to climb up and get into the Leviathon. I followed his instructions, numb to everything else that was happening. Once I was inside the serpentine coils, he placed the metal helmet onto my head.

"David, the longer you are gone, the worse it's going to be."

The room started to get dim, the sounds muffled. I heard clanking noises. A strong breeze whisked from no where, and I closed my eyes, for just a second.

chapter 24

I WAS TRYING to find a way out of Stanton. The doors were all locked. The hallways were empty. I was wandering in the hallways of Stanton's basement. There was no sign of Sal.

I found a stairwell, and with more grace and agility than ever before, I quickly raced up the flight of stairs. There wasn't a single sound, not a soul stirring. The doors were all locked, but the windows were open.

I climbed out of a window, and landed on the street. At first I didn't realize where I was, but then I saw a woman in the snug black dress. There was no one else on the streets of Brooklyn, no cars, no people, and no birds, no one except for Delfina.

The psychic was waiting for me outside her store front.

"I knew you'd come," she said.

"Delancey's gone," I said.

"I know."

"I need to get her back."

"I know."

"What do I need to do?" I asked.

"Let's get started."

We went inside her store, and she locked the door and closed the blinds.

Darkness surrounded me.

"I need a glass of water," I said.

"Of course, come with me and I'll explain what you need to do."

I sat on a couch, in the back of her store. She lit a few candles, and the room started to reveal itself. There were statues, and paintings, and antiques. I noticed relics, and knives, and various religious icons.

"Delancey is dead, but not completely gone," she said.

"Are you responsible for this? Didn't you complete a ritual with Sam that led to this?"

"Listen to me very carefully. I am truly very sorry. I can help you get her back, but it is very difficult and against the natural order of the universe. Bringing her back is very dangerous."

"Please, please," I begged. "I can't go on without her. You have to help me." I was desperate.

"Now listen carefully. Today is the summer solstice. It's the longest day of the year, which also means that it's the shortest night of the year."

"I really need some water," I said.

"You can't drink anything in this realm. You are just spirit." I was confused and asked her to repeat what she had just said.

"You are not in the physical world anymore. Wait here, I will show you."

She exited the room and returned a few minutes later with a tall glass of water. I could not see very well in the dim candle light, but she told me to try and drink it. It smelled funny, like lemon and flowers. I held it against my mouth, and it spilled all over. I was not wet. The contents of the glass went right through me.

"Now listen very carefully."

Delfina said that Delancey's spirit would still be around because she had died just recently. "Once you get to the netherworld, it's up to you to beg and plead with the powers that be to let you have her back. It won't be easy, and you don't have a lot of time. You can only enter the netherworld from sundown to sunrise. While it is still night, you have to get permission to get her back."

"How do I get started?"

"Where is Delancey's body?" Delfina asked.

"She's probably at the morgue at New York Hospital," I said.

"Then that's where she might be. That's where you should head to first. If her soul is not there, then you have to find out where it is."

I was very confused and mentally weak. Everything was becoming dim. "I don't understand."

Delfina sighed. "It's a hospital; there is always someone in a hospital that leads souls to the netherworld. You have to trust me on this. The only way for you get her back is to enter the other world. Have you heard of ascension? It's when your spirit leaves your body... you enter the astral plane. You are now in the astral plane, but you need to go deeper, much deeper to find her. It's all up to you. You have already left your body, and you are in the first astral plane. Now go find Delancey."

I had to start at the hospital. She might still be near her body. The astral plane was different. Delfina explained that Delancey may be in a holding area—a waiting area. The nether world looks like this world, but the rules are different.

"Find her, get permission to bring her back; and you must come back by sunrise, otherwise you will not come back at all. The longer you are gone, the worse it will be."

She repeated several incantations, lit several candles, and burned fragranced embers into a small fire. The light flickered back and forth. I repeated the incantations when she told me to. Strange shadows danced on the walls, and I grew drowsy. All I could think about was Delancey. I kept repeating her name. My eyes closed slowly; the room seemed to shake violently. All was quiet.

I heard a noise. Everything was dark. The noise continued, pounding louder.

"You cannot speak with your voice here. Say it in your mind."

I thought to myself, "I can hear you."

"I can hear you too," Delfina said. "The incantations just moved you into a deeper plane of the astral world. Rise up...just will yourself up. The world here is similar to when you are dreaming. Just rise up and come my way."

I floated upwards. Delfina stood in the room and I glided toward her. The pounding noise grew fainter.

"What's that noise?" I thought.

"It's your heart beat," she said.

The room was no longer dark.

"I can't leave here. You have to head out on your own. The beings that appear before you may look like faces you know, but that is your mind making them more familiar. Your mind will extrapolate any energy that it cannot resolve or decipher. Find Delancey. And hurry."

I left her store front glancing at a clock on the wall. It was after 3 pm.

The streets were empty. I walked down a vacant Flatbush Avenue. There were no crowds of pedestrians at every intersection. Brooklyn was a ghost town in this world.

At the empty subway station, I waited for a train that never arrived. I must have waited an hour. I went back to the deserted streets. Small flickering lights moved past me. I decided to go over the Brooklyn Bridge. A dark orange sunset spread over the city. Sunset already? I did not have a watch, but realized that I must be moving very slowly. I thought I had waited for the train for an hour. It was likely three hours. Time moved more quickly in this plane. That's why Delfina urged me to hurry.

Crossing the bridge was a struggle. The breeze felt much stronger, and I pushed with all my might to take each step. Someone was sitting on the guard rail, in the middle of the bridge. The person looked like he was going to jump. As I approached, his face looked familiar.

"Wilson, is that you?" I asked.

"I am Wilson."

"I thought you looked familiar," I said.

"Where are you going? Did you commit suicide too?" he asked.

"No. I'm looking for Delancey. I'm headed to the hospital where her body is."

"How are things at Stanton?"

"Well you missed the April Dance, and the prom, not to mention graduation."

"I made a big mistake, and I can't take it back. I can't believe I committed suicide. I was just overwhelmed. I was so close to graduation and leaving high school. So close to the finish line, what a mistake."

"You would've been an adult and had the freedom to do whatever you wanted. You didn't even give it chance."

"I know. I know. Such a big mistake. Things would've been better after high school. What happened to Delancey?" Wilson asked.

I explained the circumstances of Delancey's death and how I was trying to get to New York Hospital.

Before I could finish, Wilson jumped off the bridge. Horrified, I scrambled to the edge, and looked down into the water. He was nowhere. I called out but there was no answer. I turned around and Wilson was standing right behind me.

"I saw you fall over."

"I did and I'll do it again. I've been here for a while doing this over and over. This is where I committed suicide. It's the last thing I remember," Wilson said.

I kept walking. Wilson was weirder in the afterlife than he was in high school.

There was no one else on the bridge, as dusk was turning into nightfall. I thought my conversation with Wilson took a few minutes, but time was moving so quickly that it must have taken closer to an hour.

By the time I entered Manhattan, it was dark. The astral plane looked very different at night. More lights moved back and forth on the streets of Manhattan. In the material world the city was a bustling mix of sidewalks, buildings, wide streets, and cars. But here, the buildings appeared older, and the cars were missing. Light and dark sentient beings moved at a rapid pace, some floating, some walking, some gliding.

Four full moons decorated the night sky. It was unusual sight to behold. High above, beings flew past me. Some were bright colors, others were dimmer. Some were demonic and glowered at me, and others seemed angelic and benevolent.

The more I focused on the hospital, the faster I floated toward it. Minutes later I entered the hospital where she had perished just a few hours before. The hospital was not as deserted as the streets were. People were walking around. Some were old, some were young, and some appeared injured or ill. I felt nervous around these beings. Some of them looked confused.

Delancey's body was in the morgue. I called out to her, but it was no use. She was dead. I needed to find her soul. I searched the entire floor and called out her name, but there was no answer. An old woman sat in the chapel.

"Where can I find Delancey's soul?" I asked.

"Lets see...when did she pass?"

"Last night...I think," I said. My concept of time was nebulous.

"She's probably in limbo," the old woman said.

"Limbo?" I asked.

"Yes. A holding area, it's where a soul would wait until a decision is made on its destination," she said.

"Where is limbo?" I asked.

"Ellis Island is the holding area for New York."

"How do I get there?" I asked.

"You have to take the ferry from Battery Park."

I left the hospital bewildered by the notion of Ellis Island as limbo, and started toward downtown. I picked up the pace, aware of my need to spend as little time in this world as possible.

I ran and floated down Broadway, then over to West Street. I glanced upwards at the mighty Twin Towers, a familiar sight in a somewhat unfamiliar landscape. I was soon in the middle of Battery Park City.

Snakes slivered on the streets of Manhattan, but I could only see them in my peripheral vision, not when I looked directly at them. They were green and black. They moved sideways, and they moved quickly.

I raced to State Street. The ferry dock was nearby. I tried not look at the faces of the souls on my left and my right. Some were children, and looked human. Others were demonic, and their sinister facial expressions were starting to scare me. They looked angry and frustrated.

It felt like I was being followed, and whenever I looked over my shoulder, small creatures seemed to escape into the corners. They were humanoid in appearance but no more than two feet tall. Their teeth were disproportionately larger than normal. I stared further, fearing their appearance. A chill went down my spine when I noticed their feet were backwards, toes pointing behind them.

Shadows moved on the streets, like bodies walking. Some came close to me; others stayed far away.

I was hurrying but getting confused. My mental acuity was fading. Some of the street names were not familiar. Some buildings were unfamiliar. My mind was wandering, and I was no longer sure what direction to take. I spun around in circles.

Perched on a tall building were shadowy figures with human faces, wings and tails. I changed directions, and headed to the left, but was disappointed when I realized I was still lost.

I ran toward downtown, but then I found myself standing where I had begun, Downtown New York Hospital. Frustration started to take over. Composure was a struggle. I headed downtown again, counting my paces in order to maintain some semblance of mental acuity.

Along the way, balls of bright lights flew by at rapid speeds. The lights were different colors, and varying intensity. I became confused again, and struggled to remember the count. I kept going, deciding not to change directions, and not to allow the confusion to overwhelm me. Ignoring the demonic faces, and the small beings, I did my best to get to the ferry. I lost the count, but after intense concentration, I regained my count at 341 paces.

I pictured the ferry in my mind, and remembered what Ellis Island looked like. Doing so created diminished mental discombobulation. I floated faster in the direction of my most intense thoughts.

Finally, upon arriving at the ferry dock, I waited on line. This was still New York and there was a line for everything. Several women, children, and a few men waited on line ahead of me. Demonic beings were on line as well. I ran up to the front of the line, but angry faces yelled for me to go back.

The ferry arrived an hour later, and we boarded in silence. Above the skyline, high over the Hudson River, three moons and a half moon beamed in the night sky. There were four full moons when I had arrived.

The ferryman looked a lot like the cab driver from the night of the prom. Perhaps this was just my mind extrapolating, like Delfina said it would.

The ferry headed south on the murky Hudson River. Sea serpents swam in the river. In the material world, the weather had been hot, and the city was bustling. In the astral plane, it was chilly, and silent. The ferry moved through the waters without sound. I did not know how much time I had left. There were no stars, only the three and a half moons.

The wind increased steadily as we neared Ellis Island. I stood at the bow of the ferry. The souls of the recently departed remained silent. We passed the Statue of Liberty, but she had four arms, appearing like a Hindu goddess.

I asked the ferryman why there were four moons when I had arrived and only three and a half now. In a deep voice, he said that the moons told time. The ferryman explained that as the night grew older, parts of the moons would disappear, until an entire moon vanished.

Before sunrise, only a small part of one moon would remain. It would vanish in daylight.

The ferry docked at Ellis Island. A line formed for passengers to clear a checkpoint. I waited in the middle of the slowly advancing line of souls. When I approached the checkpoint, I was pulled aside by the guard.

The guard was an enormous figure, draped in a black cloak. His face was intimidating, with a large jaw line, and rough skin. His presence emitted a powerful negative energy. The guard looked like one of Delancey's doormen, and through inexplicable means, seemed to sap me of my strength.

"Why are you here?" he asked.

"I am looking for Delancey," I said.

"Delancey who?"

"Delancey..." I paused, unable to recall her last name. "Kenmare? Yuridis? Orpheus?"

"She's here, as she is supposed to be. But you are not allowed in," the guard grunted.

"Please," I begged. "I have traveled far, and I have very little time. I need to see the person in charge of Delancey's soul."

"I'm afraid that's not possible," said the guard. The passengers from the ferry filed inside. The guard stood strong, preventing me from entering.

I pleaded with him again. There was no response. I tried to push my way in, and was thrown back several feet by the guard. Only three moons remained. Time was moving quickly. I sat still, out of answers.

The guard was too strong and too unyielding. But I could not turn back and go home, not without Delancey. I thought about my guitar, and wished I had it with me. I would often play the guitar whenever I needed to think. I pictured my guitar in front of me, and suddenly, to my amazement, it appeared. I was starting to understand the impact of the mind in this world.

I strummed a few chords, sad tunes, and continued playing for a few minutes. It was melodic and I played it from my heart. The strings and sounds ached as my heart did. I sang a song of my story, of how my love was taken from me too soon. When I was finished, the guard said that I could go in.

"How...why...what changed?" I asked him.

"Your music was heard by the God of the Underworld. You have been granted permission to enter."

I entered the monumental doors of Ellis Island. In the past, I'd wondered how the immigrants arriving here must have felt, but now I knew the answer. Intimidated and afraid. The building looked ancient. The red and white colors of brick and concrete appeared faded and worn. Time had taken its toll on the massive stone facade. I walked into the center of Great Hall. The building was deserted.

Gazing at the ceiling, I was amazed by its architecture. The concrete walls were stained, covered with dark colored smoke. I waited in the center of the great hall. Several minutes passed by, and still nothing. I touched the walls. The mysterious smoke engulfed my hand. All I could hear was silence.

From the far corners, a shadowy figure appeared. There were no lights in the building; visibility was provided only by the light from the moons through the dusty windows, high above the floor. The figure came closer. I was startled by its familiarity. It was my grandfather.

"I know why you've come, and I'm here to talk you out of it," he said.

"Grandpa?" I asked happily. I walked closer to him, eager to embrace him. He was bigger and stronger than my grandfather was at the time of his demise.

"I'm not your grandfather, but this form, this image, is how your mind wants to see my energy," the apparition said. "Your mind is extrapolating; it's the only way you have to process the energies here. There is nothing in the material world that resembles what we really look like here, in this plane."

"Where can I find Delancey?" I asked with a lot less happiness in my voice.

"Delancey is no longer yours. She has died, and her soul is here, but you are making a big mistake by coming here," the apparition said.

"It's my fault. It wasn't her time. She was too young," I said.

"Listen, David, it was her time. No one passes before their time. It wasn't your fault. Even if you had done everything different, picked her up, brought her to the prom, put her in a bullet proof dress, it was her destiny to pass that night."

"I don't believe that. I could have protected her. It should've been me and not her. I should've stopped Sam!" I cried out.

"It wasn't your time yet. It could not have been you instead," he said. "That's not the way things work."

"Are you here to stop me?" I asked.

"I wish I could stop you. But that is something that occurs in the physical world, where you belong. No...I'm here to allow you stop yourself. You need permission to bring her back. Someone is waiting for you beyond the Great Hall. If you get permission to take her, which is doubtful, have you considered what she'd be like in the material world?"

"What do you mean?" I asked.

"She won't be the same. She won't be one hundred percent. Her body has already started to decay, her foot is gone, and her soul has already been gone too long. The longer you stay; the same will be true for you."

"I'd rather have some of her than none of her," I said.

"David, she could be a zombie for the rest of her life, or even a vegetable."

"That won't happen," I said.

"You're stubborn but it won't help you here."

"Where is Delancey?"

"Before you see Delancey, heed my warnings carefully. I ask you again, not to do this for her sake. You're better off just being in love with a memory, a memory of a beautiful girl, a memory of your senior year in high school. Don't bring back something ungodly to the material world."

"I really just want to see her." I was obstinate, and annoyed.

The being went back toward the shadows, vanishing from the room. A light emerged from the end of the Great Hall. It slowly headed toward a corridor. I followed the light, up the stairs, and around a stone balcony. The light floated slowly, and when it crossed into the moonlit area, it became Delancey.

She was wearing her white prom dress. She was whole, and angelic, and absolutely beautiful. Chains were attached to her ankles. I quickly ran to her and we embraced. She was happy to see me. Tears filled her eyes.

"How did you get here? Are you…not alive?" she asked.

I explained how I had traveled here and told her to come back with me.

"I can't just leave and go back with you. I'm no longer part of the material world."

"You were always out of my league, out of my realm. We were always worlds apart. This is no different. I came here to plead for your soul. I need you back. I can't go on without you. I love you so much, I'll do anything. Come back with me," I said.

"It's not that easy," bellowed a deep echoing voice. It thundered throughout Ellis Island, deafening me and filling me with fear. The voice sounded familiar. It was the most frightening voice I had ever heard.

Delancey, squeezing my hand, said that we should go downstairs. We headed to the lower level. Her chains clanged against the stone floors. I kept looking behind, but no one was following. We walked down the concrete stairs and out of the moonlight. I followed her down several flights of stairs, until we were under Ellis Island.

We entered a small room. The darkness made it difficult to see my hands just inches from my body.

"Allow me," said the same deep voice, echoing, even louder. I shivered as an icy breeze blew into the room.

A small flame lit a candle on my right side, and then a candle on my left side. The room started to illuminate. To my surprise, it appeared that I was inside the principal's office at Stanton High School.

Two large balls of light moved toward me, and stopped behind the principal's desk. One of the lights transformed itself into an all too familiar form.

"Eddie Lo?" I thought to myself.

"Not quite...but Eddie Lo for now." My mind extrapolated the energy into a familiar shape and form. But this was not an ordinary energy. It had a very strong magnetic pull, draining me of my strength and thoughts.

The other ball of light transformed into an image of Christine.

"I'm here to get Delancey back," I said by telepathy.

"Of course you are," said Christine. "Why else would you be here?"

"Dead is dead. There is no getting her back," said Eddie Lo. I did not know why I was interpreting this being as Eddie Lo. A strange accent formed the sounds of their words. All communication was telepathic.

"It's because I'm the coolest guy you know. Just like Eddie Lo was the coolest guy you knew in the physical universe." He'd read my thoughts.

"I really need to get her back. There has to be some way. She was taken too soon and I'm certain she shouldn't be here."

Eddie Lo took a deep sigh. "No one passes on before their time."

"David Orpheus, I have wanted to meet face to face for some time. You are a very talented musician, and we enjoy your music here. Music penetrates every layer of the universe, transcending all the planes of existence," the Christine energy communicated.

She moved slightly, exposing reptilian skin in the place of legs. I glanced at Eddie Lo. Both of their lower bodies were serpentine, like the scaly skin of a large python.

"I know you so well, Orpheus. I have heard your music for so long. I have heard you blame me for everything, and I have heard you say time and time again that you are not afraid of Death. I know of your talents, and how your lack of confidence has held you back. I know about your confusions, and how you second guess pursuing your dreams. Actually, you second guess everything. I know your pain, and your hunger for happiness." Eddie Lo started to uncoil.

"Delancey was too young. We were just married. We didn't have any time. I was robbed." My fear was all consuming. My nervous system went into overdrive. "You cheated me out of a life, out of happiness, just as you did before, when you took my mother."

"Delancey was your wife, for as long as she was supposed to be. Your mother was your mother for as long as she was supposed to be. Even if you had taken Delancey someplace other than your prom, something else would've happened; it was her day. Her name was on my list that day. So was your mother's, when you were eleven years old. That's how it works. I only find out who's coming here the day they are supposed to arrive on the ferry," said Eddie Lo. His tone was firm, and I barely had enough courage to make any more statements.

"Are you Death?" I asked.

"I'm more of a keeper of souls. But people see me in many different ways."

"Is this hell?" I asked.

"Hell?" Eddie chuckled. "Hell is back in Brooklyn and where you reside. This is just a waiting area. I make sure that souls are here for as long as they are supposed to be."

"I don't follow," I said.

"Well, some go to heaven, and others get reincarnated. Some leave and visit their old friends and relatives, and others go somewhere else to repent. I have no control over any of that. I just make sure that the souls that are here stay here...hence the chains on your wife." Eddie Lo grew bigger, and his face and complexion changed slightly. He looked more regal than he had just a few moments before. Christine stood by his side, not speaking.

"What is your name?" I asked.

Eddie Lo was now a towering figure, replete with a golden silk robe and crown to match. The top of his head reached the fifteen foot ceiling. A beard had grown on his face, long and gray. He resembled a middle aged Chinese Emperor. He didn't answer. Never before had I felt so small and weak. Christine became larger and older as well. She uncoiled, expanding toward the ceiling next to Eddie.

"What can I do to get Delancey back?" I asked.

"That is an interesting question," said Eddie. "You are in a room with what you most desire, and also that which prevents you from obtaining your desires. I am your opponent, and I cannot be defeated."

"I would never fight you, what would be the point?"

"If you bring her back, she'll never be the same. Anyone who is here for more than a day starts to fade," Christine commented.

"So you are saying that she can come back?" I asked, hearing only that there was a possibility.

"Every now and then it happens. Souls have managed to go back to your world—the material world. You call it earth, we call it Gaia. But they are never exactly the same as when they left Gaia." Eddie Lo was shimmering in the moonlight. He hovered above Delancey and I.

"How do I get her back?" I asked again.

"Do you know who I am?" he said.

"What should I call you?" I asked.

"If I were you, I wouldn't call me." His sinister laugh echoed. "Every time you mention my name, I hear you. If you mention it enough, I show up, and I'm afraid you wouldn't want me showing up." He glistened in the moonlight like a thousand diamonds. As terrifying as he was, he was resplendent.

"Some call me Hades, or Pluto, Yama, or Yamraj. Others call me Yima, and even Yan Lo and Enma Dai-O. I've been called Anubis, and Osiris. I have a thousand names, every culture, every people that has ever walked the Earth has had a name for me. But I urge you not to call me, not to remember my name. It's up to me if you leave with her or not, but there is always a price to pay...a great price." I gulped at the mention of this price.

"He's the Ruler of the Underworld, THE God of Death," said Delancey. "David, don't make any deals that I wouldn't want you to. I don't want to go back as a zombie or worse."

I dropped down to my knees and begged him to let Delancey come back with me. "I can't go on with her, I have nothing left," I pleaded with him, choking back tears. The Ruler of the Underworld remained silent for a while. The other figure, the version of Christine, moved adjacent to him, and whispered into his ear.

"I do like the way you play the guitar," Christine said. "I heard you play Worlds Apart at your graduation. The pain in your voice, the haunting grief that you sang with, I loved it. I truly love your agony; its music to my ears. You have a very bright future in music. The entire world will know who you are. Such God-given talent and now you have what every great artist needs—suffering, torment, and pain. You should thank us, Orpheus."

A solid gold double electric guitar appeared on the desk. Its luster was unmatched, its shine unrivaled. I picked it up, feeling the weight of solid gold in my hands. There was an unfamiliar strange feeling. The guitar was magical.

"What would you like to hear?" I asked, hearing my grandfather saying, "All that glitters isn't gold."

"Play something for me. Play something with all your heart and all your emotion. You know what I want to hear. Something you haven't played in a long time. Worlds Apart isn't the only song you sing with anguish and pain." Christine had a seductive voice. The Ruler of the Underworld grinned.

I held the guitar close. My reflection was visible in its gold luster shimmering in the moonlight. Through the dusty windows, three moons loomed in the night sky. I closed my eyes, and thought about my mother's funeral. I knew exactly what they wanted to hear.

I recalled my mother in the casket and all the people at the funeral. I could remember the flowers, and my sullen grandparents and melancholic uncles. Young Harry was sobbing. My father was standing in the back, stoic with red eyes. I was wearing a black suit.

My eyes remained closed as I recalled another image of my mother, a few years before her passing. She was happy; my entire family used to be so happy. We were on a different course then. My father was much younger, full of life. We were on a beach, playing with a colorful ball. I hadn't thought much about that day, but now it was so vivid, and so real.

The memory of how sick she became and how quickly she deteriorated replayed in my mind. I recalled her coughing. She looked like she had not slept. I remembered the hospital rooms, the chemotherapy treatments. She had lost her hair and so much weight. My mother had even lost the color in her face. I remembered coming home from school, and finding her dead. That was the day that everything changed. That was the day that my course was altered. I was on my way to becoming something special, someone happy, and that was the day it ended. At her funeral, I played classical guitar, in honor of my dead mother. It was the last time I played her favorite song. It was the last time I played Ave Maria. It was the reason why I did not want to do the school play for Mr. Zoose. I vowed I would never play that song again. But now, I had no choice. Now everything depended on my rendition, and it needed to be powerful. It had to be powerful enough to convince him to let me have Delancey back.

My chest swelled with emotion, my heart sinking with heaviness. A single tear trickled down my face. My fingers quivered as I held the pick. I played Ave Maria on guitar, and the longer I played, the more I wept silently. I kept my eyes closed, and continued to picture my mother. It was the most painful song I had ever performed, and that's why I had not played this song since my mother's death. I played without pause, without hesitation. I played despite the agony, and the extremely sad and painful feeling that the song brought from the depths of my memory, from the depths of my soul.

Someone was singing, in a haunting voice. The voice accompanied my guitar play. My eyes remaining closed, I could hear her voice.

It was celestial, coming directly from the heavens. I continued to play, and the voice continued to sing. Was it just in my head? I wept all the more, as I played the guitar with increased emotion, increased sorrow. The singer's voice was overwhelming.

When the song ended, she stopped singing. Slowly my eyes opened and my mother was standing in front of me. She was an ethereal vision of love and beauty. Her radiance emanated warmth. I wanted to reach out and touch her but I hesitated. Overwhelmed with emotions of both happiness and sadness, I burst into tears. I held my hand out to her, and all I could say in my tear riddled voice was, "I miss you." She placed her hand on my head and smiled. Slowly, a single tear fell from her eyes onto my head. She dissipated into thin air.

The Ruler of the Underworld and his consort were smiling and clapping their hands. "Well done. It's truly a gift from the heavens to play as great as you do. Fantastic performance! You have moved me, and my consort, and here is what I am willing to do for you."

I tried to recompose myself.

"There are three things you have to agree to before you can take Delancey back. The first...you can never play the guitar for anyone other than me again. You can never play for an audience of any kind, even if it's one person. I will visit you whenever I want you to play for me."

I thought about the band, and my musical career. We were scheduled to record the album the next day. This would mean the end of my musical career. I could never even play for Delancey.

"Don't do it, David. You have a God-given gift. People need to hear your music. You were given this gift for a reason. Don't let him take it away," Delancey pleaded with me.

It would mean giving away my destiny and any chance I would have to become a successful or even unsuccessful musician. I could never even play on the subway.

"Fine, I agree, if I get Delancey back," I said.

The towering serpentine empress and the God of Death laughed out loud. Their sinister laughter bellowed like thunder.

"Second, leave here and trust that Delancey will follow you back. Trust that she is behind you, and never look back to check. You have to trust that she is following behind. No second guessing."

"How can I trust YOU? You have cheated me out of every chance of happiness in my life? How can I trust anything after having lost my mother?" I asked.

"If you can't trust me, who can you trust? I'm the most consistent thing in the universe." His laughter ceased.

"And finally, you must get back to your world and your body before sunrise, or else you stay here forever. Go now! I hope you make it back in time. But if you don't, I still win. You have only until sunrise."

The God of Death and his consort vanished into the distance. There was one and half moons left in the night sky. The half moon that remained had already started to fade.

There was little time left. I started walking back toward the main hall, hearing footsteps behind me and the chains clamoring. Delancey was behind me, and I kept going. We climbed up the stairs, and left the dining hall. I ran for the main exit. In the moonlight, two shadows were on the floor. One was clearly mine, and the other looked like Delancey's figure.

"Just keep following me; I know the way out," I said. There was no answer. I ran out the front entrance, and knew not to go too fast. I had to move at a speed at which Delancey could follow. I raced past the guard, toward the ferry. I did not hear footsteps or chains behind me, but I could not look back.

No one else was leaving Ellis Island. I boarded facing forward, hoping that Delancey was still behind me. Then I heard a noise on the deck of the ferry. Her chains were audibly dragging with her movements. The ferry slowly cut through the choppy waters. I called out, "Delancey, are you still with me," but there was no answer.

The choppy waters muffled all sound on the ferry. I felt so cold from the winds. Minutes later, the ferry pulled into South Street. Stepping off the boat, I said, "Delancey, we have to head to Brooklyn. Just keep following me." There was still no answer, no reply, and no sound. I jogged slowly. In the moonlight, there were two shadows, and one was definitely mine. I felt confident that she was still behind me.

I started to imagine how great it would be to have her back in my life, and how we were going to spend the rest our lives together. Our future would be so wonderful. I imagined a new level of happiness for me, happiness for the rest of my life.

When I was heading north on Broadway, I could no longer hear anything behind me. Only one moon remained in the sky.

"We're almost there, Delancey," I cried out. We were running out of time. My heart raced with nervous anticipation. Quickly, we ran up the Canyon of Heroes, toward City Hall.

The first ticker tape parade in New York was for the dedication of the Statue of Liberty. A long list of history's most noteworthy names have been celebrated in the Canyon of Heroes. The end of World War Two saw a great celebration here, as did the astronauts returning from the moon in 1969. I didn't need a parade; I only needed Delancey.

Someone approached me, looking like Sam, only taller, and slightly older.

"She's not behind you," Sam said. "You're wasting your time."

This was not Sam, just the avatar of my self doubt in his image. I continued north on Broadway, and the same apparition popped out of a corner. Once again he shouted at me. "Look behind you, she's not there." I kept moving but his statement echoed in my head.

I stayed on course, moving closer to City Hall. The Brooklyn Bridge was near City Hall. I was growing less confident that Delancey was still behind me. It was dark, and in the night sky, the single moon was now more than half way gone. I hurried past Reade Street, and shouted out to Delancey, "Keep up with me, we are almost there." Still, there was no answer.

On the corner of Reade Street, Sam's apparition stood on the corner shaking his head "no." I kept running. I could not turn back to make sure she was there. I just had to trust Delancey, and I had to trust the God of Death to keep up his end of the bargain. The streets were deserted, and the dim light made it too difficult to read the street names. I was getting overly anxious. Was she behind me or wasn't she? I called out her name, but still no answer.

I ran a little faster, getting confused. Self doubt was creeping in. How I could trust the Ruler of the Underworld? What had I been thinking?

Sam popped out from another corner. "Only a fool would trust him; he has cheated you before and he's doing it now." I kept going, trying to ignore Sam.

The Canyon of Heroes was desolate. Dark buildings were covered in soot and decay along the route. Ironically, the pathway chosen to honor heroes in American history was for me a hurdle to the Brooklyn Bridge. I was growing weak and more confused. It was lonely, daunting, and seemed haunted.

The demonic beings and shadowy figures were visible again. I tried not to look at their faces. Snakes were all over the streets.

Finally, I was at the United States Courthouse, across the street from City Hall. Another figure was standing there. The person was medium height, with long hair. He resembled Mr. DeJesus.

"Are you sure you want to do this?" he asked.

"What are you doing here?" I asked Mr. DeJesus.

"I am here to help you make a rational decision. You have talent that less than one percent of all the people on this planet have. It is a gift given to you and not yours to give away. Yet you are willing to part with it. Pursue your destiny and fulfill your potential by becoming a great musician. Anything else would be a slap in the face of your father. You are not giving up anything for love here. You are giving it away because of guilt and regret." Mr. DeJesus stood still with a heiligenschein softly illuminating his face.

"I love her with all my heart. She is my world; she is my life. I've lost so much already. I can't lose her too." Distraught with confusion, I was no longer sure that I was doing the right thing.

"David Orpheus, you have an entire future, a bright one. You will be no better than those who take their own life; for if you trade your God-given talent for ephemeral happiness, you will have traded your life away."

"I'm trading it for a lifetime with Delancey. Is she still behind me?" I asked.

"One lifetime is ephemeral. If you had faith you would know if she was behind you." Mr. DeJesus's apparition evaporated; his words were resonating deep within my core as I continued.

I entered the Brooklyn Bridge walking along on the pedestrian walkway. Less than a quarter of the moon remained. It was nearly daybreak, and the dark night sky had started turning into a brilliant blue. "Delancey, we are almost there."

The bridge was long and it started getting cold and windy. Wilson, the jumper was still in the same spot where I had left him. "Why are you still here?" I asked him.

"It's a suspension bridge, so time stands still while you are on it. Just ask the people that sit in traffic on this bridge in the morning," Wilson joked.

"Wilson, is there a girl following behind me?" I asked.

"Don't ask me that question," Wilson shouted angrily, and jumped off the bridge once more.

I ran faster, heeding Wilson's words about time standing still. I could see Tillary Street. I was so close, just a few more blocks, and I would be back to where my body was, back to where I could leave the astral plane. I ran faster and faster; the moon was fading. I was so close to the end.

"Delancey," I called out, "just a few more minutes, we can make it." There was no answer. Sam was waiting on the corner. Everything he said increased my self doubts.

"She's not behind you. They lied to you. Don't believe them. Don't bring back something with you that isn't Delancey," he said.

I started to panic. Was she behind me or wasn't she? Was I being tricked into giving up my music career? Would Death keep Delancey anyway? I didn't know what to do. So confused, so full of doubts, I felt betrayed. I could see Delfina.

"Delfina, is Delancey behind me?" I asked.

No answer.

"Delfina, please just answer," I pleaded. Her mouth was sewn shut; her eyes were without pupils.

The moon was no longer visible, but the sun had not risen as of yet. I was almost out of time. Delfina pointed to Stanton. I had to get back to my body. I climbed through the window and headed to the basement. Quickly, I meandered through the hallways, through the boiler room, and toward the electrical room.

I had to be sure Delancey was still behind me. I only had one shot at this. I shouted out her name, again and again. There was no sound behind me. There was still no answer.

I could see my body several yards away. Sal was next to the Leviathon machine; I was back. The Leviathon was powering up, and the magnetic pull was too strong to resist. Sal yelled out that I had to return.

"Delancey, I am going to reach back; just grab my hand if you are there," I pleaded. I reached out, and reached out further, trying to touch her hand. It was then that something reached back toward me.

I felt a cold, bony hand, like that of a skeleton. It grabbed my hand sharply, and I pulled back, frightened. I involuntarily glanced back. I saw Delancey, falling backwards, reaching out to grab my hand. A single breath escaped her angelic lips. Behind her, was the God of Death, smiling, pulling her toward him, into the eternal abyss.

"David!" she screamed.

"Delancey!" But it was too late. She was gone. I had already started to re-enter the material world.

I was in my body just seconds later.

Sal was sitting next to me. I felt weak, exhausted, like I had traveled for miles. I told Sal what had happened.

"I need to go back," I said.

"There is no going back. You were gone too long," Sal said.

It was daybreak. The sun had risen. It was over. She was gone forever. I had lost her twice, and once again we were worlds apart.

Epilogue

NOT A DAY has passed in twenty years that I am not haunted my actions and my decisions. I still dream about Delancey from time to time. I never went to college. I was with the band for five years. We toured the world until our albums no longer sold.

I'm still friends with John. He never made it to college, but now owns a hundred grocery stores. John turned out to be quite the success. I hear from Carlos every two to three years. He was in the Marines for ten years, and now works as a body guard for very wealthy clients. He is married and living in California.

Sam never made it to Harvard. Due to his inability to pass the swim test he could not graduate from Stanton. But he still made it to medical school and is a doctor today in Europe. I haven't spoken to him since that fateful night.

Juan Perez was expelled from Harvard for criminal activities. He is now a State Senator.

Doreen was the big winner from our senior class. She is a successful television personality, and always has the excuse that she is too busy to socialize, get married, or start a family.

Christine and I have remained friends. She is married and living in the suburbs. She is a complete soccer mom and member of the PTA.

I think about trying to go back and find Delancey. I'm not sure if it could be done, but if I can get Sal out of Belleview Mental Hospital, I'm sure he can find a way. Sal has three doctorates. If anyone can do it, Sal can.

The End

Proof

Made in the USA
Charleston, SC
06 July 2011